ADVANCE RL

The Madwoman of Preacher's Cove
a novel
Joy Ross Davis

Pub Date: Fall 2020

ISBN: 978-1-948018-85-2
320 Pages, 5.5 x 8.5
Softcover $15.95, eBook $4.99

CATEGORIES:

FIC010000 FICTION / Fairy Tales, Folk Tales, Legends & Mythology
FIC009050 FICTION / Fantasy / Paranormal
FIC024000 FICTION / Occult & Supernatural
FIC030000 / FICTION / Suspense
FIC031000 / FICTION / Thrillers

DISTRIBUTED BY:
INGRAM, FOLLETT, COUTTS, MBS, YBP,
COMPLETE BOOK, BERTRAMS, GARDNERS
Or wholesale@wyattmackenzie.com

Wyatt-MacKenzie Publishing
DEADWOOD, OREGON

PUBLISHER CONTACT:
Nancy Cleary, nancy@wyattmackenzie.com

AUTHOR CONTACT:
Joy Ross Davis, jessarb@aol.com

**This is an Uncorrected
Pre-Publication Review Copy Only**

THE
MADWOMAN
OF
PREACHER'S COVE

THE
MADWOMAN
OF
PREACHER'S
COVE

JOY ROSS DAVIS

Wyatt-MacKenzie Publishing
DEADWOOD, OREGON

The Madwoman of Preacher's Cove
a novel

Joy Ross Davis

ISBN: 978-1-948018-85-2
Library of Congress Control Number: *to come*

Cover photography: Old house ©Tetyana Kochneva
Lightning in the sky ©John Leaver
Celtic braid illustration ©Aleksandr Velichko

Wyatt-MacKenzie Publishing
DEADWOOD, OREGON

Wyatt-MacKenzie Publishing, Inc.
www.WyattMacKenzie.com
Contact us: info@wyattmackenzie.com

Dedication

This book is dedicated to Mary Alice Nunley, my grandmother.
Thank you for introducing me to your world.
Without that introduction, Preacher's Cove would not exist.

An ancient Druidian legend holds that Cailleach, the White Maiden, swept across the circle of stones in a frenzied rage, searching for the Eye of God. The goddess snatched the light from the moon and stars and left the sky pitch black. In an instant, though, she granted mercy to the hundreds of worshippers below and blew a kiss of luminescent emerald that danced across the sky.

From this glorious radiance fell twenty long fingers of white-hot light. Ten infants and ten adults lifted high off the ground and dropped into the huge wickerwork altar in the center of the circle of stones. Their still-breathing bodies plopped one onto the other with a sickening thud. Then the White Maiden claimed her sacrifice in an enormous explosion of fire. Mercifully, the twenty burned instantly. Satisfied, the goddess commanded rain to douse the fire and wind to scatter the ashes of the dead across the forest. In her wake, she left no evidence of the cremation...except the screaming, wailing kin—mothers, fathers, wives, husbands—of the twenty dead.

Some legends, though, are lies.

"This is Alabama. Weird things happen."

—James Spann, Chief Meteorologist
ABC 33/40 News
Birmingham, Alabama
February, 2012

1

At midnight, under the veiled shimmer of a goddess's moon, she shuffled toward the worktable in the Angel Room. Her work waited under the only window in the room. One lone bulb dangling from a short cord in the farthest corner shone down upon a motley assortment of clay-fired arms, legs, and torsos intermingled with swatches of fabric strewn across the battered wooden table. Crazy Lucy worked always in the shadows.

And always alone. She went to the table, picked up a needle and thread, and began to work. She bent further over the table, closer to the creation of the dolls, intent only on the work of her hands, their skill and artistry her only salvation. As she worked, she hummed a baby's lullaby and rocked gently back and forth. Humming, rocking, oblivious to everything save the work, Lucy formed, molded, fired, glazed, dressed, and perfected the small replicas of the children of Preacher's Cove...the Firelight Angels.

The dim light of the workshop shimmered like a steady beacon in the darkness around Cove's End. For five hours, the beacon gave Lucy Addams all the light she needed to form perfect replicas of some child of the Cove, either living or dead. Lucy never knew which. She simply followed the hands. Whole or twisted, they performed with equal mastery. And the hands followed the goddess, the White Maiden of centuries before who plucked a stone from the heart of a brave priestess. With precision unequaled, Lucy honored the Maiden with a host of little angels, all beautiful, all innocent, and all alive inside the mind of a lunatic. She was lost, now, in a place where no others were allowed entry.

Bent close to the worktable, she slid white tennis shoes onto tiny feet and put the finishing touch on another of her Firelight Angels. She bundled the newly-created baby into her arms, shuffled across the room to a child-sized rocker that sat in the corner, and placed her baby carefully into the seat. The blonde, blue-eyed child, with a look of wonder on his face, a peaceful smile on his lips, seemed almost ready to speak. With great care, Lucy smoothed the boy-child's blue denim jeans, straightened his t-shirt, tipped his cap, and gently ran her whole fingers across the child's blushing cheeks. She adjusted the placard; then she took a step back, one foot dragging more slowly than the other, and stood dead still.

For one brief moment, Lucy's eyes sparkled with awareness. She lifted a hand to her mouth, as the sound of soft laughter escaped and blew gently through her fingertips. In the shadowed light, one unblemished hand as smooth as porcelain reached down and stroked the child's hair; one perfect side of a delicate, porcelain-colored face with deep green eyes feasted upon the mastery of her creation. She pulled back her shoulders, took a deep breath, and sighed. With delicate accuracy, she stepped back without a single falter.

The step backward placed her in front of the only window in the workshop. The light, a welcomed beacon only a minute earlier, now became the light which cast the reflection of the mangled left side of her face. She saw a monster with hideous scars, its neck fairly melted to the side of the face so that there appeared to be no neck at all...only a gnarled lumpy blister that drew the shoulder to the chin. One eye looked almost exposed in its socket, the tissue around it hot-curled into sagging fingers down its face. There were no eyelashes to hide the mangling of the fire, no eyebrows to soften it, and no ear to help it appear human. She saw the monster whose neck and face, fused by flames, stiffened as they had healed into one grotesque violet wave. And in that instant of recognition, Lucy remembered. For only a few seconds, she heard the cries, saw the faces pressed hard against the window. Then the sparkle of awareness left her eyes. As she retreated once again into the mindless safety of Crazy Lucy Addams, she reached over to the shelf above the rocker and grabbed a box of matches. With her gnarled hand she held the box. With the other, she opened it and took the only match from inside. She stepped closer to the child seated so peacefully in the rocker. Carefully, she slid the match across the rough edge of the box. A tiny firelight ignited.

She held it over the doll, formed a smile that resembled nothing human, and dropped the lit match square into the doll's lap. A circle of flame formed on the deep blue fabric.

2

Hap Murray strode across Channel 12's deserted parking lot in Huntsville. Fine, misting drops of rain brushed across his face. He wiped them away, glanced at his watch and quickened his steps. Beads of sweat dotted his upper lip, and he shivered despite the 70-degree air. When he came to the steps leading up to the building, he checked his watch again. He breathed deeply and took the three steps in one giant stride. He put his hand on the chrome door handle and pulled. Then, he slowed and blinked his eyes. He felt an odd tightening sensation in his head. He blinked his eyes and whispered. "Not now. Not now."

A blast of white-hot pain stabbed into his right eye then seared through his brain. He staggered backwards with his hands over his face. Distorted images—a woman, a beautiful woman, no...a hideous monster—flooded his mind. Silent screams assailed his ears. The smell of burned meat clogged his nostrils. He coughed, gagged, and hugged his arms together. The force of the gagging bent him double. He reached out blindly for the rails. Bursts of cold air slapped his face. He gasped, stumbled, and sank to his knees. He tried to open his eyes. The searing light intensified. Clouds. He saw clouds behind the light. He squeezed his eyes shut and dropped his head to block out the light. He coughed again. The light thickened into streaks of luminescent green laced with pink tendrils that wrapped themselves around him. He struggled to breathe. His heart beat so fast that he felt the beats in his throat. He leaned forward, balanced himself on one hand, and lifted his head and groaned. "Hap," he heard a voice say.

He shifted his weight and plopped down onto the cement. He could feel the dampness from the morning's misting rain seep through his khakis. He shook his head and took another deep breath.

Then he checked his watch again: 7:00am

He shouted at the air. "I've missed the phone call." He stood up, brushed his shaking hand across his backside, fumbled with his tie to straighten it, and took one long deep breath. Three more deep breaths calmed him. Hap walked into the glass-enclosed building that housed the news station. The smell of burning meat lingered in his nostrils. He coughed and wondered, for the second time since his childhood, just what was happening to him. His shoes clicked against the smooth tiled floor. He walked to the elevator, then pressed the UP button. A few seconds later, a red light blinked and a buzzer sounded. The doors slid open. He stepped inside, pressed the button for the fourth floor. The doors slid shut. The floor shuddered under his feet as it started moving. He smoothed his hair, checked his tie again, and looked around the shiny interior. Surrounded by reflections of himself, he felt somehow displaced, as if the reflections were the real person and he was merely an intruder into their space.

He shook his head, coughed, and stood waiting for his real "self" to return. "Come on," he muttered. "You can't blow it today, not today."

When the elevator doors slid open, Hap stepped out. He looked up and down the corridor. At this early hour, the place was deserted. Only the still reflections of the shining marble floors and glass-enclosed offices greeted him. He checked his watch, then shook his head. *Maybe*, he thought, *just maybe the guy hasn't called. He might have overslept.* He smiled and walked into the main office, a huge space divided into forty or so cubicles. This early in the morning, the hum of the computers sounded like giant locusts. He headed for the coffee pot, poured a cup, and hurried into his cubicle. He checked his watch: 7:33. The phone's red message light blinked. Hap felt as if someone had kicked him in his already queasy stomach. He knew he should check the messages. Without this man's story, his credibility about the Senator's abuses would seem contrived. He stared at the phone. He checked his watch one more time: 7:35. He ran his fingers through his hair, and took another deep breath.

5

Only fifteen minutes until his interview with the new station manager. In her letter to him, Mrs. Darcy James had hinted that present employees might be reassigned if necessary. He figured that if he made a good impression, he'd stand a good chance of keeping his job. But if he made a *really* good impression, he'd be first in line for the evening anchor spot. This interview, he reminded himself, would decide his future in the news business, at least with Channel 12. Right now, though, the blinking red light had higher priority. He dialed in his code, whispering a little prayer that his guy had not called.

"You have two new messages," the voice said. "Press one to listen to new messages."

One. He heard his guy and grabbed a pen from his coat pocket.

"Murray," the voice said. "Where the hell are you? Never mind, forget it, man."

Then the call ended with a clunk from the other end. He pressed for the second message. For an instant, he thought he had hope of finishing this story and getting some national coverage. Instead of his witness's voice, he heard a low screeching sound. Hap held the receiver away from his ear. He was on the verge of hanging up, but when he heard a familiar voice say his name, he listened. "Hap," his mother said.

He dropped the phone. His stomach churned, his heart hammered in his chest, and his head felt as if a bomb had exploded in it. He folded his arms across his desk and put his head down on top of them. "I must be nuts," he said, tears forming in his eyes. He reached into the top drawer of his desk and pulled out a newspaper clipping of two months earlier. He spread it carefully in front of him. His mother's obituary, in words that he had read a thousand times, lay on the desk.

"I am losing my bloody mind," he whispered.

3

By the time the portly owner of the paper, Mrs. James, arrived with her husband, the newsroom buzzed. Fingers clacked on keyboards. Impatient correspondents chattered on the phones, rustled through slips of paper and searched for pens. Hap looked up from his cubicle just in time to see the grand entrance. As she passed, he smiled at her and stood up. He held out his hand to introduce himself, but she walked by without so much as a glance in his direction. Her husband trailed behind her. He shook Hap's hand, winked at him, and whispered, "Don't worry, pal. It's in the bag."

At that moment, though, Hap wished Herb James had that bag stuffed somewhere the sun didn't shine. He smiled at Herb anyway, and when Herb motioned for him to follow him, he went along, his pants still damp. Inside Mrs. James's office, Hap stood straight to his full 6'3", making sure his posture was flawless. With his feet slightly apart and his hands clasped in front of him, he waited for the new manager to speak. After several seconds, he cleared his throat. Mrs. James didn't look up from her reading and rustling of papers. Finally, Hap spoke.

"It's, uh, it's nice to have you here, Mrs. James," he said, his hands still a bit shaky. "Thank you, Mr. Murray," she said, looking at first one piece of paper then another, but not at him. "My husband has something he'd like to tell you." Hap's stomach churned again, rumbled loudly enough for all of them to hear, and he blushed and lowered his head.

"Did our witness call?" Herb James asked. "He called, but I... I'll, uh, have to call him back."

Hap felt pools of perspiration swelling under his arms and was grateful he'd remembered to wear his jacket.

"You missed the call?" James asked, shaking his head. He stepped closer to Hap and glared at him. "You missed the friggin' call?"

Hap swallowed hard and looked down at Herb.

"He'll call back, Herb. Don't worry. He's ready to talk. I know he is."

Herb James sighed and looked over at his wife. She smirked, turned her head away and looked at her long red nails. "Yeah, well, one of us has to worry." Herb said, his voice filled with resentment. He stepped away from Hap and walked toward the large picture windows. For a moment he said nothing. Hap shifted in place and sighed. He felt his posture begin to change, yet he couldn't muster the courage to straighten up. His shoulders slouched as his self-esteem drooped. He looked down at the floor, his hands clasped behind his back. "Something happened this morning, Herb. I was here in plenty of time, but...can I talk to you outside?"

Herb looked over at his wife. Still busy rifling through papers, she didn't appear to be paying any attention to either of them. "It doesn't matter now," he said, his voice softer, almost resigned to Hap's failure. "I have another assignment for you. If you do a good job on this one, if you can manage to get some national coverage, I'll forget about the phone call." Hap straightened and smiled. "What kind of assignment?" he asked. "Preacher's Cove, Alabama, where they've had those god-awful storms."

"I know about them," Hap said, the disappointment in his voice so obvious that Mrs. James looked up at him and frowned. He rolled his eyes, shifted his weight, and waited for the rest of the story.

"Good." Herb said pacing back and forth by the windows. He waved his arms in the air. "These storms are killing people. There's even a witness, one with a videotape. You know, Hap, a real witness with *real* evidence, something with which you seem to have problems."

Hap glared back at him. The job he'd wanted for years suddenly didn't seem important.

"A witness," Herb said, his tone even and steady, "has caught a phenomenon called greenflash on videotape. If you and the crew will get the lead out of your butts, then maybe we can get another angle, find out about the others who might have witnessed either the storms or the deaths. It's worth a try. We can't be the only station in Alabama not to give this some coverage."

"I'd rather not go."

Mrs. James rose to her feet with the ponderous grace of a small rhino and glared at him. "What's the matter with you, Hap?" Mrs. James asked, her voice high-pitched and grating, like the sound of those red nails scraping across a chalkboard. "Are you afraid to go to Preacher's Cove? Or don't you want a chance to move out of the field work altogether? There might be a human interest angle, maybe an Associated Press Award. It has everything. Death, destruction, bizarre phenomenon."

"No," Hap insisted. You'll have to find someone else. Preacher's Cove is not the place for me."

"Hap!" Herb yelled, his face turning bright red, the veins on his forehead bulging. "If you cost us another spot of national coverage, so help me, I'll get your replacement in here so fast it'll make your blond head spin. I mean it!"

Hap looked at Mrs. James, who smiled with lips stretched so far over her teeth that it exposed her gum line. He looked at Herb, the faithful old friend of his father's, a man he had known since his father had first gone into business twenty years ago, but who now looked like a stranger to him. "Mrs. James," he said and nodded in her direction. He turned to grab the door handle and walk away. But what Herb said next stopped him in his tracks. "Hap, wait. I need you for this one. There are rumors about Preacher's Cove, all sorts of rumors about some unexplained deaths, deaths that don't have anything to do with the storms. You're the best bloodhound I have. Besides, I promised your dad...."

James stood there looking pitiful, his mouth forming a little pout and his eyes pleading with Hap not to make him look like a fool in front of his wife.

"My dad? My dad wouldn't want me to go there," Hap said. "No way."

"You're wrong. He's the one who gave me the lead on this one.

9

He says there's a man named Ike Madison who's the big-cheese preacher now. He's a shady character, your dad says. You're familiar with the area, you have some family ties there, and you can find out what Madison is up to. He thinks it'd be perfect for you."

Hap stared at him for a moment, then looked at Herb's wife. Mrs. James, standing with her hands clasped tightly in front of her, did not shift her gaze from him. Her jaws looked locked and Hap thought he could hear her teeth grinding together. He wondered, at that point, if any job with her as the boss would be worth the pay. Then, he remembered the morning's episode—and all the ones before it—and decided that he'd better hang onto this job while he still had his sanity. He sighed and threw up his hands. "All right," he said. "I'll go to Preacher's Cove, but I want that spot when I get back, Herb, a secure place of the evening anchor variety."

Herb smiled at him. "I've contacted the crew. They're standing by waiting for your cue," he said. The van's ready, and the equipment's checked out. Everything's set. And Hap?"

Yes?"

"Keep this one under wraps until you know for sure. Madison's an influential man. Lots of money, lots of contacts. If we air something before we have proof, our asses will be on the line."

"You know me, Herb," Hap said, straightening his tie. "I won't say a word until I know for sure."

He walked out without acknowledging either Herb or his wife. His stomach churned when he thought of going back to Preacher's Cove. He stopped by his desk and picked up the phone. His dad had some explaining to do. He replaced the receiver.

"He's got enough to worry about," Hap mumbled. "He doesn't need to think his son's a coward."

4

Later, Hap found himself crammed into the back of a news van headed toward Preacher's Cove. Squeezed in between the crew, the cameras, and the equipment, he tolerated the two-hour ride. He switched positions so often that one of the crew, Eagle, the photographer, asked him if he had hemorrhoids. "Not today," Hap said. "But it's still fairly early. There's a good chance I will by the time we make it into Preacher's Cove!"

"So," Eagle said, scratching at his scraggly beard, "how'd it go with the new battle-axe. Excuse me. Did I say that out loud?" The three of them laughed.

"Not as bad as I thought," Hap said.

"It couldn't have been too bad," Eagle said. "We're on assignment, so they must think we know what we're doing, right?"

"Hey," Joey, the young driver, said, "I bet she took one look at Hap and swooned. She probably wanted to jump his bones right there."

"Kids!" Hap said. "Gotta love 'em. For your information, kid, she didn't even look at me until she thought I wasn't going to take this job. Then she frowned like an old witch."

"Nah, you just *think* she didn't look," Joey said. "I've seen how women look at you. You walk by and their knees get all weak and rubbery. You're not too bad for an old fart."

"Well, thanks, but the perspective of a twenty-two-year-old hardly counts in the gruff world of the forty-ish Cove's End crowd."

"I hope I look as good as you when I'm old," Joey said. Hap flipped him a bird. Then he laughed and decided that they should be nearing Preacher's Cove. He was about to say something when the young driver called to them,

"Hey, guys, look up ahead," Joey said and slowed the van. He leaned forward and peered out over the steering wheel. "This fog's so thick I can barely make out the lines of the road."

"You'd better slow it down a little more," Hap said. "Looks like the fog's getting thicker."

Joey drove a few more feet, tapped on the brakes, and slowed down to 40 m.p.h.

"Careful, kid," Hap said. "There's no telling what we'll run into. Remember, this place is supposed to be plagued by some sort of storm monsters, and God, I hate storms...and monsters!"

Only a few feet ahead, Hap saw the form of something that peeped out from the fog. He squinted his eyes to make his vision sharper. Then, he stared at an enormous dark shape that, covered by fog, completely distorted the landscape. By the time he recognized the shape, it was too late. He saw an enormous tree seared straight through the middle, one large blackened branch drooping halfway across the road. The van swerved. Hap grabbed onto the handles to keep from being thrown into the floor. The tires squealed, the van lurched to the other side of the road. It screeched to a stop. Hap braced himself and his precious cargo. Without his camera and all the equipment, his story wouldn't be worth squat.

"Everybody okay back there?" Joey asked. "I'm sorry, guys, but I didn't see the blasted thing 'til it was right on me. What about the equipment?"

"It's fine. We're fine. That corker came out of nowhere!" Hap said. "If it doesn't clear up soon, we're screwed. We can't get any tape in this mess."

Hap opened the back doors and climbed out of the van. He stood in the middle of the road that led to Preacher's Cove. Some far-off sound filtered into his ears, the sound of a harmonica playing. Fog descended around him, enveloped him in an embrace so damp and thick that it was almost tangible. A low rumbling sounded in the distance. The earth beneath his feet quivered. Cocooned in the air's density, aware of the tremulous thunder and the slight shaking of the ground, Hap Murray felt isolated from the others...quite alone. His heartbeat quickened, his head throbbed. His breath burned in short spurts in his lungs. Without warning, something crashed to the ground in front of him, the sound of it almost deafening. With one long audible gasp, the reporter cried out. His knees gave way, and for the second time that day, he sank slowly to the ground. Directly in front of him lay a sign that read,

"Welcome to Preacher's Cove...God's Little Corner."

5

Hap felt the pull of a powerful force under his arm. He thought, for an instant, that one of those killer storms might be creeping in from that dense fog. He imagined the lightning hovering above, waiting to claim him. He decided he might as well bend over and kiss his ass good-bye 'cause his soul surely belonged to....

"Buddy, are you all right?" a man's voice called.

Hap stood, the man's strong hand still wrapped around his arm. He rubbed his eyes, tried to clear his field of vision, then wiped his nose with the arm of his sleeve. Before him stood a man almost a foot shorter than he, scruffy-looking and thick-necked, all garbed up in a long, tattered overcoat. Underneath the coat, a flowered shirt and striped tie peeked through. A cigarette dangled between his teeth, ashes just about to fall. "Steady now," the man said. The ashes fell and landed right on top of his left tennis shoe. "I'm fine thanks," Hap said. "You look a little pale, son, 'a might peaked' as my granny used to say. Name's Riggs, Burton Riggs. And you would be?"

"Scared as bloody heck for a minute there," Hap said, "but much better now. I'm Hap Murray. Nice to meet you, Mr. Riggs."

"You've got a ring of British to your voice."

"My mom," Hap said. "She was British."

"Think the rest of your bunch is okay?"

"Yes, I think so," Hap said.

"The fog must have given you all quite a fright. It's bad sometimes right around in here."

"Hap, what's wrong?" Joey asked, coming from around the van.

"Everybody okay?" Burton asked. "Any damage?"

"No, no damage, so don't call the cops," Joey said. "All we need is for some backwoods jerk of a cop to nose around in our business. Our van is fine, our equipment is fine, and I wasn't speeding. The fog just came out of nowhere, and that tree over there was almost in the road. I swerved, that's all, to keep from hitting it."

"Easy, son. Nobody's saying you did anything wrong. Don't go getting yourself all riled up. I was just asking if you were all okay. I offered your friend a hand. If you want, I'll pull around in front of you and lead you out of this fog."

"Thank you," Hap said. "We'd appreciate your help. Wouldn't we, Joey?"

"Yes sir, we would," Joey said and lowered his head.

"Fine," Burton said. "Any particular place you're heading?"

"We need a place to stay for a couple of nights. Any suggestions?" Hap asked.

"Oh, sure," Riggs replied. "Got just the place for you boys, unless for some reason you don't like home cooking and comfortable beds!"

"That sounds great," Joey said.

"Then, follow me," Burton said.

Hap watched Burton climbed into his car. He waved at them and smiled, then maneuvered his car slowly around the tree. Hap climbed into the news van and tapped Joey on the shoulder. "Just keep following Mr. Riggs," he said.

"Will do," Joey said. He turned up the volume on the radio and drove on.

Watching from the side windows, Hap noticed how quickly the fog disappeared once they were on the road again. Up ahead, he saw the beginnings of the town, aptly announced by a sign that read, "Welcome to Preacher's Cove, Alabama. Population: 2,000." Hap looked off to the right. Three-story brick buildings—square, red, and trimmed in white—lined the road into the main area of town. He saw one bank, one department store, and one restaurant. When the ride became bumpier, he heard Joey shout, "Hey, you guys, these old roads are cobblestone!"

Sure enough, when Hap looked down at the road, he saw the cobblestones that led into town. In front of them, Burton Riggs slowed. Hap looked out the window and saw a white marble fountain bubbling with blue-green water. In the middle of the fountain stood a large statue that looked like a large white bird, wings outstretched. He watched as Joey circled the fountain, following Riggs at a snail's pace. Ahead was an enormous white building. A sign on the sprawling lawn read: First Methodist Church of the Cove. Doric columns distinguished it as being designed by a skilled architect. A massive bell hung in a tall bell tower in the top center of the church. A steeple that seemed to reach to the sky glistened in stark white. On each side of the enormous structure were three giant oak trees with huge, gnarled trunks, each surrounded by a lush velvet carpet of green grass that seemed to extend for miles.

Along the sides of the cobblestone streets, azalea bushes with bright pink blooms rose from the ground in perfect symmetry, as if some magical gardener kept watch every hour. As Joey drove out of town, Hap noticed only two other buildings, both white and brilliant against the sky. A library stood approximately half a block from the church. Several yards away was the court house, another testament to someone's love of Doric architecture. Hap wondered who it was that designed the buildings, complete with elegant landscaping, with such precision. When the cobblestone roads stopped and the van rode smoothly again, Hap looked through the back window for one last glimpse of the story-book town.

His vision was drawn immediately to the statue in the fountain. On the way into town, Hap was sure that the statue represented some sort of large white bird, but now, on the way out, he stared at the statue unsure of what it was, exactly. As he watched, the air around the statue shimmered. In a whirling dance, streaks of green and pink light glistened. The statue seemed to melt away.

Hap blinked his eyes and stared.

Above the water, the bubbles lapping at her feet, floated the luminescent form of a woman, her arms outstretched as if she were balancing herself as she floated. Diaphanous, iridescent waves of light enveloped her gown of brilliant green and white. The woman directed her gaze at him.

"Haaaapppppp," she whispered, in a breathless, barely audible sound. Hap's heartbeat quickened. He swallowed hard and squeezed his eyes shut. Then he shook his head, rubbed his eyes, and glanced back toward the statue. No beautiful woman suspended in mid-air stared back at him. He looked across at Eagle and sighed with relief when he saw that he was busy cleaning the camera equipment.

When he glanced behind him one last time, his heartbeat still rapid, the fountain appeared normal. Eagle suddenly looked up and stared at Hap.

"Is something wrong?" Hap shook his head. Eagle nodded at him, scratched his beard, and continued his cleaning.

Hap willed his heart to slow down. He took a deep breath, ran his hand through his hair, and sighed. The van rolled along. Every few yards, another giant oak blocked the window for a few seconds, then disappeared into the mountain's morning scenery. Fifteen minutes into the ride, Hap saw an unusual sign, rusted and barely legible: The Hallows. He wondered why no one bothered to take it down or replace it. Everything else around them seemed immaculate. He saw a large residential area with nearly-perfect houses, most freshly painted with trimmed shutters and manicured lawns. Even the mailboxes, each one brightly designed, looked new.

"Eagle, did you see that sign back there?"

"What sign?"

"An old dilapidated sign that said, 'The Hallows.'"

Eagle shook his head. "What are the hallows?"

"I don't know," Hap said. "Sounds interesting, though, doesn't it?"

"Not to me. Sounds creepy, like someplace this old country boy doesn't need to be.' Course, maybe you British types might be attracted to those old haunts. Brits are a strange lot, I hear."

"Bloody hell, Eagle," Hap said and shook his fist at the man. "How many times do I have to tell you that I'm only half British? I've only visited England three or four times."

"Joey," Eagle called. "You owe me that ten-spot. Told you I could rile him."

Hap laughed with them, and when he looked out the window, he nodded. "I wondered where it was," he said to Eagle.

Funeral wreaths perched on front doors of small brick houses that lined the road. Ornately-carved wooden crosses hung from bright green ribbons draped across and tied around the mailboxes at the road's edge. Hap counted twenty. Standing guard like huge sentinels stood several massive oak trees, some burned, some scarred by fire, and some seared in half. Grass covering the lawns of many of the houses looked as if someone had taken a blowtorch to it in spots.

"Where *what* was?" Eagle asked him.

"The sign," Hap answered.

"Huh?"

"The death sign, the calling card of greenflash."

Hap shuddered, Eagle scratched his beard, and Joey coughed. "Hey," he said. "Did someone say death sign? What's going on?"

"Never mind, kid. Remember, we're here to investigate the killer storms. Notice how clean the town was? It didn't fit with the recent loss of life. I wondered, that's all, where the signs of death were."

"Oh," Joey said and frowned. "Death signs. Gives me chill bumps."

"Me, too," Hap said. He took out his pen and twirled it in his fingers.

"Yeah," Eagle mumbled and pulled at the hair on his beard. Using his thumb and index finger, he smoothed the mustache, then cleared his throat.

Up ahead, Burton pulled into a parking lot. Joey slowed the van and pulled in beside him. Hap took a deep breath and grabbed the handles of the back door. When the doors swung open, he breathed deeply as he maneuvered out. He stood and stretched, breathing in the cool, refreshing mountain air. A few yards from them, Burton got out of his car. He waved to them, lit another cigarette, and motioned toward a building that said, "Office."

Hap nodded at him and waited for him to walk over to them.

"You boys need a place for just a couple of nights, right?" he asked.

"Yes sir," Hap said. We're just here to get a little information on those storms you've been having. My boss thought it would be a good idea to try to find out more than the other stations have been broadcasting."

"A little more? Like what, exactly?"

Hap hesitated. Herb had specifically stated that he wanted this one kept under wraps. He decided to use the storms as a springboard. If he could find out about them, maybe he could find out more about the people here. And more about the people meant more about Ike Madison.

"I don't know yet," Hap said. "There must be some reason the storms keep coming back. That's what we want to find out...if there's a reason so many people die."

"There's no mystery there, I'm afraid," Burton said, the cigarette dangling from his mouth, bobbing up and down as he talked. "These storms have been going on for hundreds of years, probably longer. There've been people here on and off for as long as I can remember trying to come up with a reason to explain it. No luck. But no mystery, either. If you take a plane ride and look at the location of Preacher's Cove, you'll find your answer. Sorry to disappoint you and your boss...and all those scientists and meteorologists who are crawling all over the place right now."

Hap ran his hands through his hair and looked at Riggs. He studied the man's face and watched his eyes. Did they dart to the left to indicate lying or fabricating, or did they dart to the right... a truth-teller? Hap smiled at Riggs, certain that he was telling the truth. "Indulge us if you will," he said. "We're just here for a story."

"Let me save you the trouble, so you can get on back to Channel 12 and find a *real* story. Preacher's Cove is located at the toes, so to speak, of the Smoky Mountains. We're in the northern most part of the state, as north as you can get and not be in Tennessee. Tennessee's only spittin' distance from the Cove, you see."

"Yes," Hap said. "I've visited here before."

"Good, then you already know that we're valleyed in by those mountains on all sides except the southern. Now, you'd think, wouldn't you, that we'd be protected from the brunt of the storm systems. But the storms generated in the mountains naturally fall downward, right on top of us. We get the lightning, the flooding, and when that storm is powerful enough, we get what we call greenflash."

"That's it?" Hap asked.

"Well, you know what they say in real estate: location, location, location. Let's go in and get you boys settled for the night. Trust me. There's nothing here worth a two-night stay."

Hap walked in right behind Burton. With his hands shoved into his jeans pockets and his head downcast, he stood aside while Joey and Eagle filed in.

"Here's your jacket," Joey said. "Thought you might need it to make that all-important good first impression!"

Hap slipped his sport coat on, ran his hands through his hair, and followed Burton. On his first step into the office of Cove's End, Hap shuddered. He felt suddenly out of place. Twenty or so strangers talking in unintelligible buzzes filled the rustic office. Gleaming hardwood floors, a stone fireplace, and handmade rocking chairs took up most of the space in the large lobby area. Two large windows, eyes to the watch over the comings and goings of the town folk, both covered with white lace curtains occupied the front wall. Sunlight streamed in from both, the rays glimmering on the hardwood floors. A huge brick fireplace towered over him. Topped with an ornate hand-carved wooden mantle, it was lined with photographs, some even sepia-toned and probably from the late 1800s. The mantle drew his attention immediately. He walked toward it, but stopped when a soft voice rang in his ears.

"Chief! How nice of you to come by."

A small, attractive woman walked up to Burton Riggs and kissed him on the cheek. "Libby, just the person I'm looking for. Boys, this is Libby Arbuckle, Ms. Libby as we call her, one of the owners of this place. And I am Police Chief Burton Riggs, that backwoods jerk of a cop who not only saved your asses, 'scuse me Ms. Libby, but also led you safely to your refuge."

Joey bowed his head and muttered an apology, "Sorry, sir."

Burton took Libby's arm and patted her hand.

"Let me introduce my new friends," he said. He motioned toward Hap.

"This tall, handsome guy here is named Hap Murray, his driver there is Joey, and the other shall remain nameless since I don't have a clue what his name is. I found the whole bunch of 'em stranded on the road where that fog's so bad."

Hap extended his hand, "Nice to meet you. We're from Channel 12 News. We'll need a place to stay for a day or so, if you have any rooms left."

Libby shook his hand and stared directly into his eyes. When the handshake lasted just a little too long, Hap dropped his hand and lowered his head. His fingers tingled, and he turned his hand over to see if he could find anything unusual. Then he looked again at Libby.

"Murray. We had a family named Murray on the outskirts of the Cove. Any relation?" Libby asked.

"Yes, I'm afraid so. My grandmother lived here. I used to visit when I was a kid."

"You did?" Libby asked and paused for a moment. She studied him, looked him up and down. Then she gasped and brought her hands to her face.

"Oh, my goodness! You're Michael, aren't you? Michael Murray, Lydia Murray's grandson." He smiled down at her. "Most people call me Hap. Did you know my grandmother?"

"Certainly!" Libby said. "I lived down the street from her for years. Hap's a strange name, isn't it? Where did it come from?"

"My dad used to say that I just happened to be in the right place at the right time, so he called me Hap. The name just stuck. I'm sorry, Libby," Hap said. "I don't remember you, but then, it's been almost thirty years since I've been here. I was only ten on my last summer visit. I came back once when I was in college just to spend a week with Gigi, though from the time I was ten, she'd come visit us every summer in Huntsville. I'm sure that if I'd met you, I would have remembered."

"Oh, you've met me," she said and walked closer to him. She reached out and patted his arm. "I'm glad to see that you've recovered from the accident. And from the looks of you, I'd say that everything turned out well."

Burton shook his head and chuckled.

"Lordy," he said. "I didn't know it was going to be old home week when I rescued this bunch."

When she smiled, Hap smiled back at her. He was glad that the man had changed the subject. He certainly didn't want to talk about the accident, especially now that he was back in Preacher's Cove. He exhaled slowly and stared at Libby. He didn't remember her at all. He wondered how old she was. He couldn't quite tell for sure. Her long red hair was pulled back from her face and held tightly with a scarf that matched her black outfit. Her green eyes sparkled in contrast. He noticed the wisps of red curls straggling down along her forehead and cheeks. Her smooth complexion had a slight sheen to it and reminded him of porcelain. He guessed that she fell into the late-thirty range.

"We would appreciate anything you could do for us," he said, hoping Libby would not bring up the past again.

"Are you hungry?" Libby asked. "Cove's Inn has the best food in the South, even if I do say so myself. Let's go into the restaurant—you, too, Burton—and get you boys something to eat."

Burton bowed low, gesturing as if he held a top hat in his hand. "I must decline that kind offer, Ms. Libby. A police chief's work is never done. Besides, I'm on a diet, and there's a ton of paperwork that needs my undivided attention for about the next three weeks."

Chief Burton Riggs straightened up and turned to Hap and the crew. He smiled, walked over to them, and shook hands with each one.

"Nice to meet you boys. You take care of yourselves and call me if you need anything," he said, and handed Hap a business card. Something in the look of him gave Hap a chill that made him shudder.

"Thanks, Chief. I appreciate all you've done for us today," Hap said.

"Y'all try to stay out of trouble. And remember, this is Preacher's Cove, where just about anything can happen...and most often does."

Burton turned and looked at Hap, but he wasn't smiling this time. Hap shifted and shoved his hands back into his jeans pocket. He wondered what the look meant. With the exception of his hallucination of the woman in the fountain, coming into Preacher's

Cove hadn't been too bad, and now the lovely Libby made him feel glad that he had come. Hap nodded at Burton, unsure of the man's motive in rescuing them, uncertain as to the luck in having him show up at just the right time. He looked around the room. Preacher's Cove might be no different from any other Southern town, and with the exception of the storms and a few bizarre coincidences—his brief experience with near-death at age six among them—it was no more dangerous than Huntsville. Hap congratulated himself on surviving another day.

Someone tapped his arm. He turned around and stared at Libby.

"Are you all right?" she asked.

"Oh sure," he said. "I'm fine."

"Shall I make arrangements for a couple of rooms for you and your crew?"

"Yes, if you don't mind. We'll need two rooms for the three of us."

Hap knew he couldn't find out what he needed to know in only forty-eight hours, but he hoped that he could get enough to start the story. He hated the thought of staying here any longer than he had to.

"Two rooms for two nights, right?" Libby asked.

She walked over to the desk and went to the computer. She typed something, looked up at him and smiled, and brushed a stray wisp of red hair from her face. She came from behind the desk, smoothed the black skirt that brushed the middle of her knees, and slipped her thumbs into the waistband to straighten her black and white silk blouse. She glanced in the mirror opposite the desk. The black and white scarf that held her hair back seemed straight but several curls drifted from its hold. She looked at Hap, crooked her finger in his direction, and walked past him and the others.

"I'll select a nice table for you in the restaurant."

Hap nodded to her, looked over at Joey and Eagle and motioned them to follow. They shuffled behind her like stray pups, walked out of the office and crossed the walkway to the restaurant. Hap heard a low rumbling thunder in the distance. *Jesus Christ*, he thought, *not another storm.*

"Don't worry," Joey said. "It's like gas. It'll pass."

"What are you talking about, kid?"

"The thunder," Joey said. "I know how you hate storms. But, it's just thunder. It doesn't mean that another storm is coming through here. I'll protect you. I'm good with stuff like that."

"Sure you are, kid," Hap said. "Wasn't it you who was driving the van just a little while ago? You can't maneuver a van through a little fog, but you can protect me from lightning. That's a good one!" Hap made a fist and pretended to punch Joey on the mouth. He stopped just short of the young driver's face, smiled, and looked down at the top of his head.

"I was just teasing you, short stuff. You did a good job...well, maybe not a good job, but a passable job. No one was hurt, right. No one died. So, I'd say you did just fine."

"Thanks, Hap," Joey said and bowed from the waist. "Golf clap, please."

Eagle and Hap went along. They held up their hands, did rapid but silent claps for the boy.

"And don't worry, kiddo. When you grow up, maybe you'll be tall and handsome just like me," Hap said.

"Yes, siree." Joey rolled his eyes. "It's my dream."

They followed Libby into the restaurant and past the gift shop. Creaks in the wooden floor heralded their steps. One lone cash register marked the entrance to the gift shop, a sprawling area filled with T-shirts, jars of homemade jellies and jams, cookbooks, and souvenirs. An antique player piano stood in the middle of the shop surrounded by stands that displayed works by local artists.

Beside each display were white index cards with the artist's name and address scripted in gold. Everything from flat stones painted with landscapes and animals carved from white oak to brightly-colored afghans and handmade seasonal wreaths graced the Artists' Corner. Hap stopped briefly to look. He scanned the room, noted that it was the typical country shop, nothing out of the ordinary, and turned to follow the crew and Libby. He glanced up for only a second.

Then he stopped dead still.

6

To the right, high on a shelf that overlooked the cash register sat four small wide-eyed children, their faces frozen in gentle smiles. Two appeared to be toddlers, while the other two seemed roughly four years old.

"What are those kids doing up there?"

For an instant, Hap thought of his own child, the child he'd never seen. The only image he had of the child was one he had created in his mind: a healthy, bright four-year old girl with long red curls bouncing as she walked. These perfect dolls reminded his mind's image, a child lost from him, stranded—maybe even trapped on a ledge somewhere—without his help.

"Say hello to the Firelight Angels," Libby said.

"What?" Hap asked and stepped away from her.

"I didn't mean to frighten you, Hap." Libby touched his arm gently, curling her small fingers around it. She smiled at him. Her emerald green eyes sparkled. Behind them danced a spark of glowing light. Hap took a deep breath. His arm tingled with warmth where Libby's hand lay. He sighed and smiled at her.

"The Firelight Angels," she whispered. "That's what we call them. Beautiful, aren't they?"

"Yes. Beautiful beyond belief."

Hap shook off the guilt he felt when he realized that they were just dolls. They weren't children as he'd first thought, just works of another local artist. He moved a bit closer to the register. Up close, the dolls looked like they might move or speak at any minute. From the faces to the clothes, each one was a precise work so realistic that he couldn't bring himself to move. He squinted and read the name on one of the white index cards. "Little William, Dance on Clouds. Handmade by Lucy Addams."

"Are you all right? You look a little pale."

Libby reached up and touched Hap's face. When she smiled at him, her green eyes sparkled with life. Hap closed his eyes at her touch. A tingling warmth spread from his head to his toes, the effect of it almost dizzying. Libby grabbed both his elbows.

"Come with me," she said, the tone in her voice as soothing and refreshing as the sound of a mountain stream steadily tumbling over mossy stones. "You'll feel better once you've eaten something."

"Hey, get your butt in gear, man. We're starving," Joey called, his voice stern and authoritative. Then he smiled and chuckled to himself. Eagle scratched at his beard, frowned, and shook his head. "It'll never work for you, kiddo," he quipped. "You just ain't the givin' orders type."

"Oh well, I tried," Joey shrugged.

Hap opened his eyes, took a deep breath and walked alongside Libby. He couldn't resist one glance back. The hair on the back of his neck prickled.

"Ready to eat?" Libby asked. Libby pointed to an overhang in the doorway of the restaurant. "Watch your head now," she said.

Hap ducked his head and stepped inside, Eagle and Joey right behind him. Libby nodded at them and directed them toward the table. They walked through a spacious room with vaulted ceilings, fans whirring above them. Servers scurried from table to table carrying trays balanced with care, some just at the verge of toppling under the weight of large glasses filled with iced tea and platters brimming with homemade delicacies. The servers wore black trousers, white shirts, and black bolo ties. Hap couldn't find even one with a shirttail out. All of them seemed young and scrubbed clean, like babies just out of the bath.

Libby seated them in a small room to themselves. A server appeared armed with menus and glasses of ice water. "I hope you find everything to your liking, gentlemen."

"Thank you. We really appreciate it." Hap smiled at her. "Care to join us?"

Hap felt his cheeks flush and his heart beat quicken. "You could fill us in on Preacher's Cove, tell us all those juicy little secrets that every town has." He smiled, ran his hand through his hair, and looked down at the floor. He felt suddenly embarrassed that he'd made a move so quickly, but he found her irresistible.

"I, uh, I really need to get back to work," Libby said.

"Please, you can't turn down Lydia Murray's grandson."

Joey and Eagle looked at one another while the server stood patiently waiting for them to order. Joey raised his eyebrows in one of those something's-going-on-here looks. Then he grinned at the server, a cute teenaged girl with long, copper-colored hair, green eyes, and smooth skin. The name tag read, "Caillin." Even with her hair pulled back and not a hint of make-up, she was pretty enough to make any guy look twice. She blushed and lowered her head just a little.

"May I get you something?" she asked.

"Please give us a few more minutes, if you don't mind, dear," Libby said. "I don't think we're quite ready to order yet." Libby raised her hands as if in surrender and sat down next to Hap. He smiled again and moved over a little to make sure she had plenty of room. Then, he changed his mind and scooted closer to her.

"Thanks," he said. "We're delighted to have you join us. Right guys?"

"Right," they said in unison.

They finished the meal, and when the server appeared again, Hap noticed a resemblance between Libby and Caillin that he'd missed earlier. They had the same copper-colored hair, the same emerald green eyes, small frames and slight builds. Something else about the two of them bugged him, but he couldn't identify it.

When they all stood to leave, Caillin wrote the ticket, tore it off the pad, and handed it to Libby. As she did, Hap thought he saw an ink smudge in the palm of her hand, the first sign of "dirt" that he'd seen in this place. Hap looked at Joey and saw him staring at Caillin. He looked entirely smitten by the girl. Hap winked at Eagle, nodded toward Joey, and smiled.

"Methinks that this one is way outta your league, son," Eagle whispered to Joey. "And remember this word: *jailbait.* Trust me. It's not one you want to forget."

"I guess that must hold some weight, seeing as how it comes from a former—remember this word, Eagle—*jailbird*," Joey replied and patted him on the shoulder.

Hap laughed along with them all in one spontaneous burst. "Libby, care to take a walk?" Hap asked, seizing the light-hearted moment and counting on it to help him win Libby's trust and get the information he needed. "You can show me around this complex of yours."

Joey rolled his eyes and said, "Well, here he goes again."

"I beg your pardon," Libby said.

Hap glared at Joey. "Just ignore him, Libby," Hap said. "Sometimes he acts his age; sometimes, his shoe size!"

Libby clasped her hands in front of her.

"A short walk?" she asked. When Caillin returned with the receipt, she handed it to Libby. Hap looked carefully at her hand. In her palm was a round, sapphire-colored mark. Caillin glanced up at him, looked him right in the eyes, and seemed almost to linger inside his mind. Then, she balled her hand into a fist, lowered her head, and scurried away.

"I'm beat," Eagle said.

"Stop by the desk and pick up your keycards. Your rooms are ready. If you need anything, just call for room service."

"Thanks," Eagle said, grabbing Joey by the back of his shirt. "Come on, kiddo, time for beddie-bye. You can bunk with his highness. I snore too loud to have a roommate. 'Course, Hap already knows that, don't you, buddy?"

"Oh yeah," Hap said and rolled his eyes. "You can bunk with me," Hap said to Joey. "But no funny business!"

"Funny, real funny," Joey said and raised his hand to flip him a bird. Then he glimpsed Caillin scurrying around by the tables and lowered his hand.

"Naughty boy. What would your mama say?" Eagle chided. He put his arm around Joey's shoulder and led him out of the restaurant.

Hap excused himself to the Men's Room. He took out his notepad and jotted down several words: *blacksky, greenflash, Lucy Addams, Caillin's dot*. Large question marks by each word indicated possible information for a story. Hap washed his hands, smiled to expose his gums, and leaned into the mirror. A wayward hunk of lettuce stuck between his teeth was all that he needed right now.

Assured that his teeth were clean, he spritzed a bit of Cleen-Breath spray. He brushed off his jacket, ran his hand through his hair, and walked back into the dining room. He hoped he could charm Libby into telling him about the storms. She might be willing to talk to him, and in the meantime, to let him sit and look at her. He smoothed his jacket one more time and smiled when he saw Libby waiting for him.

Looks, don't fail me now, he thought.

7

Hap waited by the register in the gift shop. With one elbow propped on the counter, he twirled his pen in his fingers. He tried to avoid looking at the Firelight Angels.

No luck.

The hair on the back of his neck prickled again. Despite their painted-on smiles, each one looked on the verge of saying something. They reminded him of lost souls stranded on an island with no one to hear or rescue them. One in particular, Little William, magnetized him. Something about the doll tugged at his heart so desperately that he wanted to run over and save him from some unimaginable horror. Hap walked behind the counter. Each doll except William had a price tag—and a hefty one at $125—scripted in gold and taped underneath the name card. He picked up one of the cards and turned it over: SOLD. He picked up another card. Another SOLD announcement scripted in gold. Four dolls, four SOLD signs. Then he reached up and lifted William off the shelf. Heavier than he'd imagined, the doll felt like a living child. Instinctively, he cushioned it in the crook of his arm. A crushing sadness crept into his heart. He stared into William's eyes. Tingling warmth spread throughout his body. Within seconds, the warmth turned to heat, the heat to a white-hot streak of pain in his right eye. He hugged the doll tightly to his chest.

"No," he whispered.

Hap squeezed his eyes shut. The pain left him as quickly as it had seized him. When he opened his eyes, he put his arm on the counter to balance himself. He breathed in two deep breaths and blinked his eyes.

"Buggers," he mumbled.

"I beg your pardon?" a voice called to him.

He gasped and looked down at William. *No*, he thought, *it's only a doll.*

"Hap, are you all right?" Libby asked and touched the back of his arm. He jumped and spun around clutching William even tighter. "Gosh, I'm sorry. I didn't mean to scare you."

Libby stared up at him. She looked confused and frightened. "I, uh, I'm so sorry," she said, stepping closer. She held out her arms and nodded at him. "May I put him back now?"

He reached up and put the doll back in place. A chill ran through him and he shuddered.

"Someone's passed over your grave," Libby said.

"What?"

He stared at her wide-eyed.

"Relax," Libby said softly. "It's something my gramma used to say to me. Just a joke, Hap."

Hap shook his head and leaned up against a wooden beam next to the register.

"Fine," he said. "Ready?"

Hap walked toward Libby, a thin-lipped smile on his face.

"Yes, thank you for waiting."

"No problem."

He hesitated and looked back at the dolls.

"The price is a little steep for a doll, isn't it?" he asked.

"People don't seem to think so," Libby said, motioning toward the door. "In fact, we sell more than Lucy can make. The Firelight Angels are quite popular."

"So, each doll is specially ordered?"

Libby shook her head. "No, many of them are. The rest are just creations from my sister's imagination. Those we usually don't show or sell, but often we give them away if we know who they are."

"What about that one, Little William?"

Hap pointed to the shelf above the register.

"He was the first. He's not for sale," Libby said. "The others, though, will be shipped out tomorrow. Hopefully, there will be more to replace them."

"Hopefully? You're not sure your sister will replace these dolls?

I thought you said there was a waiting list."

"The dolls are usually ready when we need them."

As they walked, Hap rushed in front of Libby. He opened the door and bowed, his arm sweeping toward the doorway. "Allow me," he offered.

"What a Southern gentleman!" she giggled.

Hap followed Libby out into the fresh air of an April evening in Alabama. The parking lot was still filled, and people seemed to be everywhere, coming and going. The smell of barbecued meat lingered in the air. Sounds of chattering customers, their shoes clacking against the wooden planks beneath, lent a steady rhythm to the place. "Is it always this busy here?"

"Busy, but not *this* busy." Libby smiled and waved at a group people filing out of a car in the lot. "It's all this business about the storms," she continued, looking up at Hap. "People think that if they stay here, they might get a glimpse of greenflash. Stupid, isn't it? Our morbid fascination with all things deadly?"

She held out her hand, crooked her finger, and smiled. Hap followed her across the parking lot, eager to be near her. "The storm struck here at Cove's End?"

Hap looked up instinctively, searching for any sign of an approaching storm. A new moon shimmered behind its cloudy veil, a pearl on a backdrop of black velvet. Libby stopped and gazed into the sky. "The goddesses' moon." Hap looked down at her and shrugged.

"The ancient Celts called it the goddesses' moon." She pointed up toward the sky. "See how a cloudy veil surrounds it, almost like a sheer curtain?"

"Oh, sure," he answered and nodded his head.

"The new moon," she continued, "marked the beginning of a mystical power cycle. The cloudy veil signified the curtain behind which the modest goddesses stood as sentinels to guard their followers and to keep the moon's enemies away."

"I've never thought of a goddess as being modest." Hap shook his head. Then he looked at Libby and raised his eyebrows. He'd had a brilliant idea.

"And a full moon was the gods' moon. No need for modesty

for the guys, right?"

"Right," she squealed. "Exactly right." She clapped her hands and smiled. "Well done!" Hap inhaled and savored the lingering aromas of the restaurant. He put one hand in his jeans pocket and grabbed Libby's hand with his other. When she didn't pull away, he closed his calloused fingers around her silky smooth hand, so small that it seemed no bigger than a child's. Libby glanced up at him, then lowered her head. "You asked about the storms," she said softly. Still turned away from him, she continued, her voice low and tinged with fear. "When these storms strike, they strike all over the Cove. We're trapped here, engulfed by an electrical death cloud that hovers over us and waits."

She let go of Hap's hand and drew an imaginary semi-circle in the air.

"It waits. We've nowhere to run."

"You make it sound alive." Hap said, his eyes narrowing, his voice filled with skepticism.

Libby turned and faced him. She stared up at him, the look of fear and dread evident in her face. "You don't remember, Hap, because you were so young."

Hap breathed deeply, rolled his head around, and massaged the muscles in his shoulders. "I remember some of it. Most of it I've tried to forget."

"Well, maybe now that you're here, you can add to your memories and forget your fears. Maybe you can find peace."

Her face glowed in the soft light of the new moon, the fear and dread replaced by gentle wisdom. She smiled at him and curled her fingers around his arm.

"Maybe," he said and pulled her close to him. "Maybe."

8

Hap slid his arm around Libby's and smiled down at her. The parking lot teemed with people, but to Hap, no one else except Libby existed at that moment. He kept his hand on her arm while they crossed the lot and walked toward the back of the complex.

Libby gazed at the sky, then up at Hap. "There's a gazebo behind the swimming pool," she said. "If you don't mind the walk, we can go there. It's a little more private than the rest of the complex."

"Just show me the way," Hap said and smiled. Libby took a deep breath and sighed. It took a good twenty minutes to walk across the complex to the gazebo. From the large pool came sounds of kids squealing and parents laughing. From the tennis court came the sounds of tennis balls popping onto the court and players yelling scores. In a large open cabana across from the courts, fifty or so people sat listening to locals playing guitars, banjos, and tambourines. When one of them called out, the whole group joined in for a sing-a-long of "She'll Be Comin' Round the Mountain."

Libby looked up at him and smiled.

"The gazebo is just another few yards away," Libby said. "We won't be bothered there. Even all this noise seems to fade away."

About ten yards ahead, Hap saw the top of an enormous white marble structure graced with ornate carvings. Four Doric columns held the massive gazebo whose top curved into a sparkling white dome, another pearl against dark velvet.

"Beautiful, isn't it?" she asked.

Hap rushed ahead of her.

"Amazing," Hap said. He let his fingers stroke the smooth stone. "Absolutely amazing. Must be twenty feet tall." Hap knew marble, and he knew that a massive structure like this one required more work than anyone could imagine. He'd spent eight years "bustin' rocks" in a marble quarry before he'd made enough money to pay his way back to school. A high-school dropout, he'd gone directly to the quarry and found work. He followed Libby up the steps to the interior. Small floodlights placed strategically inside and out lit up the gazebo, a bright star in the darkness of a mountain sky.

"Let's sit, shall we?" Libby asked. "I'm a bit tired."

Seated on a row of benches, the two of them stared at one another. Hap knew he should say something, but he couldn't think of the right question to ask. Libby broke the awkward silence. "May I ask you something before we get started with your questions?"

"Sure," he said. "Fire away."

"Why did the dolls bother you so much?"

Hap reached into his pocket and took out his notebook, all the while staring down at the floor of the gazebo. What could he tell her that she would understand? What could he say that wouldn't make her hate him?

"It's a long, sad story, Libby. Not worth your time."

Libby touched him gently on the hand. "Why don't you let me be the judge of what's worth my time," she said. "I'd like to know."

He hesitated, stared down at the floor again, and wondered how she would respond to the fact that he'd abandoned his own child. But before he could stop himself, the words spilled out in a river of regret.

"Years ago," he said, "I fell in love with a beautiful young girl. We were both freshmen at Indiana State. We dated for months and hardly did anything except spend time together. Our schedules were hectic, but we found time for each other because we were so in love. Several months later, her father died. She and her mother moved away. On the day that she was supposed to leave, she came to me and told me that she was pregnant."

"And?" Libby interrupted.

"And," he said, a look of desperation in his eyes, "I couldn't see how I could support myself, a wife, and a child. I told her that I didn't know what to do, that I had to think about how we would survive. She left believing that I didn't want to marry her or have anything to do with the child."

"Did you?" Libby asked and leaned forward.

"Did I what?"

"Did you want to marry her?"

"Of course!" he said. He shifted in his seat and leaned toward Libby. "Of course I did, but I needed some time to think it through. I know that I should never have let her walk away, but I did. I made that mistake, and because of it, I never saw her again. Never saw the child."

Hap lowered his head.

"I'm sorry," he whispered. "I've never told anyone except my mother. Please don't think I'm a total jerk. I've paid for the mistake many times over."

Libby reached over and put her hand under his chin. She lifted his head so that she could look into his eyes.

"Hap," she whispered.

His eyes implored her to understand.

"Did you try to find her?" she asked.

"Yes," he said and looked straight into her eyes. "I searched for her the best I knew how back then. About a year after she left, I received a letter from her postmarked in South Carolina. I tried to find her but couldn't."

"What was in the letter?" Libby asked.

Hap looked into the sky and cleared his throat.

The veiled moon's glow cast a shadowy pink light—like a timid young girl waiting to reach full bloom. He thought of Taylor, how innocent and beautiful she had been. He remembered the look on her face when he told her he needed some time to think. Her countenance had changed, then. The beautiful smile vanished, her shoulders slumped, and the innocent life drained away, right in front of his eyes. He had transformed her from a spirited young beauty into a rejected, broken remnant.

"Hap, are you all right?" Libby asked.

"She got married," he said, the sound of his voice dull and lifeless. "She got married and had the baby."

"I'm sorry you never found her and that you never saw your child."

"Me, too," he said. "The thought of it haunts me."

Then, he sat back, cleared his throat again, and flipped open his notepad, hoping against hope that Libby would keep his secret. "Well," he said, "I guess we should get back to business. Only this time, I should be the one listening."

"What is it that you want to know?" Libby asked. Then she smiled at him and said, "Don't worry. Your secret is safe with me. I am very good at keeping secrets."

Hap cocked his head and stared deep into her emerald green eyes, sparkling even in the dim light of the witches' moon. "How did you know...."

Libby brushed at a stray curl that clung to the side of her face. She moved her head from side to side using her fingers to comb through her long red hair. Never once did she shift her eyes from his.

"It's a little warm and humid tonight," she said. "Humidity wreaks havoc with this hair. I should cut it, I guess, but I just can't bring myself to do it."

"It's beautiful," Hap said, held fast by her gaze. The sultry air relaxed him. Yet the sight of Libby running her hands through her hair almost intoxicated him. He imagined her standing naked under a waterfall, her smooth white arms reaching up as if to catch the water as it cascaded along the curves of her body.

"So, what was it that you wanted to ask me?" Her question burst into his dream like a small explosion in his brain. He blinked his eyes and sat up straight. A bell that sounded like a foghorn rang in his ears. He gasped and swiveled around to look.

"It's just the closing bell," Libby said. "We close down the courts and the pool at 11:30."

"You have a curfew?" he asked and chuckled.

Libby blushed and laughed, too.

"It's not so much a curfew as a..." her voice trailed off.

"Uh, huh, a curfew," Hap said.

"We just like to have people off the grounds before, uh, by midnight. It's no big deal. The bar, the restaurant, and the gift shop are all open until 2:00."

"So, the bell rings, and the guests have to get out of the pool and off the courts?"

"Yep," she quipped. "It's getting late. I really need to get back."

"Just a few questions? I won't keep you long. Uh, let's see," he stammered and flipped through the pages in his notepad. "Oh yes, what do you think about these killer storms, Libby?"

"That's not a very good question," she said, her hands folded primly in her lap. A coy smile crossed her lips, and she lowered her head. "Everyone in Preacher's Cove is terrified of these storms."

"Burton seems to think that they're just natural to this area because it's located as he said, 'valleyed in.' Do you agree or do you think there's something else causing these devastating storms to strike repeatedly in this area? The Chief and you have both mentioned greenflash, so can you tell me what that is all about?"

"Goodness! That's a lot of questions. I'm afraid you'll have to go slower. I'm not a scientist, but I believe that the Chief is correct. There is something about Preacher's Cove that attracts the lightning, specifically greenflash. No other place in the world has these flashes so frequently."

Hap scribbled in his notepad as Libby talked.

For a moment, neither of them said anything. Then Hap heard Libby take a deep breath and sigh. "I'll tell you about the storms," she said. "You trusted me enough to tell me your secret, so I'll tell you what you want to know."

Hap stopped writing and glanced up at her. She twisted a strand of red hair and stared down at the floor of the gazebo. "Because of the storms," she said, her voice hollow and barely audible, "I've lost two husbands, both of them charred beyond recognition by what folks here call greenflash. It's lightning, a deadly, horrid killer lightning. The word *blacksky* is what happens right before the storms. The sky turns black, that's all. No stars, no clouds, no moon, just pitch black. The thunder gets louder and louder until it practically deafens us. Then, when it stops, there's dead silence. When the sky lights up again in those beautiful colors, we know that it's time for someone else to die."

Hap leaned forward and cupped her hands in his.

"I'm sorry," he said. "I didn't know."

He heard the change in her voice and he knew that this was the wrong subject for her. He wished he'd investigated more before he asked about the storms. Now, she seemed worlds away from him. He wondered how he could change the subject without sounding like an idiot.

Libby stood and smoothed her skirt.

"I have to go," she said. "I'm very tired."

"Wait," Hap said. "Please."

She glanced back at him, shook her head, and ran down the steps.

Then she disappeared into the night.

9

At 11:40, Libby turned the lock on a battered door and waited to hear the click. She opened the workshop, turned on the light, and glanced around. Maintaining privacy—her twin sister's necessity—demanded strict attention to detail. Libby searched for signs of disturbance in each corner of the workshop. She stepped onto the wooden floorboards and walked to her sister's worktable. She ran her hand along its edges. Years of her sister's rubbing against it while she worked had worn the edges smooth to the touch. She reached across the table and picked up a white placard scripted in gold: *Swift Genevieve, Skip a Stone.*

Libby turned the card over and looked on the back. There, scripted as well in gold, was a date: May, 2017. *Sometime next month,* she thought, *little Genevieve Branson will be in trouble.* Libby wondered whether or not the little girl would understand the message when the time came. She whispered a prayer that the child would understand and follow Lucy's instructions. If she didn't, she would surely die. Her sister's warnings were never to be taken lightly. Another placard fell from underneath the first. Libby examined it. The message was clear enough: *Brave Michael, Save the Holder.* Libby surveyed the room. In one corner, seated on the edge of a table, dressed in jeans and a toddler size sweatshirt was another doll. This one had a full head of tousled blonde hair, long bangs over its forehead. The eyes shone in clearest blue. But it was the hands that drew Libby's attention. The doll held a small notebook with a tiny pencil tucked inside the spirals. Libby gasped. The notebook was identical to the one she'd seen Hap holding in the gazebo. She turned over the card in her hand. *May, 2017.*

"I'll have to watch over him so that nothing terrible happens. Perhaps whatever trouble it is will be minor."

In a small rocking chair opposite the worktable sat another doll, the Firelight Angel that looked exactly like four-year-old Genevieve Branson. Libby tiptoed to the rocking chair, glanced around to make sure she was alone, and examined the doll. Its long black hair, swept back into a ponytail tied with a green ribbon high on its head, shone even in the dim light. The brown eyes sparkled. The porcelain white complexion, a faint blush on the cheeks, and pink lips forming a faint smile gave the doll such realistic features that Libby could almost feel the child about to giggle at some fanciful idea that had filtered through her brain. Libby reached over and straightened the doll's pink shirt. She put the placard in the doll's lap securing it snuggly between the doll's lifelike fingers. She patted the doll's head.

"Read and understand," she whispered.

Libby walked past the worktable and opened a side door. She flipped on the lights and looked around at the tall metal shelves filled with boxes of different sizes and colors. "Pink and blue," she said. "A new pink box for little Genevieve and a bright blue one for Hap."

She checked her watch: 11:55; she rushed over to the shelves. She grabbed the edge of a new pink box filled with white tissue paper, slid it forward, and strained to reach its other end to lift it off the shelf. Then she grabbed a blue one and did the same. The two boxes, even empty, seemed heavy and awkward in her small arms. She walked back into the workshop and over to the rocking chair. Carefully, she lifted Genevieve out of the chair and laid her into the box. She covered her with the sparkling tissue paper, secured the lid with several strips of wide clear packing tape, and grabbed a marker from the table. "Genni Branson," she printed on the outside of the box.

Then she lifted Brave Michael, placed him gently in the blue box, and printed "Hap Murray" on the outside. When she heard the latch on the workshop door, her heart beat quickened. "Lucy," she whispered. Libby grabbed the heavy boxes, her arms aching with their weight and bulk, and waited. Lucy shuffled into the workshop without looking at her. Libby held her breath and slid past her sister as inconspicuously as possible and caught the edge of the door with her foot before it closed. She propped one side of the box against the wall, kicked the door open with her foot, and caught it with her elbow. She glanced back to see if Lucy showed any signs of recognition. Nothing.

Libby grappled her way out of the door, let out a huge sigh, and set the boxes on the ground. When she reached back to close the door, her hand brushed across something that she recognized: Lucy's apron. Libby gasped.

"Baa Bees," Lucy said and pointed to the box. "Ma baa bees." Libby smiled, stepped closer to Lucy, and brushed her hair out of her eyes.

"They are beautiful babies, Lucy, but they need to go home. They both need their mamas."

Lucy shook her head.

"No. Ma baa bees."

Libby's heart lurched.

"I'm taking them home, Lucy. You'll be too busy to look after them."

For a moment, when Lucy cocked her head and the dim light caught the good side of her face, Libby felt as if she were looking into a mirror. She hugged her sister and turned to leave. "Make us an angel," she whispered to Lucy. Lucy nodded her head.

"Anda," she mumbled, "may anda." Lucy turned and shuffled back to the worktable.

Libby walked out and shut the door. Then she leaned against it, put her hands over her face, and cried.

10

Thunder rumbled in the distance. Hap looked across the complex and strained his eyes to see any signs of life. Then he remembered the curfew. The people had vanished.

Hap bent over and picked up his notepad. As he stepped down onto the first step, a bright flash from the sky lit up the grounds. When Hap looked up at the lightning, he stepped down again and missed the second step then stumbled and fell down the remaining three steps. Sprawled on his butt, he sat at the bottom of the gazebo. He sighed, brushed off his hands, and got to his knees. He waited a few seconds to see if any body part ached. His ankle throbbed a little, but he pushed himself to his feet. Thunder rumbled behind him. As he took his first step back toward the complex, a blinding white light seared through his right eye and sent him stumbling backwards. An explosion of images flooded his brain.

"No," he whimpered, "not now, not here."

But his words did not stop the images. A woman—a monster—her mouth a gaping hole, rushed toward him. He squeezed his eyes shut so tightly that they throbbed, but the blinding white light only intensified. It felled him, and he sank to his knees one more time. He covered his face with his hands and wept.

11

Minutes later, the pain subsided, the images disappeared, and Hap struggled to his feet, wiped his nose on his sleeve, sniffed, and shook his head.

"Ya blithering idiot!" he said himself. "Get your ass in gear."

Hap pushed the side button on his watch and stared at the dial: 11:45.

"Hello," he called to the darkness. "Is anybody there?"

He squinted and looked up at the massive gazebo, shimmering like a lighthouse in the darkness of the complex. He sighed and wiped his nose again, his heart almost hammering in his chest. Alone. Alone in the dark in a place that reeked of disaster.

Hap took a long deep breath to calm himself. It was a hotel complex, after all. People didn't get lost in hotel complexes, especially one as big and busy as this one. "Buggers!" he yelled.

Another flash of light brightened the sky. A low rumbling of thunder taunted him. And in the distance, he swore he could hear that dang harmonica again. Hap trekked up one hill, then another, his shoes slipping in the grass. He wiped his clammy hands on his jeans, said a few more choice phrases, and trudged upward. Finally, as he topped yet another hill, he saw a dim light.

"Yes!" he cried.

He walked toward it. He drew closer and squinted his eyes again. Hotel lights shone far behind the one dim light. He picked up his pace and headed for the spot. His anger and fear drove him forward. His reporter's curiosity kept him running. By the time he reached the bizarre-looking building that housed that one dim light, he was out of breath. His knees ached; his lungs burned, but it was his need for safety that held him on that spot watching for help.

Hap saw someone inside. He took a few steps closer and noticed that the window was too high even for him to see into the building. He needed something to stand on. He looked around and found just what he needed. Along the outer edge of the small building were several crates. Even in the shadowy light, Hap recognized the crates. Many of the same kind passed through the marble quarry. They were used for transporting kaolin clay, a pure clay used to make porcelain. He knew they were sturdy, so he moved one of them as quietly as he could and climbed up.

He was right. There was someone inside. A woman bent over some kind of worktable. She leaned so close to it that he could see neither her face nor what she worked on. He edged along the crate, his fingers digging into the windowsill. The tighter he held on, the more his hands scraped against the crackling wood. He could feel the blisters as they formed. After only a few seconds, the woman at the worktable stopped her work. Her head turned slightly toward the window. She stopped again, as if she were listening to something.

Hap stood dead still. The moonlight shone into the work room at a perfect angle to allow him to see the woman. When Lucy Addams turned her head once again, this time further toward the window, the light caught her perfectly. She looked at the window and saw Hap Murray. And he saw Lucy. The sight of her was enough to make him gasp, let go of the windowsill and tilt the crate. He fell flat on his back, hit his head on a small stone, and slipped into unconsciousness...his last vision that of a hideous monster hiding out in a hotel called Cove's End.

12

Hap Murray woke to the sound of thunder and the flash of lightning. "What on God's green earth happened to you, boy?" Chief Riggs asked. "Seems I'm always rescuing you from something."

With a slow, deliberate turn of his head, Hap looked around. The last thing he remembered was looking in that window and seeing that woman, that horrible woman. Now, though, he was inside a hotel room. Noises from the room echoed in his throbbing head. He struggled to sit up, bracing himself on the back of the sofa. The door burst open. Joey and Eagle rushed to his side. The sounds in the room made his head swim, so he propped his elbows on his knees and cupped his aching head with his hands. One mighty clap of thunder filled the room with an almost earth-shattering sound, a bright lightning flash on its heels.

"Hey, where in the world have you been, and who beat the crap out of you?"

Hap looked up at Joey and wondered if he could muster the strength to kick his scrawny butt out the door.

"We were worried about you," Joey said. "What were you doing out there behind the hotel?"

"How did you know I was out there? How did I get in here?" Hap asked, his voice raspy. "Libby came here to talk to you," Joey said.

He sat down next to Hap and put his hand on his shoulder. "She said she needed to explain something. When we told her we hadn't seen you, she got this panicky look on her face and left. A few minutes later, someone from the office called and said that you were hurt."

Hap looked around the room again. "What time is it?" he

asked. "How long was I out?"

"It's about 1:30 and you couldn't have been out too long when Libby found you. You were still bleeding. That's a nasty little cut on your head, not deep though."

"I need to speak to the Chief alone. Can you clear out all these people for me, Joey?" Hap asked. "It's important."

"No problem, buddy. Libby put us in the next room. We'll clear out and give you some privacy." He managed a smile at the kid. He looked at Eagle and nodded. "See you shortly," he said, his head throbbing.

All except one left the room. "He's with me," Burton said. Hap looked over at the tall man standing by the window. The man turned and looked at him with a face as expressionless as bread dough, but a face that Hap had seen before. He took no notice of anyone or anything in the room, as far as Hap could tell. He just stood there in his dark suit, dead-still, staring into the dark. Something about him made Hap uneasy. Maybe it was the way he held his hands so tightly folded in front of him that his white knuckles jutted out. Hap looked at Chief Burton Riggs. "Don't I get an introduction?" he asked, squinting against the bright light in the room.

"Later," Burton said. "I'm more interested in what happened to you out there."

Hap reached up and felt the back of his head. He winced when his fingers touched the bandage that covered the gash.

"Something weird," he said. He looked down at his knee. It, too, had been cleaned and bandaged. His hand was wrapped neatly with a fresh, clean cloth. Brownish red iodine peeked out from the bandages on his knee and his hand.

"Weird?" Burton asked and lit a cigarette. One last clap of thunder rumbled through the complex. The lightning that followed lit up the sky in a white-hot glow. "You might get that storm you were looking for, after all," Burton said. "Sorry, son, you were talking about something that happened tonight?"

"Yeah, behind the hotel, I saw a...a woman. She looked more like a monster. God, she scared me to death."

"A woman scared you?" Burton asked. "She must have been doing something pretty awful if she scared you that much. What was she doing?"

"At first, when I saw her from behind, she was bending over some sort of work table, but she turned around, and..." his voice trailed off. He cupped his head in his hands. "I could use a wet cloth," he said.

Burton grabbed the cloth that hung on the arm of the sofa. "Here, this should help."

Hap pressed the cold cloth against his forehead and sighed. Burton handed him a cold soda. He took a long sip and relished the soothing feel of the liquid. "Better?" Burton asked, the ashes dangling from his cigarette. They plopped down on the carpet.

"Dammit!" he yelled. "Libby will kill me if she knows I've been smoking in here."

Hap handed him the wet cloth. "Then you'd better destroy the evidence."

Burton wiped up the ashes, put out the cigarette and told the man at the window to open the door. "Fan it," he said softly, "before she comes back. Sorry, Hap. Go ahead. Finish your story."

"I was scared. I thought she was a monster. Then I lost my balance and fell," Hap said, the pain in his head so intense that he could barely think. Burton studied his face. Then he reached over and put his hand on the reporter's shoulder.

"There's no monster here in Preacher's Cove, son. You've had a bad time of it tonight. Why don't we talk about it tomorrow."

"You don't believe me?"

"Listen to me, Hap. We've got lots of things. We've got storms that'll kill you, we've got greenflash that'll char you, and we've got snakes—little bitty ones no more than seven inches long—that'll kill you in seconds. But one thing we don't have is monsters."

"You're wrong. I saw this woman. I want to know who she is." He balanced himself on the arm of the small sofa, tried to stand, but felt his head spinning. He grabbed into thin air for something to steady him. Burton stood and steadied him, lowering him gently back onto the sofa.

"You'd better sit down. You're still a little shaky."

He sat down again, rubbed his chin with his hand, and glanced over at the motionless man standing by the window. Hap wondered if he had a pulse, or if he'd died there and nobody bothered to move him. He wondered how someone as well-groomed and well-dressed as that could be from this place, and especially with Burton, his polar opposite. Hap looked at Burton again.

"I'm okay," he said. "Why don't you just tell me who she is? Then I'll go to bed and let you get back to whatever it is that you were doing."

Burton took a cigarette from the pack, flicked his lighter, then changed his mind. He replaced the cigarette and lighter and stared at Hap. "I was sleeping. It's 1:45 a.m."

"Just tell me what I want to know," Hap said.

"There's nothing to tell, nothing of interest anyway. She's a resident. That's all you need to know. Look, you'll be gone from here in the morning. You and all those other reporters will be back at your desks filling out papers and giving 'sorry, nothin' there' reports to your station managers. In a couple of days, your head will quit throbbing and you'll feel much better. Then you'll forget about Preacher's Cove. A year from now, it'll be a hazy, vague wisp of a memory. The storm's passing, nothing to fear, nothing to find."

Burton patted Hap's shoulder again, said something to the tall man, and walked to the door. The two of them paused and looked back. "You take care of yourself, buddy. I'm too fat and too old to go chasin' after your sorry butt." He winked, smiled, and opened the door. The tall man followed him out.

As they left, Joey and Eagle walked back in. "Are you okay?" Eagle asked. "You look terrible."

"Gee, thanks," Hap said and rolled his eyes. "Just what I need, a smart ass photographer."

"Now, now," Joey interrupted. "We gotta get some sleep. I'm bunking in here with you, and I ordered a wake-up call for seven. That gives us all of five hours."

Eagle walked over to him, kneeled down, and examined the wounds. "You got any pain killers in that bag of yours?"

"I'm fine," Hap said. "I just want to sleep. You go on and get some yourself...sleep, that is." He managed a thin smile at his friend.

Eagle winked at him and called to Joey.

"Take care of him, kiddo. If anything happens to him, we'll both be out of a job."

Joey tossed a back-pack onto one of the double beds, fumbled through it for a few seconds, retrieved his "gear" and headed for the bathroom.

Hap sat on the sofa rubbing his hand across his chin. The sight of the woman lingered in his fuzzy brain. She was strange, yet somehow familiar. He wanted to know more. He wanted to know what happened to her, what she was working on so late at night. He staggered up from the sofa, steadied himself, and walked to the bed. He plopped down on it, and still in his clothes, stretched out with his hands clasped behind his head. He knew that he needed sleep, but between the throbbing pain in his head and the nagging curiosity in his mind, sleep came slowly.

He stared at the ceiling. Something about the woman made him think of his mother. He remembered how she looked only two months ago, the last time he saw her. The cancer had ravaged her body and left her only a remnant of a once-beautiful woman he had loved so dearly. He closed his eyes, thought about his mother's sweet lavender perfume, and remembered the voice on the phone. *It couldn't have been her. She's dead. My mother is dead.*

As he drifted into a blissful kind of semi-sleep, he thought one last time about the mysterious woman in the workshop and the almost supernatural perfection of those dolls in the gift shop. Then he thought again about his lost child. He decided that he would find the woman in the workshop and apologize to her. Once again, the image of her mangled face flashed into his mind, and he shuddered.

13

The welcomed relief of deep sleep descended upon Hap and carried him into a world of total strangers. He dreamt of a man, a tall man standing alone by an open grave surrounded by a circle of stones. The man looked down into the grave, his eyes as hollow as the pit itself. Dirt splashed onto the open wooden coffin deep inside and with each splay of rocks and dirt, the tall man clasped his hands tighter. The hollow eyes sparked with no hint of awareness. The dull, lifeless pallor of his face, and the steady crease of his sunken cheeks made him appear no more alive than the woman whose name was crudely carved onto a small, flat piece of board propped against the nearest tree. As he clasped his large, rough hands ever tighter, he showed the only sign of visible life: glaring white knuckles.

From deep inside the pit issued a whimper, barely audible. The tall man twitched. Suddenly, the sky darkened, thunder rumbled in the distance, and the earth trembled beneath him. The lid of the coffin slid ever so slightly. When one fierce bolt of lightning struck beside the circle of trees, a light shone inside the pit. The man's eyes widened in horror. Another cry from the grave startled him so that he took a single step back, and when the earth trembled a second time beneath his feet, he opened his mouth to scream. But it was Hap Murray whose scream pierced the stillness of morning calm in Preacher's Cove.

14

At 6:15 a.m., the sound of the screams pierced the stillness of their quarters. Hap and Joey sat straight up in their beds.

"Geez, man, you okay?" Joey asked.

"I'd be okay if I could breathe," Hap said. His clothes were drenched with sweat and his head throbbed.

"What a wake-up call!" Joey said rubbing the sleep from his eyes. "Listen, man, we gotta get out of this place. Something isn't right. Let's pack up and get out of here."

"We can't leave today," Hap said, his head ablaze with pain.

"Why not? There's no story. The storm's gone, and I don't want to stick around to go to the funerals of all those people who got killed. All the other stations are pulling out."

"Please, Joey, indulge me. I'm not in the mood to argue."

Joey swung his legs over the side of the bed, grabbed the remote, and turned on the TV. "No offense," he said, "but you're not in great shape. There's nothing here worth hurting yourself any more than you already have. Besides, I just have this feeling that something terrible is going to happen."

They both sat with their legs swung over the beds, both rubbing their eyes, trying to focus after so little sleep. "I need coffee," Hap said. "Just let me have a cup and get a shower. Then, I'll tell you why we're really here, and why we can't leave today. Deal?"

Joey sighed, got up, and went into the bathroom while Hap went to the sink and made a pot of coffee. While it brewed, he went to the nightstand, rifled through his backpack, and pulled out clean underwear and socks. He went to the hanging bag for a clean shirt and jeans.

His sport coat was missing. He shrugged it off and listened to the news broadcast. A memorial service for the ten in the storm would begin at 9:00 at Three Hills United Methodist Church.

A familiar voice rang in his ears. He walked over to the TV and saw Libby Arbuckle being interviewed by one of the local reporters.

"Yes," she said, "we are all saddened at the loss of these good people. Being a person who has lost loved ones to these horrendous storms, I feel the least I can do is offer Cove's End's services during this crisis. We'll be providing brunch for all those attending the memorial. It is free of charge, of course. All are welcome."

Delighted to see Libby on television, Hap watched her charm the interviewer, just as she had charmed him. Her poise and grace shone through the set, and he felt himself eager to see her again. He had an idea. If he helped her get additional, national publicity for Cove's End, maybe she wouldn't object to sharing information about the woman in the workshop, and especially, about Ike Madison.

By the time Joey emerged from the bathroom, Hap felt a renewed sense of purpose. As he passed by Joey, he patted him on the shoulder. Hap went to the phone, dialed 9 for an outside line, then his number. After only two rings, he heard the familiar voice.

"Hello," the voice said, fully alert.

"Dad, how's everything?"

"Good, son. I'm getting by, doing the best I can. Where are you?"

"Preacher's Cove," Hap responded. "Herb told me that you had suggested I come here for this story. Is that right?"

His father hesitated.

"I thought it was time, Hap. Your mother, God rest her soul, would want you to do this. Are you angry?"

"No, Dad. I'm not angry."

"Where are you staying?"

"Cove's End."

"What?" his father asked.

"A place called Cove's End. It's a huge place, very nice, though. You'll never guess who runs it."

"Okay, you've piqued my curiosity. Who?"

"Libby Arbuckle. Remember her? She says she knew Gigi."

"Libby Arbuckle, hmm. Can't say as I remember the name.

She knew your grandmother? Oh, wait a minute. She had a twin sister named Lucy. Libby and Lucy Taylor. They were beautiful girls, whew! Her sister used to babysit for you, boy."

"She has a twin named Lucy. There was a bunch of those girls, four, I think."

"Hmm...."

"You be careful, Hap. Preacher's Cove has a tragic history. You were one of the lucky ones, from what I heard years ago."

"Dad, please...."

"Your mother would be proud of you, Hap. She always wanted you to revisit the place," his father said.

"Speaking of mom...." Hap hesitated and ran his hands through his hair.

"What is it, son?"

"Nothing, nothing. Listen, Dad, I need to get busy."

"Take care of yourself. Nothing bad has happened, has it?"

"Everything's okay so far. I'll fill you in when I leave. I'll swing by your place with the crew and we'll spend some time together. Okay?"

"That'd be great, son. Your old man misses you."

"See you soon, Dad."

When he hung up, Hap wished he had told his dad about the episodes, the flashes of memory, the pain in his head, but he knew his dad had enough to worry about. He decided to tell him the next time he talked to him.

"Hap, get a move on. I'm starved," Joey said, towel-drying his shoulder-length brown hair. "We came here to make front-page news, right? Can't do that if we're starving."

"Eager to get to that restaurant, are we? Wouldn't have anything to do with that cute little server, would it?"

Joey smiled at him.

"I wish," he said and brushed his hair back. "You're the one with all the luck in the girl department."

"Maybe if you'd cut that stringy mop of yours, you'd have more luck, too!" Hap said and twirled the damp towel Joey had left on the sink. Joey turned to flip him a bird.

Pop...right in the midsection.

"Ouch," Joey yelled.

Hap laughed and rubbed his hand. He hadn't counted on hurting himself when he popped the towel.

"Uh, huh," Joey chided. "Doesn't feel too good on that cut. Serves you right."

The phone rang, and at the same time, someone knocked on the door. Joey answered the phone. Hap opened the door, expecting to see Eagle. Libby stood in front of him struggling under the weight of a huge tray. Crooked around her fingers was his sport coat. When she looked at him, she gasped. "You look awful," she said.

Hap reached down and took the tray from her. "I haven't had a chance to clean up yet," he offered.

"I, uh, I thought you and the others might need some breakfast. Am I intruding?"

"No, no," he insisted. "Come on in." Hap put the tray on the dresser. The aroma of eggs, bacon, and coffee tantalized his nostrils. His stomach growled.

Libby held up his sport coat.

"I took the liberty of cleaning it," she said. "It looked pretty rough."

"Thanks, I'm sure it did. I'm going to...uh, can you stay for a few minutes? I need to get a shower."

"Not now," she said and lowered her head. "I just came to apologize. I'm sorry about leaving you out there alone."

"It's okay," he said and smiled. "I'll be fine."

"I hope so," Libby said and looked up at him. "Can we talk later? I need to get ready for the service." Libby put her hand on his arm and squeezed gently. "Enjoy your breakfast," she said and turned to leave. "I'm off to the memorial service."

"I'd like to come with you," he said. "But first, who is she?"

Libby stopped, clasped her hands in front of her, and forced a thin smile. "My sister," she said, her voice barely audible. "Lucy Addams, my twin sister."

Hap stood looking down at Libby without saying a word. He found it hard to believe that the woman he'd seen was Libby's twin. The phrase, "Handmade by Lucy Addams," popped into his mind. *Of course*, he thought, *the worktable.* "She's the doll maker?"

Libby chuckled. "The doll maker, yes."

"Did I say something funny?"

Libby walked to the door and hesitated.

"The service begins in thirty minutes. I'll meet you there."

"See you then," Hap said.

15

"Come, my children," the voice echoed throughout the sanctuary. "Let us acknowledge our grief, claim it before the Lord our God, the Lord Most High Creator, Healer, Father, Friend. He alone is sufficient to hear our cries and ease our burdens. He alone can give us comfort and strength. Let us surrender our burden to God, for only by surrendering it to Him can we truly find the peace to continue. Come, my children."

With his arms outstretched, the reverend called the mourners forward.

"Come and partake of His mercy."

One by one they filed toward the altar, the reverend embracing each of them, offering a warm hug, a pat on the back, or a kiss on the cheek.

"I love you just as God loves you," he whispered.

"Let the tears flow, my children," he called, his voice trembling, his lips quivering. "Let the tears flow as we mourn our dead brothers. Let us show God how deep our grief is, flowing like a sea of daggers against our hearts."

Hap sat in the back pew of Three Hills United Methodist Church, riveted by the minister's presentation. For a moment, he forgot that he was just a stranger here. He felt the urge to get up and go to the altar, as the minister commanded. Then, back to himself, he shook his head and smiled. The minister, he reminded himself, was Ike Madison, the man he'd been sent to investigate. Hap studied him. The man looked like he'd just stepped out of a GQ photo shoot. The fine cut of his suit, the white shirt, silk tie. French cuffs, he noted, with gold cufflinks. Expensive leather shoes shined to perfection. His thick black hair, graying just at the temples, seemed perfectly combed, each hair in place. No floppy bangs fell on his forehead. Hap reached up and ran a hand through his own hair...thick, yes, but decidedly unkempt and in need of a comb. Heels clacking against the marble floor distracted him from his own appearance. Hap looked over and saw Libby walk through the great double doors. He slid down and made room for her. Then he smiled and nodded. Libby did not smile back but sat beside him, her back straight, her purse held firmly in her lap. Hap let his eyes wander from the top of her head to the tips of her black leather shoes. His gaze lingered momentarily on her lap, the spread of her green skirt short enough to reveal shapely legs.

"An evil lives here," the Reverend Madison said and took a few steps forward. He pointed straight ahead, toward the back of the church. His voice barely above a whisper, he said, "an evil that looms over our fair town and threatens all of us." The grieving mourners hushed their cries then, and an awful silence slithered through the sanctuary like a poisonous serpent. Hap glanced at Libby. She stared straight ahead. Then he watched as the dapper reverend walked toward him and put his hand on the back of the pew. Hap cleared his throat and fidgeted in his seat.

"Our brothers are dead," Madison said. "Our brothers in Christ were struck down, burned in the terrible fury of an evil that lives in Preacher's Cove. All that remains of them now is ashes...ashes, my children. We have lost our friends, our partners, our hearts to the unspeakable darkness that dwells here."

In deliberate steps, Reverend Ike Madison moved to the middle of the aisle and turned to look back to the last pew. He looked directly at Libby.

"And what shall we do now? How shall we defend ourselves against this abomination? How do we destroy an evil so vicious that it claims twelve of us in one blow? Who among you knows the answer?"

Hap glanced again at Libby. She glanced back this time with a barely perceptible smile. Then, she lowered her head and fixed her gaze on something Hap couldn't see.

"The answer, my children, is simple. We trust in God to make us warriors, hunters, finders and destroyers of evil and its whores. We trust in Him to hear our prayers and give us the strength to become the victors in His Holy War against evil."

Madison, back at the front of the church, gathered the mourners around him once more. They flocked to his side like sheep struggling for a place next to the shepherd, the guardian of their welfare, their provider.

"Hear our prayers, O Lord God, God of hope, God of mercy, God of all that is right and true and good. We ask you, O Lord, to hear our prayers and grant us strength and courage. We ask you, O Lord, for an end to this reign of evil. Let Your power be mighty before it, Lord, a mighty armor of justice."

The reverend's voice carried throughout the sanctuary. It echoed across the great hall. He lifted his arms to the sky.

"And O Lord, we beg you for your merciful grace, for the courage to face another day, and the wisdom to call upon you at every turn. We ask You, our Lord God, to favor us this day, favor us, favor us mourners for the loss of our ten brothers and as warriors in the battle against sin and death. Amen, Lord. Amen."

His petitions finished, Reverend Madison walked to the gilded, flower-laden altar and picked up a slender bouquet of roses: one red, one yellow, and one white. He read a name from a list and handed a bouquet to each of the wives, daughters, and sisters of the ten men killed by the storm.

"The red rose," he said, "for the blood they shed; the yellow for the friendships they gave to Preacher's Cove, and the white for the spirits they are now, free from care and resting in God's embrace."

The organist began a soft rendition of "Amazing Grace," and as the congregation heard, they sang, their voices growing ever louder, until at last, the sound of their singing filled the sanctuary in a perfect cadence of both grief and joy. Ike Madison's mellow baritone could be heard above them all. Hap watched from the back pew, watched this man, this near father to all his children, watched as tears fell from his eyes and ran down his cheeks spilling onto smooth black lapels, occasionally tipping a pocket square of black and tan stripes.

Hap leaned toward Libby.

"He must've paid a fortune for that suit."

Libby looked at him, smiled, and whispered,

"Everyday work clothes for him. Keeps up the image, and image is everything to Reverend Madison." Libby blushed, then, as if she'd revealed something best kept in secret.

"We grieve and we rejoice," Ike Madison shouted. "We grieve for our ten brothers in Christ, and we rejoice for their souls set aflight toward home. And in that due sense of all reverence, we most humbly thank the Lord our God, the Most Holy One, the Redeemer, the Savior, the Almighty. We thank Him now, bowing before the King, for his power, his mercy, and his grace."

Reverend Madison stopped talking, wiped the tears from his eyes, and walked slowly to the back of the sanctuary, stopping at each pew to extend a hand and a smile to those in attendance.

"Thank you," he whispered, "for coming to commemorate our dead."

When he reached the back pew, he stopped and looked at Libby. He extended his hand, but no smile crossed his lips.

"Libby," he said, his tone flat and lifeless tinged with a hint of sarcasm. Libby did not shake his hand, but instead, turned to Hap and tapped his hand, motioning for him to shake hands with the reverend.

"This is Michael Murray," Libby said to Ike. "He's Gigi Murray's grandson."

"Oh, Gigi, yes," Ike said and smiled. "We still miss her. Good of you to come, Michael."

Hap nodded and smiled, his mind clogged with images of his grandmother, with his parents...and with Libby.

"Please join us," Ike said, "for the luncheon in the fellowship hall and for the gathering afterwards at Cove's End. Our Libby is kind enough to host us."

Ike stood at the back of the sanctuary, the height and breadth of him almost filling the doorway. He stood perfectly still until silence filled the great hall. Once more, he lifted his arms toward the heavens, toward a rounded skylight in the center of the magnificent church. Sunlight beamed in and radiated throughout, filling the place with a bright warm light. Reflected on a huge cross centered above the altar, a golden spray filtered back to the exact spot where Ike stood.

"Go in peace, my children, to love and serve the Lord."

The organist played again, and at the sound of the first chord, Libby darted out a side door and disappeared. The mourners filed out one by one, each carrying a bouquet, holding it close against their breasts, like soldiers carrying shields.

Hap waited until the last one had left before he stood up.

"Come with me, Michael," Ike Madison said. "I'll show you to the fellowship hall."

Hap nodded and walked alongside Ike Madison. He chuckled when he thought of how they must look, the two of them, two tall fellows, one quite dapper, the other barely passing for suitably dressed. They headed down a narrow, glassed-in walkway thirty feet or so in length that led to another building and opened into a spacious room with several—he counted twelve—floor to ceiling windows.

"These windows must be ten feet tall."

"Exactly," Madison answered.

Each window had a stained glass, half-circle arch above it. Hap studied the design in the stained glass but couldn't quite decide what it was. He looked around the room at the round tables dressed with white tablecloths. Atop all the tables was a centerpiece of brightly-colored flowers. Hap noticed the absence of black. No black bows, no mourning wreaths.

"Colorful," he said to Ike.

"Yes, ah, you've noticed, haven't you, that there's no black in here. Now is not the time for black, Michael. Now's the time for rejoicing. Our brothers are gone. Only their memories remain, and we must honor those memories with joy."

"It's Hap," he said to the reverend. "Most people call me Hap."

"Then, Hap it is," Ike said. "I prefer a Christian given name, but I, too, bear a nickname, one from my father, so I understand how a name can become a natural part of life. Mine serves me quite well, and yours?"

"The same. My father used to tell me that I just happened to be in the right place at the right time, so he called me Hap. The name stuck, and I've been fortunate to occasionally live up to it."

Ike Madison laughed a hearty laugh and patted Hap on the back.

"That's good enough, then. And what line of work are you in, Hap?"

"Oh, I used to bust rocks," he said and held out his large, calloused hands, "in a rock quarry."

"Honest work," Ike said. "Honest day's work for a day's pay."

"Now, I'm a reporter for Channel 12 in Huntsville."

"A reporter," Ike said and stopped walking. "And what brings you to Preacher's Cove?" Then, as if he'd remembered something, Ike said, "Ah, the storms. I'm afraid the others have beaten you to the story."

"We're a little slow," Hap said. "I'm just here to see if there are any juicy leftovers in the cupboard. I do mostly human-interest stories. You know, interesting people, interesting places, stories of personal triumph...that sort of thing."

"I see," Ike said. "I see."

Libby stood beside one of the tables talking to the guests. Hap found it surprising that in a room filled with people, his eyes fixed immediately on this one small woman. But there she was, looking elegant in a green dress, her long hair pulled away from her face with a shimmering green headband. Wisps of stray curls caressed the sides of her face.

Beside her, in a younger version and only slightly larger, stood her twin. Hap recognized her immediately: the server, Caillin. Libby looked up at him, glanced over at Caillin, looked back at him, frowned, and stopped her talking. She put her hand on Caillin's shoulder and drew her close.

Hap felt his face redden.

Staring again, he thought. *Great, just great. You're about as subtle as a train wreck.*

He lowered his head, stuck his hands in his pants pockets, and looked at the floor. His reflection stared back at him. His reflection...his eyes lost their focus, swept down into a pool of images and voices. He stared, riveted to the spot where he stood. Something formed beside him in that reflected self, something dark and powerful.

A rumbling of thunder shook the floor and jerked Hap away from the vision in the pool. He gasped and held out his hands to steady himself.

Someone grabbed his arm. "You all right, son?"

Hap turned to see Burton Riggs standing next to him.

"You were kinda lost there for a minute, weren't you? It's okay. We all step out from time to time. Keeps us sane."

Hap wiped his forehead with his hand.

"Yeah," he said, "or drives us insane."

"I see you've met Ike Madison, our esteemed leader," Burton said and waved to Libby. She smiled and walked toward the two of them.

"He seems okay," Hap said. "Spiffy dresser."

Burton looked up at him and smiled.

"Yep, ever the dapper dandy."

"You're late," Libby said and kissed him on the cheek. "But I forgive you."

"Well, as long as you forgive me, lovely lady, then everything's okay," Burton said and hugged her. "Glad to see you brought along our handsome new friend," he said nodding his head toward Hap.

"Yes," Libby said. "He is quite handsome, isn't he?"

She quickly covered her mouth and blushed.

"Oh my," she said, "I, uh...I..." then her voice trailed off and she moved away from them, mingling with the guests.

Hap watched with delight when she glanced back and their eyes met. He smiled at her, raised an eyebrow, and waited for her reaction, but no return smile came. She just lowered her eyes and looked away from him. Hap felt his hands grow cold. He noticed a group of women sitting at a table nearby. The women leaned in close to each other, dabbing at their eyes with white handkerchiefs, alternately whispering, crying, and sneaking quick looks at him. He felt out of place, the proverbial stepchild of the bunch, a stranger.

When the tremulous thunder sounded again, Hap inhaled a sharp breath. Then he heard a rapping sound and looked over to see Ike Madison standing across the room beside the farthest window. "Behold," he said when the crowd quieted. "Behold the feast prepared for us this day. We thank God for it. Feast at the table of God's grace and mercy and welcome into our midst a fellow brother, a prodigal son returned to the Cove."

Ike Madison pointed at him, and when he did, Hap felt his cheeks redden.

"Hap Murray, grandson of Gigi and Henry Murray, we welcome you home and pray that you will share in our sorrow for the lost brothers and our joy for the release of their souls. Amen."

"Amen," the crowd intoned.

The feasting began, and Hap was pulled, literally, to a table full of grievers who welcomed him back to Preacher's Cove, piled his plate with food, and treated him as if he were their long-lost son. They recounted for him, as best they could, every detail of greenflash and the storm that had claimed the lives of their loved ones. In turn, each one of them made a remark about Libby. "Oh yes, she's a good enough caterer, but that whole bunch up at Cove's End, well, you have to watch yourself, boy. Just watch yourself. Something's wrong up there."

Hap asked about the Reverend Madison.

"Oh, what a lovely man," Eileen Bailey said, widow of one of the victims. "What a God-send for this town. Why, without him, I don't know what some of us would do. He—you remember this, don't you, Gracie—he stayed up with us, day and night at the hospital when..." then her voice broke and she sobbed.

"You'll not find a better minister," her daughter said. "He's given so much to this town. He's always willing to help, no matter what the problem, and he knows, you see, about the...the bad things that go on."

"Bad things?" Hap asked, his interest piqued.

"Yes, bad things. The reverend knows about them. He's fighting every day to make this place safe."

"Safe from what?" Hap asked and took a sip of his iced tea.

The girl didn't answer right away, but her mother, Eileen, reached over the table and put her hand on Hap's arm.

"It's the devil's work. We live in a lovely town with a lovely community of people. Kind-hearted, generous Christian folk who'd do just about anything for you. But there's something...

something wrong here. We don't know what it is for sure, but we know that Libby Arbuckle and that bunch up there at Cove's End, well..." her voice trailed off and she looked away.

"Well?" Hap continued, hoping to find out what this woman knew. He dabbed at his lips with a napkin, turning on a bit of Southern charm, and smiled at her.

"They're not right," Eileen said. "They're just not right."

Then she lowered her head and mumbled something.

Hap put his hand on hers, a look of utter sympathy spreading over his face.

"Please, Mrs. Bailey," he said. "I understand your grief, and I hate to intrude upon it, but I'd appreciate anything you can do to help me."

Eileen Bailey leaned close to Hap and whispered, "Evil."

Then she put a warm hand on the side of his face. "Be careful, son. Your grandmother Gigi was one of my closest friends. She would have wanted me to warn you. But then, you're the sole survivor, son. I'm sure you already know this."

Hap looked at her as if she'd slapped him right across the face.

"I beg your pardon?"

"Oh, honey," Eileen said, "surely you can't have forgotten!"

"Forgotten? Forgotten what?"

"My, my, Hap. You have a lot of remembering to do, honey. You have a long, rich history here. Best you remember some of it before it's too late."

"Mrs. Bailey, how are you, dear?" Burton asked and patted Hap on the shoulder. "May I steal this handsome fella from you?"

"Well, certainly, Chief Riggs. Just make sure he gets enough to eat. Too much food here to waste, and a big, strong man like him needs his nourishment."

"Oh, I think he's got plenty to chew on. I'll take good care of him."

Hap smiled at the group.

"Thank you so much for your hospitality," he said. "I appreciate it."

"Anytime, honey," Eileen said. "You come see us if you're here for a while. We're close by, just down the road at The Estates.

Chief Riggs can bring you."

Hap nodded,

"Yes, ma'am."

He waved, then, and felt Burton pulling on his arm, felt him reach up and put an arm around his shoulder. "In need of another rescue, son?"

"In need of a something," Hap said. "I feel like a lunatic."

"Yes, well, you've come to the right place, then," Burton said, "the right place, indeed."

After the luncheon, a gaggle of women cluttered the kitchen. Pots and pans, casserole dishes, and stray lids lined the tiled counters. Libby stood away from the others at the far end gathering the items that belonged in her own kitchen.

A procession of parishioners collected their treasures and, by 12:30, the counters gleamed; the kitchen was cleared and most of the parishioners filed en masse toward Cove's End.

"Thank you all so much," Ike Madison said to a host of women waiting for his approval. They smiled and chattered, assuring him that no thanks were needed on this most solemn but joyous occasion.

As they left, one of them called to Caillin,

"It's clean enough to eat off of, honey. Put the broom away and celebrate the day."

"She's such a little fussbudget," Ike said and shook his head. The women nodded in agreement. "Just like her mother," he added and grimaced.

"God bless you, Reverend," Eileen Bailey said and slipped her hand under his elbow. "We know your loss. We all loved her, too."

From his breast pocket, Ike drew out a crisp white handkerchief folded so that the engraved M showed prominently. He wiped at the corners of his eyes.

"My sweet Belinda," he whispered.

"There, there," Eileen said and patted his arm. "You're a good man, Reverend. God will take away this pain if you let Him."

"Yes," he replied. "He is stronger than any earthly pain, but sometimes...."

"Sometimes, it is almost unbearable," Libby said from across the room. "Sometimes, the loss of a loved one is simply unbearable."

The women stared at her.

"How dare you!" Eileen spat, "how dare you come here and pretend to grieve along with the rest of us. If it weren't for you, my Stanley would be alive."

The others gasped.

"Eileen!" one of them said and put her arms around her.

Ike Madison, silent, stood with his arms folded in front of him.

"Now, Eileen, you know that's not true. Libby had nothing to do with those deaths. It was greenflash, like always. Greenflash killed your Stanley and all the rest of the other husbands."

"She did it," Eileen said, her voice trembling now. "And if she didn't, she knows how it was done. She's evil, pure evil."

"Please, Eileen, don't cause trouble. We've got so much to deal with right now. How are we ever going to survive without our men, our husbands and fathers? Don't add to it, please, don't do it."

"My aunt is not evil," Caillin said, still sweeping.

"You're too young to know any different, Caillin." Eileen said. "You don't know what goes on up there."

"Neither do you, Mrs. Bailey."

"Caillin," Ike Madison said, his voice sharp and harsh, "watch your mouth. Don't you dare sass Mrs. Bailey. Your mother, God rest her sweet soul, would...."

"Her mother would be proud of her," Libby said. "Proud."

They turned, then—the women of the church—and walked toward the glassed-in walkway to the sanctuary. Eileen stopped and turned back. She pointed a shaking finger at Libby.

"God will have His day with you," she said. "He will reckon with you and that sister of yours."

"And what about you, Eileen? When will he reckon with you?"

The women gasped again.

"Stop it," Ike said and glared at Libby. He moved toward Eileen, his arms outstretched, a broad smile spreading across his face. "My dear Eileen," he said and enfolded her into his long arms.

"Come along. I'll walk with you."

Caillin continued her sweeping, her long red ponytail bouncing with each movement of her arms.

Libby walked up and squeezed her elbow, gently reminding her.

"Silence...."

"I've no choice but to be silent, but sometimes, I want to....

"Control yourself, my love."

Caillin's eyes narrowed as a great hiss filled the hall.

16

Cove's End opened her arms to the grief-stricken relatives of the ten dead, those who had been charred beyond recognition or buried beneath the rubble of downed trees and toppled sheds. While three hundred or so grievers—most directly from the memorial service—milled about the restaurant to gather and pay respects, comfort each other. Libby swept from room to room attending to their needs.

During her twenty years in Cove's End, she had become the premier hostess. And it was only now, in her middle age, that she recognized the powerfully seductive dance between the needy heart and the pleading soul. She had seen a time, long ago, when she would have denied that power, a time when her own heart seemed so full that emptiness in it was unimaginable.

Thirty years ago, she thought, *I married the most handsome guy in Preacher's Cove.* She recalled the day when the two of them eloped, both only seventeen years old. In high school, she was immediately attracted to Frankie Arbuckle, and for the four years that they attended Grundy County High School, the two of them were rarely apart. Libby remembered every prom, every dance and every party. She heard all sorts of gossip, then, from folks all over the Cove who said that she and Frankie were destined to be together. They said that she was the most beautiful girl and he the most handsome young man. They would have beautiful babies, folks insisted. So, the week after graduation, she and Frankie married.

For the next ten years, she remembered, the two of them had lived a simple but near-perfect life. She learned the fine points of cleaning, cooking, and gardening. Frankie, on the other hand, learned the fine art of making a living for his family while tending to the needs of friends, relatives, and neighbors. An ace mechanic, he could fix anything with a steering wheel or a pair of handlebars. And at 6'7", he was the only man in Preacher's Cove who could stand flat on his feet and fetch a kitten from a tree, or lie flat on his back and stretch the length of a Chevy pick-up truck.

Libby remembered seeing the pleasure in his face when he did both. Most of all, though, she remembered that cloudy Saturday morning, when a frantic call came from a neighbor down the way—her two hysterical little girls screaming in the background—Frankie climbed into his new '74 Chevy, waved to her, and pulled out of the driveway. As she watched him back down the long stretch of concrete, Libby heard a horrible, familiar rumbling in the distance—the devil's growl folks called it. She watched the expression on Frankie's face change and saw him hesitate for a moment. Her stomach churned, now, when she recalled the uneasiness that had settled over her like a cold, wet blanket.

An image came back to her. She could see herself motioning to Frankie to stop. Then she ran down and climbed into the truck with him.

"Did you hear it?" she asked him on that Saturday morning, the words as clear and fresh in her mind now as they were on that day.

Frankie had nodded.

"Maggie's just down the block," he lied. "We've got time."

She remembered how he had looked at her then, how he had smiled and reached over and stroked her face. He had taken her hand and gently kissed her palm.

"You're the best, baby," he said.

She smiled at him and squeezed his hand.

"Eyes on the road, honey, eyes on the road." Then she winked at him.

The rumbling in the distance grew louder until it was full-fledged booming thunder. Streaks of lightning darted through the clouds. Libby's heart pounded in her chest.

"We have to hurry, honey," she said.

When they had screeched into Maggie's driveway, two little girls were outside waving frantically. Frankie piled out of the Chevy and lumbered across the yard. The kitten, stranded in a large white oak, meowed and spewed at him. Libby remembered seeing Frankie standing on his tip-toes, stretched as high as he could stretch, reaching for the kitten. She knew from experience that grabbing a scared kitten was like grabbing a small buzz-saw. She saw the kitten squirm and claw, but her Frankie held on and gently lifted it out of the tree.

As he handed it down to the girls, a sudden blast of thunder shook the ground. Cold air burst across them all and brought with it the horror they all knew by name. In an instant, the sky blackened. Seconds later, a glorious, luminescent emerald radiance danced through the blackness, illuminating the sky. Libby recalled the radiance of flashes of soft pink light flickering about within that sky. A truly kaleidoscopic ceiling, an enormous umbrella of beautiful green light embraced Preacher's Cove...and it left her Frankie a charred mass of smoldering flesh.

Libby remembered, as if it were just yesterday, that when the rain started and the sky cleared, she ran to him. He was lying on his back, his eyes fixed wide in horror, his mouth wide open, as if at any minute he might scream.

Not one of them would touch him.

In the rain that always followed greenflash, in the wake of the destruction in Cove's End, she stood feeling as dead in her heart as the one lying in a smoldering heap at her feet.

The memories, as vivid now as they were all those years ago, rushed in upon her, and Libby felt tears well in her eyes. When she snapped back to the present, the drumming of a room filled with grieving people, made her head throb. She blotted her eyes with a tissue and turned to walk to the bathroom to get an aspirin.

"Aunt Libby, the customers are asking about hearts. We're all out of artichoke hearts," Caillin said.

"What did you say, dear?" she replied.

"Hearts, there are no hearts left."

Libby shook her head at the irony of it all.

"Caillin, dear," she said and draped an arm across her shoulder, "there are all sorts of hearts left in this room, all sorts. These folks don't care about the artichoke hearts. They care about their own hearts, and their hearts are broken today. So let's help them a little. There's plenty more in the big refrigerator. We'll give them all the artichoke hearts they can eat, and maybe by the time they leave today, they'll have forgotten, even if just for a few hours, that their hearts will never be the same."

17

Hap stood behind the display stands in the gift shop hoping to see Lucy Addams walk in with one of the Firelight Angels.

He had already decided that if she came in, he would walk up to her and apologize face to face. He convinced himself that he could look at her and show no sign of fear. He debated about going outside and finding the workshop but opted to wander around browsing through a sea of cheap souvenirs and T-shirts. He avoided the front of the shop where the dolls sat so precariously on a shelf. Their eyes seemed to look right into his soul. Thinking about it made him shudder. He almost wished that one of them would spring to life and speak to him.

One of those stranded children might call to him. He imagined the cry for help, imagined himself looking up and holding out his arms, saying "Jump, jump. I'll catch you. You'll be safe with me." He thought about how cowardly he felt when he found out about coming back to the Cove. "How could I help an innocent child? I can't even help myself," he mumbled. He looked around to make sure no one heard him and sighed when he saw no other customers. He fiddled with the price tag on an Alabama cap. If anyone came in, he wanted to appear legitimate, especially on the day of the memorial brunch. Mourners filed in within minutes, their shoes clacking on the wooden floor. Hap moved from behind the displays, looking at everyone who came in.

Every now and then, he heard Libby's voice filtering among the guests. For a small person, she had a big voice. When he heard her voice a second time, he walked in among the mourners. He smoothed his jacket, ran his hand through his hair, and took a deep breath. Hap brought his hand to his mouth and cleared his throat. He glanced behind him, then turned around again. A thin-lipped smile crossed his face, and he nodded at the crowd. His head suddenly throbbed, and for some reason, his pants felt too tight in the waist. He tugged at his waistband and looked down at the floor, then off to the side...anywhere to keep from seeing all the people in the shop.

A petite savior rescued him. In a black skirt that outlined the curves of her hips and a white shimmering blouse that draped against her narrow shoulders, and pulled against her full breast, she looked radiant. Hap felt his heartbeat quicken. He wanted to grab her, kiss her full on the lips and press her body tightly against his.

"I think most of you remember little Michael Murray. Please welcome him," Libby said.

With a sweeping motion of her hand, she proclaimed, "He's almost family, Lydia Murray's grandson."

A collective "ah" sounded throughout the guests, and all of them smiled at him. Libby walked toward him amidst a torrent of chattering, begun again since he was no longer a stranger.

"Thank you," he whispered to her.

"You're welcome."

She looked up at him, the broad smile on her face gone.

"I didn't expect to see you here."

"I came to talk to you and to...."

"Find Lucy," she said, her gaze never shifting from his face. "I can't talk to you right now, Hap. I'm on a mission to find hearts."

"Hearts?"

"We're all out," Libby said, a smile returning to her face.

Hap took her hand in his and smiled.

"I don't imagine it would be too difficult for you to find hearts," he whispered. "You have enough for everyone."

Libby pulled her hand from his and brushed at the wisps of hair around her face.

"My, uh, my guests."

Hap saw her cheeks redden.

"Sorry," he said. "I got a little carried away."

Libby nodded and brushed at her blouse.

Hap leaned down and whispered to her.

"Meet me later?"

Libby smiled at him and shrugged.

"If you're lucky."

Hap laughed out loud.

Once again, the guests turned and stared at him. His face flushed.

"I'd better go before I get into real trouble with these folks," he whispered.

Libby nodded at him.

"I can do only so much rescuing in one day. I think you've had yours for today. If you'll come back in a couple of hours, we can talk, but first...."

"I know," he said. "Where are my manners?"

Hap walked through the crowd of guests, shaking their hands, sympathizing with their losses, and apologizing for his intrusion into their private gathering.

He told and retold stories of his grandmother, each memory embellished with the retelling. Then, almost instantly, one loud voice exploded into Cove's End and turned the room dead quiet.

"My good friends!" the voice blared. "God bless you all."

Hap turned with the others to witness the entrance of the voice's owner. An elegant, dark-haired man strode into the room. Ike Madison eased through the crowd like a giant. One by one the mourners moved in waves to create a clear path for him. He looked each one straight in the eye and smiled just enough to allow them a glimpse of his perfect, moon-white teeth.

As he shook hands, he leaned in close enough to hug, but stopped just shy of touching their bodies. Occasionally, he glanced down at his suit coat, brushed it gently, and continued the hand-shaking. In a room filled with almost two hundred people, his was the only audible voice. Hap watched the man's procession through the crowd. When he was only a few feet away, the hand-some, broad-shouldered gentleman turned his head and locked his piercing hazel-eyed gaze on Hap. The roomful of mourners followed his lead, and for the second time that night, Hap Murray became the center of attention. The man held out his hand and walked close to Hap.

"Hap, good to see you again."

Hap gripped the man's hand, a little harder than he'd normally shake a hand. But in this instance, he wanted to make sure that he sported his strength. He needed a territorial victory, especially in front of Libby.

The two men stared at each other. Neither blinked.

"Ike," Libby said, "how nice of you to drop by."

She moved close beside Hap and looped her arm through his.

"It seems our beautiful little town keeps drawing media. You'd think, wouldn't you, that after a while, they'd find something worthwhile to report. Any story that prints, I guess, is worth the trouble."

Ike looked down at Libby and smiled, revealing none of those perfect teeth. He turned and motioned to the crowd. Immediately, the chattering resumed.

"Well," he said and cleared his throat, "Where's my gorgeous daughter?"

"I think we have everything under control," Libby answered. "Caillin is in the kitchen. I'll tell her you're here."

She patted Hap's arm and hugged him.

"Excuse me for a moment, will you?"

"Certainly. And don't worry. We'll be good."

Hap bent down and kissed the top of Libby's head. Then he straightened and looked right at Ike Madison. Hap cocked his head, raised his eyebrows, and smiled.

Ike's hazel eyes darkened, as if some horrible thought crept from deep within his brain and stopped just short of escaping.

"Will you be staying long?"

"Just long enough to do my job," Hap replied, his eyes never wavering from Ike's stare. "My supervisor would be none too pleased if I'd made the trip for nothing."

"Yes," Ike said, his fists clenched at his sides. "Well, I'm certain that you'll get everything you came here for...maybe more."

"Father?" a soft voice floated into Hap's ears.

Both men looked down to see Caillin standing beside them.

Instantly, Ike's demeanor softened.

"My precious girl," he said. He bent down and kissed her cheek. "How lovely you look today." A full smile spread across his beaming face.

Caillin stood on tiptoe to return his kiss.

"Thank you, Father," she said, her face blushed, her eyes lowered.

Ike reached down and lifted her chin, the smile fading from his face.

"Don't stare at the floor, child. Remember who you are," Ike said, a hint of irritation in his voice.

Libby stepped beside Hap and slipped her hand into his.

"Libby," Ike said. "I'm afraid that Caillin and I must be going. I've just remembered a previous commitment for one of our parishioners. They all need so much comforting."

"But Father, I need to stay and help...."

"Nonsense, child. Your Aunt Libby has been doing this for many years." Ike looked directly at Hap. "Many years," he said. "She can handle things."

Libby reached over and pulled Caillin close to her. With her fingers, she brushed the girl's long red hair away from her face and whispered,

"It's all right. Go with your father. Only one more hour, then everyone will begin to leave. Don't worry."

Ike made his apologies to the mourners, took Caillin's arm and walked toward the door. He stopped and turned back toward Libby. He held up his hands in frustration. "Oh, goodness, Libby. Can you forgive me?"

"For what?" Libby asked.

"I completely forgot about your lovely sister. Why didn't she come to the brunch?"

The crowd quieted, waiting for Libby's response.

Libby blinked and dabbed her eyes with a tissue. Hap's own eyes widened when he looked down at her. He saw, barely visible, a soft green light flickering behind her deep emerald eyes.

Before Libby could answer, Ike and Caillin left. Libby stared at the door, her eyes watering. She dabbed at them again. Hap bent down and looked directly into her eyes. Then he straightened and rubbed his own eyes.

Are her eyes glowing? I must be losing my mind.

18

Hap waited in the private dining room for Libby to finish with the guests. He'd sought privacy, a place to cool off, calm himself and forget about Ike Madison for a few minutes. He took deep breaths and concentrated on jotting down notes. But his concentration shattered when Libby walked through the door.

"Hi," she said in a most melodic Southern drawl. She sat down next to him and put her hand on his. Hap twirled his pen through his fingers and took another deep breath. "Are you okay?" Libby asked, leaning close to him. "You look flushed."

"Oh, I'm fine, really."

Hap smelled Libby's perfume, a gentle lavender scent that calmed and stirred him at the same time. He moved his face closer to hers.

"You look stunning," he whispered.

"Why, thank you, sir." Hap felt Libby's breath against his face. Wisps of her long red hair brushed against his cheek. He sat without moving, held fast by his longing for her. Libby cleared her throat and inched away from him.

"I'm glad you came to the brunch. Sorry about the tension with Ike, but he's the possessive sort. You made him feel like the underdog instead of the top dog!" she giggled.

Hap took a deep breath, shifted in his seat, and smiled at her. He ran his hands through his hair, winced when he touched the gash, and dropped his hands into his lap. "He's a bloody corker," Hap said and straightened in his seat.

"Among other things," she said.

"I, uh...." Hap lowered his eyes and stared at the table.

"What's wrong? Have I done something...."

"No, no. You haven't done anything, Libby. It's just that when you were looking at Ike, when he said that about your sister, I thought that—it's stupid. Never mind."

"Tell me what's bothering you, Hap."

"Your eyes," he whispered. "They glowed."

Hap cleared his throat. His fingers trembled. "I'm sorry," he said. "It's ridiculous."

"Are they glowing now?" Libby asked.

Hap looked at her and shook his head.

"Maybe it was only a reflection of light. How about a walk?"

Libby stood up and smiled down at him. She turned and walked toward the door, then stopped and held out her hand. "Coming?"

Hap stumbled out of the chair and trotted along behind her. Outside the restaurant, Hap took a deep breath and inhaled the sweet mountain air.

"Ah," he said. "Better, much better."

Libby smiled, wrapped her arm around his, and led him down the planked walkway. Hap loved the feel of her small hand on his arm. Every time she touched him, his whole body relaxed. The longer she left her hand on him, the more relaxed he became. It started with a slight tingle running up and down his arm. Then it spread through his chest and back, then along his spine and into his legs and feet. He felt as if he were floating.

"You know," he said, his voice soft and sleepy, "ever since I've been here, weird things have been happening to me. Burton Riggs showed up and rescued us from that fog. When I got here, every other reporter in the state seemed to be parked outside. Then the dolls...."

"Preacher's Cove is sometimes a strange place. We just accept it. It's all we know."

"Every time I walk by those dolls, I feel as if I should be doing something to help them. I know it's stupid, but I can't help myself. For some reason, they magnetize me."

"Maybe it's just your imagination running wild," she said, her upward gaze directed deep into his eyes. "Or maybe, you're one of us. People tell me that the dolls give them a sort of magical feeling, as if they're real, as if they could jump right up and talk."

"Really? Then, it's not my imagination."

"No, you're not imagining the feeling that the dolls give, but not a single one of us can explain why it happens."

"Before I came here," Hap said, "I thought I was losing my mind. Now that I'm here, it's worse than ever.. My mind and my body are taking a beating, Libby. I can't sleep. I had this dream about a tall man looking down into an open grave. I've seen that man before. He's the same man who was in my room, standing by the window. Something is happening to me."

"Many things happen here that can't be explained by anything your paper will accept as truth," Libby said. "I'm afraid this is not the place for your big break!" She chuckled and smiled up at him.

"This is exactly the place," Hap whispered. "I know it."

He watched Libby as she strode across the wooden planks hardly making a sound. She seemed to float along. She walked first past the office, then a long string of rooms, a paved driveway complete with a limousine, and finally, a small office called Cove's End Realty. When she came to the end of the complex, Hap felt as if he needed a rest.

She walked at such a brisk pace that it was hard for him to keep up with her. Along the walk, he looked out onto the grounds surrounding Cove's End. A backdrop of the Smoky Mountains seemed almost close enough to touch. The beauty of those natural giants called to him, and he lifted his arm to touch them. He quickly put it by his side again, remembering a time when he reached out toward the sky and ended up in a coma for almost a year. In the crisp mountain air, smells of barbecue and home cooking from the restaurant wafted into his nostrils. The sounds of his steps on the wooden planks reminded him of the steps leading to his Grandma Gigi's house. The clop-clop-clop as he took each new step brought back memories his grandmother walking down the creaky back steps, bringing him a bowl heaping with homemade blueberry pie topped with rich vanilla ice cream.

When he reached the end of the complex, he followed Libby to a long winding stairway that led to the second floor.

Beside it was a door with a sign that read, "Danger! Keep Out."

"Danger?" Hap asked. "What's in here?"

The room seemed a small one, enclosed with heavy wood, windows on all sides. Hap thought it must be some kind of shed for tools or such.

Libby stopped beside the room and smoothed her skirt.

"That's my nephew's. He's an amateur herpetologist."

"Like snakes and things," Hap said, fidgeting with the pen he still carried in his hand.

"Yes," Libby said. "He has just a few snakes in aquariums. He loves snakes. Folks around here call him the Snake Doctor."

Libby stopped, looked back at him, and started up the steps. On the second landing, a single doorway marked the entrance to her home. When she stopped briefly and glanced back at him again, Hap wondered what she was thinking. He wondered if she thought he was some sort of jerk, some news hound following after her like a puppy with its tail wagging. Libby brushed a few stray curls from her face and opened the door.

"Wheelan, it's just me, love. I have someone with me," she called. "Come and meet him."

Hap followed her into a spacious, bright room—the living room, he supposed—with elegant furnishings and a welcoming feeling. From where he stood, Hap could see the living room, the dining room, and a small kitchen, all surrounded by floor-to-ceiling windows. Gleaming hardwood floors added to the brightness in the rooms. Flowers graced every open space. Large vases filled with arrangements sat atop each open table. Floral coverings, on the largest pieces of furniture in each room, perfectly matched, as well as roses stenciled along the otherwise white walls, added to the effect. It was like standing in an open garden.

"This is nice," he said, "very nice. Peaceful."

"Thank you. It was a long time coming, but it's almost finished," Libby said.

"So, this is where you live?"

"Yes. I love it here."

"I didn't even notice that there was a house down here."

"You weren't supposed to. We have grown over the years, and when Isaiah hired me, there was no place for us to live. Of course, that was twenty years ago. Little by little, we added a room here and there, but fifteen years ago, when the business really picked up, I told Isaiah that I wanted a nice home. He built at the end of the complex, away from the business but close enough for any emergencies."

"Isaiah? Who's Isaiah?" Hap asked.

"Madison, Reverend Isaiah Madison. Ike's father."

"Oh," he said and shook his head.

"Isaiah and Ike are polar opposites," Libby said. "Isaiah owned Cove's End until about ten years ago. He let me buy it from him on the condition that I keep it and remain as its primary caretaker and manager. It's a long story."

Just as Hap was about to urge her to go on, a tall man walked into the living room. When Hap saw him, his knees felt as if they had turned to Jell-O. The color drained from his face, and he felt as if he had to sit down.

"Hap Murray, meet Dr. Wheelan Addams."

He stood head to head with the man.

"Nice to meet you," Hap said, his knees still rubbery. He held out his hand.

"I've heard a lot about you," Wheelan said and shook his hand. Hap noted the clammy feel of the man's hand.

"Yes, unfortunately, I'm sure that you have. It's nice to put a voice and a name with a face. I was beginning to think that my mind was playing tricks on me," Hap said.

"Wheelan," Libby said, "why don't you explain your theories to Hap. Maybe the two of you could investigate a little further."

"Sure," Wheelan said.

She looked at Hap and smiled.

"You're in good hands," she said. Hap watched as she patted Addams on the left arm and walked out.

The men stood looking at one another, shifting their gazes occasionally to the furnishings, then back to each other. Hap felt about as awkward as he ever had. He didn't know quite what to say, so he started with a stupid question.

"So, you're a doctor?" Hap asked. "I saw your shed outside. Libby says you like snakes."

"I'm not a medical doctor," Wheelan replied and looked down

at the floor, "and yes," he continued, "I do like snakes. I've studied them for years."

"I can't imagine anybody liking snakes," Hap said. "I'm scared to death of them. Snakes and storms...might as well put me in the bloody ground."

Wheelan had still not looked at him, so after another moment of awkward silence, Hap spoke again.

"What kind of doctor are you?"

"I'm a scientist," Wheelan said.

Sheer force of nervous habit caused him to run his hand through his hair. He knew it wasn't the professional gesture to make, but he couldn't help himself. Hap pulled his notebook out of his jacket pocket and flipped it to a blank page.

"You have some theories? Mind if I jot down a couple of them?"

"No," Wheelan said. "Would you like some iced tea?"

"Tea would be fine, thank you."

While Wheelan was in the small kitchen, Hap steadied himself and wandered around in the living room. Now he knew the name of the man who'd been standing by the window in his room. He followed him into the kitchen.

Bright and spacious with roses stenciled along the border of the walls, the kitchen fit Libby perfectly. There was no doubt in his mind that this was her house.

"You can tell that a woman lives here," he said to Wheelan.

Wheelan smiled but said nothing.

As the ice clunked into the two glasses, Hap noticed a set of handrails on the side wall of the kitchen. He looked closer and saw that the rails were part of a lift of some sort, the kind he saw in buildings that had met standard requirements for people with physical disabilities.

"Here's your tea, Mr. Murray," Wheelan said. "Let's move back into the living room, if you don't mind."

When they were seated, Hap asked Wheelan to tell him more about his theories. He listened to Wheelan, but scrawled a message in his notebook. "Elevator in kitchen?? Who uses it?"

In the meantime, he caught a word or two about the topography of Preacher's Cove, and as Wheelan had called it, "its propensity for attracting enormous fields of electromagnetic energy." It didn't take long for Hap to figure out that Wheelan Addams was a doctor of meteorology or earth science or something in that category. When he talked about it, he seemed to drift into another world. Words rolled off his tongue with none of the awkward hesitation he'd shown at first.

Now, Hap could barely get in a question. Finally, he interrupted, "Dr. Addams."

"Wheelan, call me Wheelan," he responded.

"Wheelan, I need to know what this has to do with the story about the storms. Could you be just a little more specific?"

"Mr. Murray...."

"Hap," he nodded to him.

"Hap," Wheelan said, "the point is that Preacher's Cove is a prime location for these storms. Haven't you been listening?"

"Yes, most certainly," Hap said.

The two of them reached for their glasses of tea at the same time. Hap chuckled. "Great minds..." he said.

For the first time, Wheelan smiled at him.

"Okay," he said. "Here's the history. The state of Alabama was originally formed over an inactive volcano. The volcano, while inactive, emits enormous amounts of electromagnetic energy. The geomagnetic field and the generation of extreme heat from greenflash mutually control one another and cause unpredictable fire behavior called fire whirls. Combined with the electromagnetism, the fire whirls generate erratic electrical behavior. Lightning strikes that radiate outward, then downward."

"Greenflash? Is that what you're talking about?"

"Yes," Wheelan said. "This energy attracts these killer storms and shares its strength with them. The result is an incessant stream of high-voltage storms. Anyone in their paths will die. It's the voltage and intensity that produce greenflash."

"So, what exactly is it?"

"No one's sure, although my theory is that it's a form of ball lightning...voltage concentrated so tightly that it forms spherical shapes that dance about the sky. They are deadly."

Hap followed the technical terms, but just barely. He'd actually jotted down some of the words. Wheelan knew his stuff, all right. But there remained a question.

"So, why doesn't the whole state have these storms? Why do they happen in only in Preacher's Cove?"

"The core of the activity is here."

"The core?" Hap repeated.

"Yes, something about Preacher's Cove that serves as a conductor."

"What is it?" Hap asked.

"I'm not sure," Wheelan said and leaned back in his chair, his long legs outstretched. "So, what else do you know about this natural phenomenon? And go a little slower this time so that I can keep up, okay?"

"The name greenflash originated in the Florida Keys," Wheelan continued. "People who have lived there for a long time gave it the name because of the luminescent green color that bursts across the sky. It lasts only a few moments and occurs about once every fifteen or twenty years there. Usually, any colored lightning, like red sprites or blue jets, accompany the greenflash, but in very small spurts of energy."

"There's no real evidence then?"

"Oh sure, there's evidence," Wheelan said and leaned forward. "People from the Cove have seen it for years, but the ones who've felt it are no longer around to talk. Only two people have accurate records."

"Two?"

"An American physicist, Dr. John Wincklyer was the first to photograph it. And there's Billy Ray, the guy who videotaped it."

"Do you know him?"

"Sure, but he won't be of any help to you. The video's already aired and contracted. He wouldn't talk to any of the reporters who were here."

Hap nodded and tapped his pen on his notebook.

"So, what about this volcano you mentioned?"

"I've done geological surveys of the land here, traced it through older maps, and even managed to find old cartographic and topographic data."

"Beg your pardon?"

"Maps, just old maps of the land itself, upper and lower crusts. The land bordered off as Alabama is situated directly on top of a volcanic site, probably prehistoric. When lightning from the storms releases nitrogen into the air, it enriches the soil, so it becomes a kind of food chain, of sorts. One feeds off the other."

"But that doesn't explain why it kills so many people here."

"No, it doesn't, but then I'm just a scientist, Hap. I'm not the answer," Wheelan said, and ran his hand through his wavy dark hair.

Hap sat back in the chair and tapped his pen against the notebook.

"Mind if I ask one more question?"

"Go ahead, but I think you know about as much as I can explain."

"Why do you have an elevator in the kitchen? Who uses it?"

Wheelan looked as he did when he first walked into the living room. Gone was the brilliant scientist. He had been replaced by a pale, gaunt, nervous man who wanted nothing more than to run away.

"Have I overstepped my boundaries?" Hap asked leaning forward.

Wheelan said nothing. Instead, he stood and extended his hand to Hap.

"I didn't mean to ramble on so," he offered. "I tend to do that when I start talking about the storms and such."

"No problem. I feel privileged that you shared your theory with me."

They shook hands, and as Hap walked toward the door, Wheelan called to him,

"The elevator, the lift as we call it...it's for my mother. The monster you saw in the workshop is Lucy Addams, my mother."

19

While Hap was busy coaxing information out of Wheelan, Joey was busy trying to get Caillin's attention. He had been in the restaurant for almost two hours trying to get her to talk to him. Her shyness, the way she lowered her eyes when he spoke, and her quiet manner were all too intriguing for him. He didn't know girls like that. The girls he knew giggled, talked about their hair, and gossiped about every other girl they knew. They fussed over their long nails and shiny lipstick. Caillin had none of the normal "girl" attributes. No long red nails, no puffy hair, no heavy perfume. She looked sort of innocent, sheltered maybe. Her dark red hair, pulled back from her face with a headband, fell to her waist in curls. Her nails, neatly manicured, showed a soft pink color. And her face almost shimmered with a delicate, natural look to it. Her lips were full, with only a hint of red. She was, Joey thought, the most beautiful girl he had ever seen. But she wouldn't even look at him. She served his meal, brought him whatever he requested, but never once did she make eye contact with him. When he spoke to her, she lowered her head. He called on her every few minutes and by the time he had finished his meal, he had eaten more than he would normally eat in two days, much less one meal. He even had dessert...twice. He felt as if he would burst at any minute.

Eagle left after an hour and a half, telling him to be careful. Now, he felt conspicuous. So, when he couldn't stand to smell the food for another second, he waved for the ticket. This was his chance, his last chance to talk to her. She came straightaway with the ticket, tore it off the book, then set it gently down beside his hand. He took a chance and brushed his fingers across her hand as she put the ticket beside him. Immediately, she withdrew her hand and turned to walk away.

"Thank you," he said.

Caillin stopped and turned around to face him. She looked at him square in the eyes and said, "You are quite welcome, sir." Then she smiled a sweet smile at him.

"Joey, my name is Joey Donovan," he said and stood up straight, to his full 5'9". "The food was great, but I ate way too much. I'm full as a tick on a hound dog."

He felt like an idiot with the tick statement. It sounded just like some backwoods, country bumpkin. But it got a chuckle out of Caillin. And when he saw her broad smile, he felt as though his knees would buckle. He took a step closer to her, leaned over, and said, "You are beautiful."

Then he felt his own face flushing.

"Sorry," he said, "I didn't mean to...."

"It's all right," she said, "and thank you."

"Would you, uh, like to take a walk maybe?" he asked.

Before Caillin could answer, Libby walked up beside her.

"Hello, Joey, how are you?" she asked.

"Fine, Ms. Libby. And you?"

"Fine, thank you. I'm afraid that I must steal our little Caillin away from you right now. There's so much work to do. But you understand, don't you?"

She turned to Caillin. "Come along, will you dear? I need your help."

Caillin followed her without looking back.

Joey paid the ticket and walked outside. "Dammit!"

The word echoed across the complex. He stood for a few minutes hoping that Caillin might come out.

Stupid, he thought, *stupid to stand out here waiting for her to come prancing outside just to see me!* "You're an idiot, Joey," he muttered.

"No, you're not," a soft voice replied. Joey jumped, let out a little gasp, and almost cursed again. He looked just in time to see the lovely Caillin standing in the doorway.

"I'd like to take a walk with you sometime, Joey Donovan."

Then she stepped back inside as quickly as she had stepped out. Joey headed toward the room, his heart pounding in his chest and a broad smile forming on his lips. "YES!" he shouted.

Inside the doorway, Caillin heard his shout.
And so did Libby.

20

Hap sat in his room feeling as if he'd just won first prize in a sonofabitch contest. After talking the whole afternoon with Wheelan, he'd developed a genuine feeling of admiration for the guy. He'd told him more than he would ever have guessed anybody knew about Preacher's Cove.

"What a jerk!" When he thought about calling Wheelan's mother a monster, he felt sick to his stomach. "Bloody jerk!" he chided himself again.

He decided to go back and offer a real apology instead of the stupefied look he had shown as he fumbled for the door to get out of that house. First, though, he was going to call on Libby. Then, he was going to call Burton Riggs, the esteemed police chief.

"Get a hold of yourself, Murray. These people are making your imagination run wild," he said as he grabbed his notebook and pen off the bed. It was just as Libby had said. She had warned him. He moved toward the door and stopped dead in his tracks.

In a corner chair was a blue box that hadn't been there earlier. Hap flipped on the lights and walked over to the chair. He couldn't imagine who would have left the box in his room.

Maybe it's equipment, he thought.

He reached down and removed the top of the box. White tissue paper, layer after layer, covered whatever was inside. Finally, he removed the last layer. Staring back at him was little Michael Murray.

Hap gasped and jumped back. Seeing himself as a child, a perfect replica staring at him, sent chills along his spine. He took a deep breath and reached out to touch the doll. When he bent to touch it, he noticed a white placard scripted in gold, the same kind he'd seen beside the Firelight Angels in the gift shop.

He picked it up and read the words: "Brave Michael, Save the Holder."

Hap took a few steps to the side and sat down on the bed. He leaned forward, propped his elbows on his thighs, and rested his head in his hands. "Impossible," he muttered. "She doesn't know me. She didn't know I was coming here. Bloody impossible."

His heart pounded in his chest, his head throbbed.

"I shouldn't be here," he mumbled. "God! I shouldn't have come here."

Suddenly, the door flung open and Joey burst into the room.

"She talked to me. She even said she'd like to take a walk with me!" Joey said.

"She? Who?" Hap asked and looked up at his young driver.

"Caillin, that's who. Our beautiful server. Who'd you think I meant?"

"I have better things to do, kid, than to keep up with your love life," Hap said and rubbed his eyes.

"Oh, yeah, right, as if anyone could keep up with yours. Gimme a break. As my granny used to say, 'It'd take ten men and five little boys to keep up with you.'"

"Flattery, kid, will get you just about anywhere, except around here."

"So, what's in the box?" Joey asked.

"See for yourself."

Joey walked over and looked into the blue box.

"Wow! A doll." Joey examined it further. "Hey, it's one of those dolls from the gift shop, right? You bought one of them?"

"Yes and no," Hap said and got up off the bed.

He walked over to the box and stood beside Joey.

"It's one of them, all right, but I didn't buy it."

"Oh my God, you stole it?"

Hap slapped playfully at the back of Joey's head.

"No, you little twerp. I didn't steal it. Somebody put it here."

Joey stared up at Hap, looked down at the doll again, then back at Hap.

"It looks like you, like those pictures in your wallet of you at your Grandma Gigi's house. You showed them to us, remember?

Eagle and I were surprised that you actually lived here when you were a kid.

"I remember. Read the card," Hap said.

Joey reached down, picked up the placard, and read the words.

"Brave Michael, Save the Holder," he read in his deepest voice. "Ooh, creepy."

He dropped the card back into the box.

"So, who's this holder person and what is he holding?"

Hap took a drink of his soda and sighed as the sweet liquid ran down his throat.

"Beats me," he said. "I have an errand to run. I'll be back in a little while."

"Wait, you can't just leave. We haven't talked about the story. You haven't told me anything about what I'm supposed to be doing. And Eagle needs to know something, too. He's coming over in a few minutes."

"I'll be back in a couple of hours. Just wait for me here. Then we'll talk. Promise."

Hap patted Joey on the shoulder and walked out of the door. He slowed when he heard the soft, familiar sounds of a harmonica. He had to remember to ask Libby about it. When he got to the office door, he looked inside to see if he could see Libby. She sat at a desk, going through some paperwork. A bell over the door signaled his arrival.

It reminded him of the legend from the lost books of the Bible.

A priest named Zacharias went into the temple to pray and beheld a demon, a hideous creature that was half man and half donkey. When Zacharias told the other priests what he'd seen, he was ordered to wear a bell around his neck so that the creature could always hear him approaching and hide from view. Hap wondered what creature had to hide from view when this particular bell rang.

He thought about Wheelan's mother. Maybe she was the reason for the bell, not because of the way she looked but because of something else. If there was a connection with the older Madison, maybe there was one with the younger one. He wondered if the bell might serve as some kind of warning. Then, he dismissed the idea as foolish and decided to find out for himself.

The hum of the computers and fax machines seemed odd in a place that thrived on its rustic offerings. A large modern counter for guests signing in and signing out stood to one side of the office. Three clerks busied themselves with routine procedures and phone calls. The other side of the office looked like an old parlor with several high-back rocking chairs, a couple of end tables, all centered in front of an enormous natural stone fireplace. On the mantle were several photographs of Cove's End in what looked like its stages of development. Hap walked over to get a closer look. The first photograph showed a handsome young minister standing in front of a building with the name Madison's Eatery on the door. Hap thought it looked a lot like the entrance to the restaurant. The next photo showed Libby a woman who looked almost identical to Libby stood to the side with a young set of twins. They all stood in front of a set of two buildings, a third in the background under construction. The name Madison's Eatery had been taken off and none put in its place. The third photo showed Libby, the minister, an older gentleman who resembled the young minister, and a young girl roughly three or four years old beside them. The older boy from the second photo stood in the background, his hands in the pockets of his overalls. The photo showed them all standing in front of a much larger complex this time. Three large buildings joined by a planked walkway with an office building in the middle all bore the name Cove's End. The next to last photo showed Libby again, this time holding one of the dolls and standing in the back of the hotel, not the front. The last photo had no people, just an aerial view of the entire complex, complete with tennis courts, swimming pool, cabana, and the gazebo.

"So, Hap, did you find out enough for a story?" Libby asked.

Hap was lost in the history of Cove's End when Libby's voice jerked him back into the present. He jumped and turned to her.

"I didn't mean to startle you," she said.

"These photos are great," he said trying to hide his embarrassment at being startled. "Wheelan told me a lot about the Cove."

"He's a good man," Libby said and drew closer to him. "He

had a tough time growing up, but he did well for himself. I'm very proud of him."

"The story about the storm is not the one I want to write, Libby," Hap said. "I'd like to do one about you and the history of Cove's End."

"Me? Why on earth would you want to write about me?" Libby picked at her nails and looked down at the floor.

"Because you're unlike any other woman I've ever met. I'm drawn to you and this place, this Cove's End, in a way that I can't really explain. Maybe doing a story about its beginnings will help me understand."

"I'm not news," she said, still avoiding eye contact.

"Well, my boss has this thing about human interest stories. He wants to do a serial on someone prominent, strong, and in your case, beautiful."

He watched as her cheeks flushed.

Hap bent down and put his hands on her shoulder. Then, he lifted her chin so that she had to look at him.

"Please, Libby, give me a day, one day to spend some time with you, walk the complex, and get to know the history of Cove's End. I promise you that you'll be pleased with the story. I won't print anything that you don't approve first."

Libby gazed at him for a moment. A soft light flickered behind her deep emerald eyes. She blinked and dabbed at them with a tissue. "Promise?" she asked, looking down at her dress. She smoothed her blouse.

"I promise. You get first approval rights."

"And you just want the history, how I got started, that sort of thing?"

"It's not everything. I have another assignment here, but I need your help with both," he said, hoping that she couldn't tell how attracted he was to her, how her countenance made him stir inside.

"Tell me about the other assignment. If you need my help, then you'll have to tell me more than I know right now," she said.

"I might need your help in my investigative work about someone you seem to know well."

"And who might that be?" Libby asked.

"The Reverend Ike Madison," Hap said.

Libby chuckled.

"Well, good luck with that one," she said. "But if you need my help, I'm willing."

He bent down and kissed her gently on the cheek.

"Thank you," he said.

"My pleasure," she said.

"Libby," Hap said and ran his hands through his hair. He shifted and leaned on the mantle. "Do you know anything about the doll that's in my room?"

After a minute's hesitation, Libby looked at him. Her face, that perfect porcelain-like complexion, shimmered. Once again, Hap basked in her delicate beauty. "The Firelight Angel is a gift from Lucy."

Hap stared into her eyes. He forgot about the questions, forgot about everything. Her eyes drew him into her with such force that he could not look away. He reached down and pulled her to him.

"Libby," he whispered and pressed her small body next to his. He wrapped his arms around her and savored the feel of her closeness. He felt the warm tingling of her fingers as they caressed his back. Then he took a step back, put his hands on her shoulders and bent down. He kissed her full on the lips and drifted into a world of white-hot passion.

The bell over the door jingled them both back to the real world of business. Libby jumped back, smoothed her skirt and combed through her hair with her fingers. Hap wiped his lips with his hand, brushed at his shirt, and straightened.

"Am I interrupting?" Burton asked as he closed the door.

"Goodness, no. Come in, Burton," Libby said.

Hap walked forward and shook hands with Burton. "Nice to see you again," he said, "and under better circumstances."

"You seem to have recovered from last night's adventure," Burton said. "I just came by to check on you and to see Ms. Libby, of course."

Hap cocked his head to the side and listened. "Who is it that's playing the harmonica all the time?"

"Oh, that's Billy Ray. He works for the Madisons. No mystery there, and no story. He's just a local who likes to play to amuse himself."

"The Madisons," Hap said. "Everything in this town seems connected to them."

"Yes, well, most everything and everybody is," Burton said, "in one way or another."

Hap looked at Libby. "Are you related to Ike Madison?"

"Only by marriage," she said. "Ike was married to my sister Belinda. Caillin is my niece." Hap nodded his head. "Did they divorce? Your sister and Ike?"

Libby looked at the mantle. Her gaze lingered on a picture of four girls. "No, Belinda died," she said, her voice barely audible.

"How?"

"An accident," she said. "She died from a snake bite."

21

When Wheelan Addams opened the door, Hap saw the surprise in his face and spoke immediately. "I came to apologize," Hap said. "I didn't realize that...."

"That she might be somebody's mother?" Wheelan asked. Hap looked at him square in the eyes.

"It was dark. I was scared. Out in the middle of nowhere with no lights and no clue how to get back to my room. The light in your mother's workshop helped me make it back. I saw her and it scared me. Maybe you would have reacted differently if it had happened to you, but...."

"It's been happening to me since I was thirteen," he said and looked down at the floor. "Apology accepted. Now, if you don't mind, I really have a lot of work to do."

"Can I meet her?" Hap asked.

"No," Wheelan said. "The last thing she needs is to have someone trying to get a story out of her. She can't talk to you, anyway. You'd be wasting your time."

"But maybe someone like me is exactly what she needs. She looked at me. She saw my face in the window. I'm not a total stranger to her. If I could just *see* her, I think that she would talk to me."

"Hap, we have no interest in having my mother's picture splashed all over the newspapers. The last time one of you reporters gave us that song and dance, my mother paid for it dearly. Please, go back to Channel 12 and leave us alone. Just please leave us alone."

"It would be good for business. Think of it that way," Hap insisted.

"Does it look as if we need more business here?"

"Ah, come on. Every business needs more business."

"Maybe so, but we're not like you. We're not desperate enough to use a helpless woman as target practice for anyone who's gunning for a story. No story, please. Now, if you'll excuse me."

When Wheelan shut the door, Hap stood there for a moment hoping he would change his mind. He didn't.

Hap leaned up against the building and sighed. "Well," he muttered. "On to plan B."

He walked back to the room to shower and change clothes. Joey was sprawled on the bed reading a book.

"Hey. You look awful."

"Thanks, kiddo. I feel that way, too."

His head felt as if it would literally explode. His knees ached and his hand throbbed. So, he took a couple of Extra-Strength Tylenol tablets. He wished he had something stronger; then he remembered his prescription for Lortab. He fumbled around in his duffel bag to see if it might still be in it.

"Ta Da!" he said. "Found it."

There were four left in the bottle. He popped one of the Lortab into his mouth and washed it down with a soda.

"I need a shower."

"Okay," Joey said. "I'm finishing my book."

After he showered and put on clean jeans and a shirt, he grabbed his other blazer out of the hanging bag. He wanted to look good when he talked to Libby. He splashed on a little Royall Lyme Cologne, gave his hair a final run-through with his hand, and surveyed the damage. His hand was healing; his knee was a little stiff, but he felt better. He stood in front of the mirror, turned to make sure his blazer was straight, smoothed the collar, and buttoned the two front buttons.

"Good," he said, "pretty good."

"You going somewhere?" Joey asked.

"Let's go to the restaurant," Hap said. "Aren't you hungry?"

"No, but...."

Hap picked up the phone, called next door and told Eagle to meet them outside. In a matter of minutes, the three of them lumbered into the restaurant. On the way to the table, Hap saw

Caillin and smiled at her. *Ike Madison's daughter,* he thought. *I'll have to talk to her.*

"Hey, no hittin' on my woman, Hap," Joey said.

"Easy boy, it was just a smile," Hap said, his hands stuffed into his jeans pockets.

"Yeah, but we know what happens when you flash that smile at the ladies. And that's nothin' compared to what they do when they see your buns!"

"You're a pervert, Joey, a real pervert."

Joey pouted his lips at him.

"Can we talk about something besides Joey's testosterone level and your ass?" Eagle asked.

Loud laughter burst from the three of them. Their table in the back became the focus of attention.

"Has anyone talked to Herb?" Hap asked.

"Yeah, he called this morning. He said the story needed to break before the end of the week," Eagle said, fingering his mustache.

Hap shrugged his shoulders, "I'll call him later."

"So, what's the big story?" Joey asked.

"It's still in the works," Hap said. "I've got it under control. Dr. Addams gave me some great information about the area. We can use it."

"Who's Dr. Addams?" Eagle asked.

"Wheelan Addams. He's a meteorologist. Anyway, he has this theory about Preacher's Cove. Number one, why so many storms strike here; and number two, why so many people die here."

"Wait a minute. Where exactly did you meet this Dr. Addams, anyway?" Joey asked.

"He was in my room the other night after the accident. So, I guess you could say he met me first."

"Why was he in your room?" Eagle asked.

"I don't know, now that you mention it. I forgot to ask him," Hap said.

"You forgot to ask him why he was in your room? Good goin', man. Just like an ace reporter!"

"Okay, here's the deal," Hap said. "You remember that woman

I told you about?"

"The one who looks like Medusa?" Joey said and chuckled out loud.

"She's his mother."

Joey grimaced and lowered his head. The chuckling stopped immediately.

"Sorry, I didn't know," he said.

"Neither did I until he told me. And there's more. You know those dolls in the gift shop? The Firelight Angels?"

"I remember them," Eagle said. "They're phenomenal. Just like real kids. Up on the shelf over the cash register. You remember them, don't you, Joey?"

"Sure. Once you've seen them, you can't really forget them."

"Did you happen to notice who made them? As we leave, check it out. The cards say, 'Handmade by Lucy Addams.' Wheelan's mother, the one I said looked like a monster, makes those dolls."

"How do you know it's his mother who makes them? There could be a hundred people in this town named Addams," Eagle asked.

"That woman, gentlemen, is the biggest part of our story! The woman and a man named Ike Madison."

Hap got up, smoothed his jacket, and waved to them. "Gotta run," he said.

"Hey," Joey said, "you can't just run off and leave us hanging."

"Sure I can. It's the sign of an ace reporter!" Hap said and walked out of the restaurant.

"He'd better watch himself," Eagle said. "He's headed for trouble and he's taking us with him."

"What do you mean?" Joey asked.

"I'm not sure, but I think we're all headed for trouble. I'd bet on it. Somebody will die before this one's finished."

22

Hap walked down to the office to find Libby. He needed information, needed to know more about Ike Madison. He wanted another meeting, and this time, he'd be prepared. He opened the office door, the bell sounding his arrival. Libby peeked out of her office, saw him, and smiled. She walked to meet him. Hap raised his eyebrows and whistled at her. She looked stunning. Her dark red hair was pulled up away from her face, but fell in thick curls down her back. Fine tendrils touched her cheeks and eyebrows and framed her delicate face. She wore a green dress with matching green ribbon cascading through her long hair.

"I wasn't expecting you," she said.

"Well, I've blown it with Wheelan, so I thought I'd try to see if you'd answer some questions about Ike Madison."

"About Ike? What kind of questions?" Libby asked. "Routine, I don't know much of anything about him, but let's go back to my office. It's a little quieter there." Libby motioned to Hap and led the way. Hap admired the view from behind. He hadn't realized how shapely Libby was until he saw her in a dress that belted at her small waist. She opened the door to the small back office, where the lighting and furniture made it seem larger than it had at first. A floral sofa fit snugly against the back wall. Beside it was what looked like an antique floor lamp. Across from the sofa was an old-fashioned, high-backed, roll-top secretary and a cushioned chair pulled partially out. White walls and a large floor-to-ceiling mirrored panel gave the office a bright, cheery look. Hap was impressed. He liked nice furniture; a remnant, he thought, from his parents' professions. With his mother an interior designer and his father an architect, Hap had a feel for room design and furnishings. He liked the challenge of "conquering space," as his late mother had called it. This particular hobby he didn't share with the crew or even his close friends. "You look as if you're miles away," Libby said. "Is something about the office bothering you?"

"No, the desk is nice, an antique, isn't it? And the lamp?"

"Yes, both of them have been in my family for years. I'm surprised you'd notice."

He saw a chance to share a personal secret. Maybe he would get one in return. Maybe sharing his "feminine" side would appeal to Libby enough to get her to tell him what he needed to know about Wheelan's mother.

"I, uh, don't normally tell people. Furniture, especially antique furniture, appeals to me. There's something about stepping back into the past. Guess it's rather melancholic of me."

Libby chuckled. "You wouldn't believe how steeped I am in the past, Hap. It's comforting to know that you feel the same way."

"My mother was an interior designer, and my dad is an architect, so I guess I just came by it naturally. Know what I mean?"

"Yes," she said, "I certainly do. In my family, we're very much aware of things from our ancestors. In fact, most of the residents here in the Cove are the very same way. We're big on ancestry here, so you're in good hands. Your secret's safe with me," she said and patted him on the shoulder. Her touch sent a warm tingle through his body, and before she could take her hand away, Hap grabbed it and kissed the back of it softly. Then he stepped closer to her and took her other hand. He gently kissed her palm. From where he stood towering over her, she seemed so small, so enticing. He bent and kissed her on the forehead. She, in turn, stood on her tiptoes and kissed his cheek. Then Hap thought of something his great-grandmother used to say when she saw couples who were so uneven in height. He stopped the kiss and laughed. "I'm sorry," he said. "I, uh, I thought of something funny and I couldn't help myself."

"So, in the moment when we were about to kiss, you thought of something funny? Well, that's different. Go ahead. Tell me."

"My great-grandmother used to say...I mean, when she saw a couple and the man was much taller than the woman, she used to say, 'When you're nose to nose, your toes is in it, and when you're toes to toes, your nose is in it.'"

At that, they both laughed. Libby flushed noticeably and fanned her hand in front of her face.

"It's a little warm in here. I think I'll get a soda, if you don't mind. Would you like something?"

"Soda's fine."

"Be right back," she said.

When she left, Hap wondered if he had pushed things a little too far. He wanted them both to be relaxed and comfortable, but Libby's nervous laughter and his sweaty palms didn't fit into his plan.

"Idiot," he muttered. "Take your time. Don't blow this one."

"Did you say something?" Libby asked, returning with the two drinks.

And before he could stop the words from falling from his mouth, he said,

"I don't want to blow this, Libby. I'm afraid I was too forward. I want you to be relaxed and comfortable with me."

Libby smiled at him and said, "You don't want to blow the interview, and we're both a little nervous, I think."

She sat down on the chair by the secretary and motioned to Hap to sit on the sofa. "Go ahead. I'll answer your questions."

Hap pulled his notepad from his jacket pocket, flipped it open to a clean page, checked his pen, and settled back on the sofa. He looked over at Libby; she was staring at him with eyes that seemed to penetrate his soul. The expression on her face, the slight smile, the half-closed eyes, the open posture: all of it said that she found him somewhat attractive. He could almost hear her thinking. She called to him in her mind, a call for him to get closer. Hap had a hard time concentrating on the interview. His physical desire for Libby had to be obvious to her, but he didn't want to scare her off, so he tried to hold himself in check. He knew that Libby saw him as attractive, but he knew enough about human nature to know that she probably also knew that his stay here would be brief. He would go back to Huntsville. Maybe she didn't want to get involved with him because of that. Or, maybe she didn't care. He wished he had the nerve to find out.

"You're staring at me," Hap said. "Is something wrong?"

"Sorry, I was lost in thought."

"So, tell me, Libby, about when you first started Cove's End. What prompted you to open a business out here?"

"You mean in Preacher's Cove? I've always lived here. It's my home."

"And you opened the restaurant because...."

"Because I was a widow with no job and no source of income. Reverend Isaiah Madison gave me the job as part-time waitress and manager. He owned this place and called it Madison's Eatery. It never did very much business, though, and he was thinking of closing it just about the time my Frankie died. I needed work, asked him for a job, and he let me run it for a little while to see if business would pick up. It did, very quickly. Later, he asked me to be the manager, then his partner, and eventually sold it to me for a small sum."

"Frankie was your husband? How did he die, exactly?"

"The lightning. His body was charred. The same storm killed two of my brothers-in-law and...."

"I'm sorry," Hap said.

"A lot of good people died during that storm, just like during this one."

"And you changed the name to Cove's End?"

"At the time, I thought that my Frankie and all my other relatives needed a memorial of sorts. I wasn't really thinking about the unusual nature of the name. Folks around here are familiar with it. And strangers don't really care what the name of a place is as long as it gives them more than their money's worth."

"You've done an excellent job," he said and smiled.

"Thank you. My great granny used to say...."

"She must have talked all the time, just like mine!" Hap said. They both laughed out loud.

"Well, she used to say that you can disappoint people only so many times before they begin to believe that you are simply not worth the pain. And that philosophy applies just as well to business as it does to everyday living."

"Good point. Maybe I should remember that one myself. May I use it?"

"Certainly, you'd make my great-granny proud."

"Now, tell me about the complex and how that got started. When did the restaurant turn into this mega-plex of yours?"

Libby looked at the clock on the mantle.

"It's already late evening. I hadn't realized the time."

"Just a couple more questions, please?"

"The complex started small, a little bit at a time, really. First, Isaiah knew that I needed a home, so he arranged to build the first of my houses for me and extended the bottom floor into one long stream of hotel rooms. We started our hotel business for truckers who needed lodging and food at all times of the night."

"Isaiah Madison must have been quite a man," Hap said. "How did he die?"

"Same way...bolt of lightning struck him."

"Buggers! It's not safe to be a male in this town!"

Libby said nothing. She adjusted her position in the chair and folded her arms with her hands locked behind each elbow. Hap read the non-verbal message as clearly as if she had said, "I don't want to talk about this."

"And you had the gazebo built?" Hap leaned forward.

"Isaiah loved the gazebo at Madison Manor, his home. He and Caillin spent hours sitting out there learning to love one another."

"And Caillin is the granddaughter, right?" Hap asked. "Yes, she loved that man with all her heart. She never got along well with either of her parents. She was watching out of her bedroom window during the storm and saw the lightning strike him. Such a trauma."

"The mark on her palm is a bit unusual, isn't it?"

"I've seen worse marks, much worse."

With her arms folded even tighter, Libby told Hap that this information was not relevant to his interview with her. She suggested they explore another topic.

After another thirty minutes of questions about who, what, and where, Libby began to fidget in the chair.

"Would you like to take a break?" Hap asked.

"What time is it?" she asked. "It seems like I've been answering questions for hours."

We've been at it a while. You're getting tired, I guess, and so am I.

I must leave by 11:30, so you'll have to be finished by then."

Hap could hear the fatigue in her voice.

"I have just one more question."

She smiled at him and nodded her approval.

"Where does Wheelan's mother fit into all this?"

Libby hesitated only a second. She looked at him square in the face and said,

"She is my sister, that's all. She is a great artist, too."

"Yes, most definitely. I just wondered if...."

"If you could meet her?"

Libby stood and looked down at him.

"It wouldn't do any good, Hap. Trust me. Lucy can barely manage to feed herself. Some days she is clear and has such a sparkle in her eyes. But most of the time, she's lost in Lucy's world. She was burned so badly that she won't ever be able to talk again."

"I...I, uh, am sorry, Libby. Really."

Hap stood and hugged her. Then he kissed the top of her head and ran his hands through her soft hair. When he saw tears roll down Libby's cheeks, he felt his own heart might break. He kissed her tears away and hugged her close.

"I know that loss," he whispered. "My mother died just two months ago."

Libby hugged him tighter. Hap felt the tingling begin. It spread down his back and into his legs. The warmth made him relax as if right before the moment of sleep comes knocking. They stood together, each lost in despair but safe in each other's arms. After a few minutes, Hap took a deep breath and turned around. He took Libby's hand and led her back to the sofa.

"Sorry to break the mood," he said, "but I felt a little wobbly. Something about your touch literally makes my knees weak."

Libby smiled at him and nodded. "I'll explain it to you one of these days."

Hap looked at her, his face suddenly somber.

"Explain it to me now," he said.

"Not now, but soon, when we have a little more time."

"Promise?"

Libby nodded. Hap cleared his throat and took a deep breath.

"This is changing the subject. Do you mind?"

Libby sighed with relief.

"Go ahead."

"I want to meet Lucy," he said, his tone forceful. "Just hear me out. I want to do a story on the Firelight Angels."

Libby looked up at him, her hands tightly folded in her lap.

"Why the Angels?"

"Because they're phenomenal."

"Hap, you don't understand."

Libby lowered her head and cupped her knees with her hands. Hap stood up again and paced around the office.

"What is there to understand, Libby?" His voice quivered. His hands trembled. Beads of sweat dotted his upper lip.

"I'm trying to do some good here, trying to bring you and your sister some acclaim and publicity. But every time I try to do anything, you tell me that I don't understand. Please, just tell me what I have to do to understand you!"

"Let it go, Hap. Let it go, for your own sake."

"No," he shouted. "Something here in Preacher's Cove is trying to talk to me, Libby. I won't let it go. If you don't help me, then I'll find someone who will."

His face reddened; his heartbeat quickened.

Libby rose slowly from the sofa. She spoke but did not look at him.

"Very well," she said, her voice barely above a whisper. "We're twins, we're the caul babies of Preacher's Cove."

"Caul babies?"

Libby nodded.

"It's rare. One in every two hundred thousand babies. A caul is a thick mucus covering a baby's head at birth. Being born with a caul means you're special, gifted in some way. Lucy is gifted with extreme talents, and I have a few gifts myself. Unusual gifts."

"I don't fully understand."

"Neither do I," Libby said. "Most of the time, babies born with cauls were killed. Folks believed they were evil. I have to go now.

I'm not feeling well."

Libby walked past him, but instinctively, he reached for her and put his hands on her shoulders. He turned her to him and his eyes pleaded with her. Libby reached up and touched the side of his face.

Again, her touch sent a warm tingle through his body. He bent forward and kissed her on the mouth. She returned the kiss, and in an instant of simultaneous passion, they were on the sofa together. She ran her open hands down his back and the tingling warmth overtook him. He moaned and felt such desire that he burned red-hot for her. He was barely aware that the two of them were shedding their clothes, barely aware that the sofa was uncomfortably small for him, and barely aware that beads of sweat dotted his lips and hers. Consumed with desire for her, he allowed no other thought to enter his mind. He hardly noticed that at the peak of their passion, when he felt as if he would burst, Libby moaned softly and her eyes glowed a soft luminescent green.

23

At midnight, in the darkness of the place called Cove's End, Lucy Addams reached for the red button, pushed it with trembling fingers, and braced herself for the jolt of the chair as it moved down to the ground floor. She hummed a lullaby and held tightly to a rag doll cradled at her chest. A grotesque smiled formed on her mouth, only a sliver of lip left untouched by the fire. From the misshapen hole gushed a sound.

"Baah...beh...swee...baah...beh."

One gnarled remnant of a hand patted the doll's back. When the lift jerked to a stop, one smooth, beautiful hand reached to open the gate that kept them both safe. Clutching the baby close to her chest, Lucy stood, slid her foot carefully along the edge of the lift, and stepped forward. She stood dead still for a moment listening for the sounds of any who might see her. A dead stone quiet settled over the area which was hers and hers alone. She smiled again. With her baby safely in her arms, she interrupted the silence with the swish, swish, swish of her moccasins shuffling across the hardwood floor. "Baah...beh...swee...baah...beh."

"Oh, God, what time is it, Hap? Oh, my Lord, I'm late. I just know it."

Libby jumped up from the sofa, grabbed her clothes, and rushed into the small bathroom in her office.

"Relax," Hap called after her. "It's only five after twelve. You're not going to turn into a pumpkin, are you?"

Before he'd even had time to tuck in his shirt, Libby stepped out of the bathroom, her hair hanging loosely across her shoulders, wisps of it falling down across her face. "I can't find my barrettes," she said. "My hair is a mess."

Hap looked down on the floor by the sofa and found the two large hair pins. He picked them up and handed them to her. She stepped into the bathroom again and emerged with most of her hair pulled neatly away from her face. Noticeably flushed, her cheeks a bright red, Libby took a deep breath, straightened her dress, and asked, "Do I look normal? I mean, can you tell that we, that we...."

"You look great to me. I don't think anyone will notice, especially at this hour. If they do, they'll just be envious." He laughed, but for some reason, Libby didn't.

"I really have to go," she said. "The time just slipped by. I can't believe I didn't watch it more carefully."

"I think we both dozed off. Besides, what difference does it make if you're a few minutes late for whatever it is that's ripping you away from me? You're the owner of this place, right? Rank has its privileges."

Libby just shook her head.

"I'll see you tomorrow. I have to go."

"Not so fast. You're not leaving me stranded in this place again. Wait a minute and I'll walk with you. I want to ask you something."

He stepped into the bathroom, and just before he shut the door, he called to her,

"Please, don't leave."

When he was ready, they both walked to the door and into the lobby. The night desk clerk looked up, saw the two of them, raised her eyebrows, and quickly looked down at her paperwork.

"Evenin', Ms. Libby," she said. Libby nodded.

As they walked out of the double doors leading outside, Hap said, "See! I told you no one would notice. Libby, what do I have to do to convince you to let me meet Lucy?"

Libby grinned.

"Good night, Hap. I will think about a meeting."

She hurried down the planked walkway, and before Hap could think of a good retort, she had disappeared.

Without Libby there, he knew he had the perfect opportunity.

But when he tried to take a step forward, he felt as if his legs were made of lead. Overcome with what he thought was fatigue, he decided to go back to the room.

He told himself that he was not afraid to follow Libby, that he was definitely *not* afraid of being lost in the complex. And he convinced himself enough to decide to meet her very early the next morning.

"Yeah, that would be better," he whispered.

Libby ran down the walkway, her shoes clacking on the wooden planks. She saw the door of the workshop and stopped. She smoothed her dress, patted her face, and brushed back the wayward tendrils of hair. Then she eased open the door and stepped inside.

In the soft, dim light of the workshop, Lucy bent over the worktable. Libby inched quietly closer. Another doll, dressed and ready to go, sat in the rocking chair. Libby watched as the glow around Lucy began as a tiny flicker of brilliant green light. Her hands moved with staggering speed, and as they moved, the light around her intensified until, at last, from her entire body emanated a pulsing brightness of sheer energy. Libby turned her head away from the blinding brightness.

"The Eye of God," she whispered and dropped to her knees. She bent her head and covered her face with her hands. "Embraced by God's magician," she chanted. "Seized by the Dead. Resurrected by the Goddess. Sustained by the child." In only minutes, the genius of her twin sister shone in the form of a doll, perfectly formed from head to toe.

"LeeLee," came the high-pitched wail.

Libby snapped her eyes open and looked up at Lucy.

"LeeLee."

Lucy turned and faced Libby. In her arms, she held a brown-haired doll with sparkling brown eyes, a boy whom Libby did not recognize. In the early stages of fashioning, the Firelight Angel wore no clothes or shoes. Lucy clutched the doll to her breast and opened her hand. The sapphire-colored mark in her palm glowed with brilliant but fading soft light. Libby stood up and stroked Lucy's face. Her fingers drifted lightly over the reddish-purple mass of tangled flesh that was once smooth as porcelain. With her fingers, she brushed away damp strands of long red hair that stuck to Lucy's scarred face. With one of the towels from the worktable, she wiped dots of perspiration from Lucy's forehead. "You've made another angel, my sweet sister. May I hold him?"

Lucy steadied herself on the worktable and turned away, clutching the doll tighter to her chest.

"Bahbee," she mumbled. "Ma bahbee."

"Please," Libby said. "Please let me hold him. You make the card, Lucy, and I'll hold the baby."

The soft light of the workshop framed the other side of Lucy's face, the side untouched by furious flames. Smooth and glimmering, that side seemed unmarked by age, as well. Her cheek shone with a natural blush, her green eye sparkled with clarity. But then she spoke.

"Anda," she mouthed.

Libby held out her arms and took the doll. Moments later, Lucy appeared with the placard. Libby turned it over in her hand and looked at the script. *Smitten little Joey: Take Belinda's Hand.*

Libby's eyes widened when she read the placard. "Lucy, tell me more."

But by that time, Lucy was Lucy again, locked inside a world that allowed no intruders.

Libby slid past the work table and grabbed the doll in the rocking chair.

Lucy didn't seem to notice.

Libby hurried into the storage room, retrieved a dark green box and slipped back into the work room. Just as she laid the new doll in the box, she heard a low moaning sound. She squeezed her eyes shut and shook her head.

"No, Lucy. It's time for him to go home."

But Lucy didn't hear her. The sound of her own screaming drowned out any sound Libby made. Lucy stamped one foot on the floor and screamed in a high-pitched wail that made Libby's head and ears throb.

"Stop!" a deep voice boomed through the workshop.

The wailing softened barely.

"Mother, stop it!"

Immediately, the screeching wail stopped. Wheelan walked into the room, grabbed the box, took Libby by the arm, and pulled her with him.

He stopped beside the door and turned to face Lucy.

"Don't worry, Mother," he said, his voice firm but gentle. "I'm taking the angel home."

By the time he and Libby left, Lucy stood beside her worktable humming a soft lullaby.

24

Hap fumbled with the key card and finally managed to see the small green "enter" light appear. It reminded him of something—he couldn't say what—and he shuddered slightly. Sounds of Joey's snoring filtered through the air, so Hap undressed as quietly as a tired man can and slipped into bed. While he crooked one pillow between his elbow and body, fluffed the other one under his head, and stretched his legs as far as the bed allowed, he thought of that green light again. There was something that he knew he should remember, but he was so tired that his brain said,

"Go to sleep, man, it ain't worth the hassle right now."

Within minutes, he drifted off again into the world of strangers. This time, though, there was one familiar face. He dreamt again of the tall man standing alone by an open grave listening to the splatter of rocks and dirt atop the wooden coffin. As before, the earth trembled beneath his feet as the sky lost its brilliant blue and turned, instead, a grayish black. The tall man watched as the top of the coffin slid slightly askew. When the earth trembled once more and thunder bellowed in the distance, the top slid again, this time just enough to reveal the blood-stained hem of a plain green dress. A bolt of lightning struck the ground between the circle of trees where the body lay, but the tall man did not budge. He watched.

Huge, billowing dark clouds whirled in the sky above him, the air heavy with their tears. When the thunder boomed again, the earth beneath his feet heaved in one last climactic shudder. Dirt fell from atop the open grave, its weight moving, once again, the top of the coffin. With one creaking thud, the top slammed against its catacomb. The body of the woman he loved lay lifeless, its eyes fixed open. Suddenly, a brilliant green light shone from those eyes, flickered, and went out. The mouth moved and cried, "Help us, Sydney." Blood-soaked and stiff on its back, its eyes open, too, the body of a baby lay against its mother. Covering its head and face was a thick, clear substance that distorted the face and made it seem almost inhuman. Stealing the last light by which the tall man mourned, the sky turned pitch black. A moment later, greenflash danced across the sky, filling it with brilliant, luminescent green light. Sporadically, hues of bright pink and deep purple streaked through and intermingled, creating a kaleidoscopic ceiling of lethal beauty. In an instant, lightning crackled through the sky, as though a goddess had swept past, leaving in her wake a shimmering, translucent stream of light.

Staunch and straight, his eyes wide with terror, the tall man turned away from his green-eyed wife and walked toward the woods behind the circle of trees. He did not stop, but as he approached the edge of the woods, he turned and looked back, his face in full view lit by one blinding flash of lightning. It was a familiar face. Staring dead-on in the dreamer's eye was Wheelan Addams.

Hap gasped in his sleep and sat straight up.

"Buggers!" he yelled.

"Don't you ever sleep?" Joey asked, his voice thick with his own sleep.

Hap practically jumped out of the bed.

"Hey, what's the matter?" Joey asked. "You've been calling out in your sleep for over an hour."

Hap looked at bedside clock. His head throbbed, his hand ached, and his knee felt as if it were on fire. He sat on the edge of the bed and ran his hand through his hair. He struggled onto his feet, moved slowly over to the dresser, and searched through his bag. When he found the Lortab, he wrestled off the cap and took one pill from the bottle, and with the same stale soda from earlier in the afternoon, he swallowed the pill.

"Sorry, kid," he said. "Try to get some sleep. Oh, and by the way, have you ever heard of a caul?"

"Caul? Yeah, I've heard of it." Joey sat up and rubbed his eyes. "My great-grandma used to tell a story about witch babies. You could tell they were witches because they were all born with this slimy stuff over their faces. I've heard her talk about it a lot. Country talk, mostly. You know, old wives' tales and such. But Gran was scared of those tales. She believed in them."

"Witch babies, huh?"

"Well, that's what Gran said. I've never seen one, though. Gran swore she knew a couple in Jackson County who had a witch baby. It was stillborn, and when folks saw it, they ran that couple out of town. Right after, some sort of sickness struck the women in the County. They all swore it was a curse of those witches."

"Thanks, kid, for sharing that bizarre tale with me!"

"Well, hey, you asked and I explained. Oooh eee oooh...did I scare you?"

"Go to sleep, kid."

Hap sat back down on the edge of the bed. Images from his dream crept into his mind. The woman with the blood-stained dress, the dead baby, the storm, and Wheelan's face. But the one image that kept him from stretching out on the bed and trying for a few more hours of sleep was that of the woman's eyes, those glowing green eyes. He had seen them before. Now, sitting in the darkness, the thought of them scared him blind. He shuddered.

He wanted a warm shower. It would help clear his head and loosen up his stiff, aching joints. He walked into the bathroom, flipped on the fan and light, and pulled back the shower curtain.

When he heard the rattling sound, he jumped back. Coiled inside the tub was a snake, its rattlers straight in the air and moving so fast that they seemed like one small blur. "Joey" he yelled. "Get in here!"

As quick as lightning, Joey was standing right behind him. "In the tub," he whispered. "It's in the tub."

Joey stepped forward and peeped over the side of the tub. The snake hissed, its mouth open, and struck at the side of the tub with a distinct thud.

"Holy crap!" Joey cried. "Call somebody."

They stumbled out of the bathroom, pulled the door tight, and shook. The snake hissed and struck again at the side of the tub.

"Did you hear that?" Joey asked.

"Yes. I'm calling Addams."

Hap fumbled with the phone, dialed the front desk, and asked for Wheelan's number.

"I'm sorry, sir," the night clerk said, "I can't give out that number."

"Listen," he yelled, "and listen carefully. There's a snake in this room and if you don't give me that number so I can reach Dr. Addams, I'll make sure you don't work here long enough to draw another paycheck. "

"I'll ring it myself, sir."

Hap heard the phone ring once, then twice. On the third ring, someone picked up.

"Hello," Wheelan answered in a hoarse whisper.

"Addams, Wheelan Addams?"

"Yes, this is Addams. Who is this?"

"This is Hap Murray. Listen, get down here to room 212 as quick as you can. There's a snake in the tub. Hurry!"

"I beg your pardon. Did you say that a snake was in the tub?"

"Buggers, Addams. Get your ass down here…NOW!"

"I'll be right there. Did it bite anyone?"

"No, we've got the door closed."

"I'm on my way."

Hap and Joey stood against the dressing room wall waiting for another sound from the creature. Once again, it struck the side of the tub.

"You afraid of snakes?" Joey asked.

"No, what I feel goes way beyond fear. It's more like pure horror. They terrify me. I'm the original ophidiophobe."

"Huh?"

"Ophidiophobia, fear of snakes. That's me."

"Then I guess we're just out of luck 'til Wheelan gets here."

A sudden banging at the door startled them even more. Fear coursed like ice water through their veins.

"Hap, it's me, Wheelan. Open the door!" he called.

"Geez, that was fast!" Joey said.

Hap fumbled with the handle, his fingers shaking as hard and fast as the rattlers on that snake. He jerked it open. Wheelan stood holding a large bag in one hand, a stick in the other.

"It's in there," Hap said, pointing toward the bathroom.

Joey stood stiff against the wall.

"You'd better step back, son," Wheelan said. In one stride, Joey cleared the dressing area and moved to the opposite wall.

"Oh, God," Joey said, "he's gonna try to catch it."

Wheelan edged open the door of the bathroom. He glanced around at the floor, listening for any sound. Then he leaned over and looked into the tub. With a quick thunk, the snake struck at the side of the tub one more time. Wheelan jumped back. He grabbed the bag, removed the hook stick, took a deep breath, and walked to the tub. Trembling, he lowered the hook in place, the snake in a desperate wiggle to get out from under it. He pressed down as hard as he could to get exactly behind his head and hold him there.

"Hap," he called, "get me that jar out of the sack."

"I'm not coming in there, Wheelan. Sorry, you're on your own."

"Oh for mercy's sake, be a man. Help me out here," Wheelan yelled.

Hap moved slowly over to the sack, reached inside, and felt for the jar. His fingers found something cold and round, grabbed it out of the sack, and held it up: a Mason jar filled with cotton balls. "Open it, please, but keep it away from your nose."

He carefully twisted off the lid, tossed it on the floor, and keeping it at arm's length, handed it to Wheelan. Wheelan leaned back to keep it away from his own nose, turned the jar upside down and in one swift expert movement, caught the snake's head under the jar. Within seconds, the snake uncoiled and lay quiet, as quiet as stone. Wheelan nudged it with the hook stick just to make sure. Then he bent down, grabbed its tail, and pulled it out of the tub. Into the bag it went. He bent over again and got the jar, being careful to keep it upside down and pressed against the bottom of the tub. "Quick!" he said to Hap, "hand me the lid."

Hap snatched the lid from the floor and handed it to Wheelan. He bent over, carefully tightened the lid, and washed his hands and the jar under the faucet. He struggled up off his stiff knees and walked out of the bathroom. "You're safe," he said to the two men standing stiff as statues in front of him.

Wheelan motioned to Joey, "Why don't you open the door and let it air out in here. Ether's not going to hurt you if you get plenty of air."

Joey did as he said and breathed deeply as the early morning May air rushed through the door. Wheelan picked up the sack, grabbed the jar, and headed toward the door.

"Better go put this thing away," he said.

"That's it?" Hap asked. "No explanations, nothing? You're just leaving?"

"I need to get back to make sure it's dead. I need to examine it, figure out how it got here, and what we should do about it. I'll have your answers tomorrow. Okay?"

"Sure, I guess. I'll see you tomorrow then. And thanks."

"No problem," he said.

When he'd left, the two them sat on the edge of the beds shaking.

"I've never been that close to a snake before," Joey said.

Another banging on the door caused them both to jump.

"Open up."

They both recognized Eagle's voice. Hap got up and opened the door.

"What in Sam Hill is going on here?"

Eagle flipped on the overhead light. Then, the three of them stared at a chair in the corner of the room. "What *is* that?" Eagle asked.

"Looks like a big green box," Joey said, his voice flat.

"Astute observation," Eagle said. He twirled the ends of his mustache.

"I know what it is," Hap said. His fingers still trembled. Now, his stomach churned, as well.

"Eagle, look in that bottom dresser drawer," he said. "There's a big blue box in there. Take it out, will you?"

Eagle walked to the dresser, opened the drawer, and pulled out the box. He laid it on the bed. Then he looked at Hap, opened his hands, and shrugged.

"Go ahead," Hap said.

Eagle removed the top, pushed back the layers of tissue, and stepped backwards.

"Whoa," he said. "It's you."

"Read the card."

Eagle picked up the card and read aloud:

"Brave Michael, Save the Holder."

Hap walked over to the other box, opened it, and lifted out another Firelight Angel. Eagle coughed and chuckled. "Well," he said. "It's definitely too cute to be me!"

Hap reached in, retrieved the card, and handed it to Joey. Joey took the card without reading it. He looked only at the doll. "I know you're not going to believe this, but when I was a kid, I had a shirt that I wore everywhere. It looked just like that one," he said. He pointed to the T-shirt the doll wore. It had an Auburn Tigers logo, orange and blue, imprinted on the front. "I, uh, I guess lots of kids had those," Joey said and looked at the card he held. He studied the message scripted in gold. It made little sense to him, so he read it to Hap and Eagle.

"Smitten little Joey: Take Caillin's Hand."

Hap went to the dressing area, pulled on a pair of jeans, and headed for the door.

"Where are you going?" Eagle asked.

"I've had enough. I'm going to find out about these dolls. Libby said they were gifts, just gifts. But I don't buy it. There's something else going on here. I'll be back in a while."

"What about your shoes?"

Hap shrugged and waved to them. "Don't worry. Tough hands. Tough feet. Even in a place full of monsters."

25

The dim light of the workshop shone like a beacon in the darkness around Cove's End. For five hours, the beacon gave Lucy Addams all the light she needed to form perfect replicas of some child of the Cove, either living or dead. Lucy never knew which. She simply followed the hands. Whole or twisted, they performed with equal mastery. The hands simply followed the goddess, the White Maiden of centuries before who plucked a stone from the heart of a brave priestess and changed the lives of women...gifted women like Lucy. With precision unequaled, she honored the Maiden with a host of little angels, all beautiful, all innocent, and all alive inside the mind of a lunatic. She was lost, now, in a place where no others were allowed entry.

Bent close to the worktable, she slid black patent leather shoes on tiny feet and put the finishing touch on another of her Firelight Angels. She bundled the newly-created baby into her arms, shuffled across the room to a child-sized rocker that sat in the corner, and placed the baby carefully into the seat. The blonde, green-eyed child, with a look of wonder on her face, a peaceful smile on her lips, seemed almost ready to speak. With great care, Lucy fluffed the child's bright blue dress, straightened the white pinafore, and gently ran her whole fingers across the child's blushing cheeks. Then she took a step back, one foot dragging more slowly than the other, and stood dead still.

For one brief moment, Lucy's eyes sparkled with awareness. She lifted a hand to her mouth, as the sound of soft laughter escaped and blew gently through her fingertips. In the shadowed light, she was Lucy Addams again, the beautiful young wife and mother. She beamed with pride at the child seated in the chair. In that same shadowed light, one unblemished hand as smooth as porcelain reached down and stroked the child's hair; one perfect side of a delicate, porcelain-colored face with deep green eyes feasted upon the mastery of her creation. She pulled back her shoulders, took a deep breath, and sighed. With delicate accuracy, she stepped back without a single falter.

The step backward placed her in front of the only window in the workshop. The light, which shone like a welcomed beacon only a minute earlier, now became the light which cast the reflection of the mangled left side of her face. She remembered the black sky, the green flashes, the wailing, and the deaths. The horror of that night flashed into her mind like the lightning that killed her husband. For only a few seconds, she heard the cries of the twins and saw their faces pressed hard against the window.

"Bah...bee..." Lucy said, "Swee...bah...bee."

But when someone grabbed her from behind and pulled her away from the doll, Lucy dropped to her knees and wailed. Out of breath and stumbling over his own lanky body and big feet, Wheelan grabbed a bucket already filled with water and doused the flames. He yelled so loudly that Lucy stopped the wailing and slowly cocked her head to the side to glare at him. For the first time in many years, she saw her son, she recognized the boy-turned-man, and she smiled inside. Her mouth, however, would not cooperate. No matter how hard she tried, she could not call out his name. Only a jumbled mush of sound escaped her lips. On her knees, with her head turned to the side, the smooth side of her face lit softly in the dim light, Lucy raised her arm. One small, slim, perfect hand struggled to touch the son whose life the fire did not claim. She thought if she could touch him for only a moment....

"No more, Mother, no more!" he yelled and threw the empty bucket right through the window. The bucket whizzed beside the lone hanging light bulb, set it swinging, then barreled through the window spraying shards of glass throughout the workshop. Still on her knees, bits of glass showering across her back, Lucy continued the wail.

"Why can't you just leave them alone? Why can't you just forget?"

"Wheelan?" someone called behind him. Startled by the intrusion of another voice, Wheelan gasped and tripped over the rim of the rocker. "What's going on in here?"

When Wheelan did not respond, Hap stepped over closer. On one side of the room was a sobbing woman on her knees. On the other was a crouching man, also on his knees. But he wasn't moving. Hap moved forward a little more. Wheelan turned his head slowly and brought up his hand.

Stop! He signalled.

Lucy stopped her wailing. The room stilled and grew deadly silent...except for the furious rattling, a sound so familiar to Hap that it made his knees buckle. He caught himself on the edge of one of the work tables. The movement was enough to incite the tiny rattler into action. Lightning quick, it slithered underneath the very table on which the young reporter had braced himself.

"Get out of the way, Hap. Hurry! It's going right toward your...."

By the time the reporter heard and registered Wheelan's words, he felt the fangs sink into the soft fleshy spot under his inside anklebone. At first, he thought someone had shoved a piece of red-hot charcoal into his foot with such force that it burned right to the bone and all the way up to his groin. He took a deep breath and another. His lungs felt stuck, unwilling to bring in the air that he needed. The room seemed so much colder.

He dropped to his knees and gasped for air. He tried to put his head back, to clear his passageway so that he could breathe easier, but when his head dropped back, so did his body. It crashed right at the feet of the woman he'd seen as he came in. She had such a pretty face, such smooth skin. He wanted to touch her, but his arms would not obey the command given by his brain. He wondered, only briefly, what had happened to the monster he'd seen in this place. Where'd it go? he wondered.

Wheelan was up in an instant. He grabbed a rusty hatchet that had been hanging in the workshop for years. In a split second, the tiny massasauga rattler lay in two pieces. Awkwardly maneuvering his tall body next to Hap's, Wheelan felt for a pulse. It was there, but fading. Hap breathed with short, raspy wheezing sounds. His eyes were glazed, pupils dilated, and his skin felt clammy and cold. Wheelan scrunched himself down to see the wound and pulled off his T-shirt, ripped it in half, and tied a tourniquet of sorts above the kneecap. When there was no response from Hap, Wheelan knew he wouldn't live more than a few more minutes. With no phone in the workshop, he had to leave to get help.

He bent close to Hap and said, "I'm going for help, but I'll be right back. You stay right where you are. Don't give up on me, now." He looked at his mother, imploring her with his eyes to do something. Then, he was up and out the door. By his calculations, it would take about five minutes to reach the office, if he ran like the wind, another fifteen to twenty for help to arrive, and another five for the paramedics to...pronounce Hap dead.

"Jesus!" he said and ran as fast as his long legs had ever carried him down the long corridor.

26

Crazy Lucy cowered in the corner of the room, staring at someone's blonde hair. The thick shiny hair reminded her of something familiar, something that felt warm and soothing. She reached out to touch it, but drew her hand back when the large body attached to the hair jerked once and gurgled.

Lightning quick, Lucy's eyes burned, her hands reddened, and her heartbeat quickened. She crawled around in front of the body and stared down at its face. Then she stretched herself out alongside it and slid her hand down the body, searching for the hot spot that would tell her what to do. The swollen ankle drew her hand like a magnet. She sat up again, wrapped both her gnarled lump of a hand and her smooth perfect one around the ankle. But she needed more heat to help this lifeless body, and as she swayed back and forth, demanding more energy, the temperature in the room dropped almost ten degrees. When her eyes glowed a soft luminescent green, Hap Murray jerked once more. Lucy stretched out alongside him again, ran her hands up to his chest, and pressed down hard. Nothing happened. She moved again, straddling him. Then she pressed her gaping mouth to his, wrapped her smooth hand around the back of his neck, and closed her eyes. Within seconds, Hap jerked again. This time, his hand moved, then his arm. Lucy moved her hand from behind his neck, opened her eyes, sat up straight, and ran her hands down the sides of his arms and up again across his chest. Down the arms, up again and across the chest. Down the arms and up again....

When he opened his eyes, Hap Murray stared into the face of his monster. Too weak to fight, he watched as its eyes glowed a brilliant green and its gaping mouth twitched back and forth as in some silent song. But then, the monster turned her head, as if it had heard something in the distance. Hap saw Lucy Addams, but this time, she was a vision. The dim light of the workshop softly illuminated a beautiful, porcelain-like face framed by thick auburn hair, and two perfect emerald green eyes, glowing softly. She moved her hand to caress his hair.

"Bah...bee," she mouthed. "Swee...bah...bee."

She was off of him, after that, sitting beside him.

He struggled to sit up but had no energy.

"Please, don't leave me," he whispered.

Lucy reached down and stroked his hair.

When Wheelan barreled into the room, he saw his mother stroking Hap's hair.

"Oh, God," he said. "I'm too late."

He walked over expecting to see the eyes staring wide in the death watch.

"Took you long enough," Hap whispered as a coughing spell assaulted him in spasms so hard that he had to turn on his side and vomit. Green bile spilled from his mouth. "Help's on the way. Just a few minutes and they'll be here." Wheelan pulled a small towel off the worktable, stepped over to the sink and wet it, and wiped Hap's mouth and forehead. Then he grabbed him under the arms, and pulling him gently away from the mess on the floor, cradled his head in his lap.

"It's cold in here," Hap whispered. "I know," Wheelan said. "It's always cold afterwards, but the room will be warm again soon."

"Mother," Wheelan said softly, "people are coming, Mother. You'd better go back to your room." She looked in his direction. Wheelan smiled at her, and when he did, she remembered a young thirteen-year-old boy who stood helplessly as his father and brothers burned alive. She reached across to touch his face.

"Mother, go on. Get out of here before they come. I know you can understand me. You have to leave."

Lucy pulled her hand back, got to her feet, and shuffled toward the door.

"Thank you, Mother," Wheelan said. "Thank you."

But by that time, she had retreated once again into the mindless safety called Crazy Lucy Addams.

27

By the time the paramedics arrived at Cove's End, the work-shop teemed with anxious visitors: Burton Riggs, Libby Arbuckle, and Caillin Madison crowded in to find out how the young reporter was faring. Soon, Joey and Eagle shoved in, as well. When Libby noticed the gathering of so many, she immediately motioned to Burton. "Okay, folks, show's over. Let's clear the way for the paramedics. Joey, why don't you and Eagle go back to the office. We'll meet you there in just a few minutes."

"Well, I'd at least like to know what happened to him," he said.

"It was just an accident, son, just an accident. He'll be fine. I promise you. Now, run on down to the office. I'll fill you in on all the details just as soon as I'm through here," Riggs said.

"No offense, sir, but I'd rather ask him myself. I'd like to talk to him."

"I know he's your friend, but he's not in much shape to talk right now. Please, clear the way so that the paramedics can get in here and help him."

"Joey, would you like for me to walk down with you?" Caillin asked. "Is that all right, Aunt Libby?" Libby smiled her approval as the girl walked over and ushered the crew out of the doorway just as the four paramedics headed inside. Outside the complex were two rescue vehicles, one fire truck, and two police cars, all of them with lights flashing. "Chief, good to see you," a police officer said. "Heard we had some sort of freak accident here."

"Yes," the chief said. "Look, do me a favor. Turn off some of those lights. The place is booked solid. We can handle this in a more discreet manner, don't you think?

"No problem, Chief." The officer walked over to his own car and switched off the lights. Then, he signaled the other officers who did the same.

Inside the workshop, one paramedic managed to squeeze into the tiny space between Wheelan, Hap, and the corner table.

"What happened to him?" the paramedic asked.

"Snake bite," Wheelan said. "Shine your flashlight over there and you can see the culprit yourself.

While one paramedic cuffed Hap to take his blood pressure, the other shined a light into the corner of the room. The light bounced off the chair, searching for the perpetrator. Then, it skimmed along the floor, still searching. In one lightning quick move, the light found its target and came to rest on the open mouth of a creature that, in the dim light of the workshop, seemed a giant.

"Jesus Christ!" he screamed and dropped the flashlight. "It's huge."

"It's dead," Wheelan said. "And it's not huge. It's a pygmy rattler called massasauga."

"Your friend here was bitten, you say? And how long ago was that?" the medic asked. "Yes," Wheelan said and pointed to the marks. "About thirty or forty minutes ago."

"What's his name?"

"Hap Murray. He's from Channel 12 in Huntsville, a reporter."

"Too bad he had to get a story this way. Let's get him outta here."

After a few more minutes of struggling to squeeze all of Hap through the small space between the tables and onto a gurney, the paramedics finally loaded him into the ambulance.

"I'm coming with him," Wheelan said.

"Me, too," Libby insisted.

"Libby, why don't you ride with me?. We need to talk to the crew for a minute before we leave. I promised them."

"Goodness, I forgot about them, Burton. You're right, of course," she said.

As soon as the words were out of her mouth, she sort of sucked in the corner of her lower lip and bit gently. Her teeth showed over the portion of her lip that had disappeared. Burton knew her well enough to know that when the lip went, the nerves were frayed.

"Was Lucy with him?" Burton asked.

"Yes, for a few minutes, I think."

"Then, don't worry. He'll be fine."

"But what if he remembers?"

"Look, Libby, he won't remember. He's off in dreamland, sleeping the sleep of the newly born. He won't remember anything. He probably won't even remember being bitten. You've got nothing to worry about. If he does remember, we'll just tell him he dreamed the whole thing, like before."

They reached the entrance of the office, and Burton paused before he opened the door.

"Besides," he said, "we've got bigger troubles than Hap. Right now, he's the least of my worries. Lucy could have been killed tonight. Or Wheelan. Or Murray himself. I don't think these were accidents. We have a killer on our hands."

28

He slid the box into the nursery and listened for the slightest sound. He listened, in particular, for the warning sound of an angry little viper. One, then two more. They were riled. He reached into his pocket, drew out his harmonica, and cupped his hands just so around it. When the sounds of "Edelweiss" echoed through the nursery, Billy Ray did the impossible. He quieted the vipers with an old mountain tune.

After a few minutes, Billy Ray stopped his playing and gently removed the top of the crate. Twelve tiny snakes lay curled under nests of hay. Billy Ray walked over to the first fifty-gallon aquarium tank and prepared it for the new arrivals. He reached up and turned on the mister and set the temperature at 60 degrees, any hotter would raise the body temperature too high. To him, these special babies required extra care. They needed a constant body temperature of 35 degrees. When the mist cooled in the air and fell on these little ones, it would keep them just right. Billy Ray positioned the rocks and grasses in the tanks so that there would be plenty of space for the tiny snakes. They would grow rapidly, but this specially-bred massasauga would reach no more than a foot long. When he'd finished with Tank 1, he put on his thick work gloves and reached over into the crate. Gently, he grasped the first of the pygmies. He turned it quickly to its side to look for the tiny bulge under its skin. He smiled when he saw that the PIT tag had been implanted. He stroked the tiny head and placed the baby into the tank, covered it with grass and moved on to the next. When all twelve babies had been transferred, Billy Ray walked over to Tank 8, reached inside and, in one swift motion, grabbed two dime-sized tree frogs. He put them into a plastic garbage bag, grabbed two more and did the same. He repeated this process until twelve frogs lay tucked into the bag. Then, he walked over to the new arrivals, lifted the lid, and dropped in the frogs. He stood there for a few minutes hoping to see one of the babies come out and strike. Like all other pygmies, these babies would lie motionless when they smelled prey. When he detected a slight movement on the side of the tank, his heartbeat quickened. A small dark brown head, twitching from side to side, appeared from underneath one of the large rocks. A tiny tongue flicked out. Then, in one lightning-quick motion, the viper struck, released the frog, and retreated to wait the few seconds it would take for the venom to paralyze the victim. One minute later, the tiny snake slithered along the tank, its tongue scent-tracking the frog. With all chance of injury cast away by the deadly venom, the snake opened his jaws, slid them over the frog's body, and swallowed. Billy Ray smiled. What these babies lacked in size, they made up for in speed, cunning, and potent venom.

"Way to go, little darlin'," he said. Confident that the others would follow suit, he replaced the holed lid and softly patted the sides of the tank. He checked the inside temperature again, put the empty crate in the back of the nursery, and turned out the lights. When he walked out of the chambered hidden room, he felt good.

29

A young bearded man wearing blue scrubs walked toward them. He ran his hand across his head and slid off the surgeon's cap. Libby jumped to her feet as he neared.

"Is he all right?" she asked, fidgeting with a Kleenex wadded in her hand.

The doctor motioned for them to sit.

Libby glanced at Burton and Wheelan, looked over at Joey and Eagle, then lowered her eyes and sat down.

"I'm Dr. Mears," he said. "Mr. Murray is going to be fine. He's sedated now, but you can see him shortly." The doctor looked at Burton.

"I understand," he said, "that your friend was bitten by a snake. Is that correct?"

"Yes," Burton said then turned to Wheelan. "You saw it, didn't you?"

"Sure," Wheelan responded. "I was right there with him."

Dr. Mears leaned forward and propped his elbows on his knees. He directed a question to Wheelan.

"So, you saw this, uh, snake?"

Libby, Wheelan, and Burton stared at Dr. Mears, their faces reflecting a gnawing disbelief.

"Wait a minute," Burton said. "I don't like your tone. You trying to tell us something?"

Dr. Mears slid back and sat with his elbows propped on the chair arms. He cleared his throat.

"There was no venom in his bloodstream," he said. "None."

"So?" Wheelan asked. "Your tests are wrong."

"Possibly," Dr. Mears said, "but I don't think so. What we found instead of venom was a heavy concentration of narcotics. Venom didn't cause the symptoms you witnessed. Drugs did."

"No way!" Joey blurted out. "Hap doesn't use drugs."

"According to our tests, he does, sir. My guess is that the, uh, snake might have grazed him, but he was too drugged to know what happened. Just let him sleep it off."

Joey jumped up from the chair, ran over to Dr. Mears, and grabbed him on the front of his scrubs. He jerked him to his feet. "You son of a bitch!" he yelled. "My friend's not a druggie."

Eagle stepped forward, grabbed Joey by the belt loops of his pants and pulled him off Dr. Mears.

"Easy, kiddo," he said and put his arm around Joey's shoulders. "It's okay."

Dr. Mears, visibly shaken, his hands trembling slightly, smoothed the front of his scrubs and walked away.

Burton trotted behind him. "We can see him?" he asked.

"Yeah, in a few minutes. Just tell the nurse."

Mears strode down the long corridor toward the swinging double doors that separated the waiting area from the emergency room. He reached to push the large OPEN button on the wall, then stopped. He turned back toward Burton.

"You really should get him some help."

Joey heard and charged forward again. Burton caught him by the shoulders and swung him around. "Stop it! He's only trying to help us, Joey. Get that through that thick skull of yours."

Burton looked at Eagle.

"Get him out of here," he said. "Enough's enough."

Joey shook off Burton's grasp, smoothed his shirt, and took a deep breath. "Sorry," he said to Burton. "It won't happen again. I just want to see Hap before I go."

Libby stood back from the group still fiddling with what was left of the ragged tissue. She thought about what Hap's reaction to the accident—especially Lucy—would be. She wondered whether or not he could remember that day so long ago when he almost died, when the lightning bolted at his feet. Would he remember her and Lucy?

"You still with us?" Burton asked. "You were staring off into space. Again!"

Libby smiled at him and looped her arm through his.

"Let's get this over with," she said.

"Don't worry. I'm telling you he won't remember anything."

A nurse in a starched white pantsuit approached them.

"Mr. Murray is in Room 2. You can see him now," he said. "First room on the right."

The five of them walked together down the hall and stopped in front of Room 2. Burton tapped on the door and eased it open. Hap lay in bed hooked to a heart monitor, blood pressure cuff, an IV, and an oxygen stream.

Libby whimpered when she neared the bed.

Hap's eyes flickered open. He glanced around the room, managed a weak smile, then closed his eyes. He heard the buzzing of their words around him, but the words didn't register. So, while they talked about him, he paid another visit to a world full of strangers.

30

He dreamed of a hollow man, old and bearded, brandishing a rifle. He stood at the edge of a rushing stream of water. Midstream in water up to her knees, a young girl, naked and sobbing, thrashed about, desperately grabbing for her clothes. She stretched as far as her balance allowed and grasped her blouse as it whirled in the strong current. Blue-lipped and shivering, she struggled with the dripping cloth and coaxed her trembling arms through the material. Her long skirt, caught in a whirlpool, swirled about her knees and knocked her off balance. Flailing her arms, she took a step backwards and straightened herself.

The bearded old man yelled at her, "You can come out now, girlie."

A noise filtered through the sound of the rushing water and the old man's voice.

Another sound was right behind it. The girl stopped dead still.

Something was in the water.

Something huge was in the water. It brushed across her foot then wrapped itself around her ankles. At first, in a foolish glimmer of hope, she thought it was a log that drifted down stream. It was heavy, even in the water. She tried to step over it, but as soon as she moved, a head the size of her own rose out of the water. Two large gleaming white fangs appeared for only an instant. Then they were gone, imbedded in the soft sweet flesh of her left knee. When the girl fell, almost instantly, the fresh spring water worked alive with giant rattlers that slithered around and across her dying body. She could not move away from them. She struggled to gasp for air. Then her eyes were fixed in a glazed stare. She felt the snakes crawling on her legs and stomach, over her arms, and finally, along her neck. The eight-foot rattler's head moved up to her ear.

A hissing sound, the sound of hot steam gushing from an engine, signaled the rattler's next move. The last things the girl saw were two huge white fangs that curved to fine sharp points. The last thing she felt was the searing pain of those fangs buried in the soft flesh right beneath her eye. "Too late now, girlie," the bearded man yelled. "Too late now...."

Hap Murray gasped and sat straight up in bed. His heart felt like a hammer in his chest.

"It's too late now. I'm afraid you can't go in. Visiting hours are over," a gruff voice insisted. "Please, I won't stay long," the female voice begged.

The door opened slowly. "Hap?" she called softly.

Libby walked closer to the bed. When she saw Hap, she cried out, "Hap, what's wrong with you?"

He was sitting up, his eyes wide open, his breath coming in sharp rasps. Beads of sweat dotted his upper lip. "Hap!" Libby called. "Look at me. You're all right. You're safe."

She grabbed a washcloth out of the bathroom, wet it with cool water, and went back to his bed. She wiped his forehead and then his face. "You're all right, Hap. I promise you."

Libby curled her fingers around his hand. Immediately, she felt the warmth spread into her fingertips and surge into him. She bent down and kissed him gently. "Another one of those dreams?" she asked.

He looked at her and nodded. "The worst yet," he whispered. "I'm going to have to leave this place, Libby. It's hazardous to my health." He chuckled and shook his head. When the warm tingling sensation began to run up his arm, he felt suddenly relaxed and light-headed.

"Well, on the bright side, it would make a great story," she said as the first smile crossed her lips.

"No one would believe it," he said and smiled back. "Speaking of which, why don't you tell me exactly what happened in that workshop. I was bitten by a snake, the same kind of snake that was in my bathroom. Wheelan told me the snake's venom kills in seconds. So, what happened? Why didn't it kill me?"

"What do you remember?" Libby asked and scooted onto the bed beside him. "And don't leave out any of the juicy details!"

Someone knocked on the door and slowly pushed it open.

"Visiting hours are over, Ma'am. You'll have to leave," the nurse said.

"Family members can't stay with their sick loved ones in this hospital?" Hap said. "I'll be sure to put that in my story about Preacher's Cove. Inquiring minds will want to know...."

The nurse sighed. "Have a good night, Mr. Murray," she said and walked out of the room.

Hap looked at Libby and winked.

"You use what you've got to get what you want," he said and yawned. "I'm so sleepy."

"Yes," Libby said. "Why don't we wait until another time to talk about this. I can come back in the morning, if you like."

"No, no. I'm sleepy, but I want to talk about this," he said and ran his hand through his hair. He took a deep breath and started again.

"Okay, here's what happened. I got lost again and ended up on the back of the complex. When I saw the light on in the workshop, I followed it and heard Wheelan's voice. I walked in and saw him bending over one corner of the room. A woman crouched in the opposite corner. I took another step and saw Wheelan motion me to stop. Then I felt a sharp sting in my foot. I could feel myself falling, but I don't remember hitting the floor. I only remember opening my eyes and seeing a beautiful woman leaning over me. She looked like you. Then I felt warm...kind of calm and sleepy."

Another big yawn followed.

"Buggers!" he said. "I'm putting myself to sleep! Anyway, all I remember after that is waking up after that awful dream tonight and seeing you standing by my bed."

Libby was silent for a moment. Her silence proved a bit too awkward for Hap.

"Okay, I told you mine. Now, you tell me yours," he said. "And don't leave out any of the juicy details!"

"What do you want to know?" she asked.

"That was Lucy, right?" Hap reached over and ran his fingers along Libby's face. Her skin felt like velvet. Libby nodded and cupped her hand around his. She held it to her face and nestled against it.

"What happened to her?" he asked.

"A fire," Libby whispered. "A terrible fire. Her beautiful face burned beyond anything I imagined. The other side wasn't burned at all. Depending on the angle at which you see her now, she is either a beauty or a monster."

"I shouldn't have called her that. I'm sorry," he said in the midst of another yawn.

"It's all right. I'm used to her scars, but most people are horrified when they see her. That's why we have the workshop so far out in the back. We don't want people to see her. She doesn't do well with other people."

"And what did she do to me?" Hap asked.

"Some form of CPR, I guess. Lucy is different from most people. The accident took her mind, as well as her family and her face."

"Look, I know CPR, and what she did was not it. And as far as her mind goes, the woman who helped me, who is the same woman who makes those dolls, was not out of her mind. She knew exactly what she was doing. So, just be straight with me. I deserve the truth."

"The truth? You mean like the truth about my first approval rights? Is that the kind of truth you're talking about?"

If she hadn't smiled, Hap would have worried that he'd pissed her off.

"I apologize for that, too. There's no such thing as first approval rights. But there is such a thing as honesty between friends and, uh, lovers."

He could feel his face turning red, and he could see that hers was, too. "I'm not sorry about that part," he said.

"No, neither am I. It was wonderful," she said. "Embarrassing, but wonderful."

"Embarrassing, why?"

"It's been a long time since...."

Her voice trailed off.

"Anyway," she continued, "my men all seem to die on me, and I am a little older than you are, Hap."

"Don't be embarrassed. I'm not going to die, not yet anyway. I don't care about age. Age is only a number. It's not what a person is on the inside. Besides, you're still a babe."

She grinned and kissed him gently on the lips.

"And you're quite a hunk," she said. "A babe and a hunk...a perfect pair."

Hap ran his fingers along the side of her face, then took her hand and kissed it.

"When I'm out of this bed," he said, "you'll have a hard time getting rid of me."

"I don't want to get rid of you," she said. "I can always use more help in the kitchen."

They laughed, kissed again, laughed some more. "Now, you'd better get some rest. You'll feel better in the morning."

"I feel pretty great right now!" he said.

"Hap?" she asked as she walked to the door.

"Yes?" he said.

"She used to baby-sit for you."

"Huh?" he asked struggling to sit up.

"Lucy," she said. "She used to babysit for you when you visited your grandparents. Your mom and dad would go into town and drop you off with Lucy. You used to love staying with her. Don't you remember?"

He tried to recall the days when he visited his grandparents. Sketchy details came into his mind, tickled his memory, then vanished.

"No," he said. "I don't remember much about those days."

"Then you don't remember what you used to call Lucy?" she asked.

He looked at Libby, tried to recall the days in Preacher's Cove, but sighed instead. "You used to call her the angel lady."

For the first time in almost thirty years, Hap remembered Lucy Addams. He remembered running around in the front yard, having Lucy chasing after him, giggling and tickling him. As Lucy ran around the yard, her hair bouncing in long curls down her back, her green eyes sparkling, she lifted her arms to the sky and twirled around in a circle. Hap remembered watching her, wondering if she would lift off and fly. And every time Lucy lifted her arms, behind her floated a beautiful lady in white, her gown swaying with the breeze, her face glowing. He could see himself as a boy of six, watching in wonder as Lucy's angel hovered above them. He wanted desperately to touch her, to see what an angel felt like. But, when he lifted his own arms to the sky, the angel vanished.

"Hap," Libby called. "Are you okay?"

"The angel lady," he said. "I remember."

"Think longer," Libby said, "until you remember the whole story. Then, you will know why you're here."

Hap pictured himself running in the yard with the angel lady. The sounds of their laughing seemed to reverberate through his mind. He took a deep breath and thought, just for a moment, that he could smell the lavender perfume she wore. Then, the scene changed in his mind. He saw himself alone in the yard reaching toward the sky. He saw the sky blacken, wiping out the light from the sun. A strange prickling sensation crawled across his spine and up to his neck. Then, he remembered the beautiful lights dancing in the blackened sky. First a brilliant green, then a blazing pink, the lights seemed the most beautiful sight he'd ever seen. He wanted to touch them, but when he reached up again, he heard a sharp crackling sound. He could picture himself drawing in his hands. The thunder roared behind him. He thought he heard a screen door slam and his mother's voice wailing. When the earth trembled and his feet began to burn, he fell backwards and smashed onto the ground, the smell of burning flesh flooding his nostrils.

"Hap!" Libby cried. "What's wrong?"

He heard her calling his name, but the strength it took to answer had vanished, just as it had when he heard his mother's voice screaming to him on that day when the lightning claimed him. "Hap!" Libby screamed. "Answer me!"

Hap opened his eyes and saw a wondrous sight. Beside his bed was the angel lady, and above her...the beautiful woman dressed in white who floated in mid-air and called his name. "Hap," she said. "Wake up."

He sucked in a deep breath, rubbed his eyes, and tried to clear his vision. He could feel someone shaking him.

"Come back. You're all right, Hap."

He could feel her rubbing his arms, a warm tingling touch that soothed him.

"Can you hear me?"

"I can hear you, Libby," he whispered.

He inhaled her sweet breath as if blew across his face.

"What happened?" she asked.

He looked at her and closed his eyes again, his body and mind exhausted.

"I'm all right," he whispered. "The angel told me."

He sighed, snuggled down into the bed, and fell asleep.

31

It was a highly charged morning in the Cove. Burton and Libby sat in the restaurant eating breakfast. Even at 6:00 a.m., the servers had already worked two hours and were scampering around trying to accommodate every customer. The unusual size of the crowd on this particular morning heightened the tension in the restaurant. Combined with the clanging in the kitchen and the clamoring of the servers, the myriad sounds from the customers sparked the air with crackling electricity. They had all heard about the snake bite.

With her arms folded in close to her chest—the language of a body screaming "leave me alone"—Libby answered all of Burton's inquiries into Hap's condition. Though her tone was clipped, she answered all of Burton's questions.

"You don't have to get your hackles up, Lib. I'm just trying to cover all the bases. It is my job, you know."

"I know," she said.

"We've got bigger problems than Hap Murray. Can you think of anyone who would want to kill Lucy? It doesn't make sense. And that snake in Murray's room. That doesn't make any sense, either."

"Burton, isn't there a chance that these were just accidents?"

He looked at her as if she had lost her mind.

"Oh, sure, there's a chance...about a million to one, I'd say. When was the last time you saw a rattler around here? I don't mean in the Cove. I know they're here in these parts, but snakes don't like people. Think about it, Lib. Two 'accidents' in one night? Highly unlikely."

"And what is the likelihood that someone wants to kill Lucy and Hap? Also highly unlikely."

"Then, what's the answer? I don't have the slightest clue about where to start. I need your help."

Libby looked at him and lowered her head. She knew what he meant.

"I hate to ask you, but I'm running out of time, Lib. Another one of those little assassins could be anywhere. Whoever started this means to finish it, I believe. It wasn't a joke. But the plan failed. Our killer will strike again, until the job's done. So, will you help, Lib? Will you sleep on it for me?"

"Burton, I...it's been a long time. I don't know if...."

"Please. I'll be close by. Wheelan and I will help. I promise."

She rose and nodded to Burton.

"I'm supposed to be helping out in the gift shop today," she said. "I really should get started."

"Hold up. I'll walk with you."

They crossed the expanse of the restaurant into the adjoining shop. Burton looked up at shelf which held the latest Firelight Angel as Libby walked back behind the counter. "You'd think I'd be used to them by now," he said. "But every time I see them, I am still amazed. She's quite an artist."

"She's getting better and faster," Libby said.

"Do you think she's...."

"No, she's not improving physically. Each time I think she's coming back to me, she sets another one on fire."

"She will get better, Lib. She's already much better than two years ago. She can walk, get around by herself, come and go with some measure of certainty and safety. Just think how much she's improved. Look at where you were five years ago. You couldn't even let her out of your sight. So, just remember that when you begin to think that she's not getting any better."

"I didn't mean to complain," Libby said. "Since Wheelan's been here, things have been a lot better. He's a big help. I know that she's better, Burton. I look at these dolls, and I see such a remarkable skill buried underneath all those scars. She is truly gifted. The fire did that much for her. It released her gifts. But you know what? I'd much rather have her back. These dolls are wondrous creations, but I'd rather have my sister back."

"Well, you really can't tell about Lucy. You don't know what she's thinking or feeling. You could very well have her and not know it. Maybe you should...never mind."

"Maybe I should what?"

"Treat her more like your sister, more like the old Lucy. Forgive me, Lib. I know you've done more than anyone else would or could have. I'm sorry."

Burton looked up at the dolls one more time before he turned to leave. "This one looks a lot like Caillin, doesn't it?"

"Yes, it reminds me of her when she was a child."

"It's remarkable considering that Lucy doesn't know her."

"What? Of course, she knows her, Burton! Don't be silly."

"Caillin wasn't born until after the accident, Lib. Our Lucy never saw her. I'm sorry, Lib."

"It's all right," she said.

"Sometimes we all need a little reminder. Now, go get to work on this case. You're the Chief. We're depending on you." As he left, Libby stared up at the Firelight Angel that looked so much like Caillin. Since she had not seen it before today, she assumed that Wheelan had done the rescuing and the packaging.

She looked up again and felt such heaviness in her heart that she caught onto the side of the counter to steady herself.

Oh God, she thought. *What horrible prediction will there be for my sweet Caillin?* Even the dress looked exactly like something Caillin would have chosen for herself: not too feminine but dainty and brightly colored. She was posed with one hand in her lap and the other close to her lips. Libby had not noticed, before, that the doll looked almost as if it were saying, "Shh...." In a moment of irresistible curiosity, Libby called to one of the taller servers to get the doll off the shelf for her. He handed the white index card first, then the doll, and went back to his duties.

When Libby was sure that no one was looking, she turned the doll's lifted hand ever so slightly. She gasped at the sight of it. The blood in her veins seemed to turn to ice water. She grabbed the side of the counter again. She cradled the doll in her arms and carried it back into her office. Once safely inside, she positioned the replica in the chair beside her desk. She went into the bathroom, grabbed a washcloth, wet it with cold water, and wiped her face. From where she stood in the bathroom, she could see the doll seated so primly in the chair, its small hand raised to its mouth bidding her not to tell, not to reveal the secret which bound the women together, the thing that kept them linked eternally to one another. In that perfect palm was the small rounded mark of the White Maiden, the goddess whose treasures had been bequeathed to her family, the goddess who had saved their ancestors from persecution so many years ago, and marked one special woman with a blue dot in her palm. Each generation, the mark showed, and the very special person who bore it became the protector of the Eye of God—an invaluable stone still today protected from harm by the one chosen and marked by the White Maiden. The White Maiden, their goddess of light and love. And for the second time that morning, Libby Arbuckle confronted a stark reminder of her heritage. As she opened the door to leave, she glanced back at the doll...the perfect little protector, the holder of the Eye of God. When the door clicked tightly into place, she looked out at the bright glow of the morning light.

A chill settled over her.

32

When the doctor walked into his room, Hap was sitting on the side of the bed struggling to maintain his balance. He had pulled up his leg and propped it over one knee in a clumsy, desperate attempt to see those fang marks. Finally, with the young doctor's help, he looked down at the wound. Two barely distinguishable pink marks dotted his skin. "That's it? That's where the snake bit me?"

The doctor nodded. As he did, his bangs fell down over his eyes. He brushed them away. "Not much of a battle scar, I'm afraid. There, uh...."

The young doctor lowered his head and busied himself with Hap's chart.

"What?" Hap asked. "Go ahead. Say what's on your mind."

"There was no trace of venom in your bloodstream, Mr. Murray."

Hap looked up at him, his eyes wide with disbelief. He shook his head and ran his hand through his hair.

"That's impossible!"

"It's the truth, however impossible it may seem to you. Look at the marks, Mr. Murray. I admit that what appear to be puncture wounds from fangs are present, but take a closer look. The marks are healed. They are not fresh puncture wounds."

"I felt the bite. I know the snake bit me."

Small and spindly, with shoulder-length hair, one earring, and a small cross tattooed on his hand, the doctor reminded Hap of some punk rock kid. *I always get the rookies,* he thought. "Mr. Murray, I can't explain what happened to you, but I do know that no venom was found in your bloodstream. All we found was an unusually high level of drugs," he said, once again brushing his stringy bangs from his face.

"Drugs? You found drugs? What kind of drugs?"

"Lortab," the doctor said. "You were saturated with it."

"Not possible," Hap insisted. "I took one that morning, one that night. That's all. Your tests are wrong, Doc. Don't you think I'd know if I was taking too many of those pills?"

"We can help, if you have a problem."

"Look, I don't do drugs!"

Hap moved to get up off the bed, but when everything in the room began to spin, he plopped back down. Disgusted with his frailty, he glowered at the young doctor.

"Just sign my release forms and let me get out of here."

Just as the doctor opened his mouth to answer, someone knocked softly on the door, then pushed it slightly ajar.

"Hap?"

"Libby! This idiot thinks I'm a drug addict. Get me out of here, will you?"

An hour later, with release in hand, Hap climbed into Libby's car bound once again for Cove's End. He said nothing during the twenty-five-minute drive. When they reached the hotel, Libby turned to him. "Don't feel bad. We know that you're not on drugs. We were there, remember? We know what happened."

He opened the car door and moved out slowly. When Libby got out of the car, she rushed around to his side and offered her hand to help.

"I don't need your help, Libby. I need the truth. I need to know more about Lucy. How could she have the power to heal me? Where did it come from? Maybe you *do* know what happened, but I wish you'd tell me because I sure don't."

Biting her lower lip and picking at her nails, Libby turned away from him and walked toward the other side of the car. "Those are not fresh puncture wounds. Anybody can see that," he called to her. "Please tell me."

"Aunt Libby, Hap, hello!" Wheelan shouted.

He walked around from the corner of the office building, grabbed the reporter by the shoulders, and gave him a brisk squeeze. "It's good to see you," Wheelan said. "Need any help getting to your room?"

Hap smiled and shook his head.

"No, thanks."

"Are you hungry? Why don't you come to our place? I'll order some lunch."

The look on Wheelan's face hinted that perhaps this would be no ordinary lunch. Hap wondered what Wheelan had on his mind. "Sure," he said. "I'd enjoy the company. But let me check in with Joey and Eagle first. How about if I meet you there in an hour?"

"Good," Wheelan said. "I'll have lunch waiting. Burger and fries okay with you?"

"Yeah, that'd be great. I'm starved."

Wheelan left and turned back to wave as he walked away. "I've never seen him so outgoing," Libby said as she walked back toward Hap. "He's usually so quiet, keeps mostly to himself. He must really like you."

"We've had our moments," Hap said. "Libby?"

"Yes?"

Hap held out his arms. "How about a hug?"

She stood on her tiptoes, wrapped her arms around him and kissed him on the cheek. She gently stroked the side of his face with her fingertips.

"I'll see you in a little while," she said.

She turned and walked around to the other side of the car.

"Libby?" Hap called.

She stopped right before she slid onto the seat.

"Would you like to have dinner tonight?"

A smile spread across her face, and she breathed such a loud sigh of relief that even Hap could hear her. She nodded and chuckled. Then she slid onto the seat and drove away.

"See you at eight," Hap called after her.

On his way to the room, he wondered what secrets Libby was still hiding. He decided that he had to know the whole truth, not just part of it. Lucy had saved his life twice. He wanted to know how...and why.

33

When Hap knocked on the door, Joey answered and squealed like a kid. He patted the reporter on both shoulders, then hesitated only a second before giving him a hug. Then he pointed to the beds, each of which held packed suitcases and hanging bags. A bright blue box and a deep green one stood like gemstones in the midst of their baggage.

"We're all ready," Joey said, the excitement in his voice almost contagious. "Eagle's loaded the van. And Libby wouldn't even take any money for the rooms. Can you believe that? Let's get out of here. Let's go home."

"Have you talked to Herb?" Hap asked.

He plopped down into one of the plush chairs in the room. "Of course. He's chompin' at the bit to talk to you."

"Will you hand me the phone?"

Joey stretched the cord as far as it would go and put the phone in Hap's lap. He watched while Hap dialed the number and listened to a one-sided conversation which ended with the words he'd hoped he wouldn't hear: "See you in a couple of days."

"You're not serious, are you? Two more days here? No! We're ready to leave this place. It's too creepy here, and besides, there ain't no story. Good lookin' women, but no story. Haven't you had enough?"

"Bear with me, kid. Just bear with me for two more days, and I guarantee you that we'll go back with a story that will make us all famous. Human interest heaven. I'm talking Pulitzer Prize-type famous. Big spot for me as anchor. Big spot for you and Eagle as my crew. But I can't do this by myself. I need your help. Joey, we're not really here about the storms. You've figured that out by now, right?"

"Huh?"

"I might as well tell you the truth. Seems there's very little of it going around these days." Joey paced in front of him, hands in his pockets.

"The truth?" Joey asked, a look of utter surprise and confusion on his face.

"If you'll just sit down," Hap said.

"I take the truth better when I'm pacing," Joey said.

"Okay, here it is," Hap said. Hap leaned forward and propped his elbows on his knees. He clasped his hands together and propped his chin on them. "The real reason we are in Preacher's Cove is to find out about a man named Ike Madison. He's Caillin's father, Joey, so you must swear to keep this to yourself."

"Caillin's father?" he asked as if he didn't believe a word Hap had said.

"Yes," Hap said. "He's involved in some shady business dealings, or so Herb says. I'm here to find out exactly what he's up to. That's why I need your help."

"Why would Mr. James be interested in what goes on in Preacher's Cove, especially with a small-town minister?"

"Because he's not just a small-town minister. Herb thinks he may be involved in some...."

Hap hesitated. He wondered about Joey's feelings for Caillin and how this "truth" might affect him.

"Go on," Joey said. "He might be involved in what?"

"There are some cases of mysterious deaths that Madison might be linked to."

Hap stood, walked to the dresser and took out a cigarette. He lit it and took a long, deep draw.

Joey paced even faster. "Please, kid, you're making me dizzy," Hap said.

"What about Caillin?" Joey asked. "Is she in danger?"

"I, uh, I don't know. I hadn't thought about it until now. I was thinking more along the lines of maybe she knew something...."

"NO!" Joey shouted. "You can't possibly mean that she knows about these killings. You've lost your mind. She's a sweet innocent girl. She is not involved in anything!"

Hap stood up and put his arm around Joey's shoulders.

"Relax. I didn't mean to insinuate that she was involved. I'm sorry." Joey sighed and looked up at Hap with a weak smile on his face.

"Okay," he said. "But we should tell Eagle. He has a right to know what we're doing. I'll go next door and get him."

"Tell you what," Hap said. "Why don't *you* tell him?"

"You want *me* to tell him?"

"Sure, why not?"

Joey stood up very straight. Then he smiled a broad smile and nodded. "You're right," he said. "I'll go break the news to him. He thinks there's something evil here. Said he had a gut feeling that something bad was going to happen. He's gonna be real mad."

"It won't kill him."

With the shades drawn and the air-conditioner running wide open, the room, dark and cool, lulled Hap into sleep. When Joey walked in, sunlight burst through the room. The brightness hit Hap square in the eyes, and he squinted and turned his head.

"Too much sunlight for ya?" Joey asked. "You're not turning into a vampire, are you? That's all we need. Our star reporter turned vampire. Now, that would be a story. *Ace Reporter Visits Small Town, Comes Back a Vampire.* Great headline."

"Too many words," Hap said, sitting up and rubbing his eyes. "What did Eagle say?"

"Let me see how I can phrase this nicely," Joey said and smiled. He was about to speak when he looked up and saw Eagle standing in the doorway, his large frame blocking out the sun's light.

"Gosh, it got so dark in here I thought we'd had an eclipse," Joey said and laughed out loud.

"Very funny, kid," Eagle said and walked into the room. He sat down in one of the chairs next to Hap and looked him square in the eyes. "There's no reason to stay here."

"Herb gave me this assignment. I have to stay." Hap reached over and punched Eagle lightly on the shoulder. "Trust me," he said. "In two more days, you'll be thanking me for keeping you here. I swear on my mother's grave."

Joey and Eagle stared at him. Both of them shook their heads.

"There's something wrong here, Hap," Eagle said. "Somebody's going to die if we stay here. Why don't you be the one to trust *me*, for a change?"

"It's just two more days, probably not that long. I promise that we can leave as soon as I'm finished, but I have to do this."

Hap got up and went to the sink. He splashed cold water on his face, fixed a soda with ice, and walked back to the bed. "There's one other thing that I need to tell you."

Hap sat down on the edge of the bed, put his drink on the nightstand, and sat with his long legs apart, his elbows resting on his thighs. He locked his fingers together and rested his chin on them. Joey and Eagle sat opposite him on the other bed and assumed the same position. "Years ago," Hap started.

"Once upon a time," Joey interrupted and smiled.

Hap smiled back.

"Yeah, once upon a time, I fell in love with a girl named Taylor Winters. She was beautiful, long red hair, green eyes, dainty little frame."

"Like Caillin," Joey said.

Hap stopped and thought about it. It was true. Taylor, Libby, and Caillin all looked a little alike, all of them petite, red-headed, green-eyed and beautiful. He nodded at Joey. "Yeah," he said, "like Caillin and Libby, too."

"Must be some genetic code or something," Joey said. "Was your girl from here?"

"No," Hap said. "She was from Indiana. I met her at the University."

"Where is she now?" Joey asked.

"I don't know. She left and moved away."

"And?" Joey urged him on.

"And, she was pregnant. So, somewhere out there is a child I've never seen. My child."

"So, what does that have to do with this place?" Eagle asked.

"I'm not sure yet. Those Firelight Angels...."

Hap paused and took another sip of his drink. "The dolls hypnotize me. Memories and longings flood into my mind. I keep thinking that there's something I should be doing to help them.

Then, when we both found them here in the room, I...."

"Spooky, isn't it?" Joey asked. "It sounds crazy. I know."

"It just sounds like you're under too much stress to me. I know I'm younger and all, but seems to me like you need some rest... away from here." Eagle twirled his moustache and took a deep breath.

He rifled through his duffle bag until he found what he was looking for.

As Joey watched him, he said, "Your Lortab are in the dresser," Joey said. "I put them up for you."

"Lortab? Why would I want Lortab? I'm looking for my journal. That's all."

Hap paused and looked Joey square in the eyes. "Oh, I get it," he said. "You talked to the doctor, didn't you? So, now you think I'm a druggie. Fine! Think whatever you want to think."

"Hey," Eagle said. "We don't think anything. All we know is what the doctor told us. It's his word against yours, so to speak. But we trust you, so that's good enough."

His hands trembling, Hap fumbled around in his duffle bag and found his journal at the bottom. He grabbed the journal and left, making sure he slammed the door on the way out. The door-frame rattled as the door slammed hard against it. Joey flinched and stood, the rebuked child.

"Don't worry," Eagle said. "He'll be back. He can't leave 'til he figures out what's going on."

Hap stormed past the office at Cove's End. His heavy steps thudded on the wooden planks of the walkway. He passed one room after the other, each with the numbers hand painted in ornate script on the doors. Each room had a large plate glass window at the front, some clear and open while others were covered by heavy drapes that blocked the sun and looked white from the outside. As his footfalls echoed on the planks, Hap noticed, for the first time, that the blue-planked siding on the outside of the hotel matched the color of a clear, blue sky. Blue outer covering blotched with patches of white.

Along the walkway, neatly-trimmed hedges formed a precise line of little soldiers guarding the Cove from intruders. He stopped and looked across the parking lot. He hadn't noticed the straight line of enormous oaks that grew directly across the street. *Another sentinel of guards*, he thought. As far as he could see to his left and right, these lush white oaks, some probably forty feet tall and as big around as an elephant, lined the roadway. Hap took a deep breath and smelled the aroma of bacon wafting from the restaurant. He remembered his grandmother, Gigi, always in the kitchen cooking. What he loved most about Gigi's house was the front yard. The color of emeralds, each yard in the Cove claimed its own white oak, old gentlemen trees rooted in grounds that had been a part of the Cove before any of the residents drew a first breath. The sturdy monoliths made for good climbing, and Hap remembered when he would spend hours perched on a limb bigger around than his arms could reach. Along the front of Gigi's house were giant azaleas in bright pink, lavender, and red. He could almost hear her admonishing him, "Don't trample my prize azaleas, sweetie," she would call as he played, careful to stay on the long, paved driveway and away from Gigi's flowers. Hap smiled and slowed his pace. In the background, he heard giggling children splashing about in the pool. Great trucks roared past on the highway, but above it all, the sound he loved most was that of the birds cawing from the majestic oaks. Giant shiny black birds, fat from the continual feast of the restaurant's leftovers, stood guard in the trees, and like small trumpeters, sounded the alarm as Hap walked by. He could remember hearing the same sounds as a child. Gigi always told him that the crows came in May when the flowers bloomed. "They can't resist my prize azaleas," she would say. "How beautiful they must look from the treetops!"

Hap smiled, changed his direction, and walked to the edge of the parking lot. He waited until the highway cleared, then trotted across. He stood beneath one of the old gentlemen trees. Now, he didn't have to climb up to reach a branch. He just stretched his arm and patted one of the huge limbs. The bark, rough and gnarled against his hand, felt strangely cool to the touch. Then a crow cawed, signaling him. "Stay away," it seemed to say. Hap brushed his hand against his jeans and turned to walk back across the highway. He looked up one more time, and when he did, he noticed an odd growth high amidst the lush thickness of leaves. He walked four steps around the trunk of the tree. He stood very still and focused his sight high up into the oak. Silvery-green pointed leaves dotted with bright red berries peeked from beside the oak's natural foliage. Hap wrinkled his brow and tried to remember what Gigi had told him about the white oaks. As he thought, he walked down to the next tree. He put his hands on the giant trunk and looked up. The same silvery leaves dotted with red berries grew beside the oak's leaves. He tried a third and a fourth. On his walk down to the fifth tree, he remembered what Gigi had said. "It's mistletoe," he said aloud. "Mistletoe." He repeated Gigi's words, just as he remembered them. "From the Druids comes the legend of the mistletoe and the white oak. The delicate mistletoe..." he stopped and tried to remember each word correctly.

"Mistletoe curls 'round the mighty oak. Lifelong companions they. Berries spring forth as mystics of old, ever guiding the way. Sacred ground waters the soul. Sacred ground hides secrets of gold."

"Sacred ground," he repeated and looked across the street, along the highway, down both sides of the complex and beyond. "Sacred ground?" he asked the trees. Without warning, a throbbing pain began in his right eye. A blinding white light invaded his brain. He covered his face with his hands.

"NO," he shouted. "Not again."

Distorted images flooded his mind, screams assailed his ears, and the smell of burned meat clogged his nostrils. He coughed, gagged, and hugged his arms tightly together. The force of the gagging bent him double, and in his panic, he reached out into empty air, desperate for something to hold onto. Bursts of cold air slapped at his face. He gasped, lost his balance, and sank to his knees. When he tried to open his eyes, the searing light intensified. He squeezed his eyes shut, then dropped his head to block out the light filtering through the clouds. When he coughed again, streaks of greenish white light laced with pink tendrils overpowered him. He struggled to catch his breath, his heart beating so fast that he could feel the beats in his throat. He leaned forward, balanced himself on one hand, and lifted himself up. He stood against one of the white oaks, trying to catch his breath.

He heard a car door slam. "Hap, you okay, fella?" he heard Burton Riggs ask. "You look like you've seen a ghost. You're pale as can be, son. Let me help you to the car."

Once again, Hap felt Burton's powerful arms brace him. He wondered briefly how many times this man would have to rescue him. Burton helped him into the car, rolled down the windows, and lit a cigarette. Then he reached into the back, made some sort of clicking sound, and brought out a cold drink. "Here, have a soda. It'll be good for you."

Hap took a drink. The icy sweetness made his mouth tingle. He wrapped his warm hands around the chilled can and let out a long breath. "Don't drink too fast or you'll puke," Burton said. Burton handed him a clean handkerchief. Hap wrapped the cloth around the can, waited a few seconds, then removed it and wiped his face. The cool, wet cloth refreshed him.

"Thanks," he said to Burton. "I'm sorry about this."

Burton took another puff of his cigarette and looked at Hap. He turned his head and blew the smoke out of the window, then glanced over at Hap again.

"What?" Hap asked, uneasy at the way Burton looked at him. Burton threw his half-smoked cigarette out, cleared his throat, and curled his fingers around the steering wheel. He stared out the windshield.

"Are you sick?" he asked without looking at Hap. "I mean... something terminal?"

Hap thought for a few seconds before he answered. He was too tired and too weak to cover up the truth. "Terminal? Only if you call a mental breakdown terminal," he said, his voice flat.

He looked over to see Burton staring at him again.

Hap shrugged. "You might as well know the truth. It started years ago, but since I've been here, it's become almost constant."

Hap ran his hands through his hair and wiped his mouth with

the back of his hand. Beads of sweat popped out along his forehead. He dabbed at them with the cool soda can.

"Tell me more," Burton said. "Maybe I can help."

Hap shook his head. "You can't help, Burton. No one can help."

"Try me!"

Hap took another drink, scooted down in the cushioned seat, and leaned his head on the headrest.

"You can trust me, Hap." Burton stared out the window again.

Hap sighed and wiped the perspiration from his upper lip. "It started after the lightning accident when I was six. Pain in my eye, my head about to explode, images flooding through my brain."

"Images?" Hap chuckled.

"Yeah, of women, mostly, but horrifying and very painful. A bright light feels like it's searing my brain. I've been to doctor after doctor. First it was called migraines, but these are not migraines. They're something much different."

Burton looked over at Hap. "Is that what was wrong with you that first time I found you?"

"It puts me on my knees," Hap said. "The pain is unbearable." He rubbed his forehead and took a deep breath.

"And you've tried to get help, I assume?"

"Oh sure," Hap said, "I had years of it when I was growing up. Shrinks, neurologists...and all for free. They were fascinated by me. Hap the Wonder Boy...the kid who just happened to be standing in the right place not to be killed by greenflash."

"Finally," Hap continued, "after years, I understood, sort of. Survivors of severe lightning strikes almost always suffer lifelong side effects. I found a professor at one of our universities who'd also been struck by lightning and survived. He told me that he suffers from horrific headaches and recurring nightmares. He named other effects, as well, but it was the headaches and nightmares that convinced me.

Burton straightened up and turned toward Hap. "I see. "Greenflash? The strike was greenflash? With a strike that powerful, I can understand about the headaches.

Hap nodded.

"Amazing, isn't it?" he asked. "I'm the only bloody survivor on record."

Burton gestured with his hand, a mock bow to the waist.

"I'm in the presence of greatness!"

Hap laughed out loud. "You better believe it," he said. "Now, if I could just convince Libby of it...." His voice trailed off.

Burton smiled.

"Well, I do have considerable influence in that area."

"Yeah, I've seen you two, those looks between you. What's the deal?"

"She's a special person. You should tell her what you've told me. She would understand."

Hap nodded then shook his head. "I don't think I can do that," he said. "Not now."

"You think you're losing your mind, don't you?"

Hap stared out the windshield.

"Well, maybe you're finding it," Burton said. "Maybe being in the Cove is just what you need."

"I don't understand."

"There are ancient secrets here, son. You're here for a reason."

Burton started the car and pulled out onto the highway. Hap looked over at Cove's End and saw Libby standing outside in front of the office. She waved, dropped her head, and went back inside.

"Wheelan's making lunch for me," Hap said. "I can't be late."

"I want to show you something," Burton said. "It won't take long, and it will answer one of your questions."

They drove about three miles down Monteagle Road until they approached a large set of brick columns, an ornate black wrought-iron gate between them. In gold letters was a scripted sign that read, "Clifftop Estates." Beyond the gate was a straight paved road lined on both sides with enormous white oaks. "More sentinels," Hap said.

"What?" Burton asked.

"The oak trees. They look like giant sentinels guarding the place, just like the ones across the street from Cove's End," Hap answered.

Burton stared at the precise order of the trees. "I've lived here for twenty years, but I've never thought of these trees as guards before. An astute observance...for a reporter!" he said. "Watch it, son. When I start using three-syllable words, I'm apt to talk about anything."

Burton got out of the car, pushed a large black button on the side of one of the columns, and watched the gate swing open. He climbed back into the car and said to Hap, "Mind if we take a spin through Clifftops?"

"No, not at all," Hap said and sat up straight.

Burton drove down the road that led into Clifftops. Hap savored the richness of the landscape as they passed by first one tree, then another. Twenty huge trees, ten on each side, lined the road. Encircling each tree, an array of roses grew in rainbow colors, each garden precisely protected with white picket fences about a foot tall. Beyond the short fences, the grounds spread in bright, rich green. Each blade of grass seemed perfectly measured so that none rose taller than the others. Hap took a deep breath. The smell of roses lingered in the air. "Smells good, doesn't it?" Burton said.

"Yes, pungent but sweet."

As they drove along, Hap heard the sound of a harmonica playing, this time a melody that he knew but couldn't name. "What's the name of that song?" he asked.

"Edelweiss, I think. It's his favorite. He plays it so often I hardly hear it anymore."

"Somehow, a harmonica doesn't seem to match these surroundings," Hap said. "A violin or a harp, maybe, but not a harmonica."

"Billy Ray's been playing that thing for a couple of years now," Burton said. "Sometimes, it's soothing."

At the end of the long drive into Clifftops the road forked. Burton stopped before turning. Hap noticed the enormous estates, all three-story brick structures, each with attached garages, manicured emerald lawns, and most with something Hap hadn't seen in too many other homes—stained glass windows. Though the homes were constructed in different designs, virtually all of them had the same design located in the same place. At the front of each home, on what seemed like the second story, appeared a large round stained-glass window. The windows, bright and colorful, marked each home with its unique depiction of style and hue. Hap couldn't distinguish the individual designs, but he could see well enough to know that they were all the same in form. As he watched, he felt that something stared back at him. Then, it occurred to him that it was the homes themselves, each with its own eye watching for intrusive strangers. "Creepy," he said and shuddered.

"What's creepy?" Burton asked.

"The houses have eyes," he said. "They're watching us."

Burton cleared his throat and searched Hap's face for some hidden message that he couldn't decipher at the moment. He found nothing but a blank stare. Burton turned to the right and drove about a mile down the road. He stopped in front of a sprawling mansion with a large "M" scripted on one of the brick columns that lined its steep driveway.

Hap looked over at Burton and shrugged. "Madison," Burton said. "This beautiful place is Madison Manor. The good reverend, Ike Madison, calls that stained-glass window of his the Eye of God. What a laugh! Anyway, this is the home of Ike and Caillin Madison."

The look of surprise on Hap's face brought a smile to Burton's mouth.

"Just thought you'd like to see where he lives," Burton said and drove back onto the main road. He stopped the car just before they reached the exit to the estates. Then he turned and looked at Hap.

"Let me level with you, son," he said. "I know your boss, Herb James. We go way back."

Hap's mouth dropped open and his eyes widened.

"Yes, I know," he said, "I'm just some backwoods jerk of a cop, but I'm the Chief here. I'm not really as stupid as I look, although looking stupid can be quite an asset in my business. If you look stupid, people naturally assume that you ARE stupid. I've been after Ike Madison for ten years, on and off, but the problem is that he's very well connected...and extremely cunning. His hands don't get dirty, if you know what I mean."

Hap couldn't think of anything to say. He couldn't believe that Herb James and Burton Riggs had planned this and set him up.

He thought he knew what he was doing. He thought he was in control of some things, but now....

"Herb says you're the best bloodhound he's ever seen, but frankly, son, I've seen better work from my rookies. This story is falling out from under you. All the answers you need are right here in Preacher's Cove. You just have to get off your butt and find them."

Burton reached into his coat pocket and drew out a yellowed, wrinkled envelope. He turned it over in his hands and finally held it out to Hap.

"Maybe this will help. It might answer some of those questions that have been dropping you to your knees."

"What's this?" Hap asked and reached for it.

Burton held on to the envelope.

"Before you read this," he said, "I want you to understand the story behind it, and I want you to understand that you know more about Ike Madison than you think. You're connected to him in a way that you'd never have believed if you hadn't come back here."

Burton held the envelope tightly in his fingers. "Ike Madison is just this side of the right side of the law. I can feel it in my gut. And, I think he's been watching you for years. He's been waiting for you to come back here. You're a target now."

"Wait a minute," Hap said and shook his head. "Ike Madison doesn't know me. We met at the brunch. But...."

"The letter in this envelope will explain some things. Not everything, but some things."

Burton still held the envelope away from Hap. "There's something else...."

"Go ahead," Hap said. He fumbled in his pocket for a cigarette, found none, and stared at Burton.

"Libby likes you, Hap. Do you know that?"

Hap frowned at Burton and shrugged his shoulders.

"Do you know it?" Burton insisted.

"Yes, I know it. I like her, too, but what does that have to do with this?"

"Libby is a special lady, a very special lady. And she's intelligent, Hap."

"Okay, I know that," Hap said. "But I can't for the life of me figure out why you think this is your business."

"I don't want Libby hurt, that's all. She's family."

Burton released the envelope and gave it to Hap. Inside was a piece of yellowed paper with a scripted "M" embossed on the front of it. Hap turned around and looked back at the Madison home. "Madison," Burton said and pointed to the house.

Hap gently opened the letter, afraid that he would tear the crisp worn folds. It read:

> *Dear Juls,*
>
> *His name is Michael Murray. If you find him, tell him that I'm sorry. I had no other choice. I will always love him.*
>
> *With love,*
> *Belinda*

Hap read the letter again and again. He tried to make sense of it, tried to imagine why his name was in it, and tried to fit together pieces that just wouldn't fit. Finally, he looked over at Burton.

"I...I don't know what this means. I can't fit the pieces together."

"My wife, Julianna, was Libby's sister."

Still, the information didn't help. Hap sat dumbfounded and stared at the brown dashboard of the car. He felt as if someone had punched him in the stomach, and then reached in and grabbed hold of his heart, squeezing it until his chest seemed ready to explode. His hands felt like ice, his head throbbed, and he grew dizzy at the thought of another onslaught of another blinding flash of light.

"The reference to Juls is to my wife. Then you see your name, Michael Murray, and finally, a signature: Belinda."

Hap said nothing. He waited. When the images didn't flood his mind, he let out a deep breath. Finally, he put his head back on the headrest and closed his eyes.

"Take another drink, son. You're looking pale again."

Hap did as Burton told him. The drink cooled him as it washed down his hot throat. He took a deep breath and told Burton to go on.

"Belinda's full name is Belinda Taylor Winters. She was Libby's younger sister. Libby's mother married a second time when Libby and Lucy were thirteen. Julianna was ten. Belinda was born a year into that second marriage. Her father was transferred to Indiana, and Lib's mother moved with him and took the baby...Belinda. We learned that Belinda went by her middle name, Taylor. She grew up in Indiana, went to school there. You know the next part," he said.

"But," Hap said. "No, this is too farfetched. It can't be the same girl. She moved to South Carolina. I got a letter from her post-marked in South Carolina. "

"I don't know about that. She traveled all over with the Madisons. She probably mailed your letter on one of their trips, possibly to keep Ike from finding out. I'm not sure about it, you understand. When she came back from Indiana, pregnant and without a father for her baby, she married Ike Madison."

"She told me she was pregnant," Hap said and lowered his head. "I acted like a jerk, but when I went to find her, to explain and ask her to marry me, she was already gone. I couldn't find her."

Burton patted Hap's shoulder. "We all make mistakes that hurt other people."

"Is Taylor, uh, Belinda. Is she here? Can I see her?"

"Look, Hap. Hear me out. Then you'll have your answers. Ike's father, Isaiah, and Libby were, uh, close friends. Libby and Isaiah arranged the whole thing, and Ike was more than happy to oblige. He thought Belinda was beautiful, and when he found out that she was pregnant, he liked it even more. By the time the child—Caillin—was born, Ike claimed her as his own. No one else, except Libby and Isaiah—and Julianna and me, of course—knew any different."

"Caillin is...."

"Your daughter, and she's living with a killer. I can't prove it, but I know it."

"Caillin is my daughter," he whispered, the iciness returning to his hands. While he listened to Burton's story, his headache faded, his breathing slowed, and he felt better.

"Yes, she is. But, if you think you'll ever convince Ike Madison of that, you're wrong. He'll never give her up."

"What about Taylor? Where is she?"

"I'm sorry, Hap. She died three years ago."

Hap put his face in his hands.

"NO!"

After a few seconds, he looked at Burton.

"How?"

"She was hiking in the woods behind the house. A snake bit her...."

Suddenly, Burton's voice trailed off. He opened his mouth to speak, but no words came out. He and Hap stared at each other, their mouths open, their eyes wide.

"And my Juliana," Burton whispered. "My poor Juliana."

"Huh?"

"Snakebite. Two beautiful sisters, dead to some little assassins. But those years were bad years for the Cove. The snakes appeared and infested this area. They were everywhere. But then, the exterminators came in from the Army, wiped them out. We've been clear of them for three years." Burton looked over at Hap.

"Maybe," Hap said. "Maybe not."

Burton frowned and cocked his head. "How could I have been so stupid? More snakes...." Burton floored the accelerator and sped out of Clifftops. He knew what he had to do next.

Hap held on to the dash. For the first time in months, his headache completely disappeared, and renewed strength returned to his body. He flexed his fingers, stretched out his arms, and inhaled. Then he slapped his hands on the dashboard, and smiled at Burton.

Burton raced down the highway and screeched to a stop in front of Cove's End.

"Herb is right, Burton," Hap said, "and so are you. It's time for me to get off my butt and get to work. It's time for me to rescue my daughter from the killer she's living with."

34

With a clear agenda, his strength and courage renewed, Hap took the steps to Libby's house two at a time. He would ask Wheelan about Lucy and find out exactly what happened that night in the workshop. He'd find out why the doctors thought he was a drug addict. Then, he'd ask for Wheelan's help. He needed someone who knew about Ike Madison, someone slightly removed from him, but close enough to know the scoop—someone like Wheelan Addams. Then, he would talk to Libby. He needed to tell her about his relationship with her sister. He hoped she'd understand, but even if she didn't, he had to clear his mind and conscience. He had to tell the truth, even if it meant giving up the woman he.... Hap paused as he climbed the steps. *God, I think I'm in love with her. Just my luck. I fall for her just when she's about to throw me out with the trash.* He took a deep breath and stood outside the door. He tapped quietly, hoping that Libby would not answer. He needed a little time to think. After only a few seconds, Libby opened the door. Surprise showed in Hap's face, and he opened his mouth to speak, but the words wouldn't come.

"How quickly we forget," Libby said and brushed past him.

"Libby," he said, "I, uh, we're staying a couple of days longer. Are the rooms still available?"

"I'll make the arrangements," she said and brushed a tendril of hair from her face.

"Dinner at eight, remember?"

Libby looked up at him without speaking.

"Please?"

"Who could resist a gorgeous blond begging for a date?" she said. "Okay, I'll meet you in the restaurant." Hap smiled at her, bent down and kissed her gently on the forehead.

"I have some things to tell you. Important things," he said.

Wheelan appeared at the door. "Hap, how are you feeling? Come in, won't you?" Wheelan asked. "Lunch is ready and waiting."

He looked at Libby, smiled, and walked into the house. As she left, Libby looked back at Wheelan, the expression on her face changing from giddy smile to dead-serious stare. Wheelan nodded and smiled an I-understand-smile as he closed the door.

"Let's go into the dining room," he said to Hap.

Signs of Libby showed all over, from the formal table setting with elegant china, silver, and crystal to the precisely folded cloth napkins and a centerpiece made to match the floral pattern on the tablecloth. "Wow," Hap said, "all this for hamburgers! She does it right, doesn't she?"

"Always," Wheelan said. "She's a perfectionist, doesn't like loose ends, quite the show-person. She's made Cove's End a success."

"With your mother's help, too. The dolls must have helped. They're so lifelike, so perfect. She made one for me and one for Joey. Scared the beejesus out of me when I first saw them."

"They can do that. They have helped make money, but not at first. People from the Cove were afraid of them."

"Why?" Hap asked.

"Weren't you?"

Hap didn't answer right away. Wheelan was partially right. He had been afraid of them, but now he realized that those dolls seemed to call to him because of his own child, trapped in this town with a killer.

"The locals were afraid of them because the dolls looked too much like their own children. And the messages frightened them. But the first time the message proved accurate, when the first child's life was saved, they weren't scary anymore."

Hap looked startled, but Wheelan continued. "Each doll is an exact replica of some child here in the Cove. And the fact that they were hand made by a monster...."

"I'm sorry, Wheelan."

Wheelan shrugged. "Don't worry about it. Everyone thinks it.

They just don't have the guts to say it. Anyway, it was good for business. Nothing quite like having a local monster. She makes everybody else look pretty good."

"I am truly sorry...."

"You're not the first, Hap, so don't feel so bad. Actually, I was probably the first one to call her a monster. So, don't let it bother you. You never did tell me how you were feeling."

"I'm okay, surprisingly," he said. "Of course, according to the doctors, there was never anything wrong with me except that I was strung out on drugs. I guess they're out of my system by now."

"Let's eat," Wheelan said.

They sat at the table, both too hungry to talk. They devoured the thick homemade hamburgers stacked high with fresh lettuce, tomato, and onion. A side of fries, a glass of iced tea, and fresh blueberry cobbler topped with vanilla ice cream completed the feast. When the two of them were finished, they sat back in their chairs and sighed.

"I'm stuffed," Hap said. "But, man, it was good!"

"I didn't realize I was so hungry," Wheelan added. "I haven't eaten like that in a long time."

"Me, either," Hap returned. "Must have been the good company."

"Grab your tea and let's go into the living room. Just let me clear away some of this mess. I don't want Aunt Libby coming in to find we've not been gentlemen enough to clean up!" he added with a wink. They cleared the table, rinsed the dishes and loaded them into the dishwasher. Wheelan straightened the placemats, adjusted the centerpiece, and replaced the napkins with clean ones from the bureau. Then, he stood back to see if he'd left anything undone.

"Boy, somebody sure trained you right," Hap said.

"Force of habit," Wheelan replied. "My wife always insisted that a Southern gentleman always leave things as clean as he found them...or be prepared to marry them!"

They both laughed.

"Your wife? I didn't know you were married."

"Claire, my wife. She, uh, she died two years ago. Leukemia."

"I'm sorry. I had no idea."

"I moved back here when she died. Couldn't stand being in the house by myself. Even with the servants, it was too lonely. It was Claire's house. She was everywhere I looked. So, I sold it and moved back here."

"Where did you live?" Hap asked.

They walked into the living room, set their glasses down on coasters, and sat on opposite love seats. "Memphis," he said.

"Oh, nice place. How long were you there?"

Wheelan told Hap that he'd left Cove's End when he was sixteen and that his Aunt Libby had found him a job with one of her friends in Memphis. He traveled by bus, went directly to his new job, and stayed. He said that his employer, Claire McFerrin DuPont, recently widowed and heiress to both her father's mining fortune and her dead husband's jewelry empire, took an instant liking to him. After a year, Claire decided that he needed some "grooming," as she called it. She taught him about elegant dining, table settings, table manners, proper attire, proper speech. She managed to turn a young buck redneck into a refined Southern gentleman. Hap listened intently. "By the time I was eighteen, I had a new Mustang, expensive clothes, and was head over heels in love. Claire sent me to school. It was the greatest gift anyone could ever have given me," Wheelan said. "Not bad for a redneck."

"You're anything but a redneck, Wheelan. Don't kid yourself. I don't know a single redneck who wears a Rolex watch, Armani suits, and sports a vocabulary worthy of mention in Webster's."

Wheelan chuckled and lowered his head.

"So, go ahead with the story. I'm lovin' it so far."

"Well, I finished with a Bachelor's in Earth Sciences at Sewanee University. Perfect grade point average got me a scholarship to Yale. And Claire paid for everything that the scholarships didn't cover. She was great."

"And?" Hap asked.

"And when I graduated with my doctorate, we got married. I was twenty-six. She was thirty-seven. We had a perfect life for ten years, the best marriage on the planet. We were crazy in love until the day she died," he said, a single tear falling down along his cheek. He brushed his bangs out of his eyes and wiped his nose on the back of his hand.

"Let's change the subject, shall we?"

"Sure. Claire sounds like quite a lady. You're a lucky man, Wheelan, to have found that kind of life, no matter how short."

"She was always the most gracious, most elegant lady I've ever met," Wheelan said. "She wasn't what most people would call beautiful, but there was something about her that made you take notice. She commanded a room from the moment she walked in."

They drank some more iced tea, and then Hap opened up his journal and slid his pen out of the holder. "So, are you ready for another round of questions?" he asked. "Last one, I promise," Hap said.

"I guess so, though I don't know anything more to tell you about the Cove."

"I want to know exactly what happened to me in the workshop, Wheelan. That's been bothering me. Libby said it was CPR, but it wasn't. I need to know everything. But mostly, I need to know that what those doctors said isn't true. I wasn't strung out on drugs. You were there. You saw it all, and you're the only one besides your mother who can tell me what happened."

"And you want to write your story about it?"

Hap lowered his eyes and doodled in his notebook. "Not really," he said. "I'd just like to know what happened out there. And one other thing."

Wheelan looked at him and nodded.

"I need to know what you know about Ike Madison."

Wheelan's eyes widened. "Ike? What do you want to know about him?

"How about if we go down to my room," Hap said. "Joey will be there, but all he's interested in is trying to get Caillin's attention." As soon as the words fell out of his mouth, Hap stopped. He felt a strange churning in his stomach.

"What's wrong?" Wheelan asked.

"Nothing," he said. "I guess I'm just tired."

He couldn't tell Wheelan about Caillin, not yet. He had to tell

Libby first. "Let's get out of here," he said. Wheelan and Hap left the house. They passed by the office on their way to the room, the two of them like tall gods surveying the land. As they went past the window, they waved at Libby, who was working the desk, checking in a crowd of new customers. When she saw them, she barely smiled. Hap wondered if she remembered their date tonight. *Maybe she's just tired*, he thought. But there was something in that smile that he didn't like.

35

Hap and Wheelan decided to get some fresh air. The room proved too stifling for both of them. "Let's take the van," Hap said. "I'd like the chance to drive around myself and get reacquainted with the place."

He scribbled a note to Joey to tell him he'd be back soon, then taped the note to the mirror.

"I need to make a call before we go," Wheelan said. "Let me speak to Libby," he held for a second and waited for the Libby's voice. "Hi, I'm going for a drive with Hap for an hour or so. Do you need me for anything?"

Wheelan looked at Hap and smiled. He covered the phone with his hand. "Have to check in," he said and winked. Then he went back to his conversation with Libby. "No, don't worry. She's sleeping, and I'll check as soon as I get back. In fact, I'll go by there on my way out, just to make sure."

He hung up the phone and looked at Hap.

"You don't mind if we go by the house, do you?"

"Let's get going."

They went outside and climbed into the van.

"Wait," Hap said before he started the engine, "do you hear that harmonica?"

Wheelan turned his head and listened. "Sure, I guess I'm just used to it."

"Don't you think it's weird?" Hap asked.

"Weird to play the harmonica? No, not especially."

"I know. I'm being paranoid, I guess. Pay no attention to me."

They drove down the side of the complex to the house. Wheelan got out and called back, "I'll just be a minute. Wait right here."

Wheelan went up the stairs, unlocked the door, and stepped inside. He listened for any sound out of the ordinary, but heard nothing. He walked back to the end of the long hallway to bedroom number three. He stood for a moment listening, and slowly opened the door. His mother was asleep, as usual for this time of day. She seemed to be resting peacefully. He closed the door quietly, almost holding his breath so as not to make a single sound. Then he left, locked up again, and went to the van.

"Everything okay?" Hap asked.

"Yes, fine. Head out down 24. It's about two miles south straight down this road. I'll tell you when to turn."

"Did Libby tell you that your mother used to baby-sit for me when I visited my grandparents?" Hap asked.

"No," Wheelan said, obviously surprised. "You're kidding, aren't you?"

"Not at all," Hap said. "In fact, I remember playing with her, running around in the front yard. I used to call her the angel lady."

"Why?" Wheelan asked.

"Promise you won't laugh?"

"Sure," Wheelan said.

"Whenever we ran around outside, I thought I saw an angel floating above your mom's head."

Wheelan stared at him, his mouth open, his eyes wide.

"It's the truth. I swear."

"I believe you," Wheelan said. "I used to see it, too, when I was young, but I always thought I was crazy."

They drove for about thirty minutes. Hap watched as he drove by the giant sentinels, still guarding the restaurant. In the warm May air, a gentle breeze pushed past him, ripe with the smell of roses. Hap marveled at the beauty of this place, the sky a magnificent clear blue, dotted with cottony clouds, and the grounds as green as polished emeralds. Every few feet another white oak hailed as they passed. Hap remembered the sign that had crashed in front of him when they first arrived. "God's Little Corner." It was, indeed, a wonder of creation.

"Turn left at the sign ahead that says, 'The Hallows.'"

As they neared an obvious turn-off, Hap saw a small white

sign with the letters THE HALLOWS printed on it. He turned down a long stretch of dirt road with no houses or buildings in sight. Gigantic, looming oaks lined the road, more mighty sentinels guarding a sacred plot of ground. "They're white oaks, very rare in this area. Beautiful, aren't they?" Wheelan asked, his face almost aglow with wonder.

"Yes, I remember them from my childhood. My grandmother used to tell me stories about the white oaks."

"I had just about forgotten that you visited here as a kid. I knew your grandmother, but not very well. These trees have been here longer than the Cove itself. You say your grandmother told you stories about them?"

"Yes, she did. I remember something that she used to say to me. She talked about the Druids and trees filled with mistletoe."

"Another turn right up here. See it?" Wheelan asked.

Hap turned onto a small dirt road nestled among the gigantic sentinels. He drove for about thirty yards. Then Wheelan told him to stop. "Let's get out. I want to show you this. You'll appreciate it, given your history here in the Cove."

Even in broad daylight, the enormous oaks blocked most of the sunlight, casting an almost ominous darkness around them. The two men walked for almost a mile into the deep forest along a path that seemed as old as the trees. On both sides of the path, the sentinels stood guard. Occasionally, when Hap walked by one of them, he noticed a patch of red berries growing so far above the ground that no man could reach them. The berries seemed to be growing directly out of the tree itself, as if berry and tree fed on one another. When they came to a steep upgrade, Wheelan told him that it was only a few more feet away. "Just at the top of this grade. Then, we'll be there."

As they neared the top, Hap stared at the spot. It was almost completely clear of brush and leaves. Someone had obviously been working here.

"There it is," Wheelan said. Still surrounded by white oak monoliths, the two of them walked toward the place. A small clearing marked with flat boards in square shapes lay just in front of them. "I've been working up here," Wheelan said. "Surveying and digging, as you can see. This is the point of origination, I believe."

Hap walked around each square. He'd seen these squares many times on television, on Discovery Channel, when archaeologists were on digs and marked each important space with these boxes. There were at least five that he could count, the earth upturned in some of them, perfectly in place in others. A large covered barrel stood in the middle of the diggings. Hap walked over to it, removed the lid, and found small shovels, spades, and gloves, along with rolls of paper. "You did all this by yourself?"

"Yes. This site hasn't been excavated before. You'd think that with all the people who've come here to find out about the storms, someone would have found it."

"How did you know about it?" Hap asked.

"I've been playing up here since I was a kid. If you look closely through those trees, you'll see the area that really is The Hallows. It's a very old cemetery surrounded by a large stone formation, a circle of stones. All the locals know about the Hallows, but not many of them venture this far back, and no one I'm aware of has been here. Everyone's too scared to come here. Besides, they can't defy the good reverend."

"Who?"

"The good reverend, Ike Madison. He believes that this place is evil, and there are not many of his parishioners who will outright defy him. Our Caillin is nothing like her father. He is a piece of work. He's THE preacher around here. One church, one preacher in the Cove."

"She has a strange mark in her palm. Have you noticed it?"

Wheelan nodded. "Unique, isn't it?"

Hap waited for more information. When none came, he said, "Joey thinks she's beautiful. He's entirely smitten."

"You'd better tell Joey to back off. If Ike finds out about him, then there will literally be Hell to pay."

"Why?"

"No one fools around with Caillin. She's the original sheltered teen. Ike barely lets her out of his sight. He's mean, Hap, really mean. So, tell Joey to forget about Caillin."

Hap looked at him. The smile on his face changed to a frown.

"What's wrong?" Wheelan asked him.

"Does he hurt Caillin?"

Wheelan shook his head. "No, I don't think so. He loves her in his own warped way. He won't tolerate anyone even talking to her. He's so protective that he has Madison Manor wired like Fort Knox. Nobody gets in that place without a pass, so to speak."

Wheelan stood up and walked closer to the dig site, motioning for Hap to follow. When they reached the site, Wheelan squatted down and scooped up a handful of dirt. Hap watched as he let it fall through his fingers again. Wheelan said. "It's hallowed ground, you know." Hap bent down and brushed his fingers across the ground. Then he, too, scooped a handful of smooth dirt and let if fall through his fingers. The earth felt cool and clean in his hands and smelled like flowers instead of dirt. "The Hallows," Wheelan said. "The name came from Druid worshippers."

"I remember Gigi talking about the Druids. I always imagined bearded old guys in white robes, tree worshippers or something."

"The Hallows is a name used to signify stone altars. The Druids recorded very little of their history, though there was an ancient alphabet called Ogham which consisted of lines carved into stones and trees. The Druids believed in the oral tradition of preservation and relied on their memories."

"It's a good thing I don't have to rely on mine," Hap said and chuckled.

"What's wrong with your mind?"

"Nightmares, headaches...just standard stuff."

Wheelan nodded. "Been there, done that."

Hap smiled and shook his head. He reached into his pocket and took out his notepad. "This looks story-worthy," he said. "Mind if I take some notes?"

"Not this time!"

Both of them laughed aloud. "Actually," Wheelan said, "I've been researching the history and the Druids, but the closest I can get to anything that points to the Hallows is an old letter from the Alabama Archives written from a man to his son in 1723. The letter speaks of a place in this area where five enormous stones stood deep in the forest surrounded by white oaks, some with mistletoe vines entwined in them. The stones sat atop a hill, and as the story goes, the man said that whenever there was a storm in the area, the stones "danced" with the lightning. I do know, from one reference in that same letter that many years before the letter was written, a group of immigrant Irish settlers, who somehow found their way here, supposedly built a stone dolmen...."

"A what?" Hap asked and scooped another handful of smooth dirt. He liked the feel of it in his own hands.

"Dolmen, it means altar. Irish folk, using considerable labor and time, built a stone altar to the goddess Cailleach, the White Maiden, and patroness of the Druids. Cailleach was the Mother Earth goddess, very powerful. When the Druids were forced into hiding by the Romans in about 50 B.C. and then by the Christians a few years later, they kept their rituals. Many of them converted to Christianity on the condition that they be able to retain their gods and goddess."

Wheelan drew a small circle in the dirt. "The Christian priests, knowing they were unable to bend the wills of these people, made some of their gods and goddesses saints of the church. That way, the Druids kept their deities and the Christians got the converts. A power play, don't you see, between two powerful forces."

"So," Hap said, "this whole area is an altar?" He decided to sit down on the ground. He cleared a place with his hands and sat on the cool earth. He breathed in a long breath, sweet with the aroma of flowers.

"That's what the legend says. The stones are evidence of an earlier culture, but the frequency of storms here prevents extended digging around them. I've seen those storms plenty of times, and last year, I did exact markings linking them, physically and geologically to this spot. That's why I'm digging. To find out if this is the point of origination."

"Origination of what? I don't follow," Hap said.

"Origination of the storms. I want to find out if the secret stone is buried here. If it is, then I'll have the answer."

"Okay, one more time," Hap said and raised his eyebrows. "You're too far ahead of me."

Wheelan explained that in Tuscaloosa, Alabama, three hundred miles away, there is a site called Druid City Hospital, and in the middle of the grounds are two stones, large and ancient. Underneath the large stones, a few yards away, is a smaller stone that the worshippers called the Secret Stone, the most powerful and always buried so that it would be in direct contact, at all times, with the energy of the earth. Both stones are on a lay-line with the Hallows, a direct lay-line which establishes a link between the two stones, an electromagnetic link.

"So, you're telling me that there is a connection between this site and the one in Tuscaloosa? And this connection has something to do with the storms?"

"Yes. It has everything to do with them. The killer storms here are not just a freak of nature. They are killers for a reason. Remember that I told you that Alabama sits directly over an inactive volcano?"

"I remember."

"Combine the electrical field of a volcano with the powerful magnetism of these huge stones, and you have a combination for disaster. And this is the point from which it all comes forth. *This* is the point of origination."

"But how do you know the stone is here? No one's ever seen it, right?"

"Right, but I have some very old records that indicate it is buried deep beneath this soil. And many people did see it, just not anyone who's still alive."

A low rumbling of thunder in the distance startled both of them. A tiny ripple in the ground beneath them brought Hap to his feet. "Buggers! Did you feel that?" Hap asked as he dusted off the seat of his pants.

"Yes, as I said, the point of...."

"I know, the point of origination."

Wheelan looked at his Rolex and pointed to the van. "We'd better get back. We've been gone over an hour."

As they approached the van, another rumbling of thunder, another trembling in the ground made Hap feel as if he would lose it any minute. His heart pounded, his pulse quickened, and his head throbbed. He took a deep breath and prayed that the two of them would make it out of this place alive.

36

Gnarled fingers of lightning spread across the sky. Thunder bellowed around them. On the ride back to town, Hap's stomach churned. The thunder and lightning brought back memories he'd just as soon forget. He occupied his mind with talk...about the stones, Preacher's Cove, and Ike Madison. When they were just about to pull into the parking lot, Hap looked at Wheelan. "Another storm is coming, right?"

Wheelan leaned out of the van and looked up at the sky then shook his head. "Not a bad one, not one with greenflash. Relax."

Hap sighed and smiled. Then he remembered what he had wanted to ask Wheelan in the first place. "Can we go to your mother's workshop? Maybe I can remember something."

Wheelan stared out at the parking lot. He rubbed his forehead with the back of his hand and wiped away the droplets of sweat that covered it. Hap reached over and put his hand on Wheelan's shoulder. "What is it that you're all so afraid of? You and Libby and Burton...you act like I'm asking you to cut a vein or something. I just want the truth. That's all. I want to know that I wasn't strung out on drugs. My career depends on this story, but my sanity depends on the truth of it. Can't you see that?"

Wheelan looked at Hap. Simultaneously, they both ran their hands through their hair. Then, they chuckled. Wheelan checked the time. 5:50. He took a deep breath. "Come with me," he said.

Hap followed him out of the car and down toward the back of the restaurant. At the end of the complex, right below Libby's house, was a small breezeway, closed on the outer side. They turned into the breezeway, rounded the inner side to find a door. Wheelan took out a key, unlocked the door and pushed it open. "This is the workshop, the Angel Room, as we call it. Come in."

"It's so dark in here."

Wheelan flipped a switch near the door. A bright light spread throughout the workshop. Hap winced at the glare of it.

"Mother is very sensitive to light. When she's in here, she uses just that old light bulb dangling from the cord. There's plenty of light. She just can't tolerate it. Oh, and don't move anything. She's also very possessive about her things. She leaves them in particular places so that she can find them. She gets very upset if we move anything."

Hap felt like a disobedient child doing something that he'd been told not to do. As he looked around the workshop, he noticed tools of all sorts, small ones for doll making, he supposed. In the bright light, the workshop seemed much bigger. He walked over to the table where he'd seen Lucy that first night. Littered with scraps of material, scissors of every size, string, ribbon, and dried pieces of clay, the table seemed hardly the place for the creation of these perfect dolls. "Who makes the dolls, the bodies, I mean? Don't you need a kiln or something?"

"Mother does it all, Hap. There is a kiln here. You just can't see it. That little side door there leads right into the firing room. Go ahead. Open it."

When Hap opened the small side door, he saw a large room filled with clay, ceramic molding pieces, and at the far end, the kiln. Shelves lined the room. On each shelf, labeled boxes stacked one on top of the other took up every inch of shelf space. A potter's wheel stood toward the far corner of the room.

"We import kaolin clay from Georgia every two weeks," Wheelan said. "She always has a fresh supply."

"What kind of clay?"

"Kaolin, originally from China. It's used to make the finest porcelain, like Lenox. You know the name? There is a kaolin mine in Georgia."

"Your mother uses it to make the dolls?"

"Yes, that's part of the reason the dolls are so beautiful. The clay is the finest money can buy."

"Who taught her how to do this?"

"My Uncle Alton. When he and Aunt Libby married, my mother

was in terrible shape. It was only a year or so after the accident. She couldn't speak, wouldn't respond to anyone. She just sat in that rocker and rocked. Most of the time, she slept or wandered around the restaurant's kitchen, scaring folks. Uncle Alton lived in Georgia, had lots of friends there, and had this idea that he could teach my mother how to mold clay. He thought it would keep her occupied. He didn't know that she would catch on so fast and so well. Uncle Alton started it all."

"He must be a wonderful guy," Hap said. "He somehow knew that my mother could mold the clay. She'd always had a way with painting and sculpting. We all knew that, but after the accident, after the fire, she lost interest in everything. She was hospitalized for a very long time, almost a year, trying to recover physically from the burns."

"I'm sorry to hear that."

"But then she came back here and she was just not the same person. It was Alton who talked her into trying her hand at sculpting again, and honestly, after losing the boys, I think she was desperate to occupy her mind...what was left of it."

"So, making the dolls was Alton's idea?"

Wheelan nodded.

"When Mother finished the first doll, Aunt Libby ordered doll clothes from a Sears catalog. Then, she contacted a doll maker in Atlanta and ordered eyes and hair. Eventually, the doll maker sold her business to Aunt Libby and shipped all the products here. That's what you see in the boxes. Mostly hair and eyes, the very best. The hair is made from human hair. The eyes...."

"God, don't tell me they're made from human ones!"

"No, but they're made with lasers and crystal. Very expensive and of excellent quality. The colored parts are actually finely ground gemstones."

"Gemstones? True gemstones?"

Wheelan nodded.

"Yep, true gemstones."

"Well, at least now I know why the dolls are so expensive. So, where does the heat from the kiln go?"

"Actually, that was Alton's idea, too. The heat vents go into the pool area. So, even when it's cold, during firing time, the water is warm. If you noticed, signs are posted that tell customers that the pool is heated during certain hours."

"Yeah, I saw that. This Alton's quite a guy. Where is he now?"

"He, uh, he died. One of the storms got him."

"Wait a minute. I thought the storm killed—what was his name—Frankie?"

"Yes, him, too."

"So, the storm killed Alton and Alton was Libby's second husband?"

"Yes, Uncle Alton was our savior, in a way."

Wheelan thought of that night, that horrible night when his whole world fell apart. He remembered the trips Alton made every weekend, just to teach his mother how to use the clay. He remembered how Alton loved his Aunt Libby, how, with such soft eyes, he watched every move she made and how he smiled with utter joy whenever she entered the room. Alton was the only person besides Libby who understood his mother's incoherent babbling, who didn't mind the constant swaying, and the sporadic, frantic brushing of her skirt against flames that only she could see. When she bit her nails to the quick and drew blood, Alton gently moved her hand from her mouth. And when she clawed at the little mark in her palm until it, too, bled, he stopped her. He looked at her, not always square in the face, but close enough. He didn't look away or grimace, not even the first time he saw her. Not even Crazy Lucy Addams could deter him. He made those trips from Georgia, without fail, every weekend until Libby gave in and married him. Because of Alton, Libby and his mother found new life.

"Let's go back into the workshop," Hap said, startling Wheelan out of his temporary mental refuge.

"Sorry," he said. "A short trip to the memory bank. Made a withdrawal."

Hap chuckled. "Been there, done that, got the T-shirt," he quipped.

They walked back into the work area, squeezing past two large tables. In the workshop, the two of them seemed like awkward giants. As Wheelan knocked over a small can of water, Hap stepped on something glass that crunched under his shoes.

"Bulls in a china shop," Hap said. "I've always been clumsy. My good looks make up for it, though!"

They both laughed. "Sure they do," Wheelan said. "Handsome and humble. It's a winning combination."

"So, show me where that snake was," Hap said.

"Right over there in the corner," Wheelan said.

Hap squeezed past the table, bent over and looked for any signs of the snake. He didn't really know what he was looking for, but he felt sure there was something that would jog his memory.

"And where were you?"

"I was by the corner, by the table. That's how I saw it."

"Was it one of yours?" Hap asked.

"No, that's the first thing I checked. I promise you, Hap. That snake wasn't mine. I'd never keep something that venomous around all these people."

"And where was your mother? No, wait." He held up his hand to ask Wheelan to be quiet. He pointed at the corner. "I know where she was," he said. "Sitting over here, huddled up. She was crying. Then you found the snake and indicated I should stay still. The next thing I remember is feeling a sharp sting and falling. Is that right?"

"Yes, that's right. You fell."

"Then...." Hap turned around and surveyed the small room, "then I was lying on my back and someone was on top of me or beside me. A beautiful woman. No, a hideous woman." Hap lowered his head and stared down at the floor. "I thought I was floating. Then a horrible mouth came down on mine, and those eyes...they glowed. I'm sure of it. I remember seeing those eyes." His hands shook and his heart pounded.

"Hap, it's all right. The woman was my mother. When the lights cast just right, you see the side of her face undamaged by the fire. Then, if she shifts slightly or if the light changes, you see the mangled remains of the other side."

"But why did she try to kill me?" he asked as sincerely as he had ever asked a question.

Wheelan looked at him for a moment, then lowered his head.

"She didn't try to kill you, Hap. My mother saved your life. She kissed you, called you a sweet baby, and with her weight, kept your heart pumping. She saved your life."

"And the eyes? Those orbs I saw?"

"Well, by that time you were unconscious. I was watching you, remember? I was right next to you. You passed out. I can't explain the orbs you saw. I didn't see them, but I can tell you that Mother saved you. She loves your blond hair. It reminds her of her babies." Hap looked at Wheelan, glanced up at his jet black hair, and raised his eyebrows. "Her younger ones," he replied. "The ones who died."

"So, can you tell me, Wheelan, why the doctors swore I was on drugs and there was no sign of a snake bite? No offense, man, but your story just doesn't quite cut it. I was there, too, and I know what I felt and what I saw."

Wheelan stared down and moved his foot across the smooth floor. "Remember this, Hap. What my mother does is a gift. I know that the force that guides her does three things: destroys, builds, and magnifies. She's the angel lady, remember?"

"I don't understand," Hap said.

"It's simple. My mother has the power to destroy, to build, and to magnify whatever is inside your body. Just think about it. It will make a warped kind of sense after a while."

Hap looked at Wheelan's eyes. They betrayed no sign of lying or even exaggerating. Hap decided he was telling as much of the truth as he knew. He smiled at him. "I'm having dinner with Libby," he said to Wheelan. "I guess I need to get ready. Thank you for telling me the truth. I can't say that I fully understand it, but I appreciate your honesty."

Hap turned to leave, squeezed back through the tables, and out the door with Wheelan right behind him. Just as he rounded the corner to leave the workshop, Wheelan grabbed his arm. "My mother is...special. She can do things, see things. She's not your average person. The women in this family are all special. Each one has her own qualities. Mother's a healer. That's as much as I know."

The two of them stood inside the breezeway, two handsome,

towering figures ready to butt heads. Finally, Hap shrugged his shoulders and nodded. "Well, that's a start. Maybe tomorrow we can talk again?"

Wheelan smiled and felt almost relieved at the prospect. "Maybe," he said. "If you're really lucky, I'll order lunch again."

Hap turned and walked down the breezeway and out into the open air. "I'm gonna head to the room," he said. "See you later." Wheelan watched him walk away. He shuddered. "Methinks the Cove's about to crumble," he muttered.

37

Worn out from the long day of half-truth telling, Wheelan lay on his bed, staring up at the ceiling. He needed a nap, but sleep eluded him. The dark hardwood floors and the deep cherry wood, four-poster bed, dresser, and nightstand did little to dull the brightness of the room, which was newly painted in stark white and the woodwork trimmed in light blue. Even at night with the heavy draperies drawn fully closed, the edges lapped over so that none of the light from the parking lot filtered in, the room still seemed to shine. It was a room designed for thinking, not sleeping. Foremost in his mind were the memories of Uncle Alton...and the storm that claimed him. It had started just as they all start: first, the low rumbling of thunder—folks called it the Devil's Growl— then the darkening skies. Next came the utter blackness, the void that enveloped the entire area, then, at last, the beauty of the killer known as greenflash.

On that dreadful evening, something almost as horrible happened before the storm. Wheelan remembered that night as clearly as he remembered anything. It was, unfortunately, his most vivid childhood memory. Even now, after all the years, he could hear the lightning crackle, see the skies turn black, and smell the stench of burning flesh as if it had just happened. He remembered that dreadful day's events, of some twenty years earlier, with utter clarity. He had been napping on his bed when he heard his mother's shuffling beside him. He looked up to see her standing by his bed, a hideous grimace of a smile on her face. She reached out to touch him, holding something small and straight in her hand. Then, she drew back her hand, and he closed his eyes to doze again. At that moment, he heard the match light, its flame the only light in the room. He saw it drop onto his bed in a kind of slow, torturous motion. The flame grew longer and hotter as it dropped. When it landed, his mother stood over him humming the lullaby she used to sing to the babies. When his Aunt Libby burst through the door, she screamed. Wheelan remembered seeing himself in the shadows cast by the fire's light as he struggled to get out of the flaming bed...his mother holding him down as tightly as she could. Alton and Libby managed, just in time, to pull them both to safety. The three of them doused the flames with pitcher after pitcher of water until all that remained of the flames were wisps of rising steam. Wheelan sat up and shook his head. He squeezed his eyes shut, ran his hands through his hair, and put his feet onto the floor. *Too many memories are bad for the soul,* he thought. He walked into his bathroom, reached under the sink, and pulled out a bottle.

"Stoly's," he muttered. "My old friend."

He poured a small glass half-full of the vodka, filled it the rest of the way with water, and drank it down. "Ah," he said. "Better, much better. Tomorrow, old friend, we will tell Hap the truth and see if the place crumbles around us. Tomorrow."

He walked around the bedroom humming the tune to the song from *Annie.* For some reason, he couldn't get it out of his mind. He decided to have another drink, and while he poured it, he looked at himself in the bathroom mirror.

"It's only a day away," he muttered.

38

At 8:00, Hap met Libby in the restaurant at Cove's End. When he saw her, his heart literally pounded in his chest. His palms began to sweat. Dressed in an emerald green pants suit, her hair swept up with long curling auburn tendrils drifting along her face, she looked beautiful. She smiled as she approached him. He bent down and hugged her tightly.

"Careful," she said. "You'll crush me."

"I'm so glad to see you, Libby."

"I'm glad to see you, too. Let's sit down, okay?"

Servers scurried back and forth. Caillin stopped at their table.

"Caillin, honey, would you bring us some iced tea?"

"With extra lemon, in mine, please," Hap said, and for the first time, made direct eye contact with Caillin, but only briefly. She looked at him, holding eye contact for a few seconds, then jumped as if she had been startled and looked away. After that, she kept her eyes on the pad in front of her until she nodded at Libby and left without speaking. Hap followed her with his eyes, noticing everything about her that reminded him of Taylor Winters, or Belinda, as the Chief had called her. Caillin looked so much like her mother that Hap couldn't imagine that he hadn't paid more attention at first. Libby watched him watching Caillin. When he looked over at Libby, she had a somber look on her face. Hap wondered if she thought he was trying to flirt with Caillin...or worse, if he had some perverted designs on her. He smiled at Libby, then, hoping to soothe her. "It's amazing how similar you are in appearance to her," Hap said. "She's very quiet, though, isn't she?"

"She's very shy," Libby said. "She's had a rough time."

"Joey thinks she's wonderful. I think he's smitten. He's got one heck of a case of puppy love."

When Hap realized that he was talking about his own daughter, he felt a sinking feeling in the pit of his stomach. He swallowed hard and tried not to think about Joey's feelings for Caillin.

"He'll get over it and move on," Libby said. "Besides, you're leaving in a day or two, aren't you?"

"Yes, I think so. It depends, really, on...."

"On what?"

"On you, Libby. It depends on you."

Hap could tell by the broad smile that Libby liked what he had said. Caillin brought their tea and set the glasses down. She placed a saucer of sliced lemons in front of Hap, but again, kept her eyes away from his. As she pulled her hand away from the saucer, he noticed the mark in her palm. As if she knew exactly what he saw, Caillin closed her fist and walked away.

"What would you like to eat?" Libby asked. "The trout almondine is especially good. Do you like fresh fish?"

"Yes, that will be fine."

Libby caught the attention of one of the servers who came immediately to the table. "Two trout almondine with baked potato and salad," she said.

"Help yourself to the salad bar," the server said, then flushed as if he had forgotten who his customer was.

"Follow me to the salad bar, Mr. Murray," Libby said and winked at him.

"Yes, ma'am," he said.

When they had finished piling their salad plates, they walked back to the table, Libby leading. Hap watched her walk and marveled at the petite figure proportioned perfectly. She swayed a little when she walked in a feminine, delicate way. Her steps seemed so light that Hap thought for a moment that she might be floating across the floor. He set his plate down, moved Libby's chair for her, and then sat down himself.

"So, why does your leaving depend on me, Hap?" Libby asked immediately.

"Because...because I need you to tell me more. Wheelan took me to the workshop and we talked a little about Lucy...."

Libby inhaled sharply, coughed when she tried to swallow her tea, and dropped her fork. It clanged onto the plate. Immediately, a server scurried over to help with any clean-up.

"It's fine," Libby said as she tried to clear her throat and get the tea down. "No mess, but thank you for being so attentive."

"Are you all right?" Hap asked.

She cleared her throat again, coughed once more, and wiped her mouth with the napkin. "Yes," she said in a gravelly voice. "I'm fine. Went down the wrong way."

"Hold your head back," he said. "All the way back. Go ahead."

Libby did as he said and immediately she could speak. "It works every time," he said. "One of my dad's many contributions to my survival."

"Thank you," she said, the look on her face much more serious. Hap smiled again, but he couldn't help but wonder why the very mention of Lucy's name was enough to make the lot of them jittery. He wanted to stand up and yell, "What's going on in this place? Why is everyone so bloody protective? Will the earth crumble if I know the truth?" Instead, he sat quietly and waited. The servers brought the rest of the meal, a large helping of fried trout topped with almonds, huge baked potato on the side and piping hot fluffy dinner rolls. Crocks of real butter and smaller ones of homemade apple butter sat alongside the rolls. "If I ate here all the time, I'd be big as the side of a barn."

"No, you wouldn't. You'd work it off. There's a ton of work to running this place. It helps me keep my girlish 'figga.'"

"It works like a charm," Hap replied. "You've got one heck of a girlish figga. You're perfect."

Libby blushed, lowered her head, and smiled.

"It's true," he said. "You're a knockout, Lib," he said.

Libby just shook her head.

"You don't have to try so hard, Hap. I like you. All this flattery is, well, nice, but...."

"Why can't you just accept the compliment without making it some sort of scheme on my part? You are a beautiful woman. Face the fact and enjoy it. I certainly do. It's my great pleasure to sit across from you and admire you."

"Wow," she said. "What a charmer you are and great looking, too. What more could a girl want?" They laughed and finished the meal in such a pleasant fashion, with such light conversation, that Libby almost forgot what Hap had said earlier. Almost.

It was 9:00 when they finished, and Hap asked, a little sheepishly, if they could go back to her place. "Why don't we take a walk and then go back to my office?"

"Sure," he said. "Whatever you want is okay with me."

They strolled leisurely down the wooden planks of the compound past each room. Each time they took a step, the planks creaked. By the time they reached the office, a chorus of squeaks and creaks sounded around the two of them. Hap noticed that the complex extended far beyond his range of vision. Three hundred rooms, he remembered Libby mentioning. He glanced across the street. The sentinel of trees stood guard against the ne'er do wells. *Sacred ground*, he thought. The sky, clear and speckled with glittering beads of light seemed a perfect sort of halo for such sacred ground. The air was warm and heavy with moisture. Every time he took a breath, Hap felt as if the air—still thick with the aroma of cooked food—clung to the inside of his nose, then slowly filtered down into his lungs. Drops of perspiration dotted his upper lip.

Several couples passed by as he and Libby walked to the office, all of them dressed in standard tourist garb—casual pants or sweats, loose t-shirts, and flip-flops. All of them spoke as they passed, some in lazy Southern drawls and some in quick high-pitched pecks. From the parking lot came sounds of engines idling, doors slamming, and children giggling. Darkness fell on the Cove, and in the distance, a low rumbling sounded. "I hope that was your stomach," Hap joked.

"No, it wasn't. There's another storm coming, I think."

"Maybe I'll be gone by then."

When they reached the office, Libby told Hap to wait at the door. When she came back out, she jangled something in her hand.

"What do you have, there?" Hap asked.

"Well, it looks like a key to me. Doesn't it to you?"

"You got us a room? Great!"

They walked up a set of stairs, down a long corridor, and creaked to a stop in front of one of the rooms. Hap looked out over the balconied walkway. He leaned against the rails and took a deep breath. In spite of the things that had happened to him, he thought this was probably one of the prettiest towns he'd ever seen: pristine, secluded, yet humming with a peaceful buzz of activity. In the distance again, the low rumbling became louder. When another sound assaulted his ears, he cocked his head to the side and listened. Strains of Edelweiss filtered through the air.

"That harmonica gives me the creeps!" Hap said.

"I guess we're used to it," Libby said. "I don't really pay any attention to it anymore."

He followed Libby into the room, shut the door, and stood beside her. When she reached to flip on the lights, he took her hand. "We don't need them," he said. As soon as Libby reached up and touched him, Hap felt his skin turn warm and tingle. Her touch was like magic to him. He was, once again, overcome by passion. The next hour brought utter bliss and complete satisfaction. He drifted off to sleep with Libby's head on his shoulder. He hugged her tightly, but after only a few minutes, she woke and jumped up, startled that she had fallen asleep. When she announced, at 11:00, that she had to leave, Hap was disappointed.

"What's the matter? I thought we could stay a little longer," he said. "I have something very important to tell you about, Libby. Please, don't go. Stay with me. Let's talk and then sleep. Stay the night, Libby. Please."

"I don't want to sleep, Hap. Sleep is not really my thing, and besides, there's something I have to do," she said. "I have to go home and check on Lucy."

"You don't like sleep? Come on. Everyone likes to sleep."

"Not everyone," she said. "I have to go check on Lucy."

"Isn't Doc there? Can't he check on her? I'm sorry. I know that sounds really selfish, and I have no right to...."

"It takes both of us. If you want to wait here for a while, maybe I can come back later and you can tell me whatever it is that is so important. Okay?"

"I have a better idea. Let me come with you. I won't get in the way. I'll just hang out behind you."

"No, Lucy doesn't like strangers, Hap."

"Strangers? She used to baby-sit for me, and she saved my life, for God's sake. I'm no stranger to her."

"She won't remember."

"Then let me take my chances. I won't get in the way, I promise. Let me come with you."

"For your story?" Libby asked.

"No, Libby, not for the story. For myself and for Lucy. I'm going to thank her for helping me. Whether you think she'll remember or not, I want to thank her."

After a few seconds, Libby agreed. They dressed and left. Hap hoped he'd made the right decision.

Libby hoped that Lucy wouldn't try to burn him alive.

39

At ten minutes to midnight, Wheelan heard his mother's shuffling steps in the kitchen and went to make certain that she operated the lift correctly, without hurting herself or anyone else. He went into the living room to watch just as someone turned the key in the front door. Libby came in, with Hap close on her heels. Wheelan's look of surprise startled them both. Instinctively, Libby reached up to straighten her hair and smooth her blouse. Hap ran his hand through his hair and coughed. *Classic signs of hanky-panky*, Wheelan thought.

"Hi," Libby said. "Did I make it in time?"

"Yes," Wheelan answered, "she's gone to the lift. I'm just listening to make sure she doesn't fall."

"You're a good son, Wheelan, honey."

"No, I'm not a good son, Aunt Libby. I'm just a watchful one," he said with a hiccup and a belch. "Excuse me."

Libby walked into the kitchen to see how Lucy was faring. She watched as her sister shuffled those baby steps toward the lift, scooted toward the chair, held the bar, and lowered herself onto the seat. Before she could hit the red release button, Libby spoke to her, "Lucy? Will you look at me, Lucy?"

Libby put her hand over the red button so that Lucy could not release the lift. Then she spoke again.

"Lucy, please look at me."

Her sister looked up at her with eyes so devoid of expression that Libby wondered if she were thinking at all. "Lucy, I've brought someone to see you."

She turned and called to Hap to come into the kitchen. When she turned to call to him, she removed her hand from the release button. Lucy reached up and pushed the button. The lift door closed and locked, and the lift began its descent. "Lucy!" Libby called. Wheelan and Hap came into the kitchen just as the lift reached the first floor. "We'll have to go down to the workshop. She left before I could stop her."

"I'll let you folks have that pleasure," Wheelan said. "I'll stay here, if you don't mind."

"I do mind, Wheelan," Hap said. "I'd like for you to come with us."

Wheelan shrugged, hiccupped again, and walked over to the front door. "I'll lock up," he said. The three of them used the back door and walked down the steps to the side of the workshop. Lucy struggled to get out of the lift. Her long purple robe caught on the door, and as she tried to move forward, she reminded Hap of one of those cartoon characters who tries to step forward and is pulled back, tries again and is pulled back again. Lucy seemed unaware that her robe was keeping her from moving. "Goodness," Libby said. "Her robe is caught. I've told her not to wear that long robe, but she puts it on every time. I thought I'd put it where she couldn't find it."

"My fault," Wheelan said. "I saw it hanging in the hall closet and put it out for her."

Hap walked over and bent down to release the robe. Lucy paid no attention to him, and as soon as the robe released, she shuffled out of the lift and walked toward the workshop. When she entered, she reached up and flipped the light switch. The one dangling bulb spread such a weak light into the room that Hap wondered how she could see to do anything, much less create one of those perfect dolls. Without room for all four of them in the workshop, Libby indicated with her hands that Hap and Wheelan should stand outside while she went in to try once again to talk to her sister, already busy at the worktable. "Lucy, look at me," she said. "I have a surprise for you. A sweet new baby."

Lucy stopped her work and turned to look at her twin sister. "Bah...bee...." she muttered.

Libby motioned to Hap and Wheelan. As they started in, Libby walked past them. The minute they stepped into the workshop, thunder rumbled in the distance.

The thunder outside grew louder. When Lucy heard it, she wailed. Chills ran down Hap's spine.

"She doesn't like the thunder," Wheelan said. "Better talk to her while you can."

Hap moved closer to Lucy. He was thankful for the dim light which camouflaged her appearance. He didn't want to grimace or look away from her. In spite of what Libby said, Hap was sure that Lucy understood more than people gave her credit for. He stepped beside her and spoke.

"Hello, my name is Hap," he said so loudly that Libby heard him outside.

"She may be crazy, buddy, but she's not deaf," Wheelan said. "Talk softly and you'll get her attention. Tell her you're her baby."

Hap lowered his voice and spoke again, almost in a whisper.

"Hi, Lucy. I, uh, just want to thank you for helping me."

Lucy looked up, all the way up to his face. She cocked her head so that the light caught the beautiful side of her face. He looked down at her and smiled.

"Thank you for helping me. You saved my life."

"Bah...bee," she muttered. "Swee...bah...bee."

"Yes," he said. "Sweet baby. You saved your sweet baby."

He reached down to touch her face, but as she cocked her head the other way, the light shone on the mangled remains of her once-lovely image. Instinctively, Hap inhaled sharply, pulled his hand away, and looked down at the floor. When he looked up again, Lucy was looking right into his eyes, as if her eyes had never left him.

She turned away, back to her worktable and muttered something that Wheelan had never heard her say before. As she worked, she muttered repeatedly,

"Mon...tah, mon...tah, mon...tah."

"What is she saying?" Hap asked.

"Monster," Wheelan said. "She's saying monster."

"Oh, God," Hap said, "how did she know I said that? How did she know?"

"She read your mind," Wheelan said.

"What, so now she's a healer and a mind reader?" Hap asked.

"The tip of the iceberg, my friend. Just the tip of the iceberg."

Hap left the workshop feeling worse than ever. He had messed up royally. Not only had he hurt Lucy's feelings, but he had also underestimated her abilities and failed to find out about the eyes... the main reason for his trek to the workshop in the first place. He was grateful that Libby trusted him enough to let him go with her, but he was angry at himself for having lied to her again. And while it was true that he wanted to thank Lucy for helping him, he was not convinced that she had saved his life. All he knew for certain was that while she was helping him—"healing" as Wheelan called it—her eyes glowed green. He knew it for certain, and he wanted to know why and how. *What kind of human being had eyes that glowed? How could that happen?* The reporter in him felt such compulsion to find the answer that he couldn't let it go. He had to visit Lucy again, somehow. He was becoming a desperate man, hungry for answers.

40

At 1:00 a.m., with the thunder rumbling and the tune of Edelweiss playing in the distance, Hap and Wheelan stood outside in the parking lot of Cove's End.

"I'm sorry, Wheelan. I didn't mean to hurt her feelings," Hap said.

"I know you didn't. So, what else is bothering you?"

"What do you mean?"

"Well, you look as if you've lost your best friend," Wheelan said.

"I, uh, I haven't been totally honest," Hap said, running his hand through his hair.

"Is anyone ever totally honest?"

"I didn't tell the whole truth. To Libby, I mean, and to you. I didn't tell all of the truth."

"Let me guess. You told Aunt Libby that you wanted to thank my mother for saving your life, and you did, but you also wanted to find out some answers to your questions, questions we didn't bring up while we were in the workshop."

Hap looked at him in absolute wonder. Wheelan adjusted his collar and brushed his bangs out of his eyes.

"Hap, do you really take me and Aunt Libby for such back-woods fools? Don't you think we've been dealing with this for years? You came here for a story. Coincidentally or not, you've been involved in an accident, plagued by nightmares, bitten by a snake, and hospitalized. And, you've seen face to face a woman named Crazy Lucy Addams, the likes of which you'll never meet again. So, my friend, you have plenty of material for a story. But you're still here because there's that one nagging little question, isn't there? You want to know how she can do what she does.

Am I right, or am I *right*?"

Hap felt about as stupid as he'd ever felt. He had thought he was masking his intentions, but all the time, Libby and Wheelan, and probably Lucy, knew exactly what he was doing. Shame and embarrassment washed over him like a flood of dirty river water. He stared at the ground, too weak-spirited to look at his friend.

"Would you like to go up to the Hallows?" Wheelan asked.

"At this time of the morning?"

"Can you feel the spark in the air? A storm's brewing, I think. It would be the perfect time to go. I'll take my Jeep. It has flood-lights, and we can get in close enough to do a little investigating."

Hap took a deep breath and agreed to go. He followed Wheelan around to the back of the complex and saw a new Jeep Wrangler with huge floodlights mounted onto the front and top, with long chrome beams holding a third set of lights at the rear. The back seat was filled with miner's headlamps, big flashlights, shovels, and even a couple of pick-axes. "You mind if we stop by so that I can tell Joey where I'm going?"

"No, not a bit," Wheelan said.

They drove around to the front parking lot, pulled into the spot closest to the room, and parked.

"I'll just be a minute," Hap said.

Hap knocked on the door to the room, trying to be quiet enough not to disturb the other guests, but loud enough to wake Joey. After a few seconds, he knocked again, a little louder this time. He fished around in his pockets for the keycard. While he was still searching, Joey came to the door and opened it. He stood there in his boxer shorts and T-shirt, and from the look in his squinted eyes, Hap could tell that Joey had been sleeping. "Sorry, kid. I just wanted to let you know that I'm going up to the Hallows with Wheelan."

"What?" Joey said.

"The Hallows," Hap answered. "Never mind, go back to sleep. Just let me get something out of my bag and I'll be gone again."

Joey opened the door a little wider as Hap stepped through. He fumbled in his backpack for a decent pen. Then, he turned to say good-bye to Joey, but found that the kid had gone into the bathroom. Hap stepped to the door, held up his index finger to signal just one more minute to Wheelan. A nod gave him the okay to go ahead, so he walked back to the bathroom, tapped on the door and said, "Don't wait up, kid. I'll be back when you see me walk through the door."

He turned to walk back to the truck, heard Joey yell, and stopped. "You okay in there?" he called.

Nothing except a muffled thud came from the bathroom.

Hap knocked, turned the handle, and tried to push the door open.

"Joey, what's wrong?" he called. "Are you all right?"

With a heftier shove this time, Hap slid the door open only slightly. "Joey!" he yelled. "Answer me."

The door wouldn't budge. All Hap could see was Joey lying on the floor, but the harder he shoved the door, the more it wedged Joey into the room. He ran outside and waved for Wheelan to come in. "Something's wrong with the kid," he said. Wheelan jumped out of the Jeep and ran inside with him. "I can't get the door open," Hap said. "I've got it just enough to see that he's on the floor, but I can't see anything else."

"Dial 911, just in case," Wheelan said. "Then dial home, extension 741. Get Libby to the phone and tell her to call Burton. I'll see what I can do with the door."

After he'd talked to the paramedics and to Libby, Hap ran next door and pounded until he heard someone rustling around inside.

"Eagle, get out here!" he called. "Something's wrong with the kid."

He ran back to the room to see if Wheelan had made any progress with the door. "We can get to him," Wheelan said, "if we can just move his feet around. Bend down and try to move his legs."

Hap did as Wheelan said, but had little luck in moving the kid's legs. The more they did, the more the door wedged him in. Finally, Wheelan got down on his knees, reached in and grabbed Joey's leg. He pulled forward with all his might. Nothing. He tried one more time, pulled forward, and felt Joey's body shift and his head hit the floor. With one last effort, he put his hand under the kid's butt and rolled him over.

"Now, reach down and try to grab his arm," he said to Hap. "Pull him up so that we can edge this door open a little more."

After another five minutes or so, the two of them were able to pry the door open while holding onto the kid. Hap grabbed him under the arms and pulled him out of the door. As Joey's feet brushed across the bathroom floor, Hap and Wheelan stopped dead still. "Hurry, get him out of there," Wheelan whispered. "Just pick him up if you have to."

With a more powerful force than Hap ever thought possible, he pulled Joey out of the bathroom and let him drape over his arm. He lowered him gently to the floor. As soon as the kid's feet were free from the doorway, Wheelan slammed the door. "Did you hear it?" he asked

"I heard it," Hap said. The two of them were breathing so hard that they could barely speak.

"What do we do now?" Hap asked. "And where in God's name are those paramedics?"

"They'll be here soon," Wheelan assured him. "All we can do is keep this door closed. I don't have anything with me. My handler's back at the house. How's Joey?"

"Not good. He looks pretty bad and his breathing's shallow."

On his knees, Hap bent over the kid and felt his pulse. "Kid," he whispered, "wake up. We're going to get you to the hospital, so you hang on for me. Joey, can you hear me? Answer me."

Hap cradled him in his arms and rocked back and forth.

"Joey, hang on, just hang on."

"How's his pulse?"

"Slow, real slow," Hap said.

He patted Joey's face and said, "Come on. Open your eyes."

When Wheelan looked at the boy's feet, his stomach felt as if it did a somersault. Two bites, one above the other on the right ankle.

Eagle came running into the room.

"What's the matter with Joey?"

"Snake bite."

It was all Hap could manage.

Just as Wheelan began CPR, the paramedics arrived and ushered them both out of the way.

"What happened to him?" the one with the metal notepad asked.

"Snake bite. The snake's still in the bathroom," he said.

Several of them looked at one another in disbelief.

"The snake's in the bathroom?" one of them repeated.

"Yes. I can get it out, but I'll need about fifteen minutes to go back and get my handler."

"So, what are you waiting for?" one of them asked. "We don't do snakes, so somebody better do something."

Three of them worked on Joey. Hap sat across the room on the bed, his head in his hands. He heard all manner of medical terms, recognized a few, and knew from the sound that they weren't good.

"If it's any help," Wheelan said, "I believe that the snake is a viper, specifically a massasauga."

Wheelan left quickly then, leaving Hap alone to cope with the snake, the paramedics, and his buddy, Joey. The paramedics asked him all sorts of questions, none of which he could answer coherently. He was much too concerned about the kid. He got up twice and went over to him, just to watch for signs of life. On his second trip, Hap found Joey with purple lips, pale skin, and wide-open eyes.

He stumbled backwards and slumped into the chair beside the dresser. The room seemed to be working alive, ants scurrying upon and devouring a carcass. The noise made his head feel as if it would split wide open at any second. Burton, Libby, and Eagle all stood around conjecturing, questioning, and wondering exactly what had happened. Their voices almost shook the room apart. Finally, Libby asked Hap and Eagle to leave. Hap could tell from the sound of her voice that she had lost all hope for Joey. For only the second time in his adult life, tears rolled down his cheeks.

"Hap, why don't you and Eagle go next door," Burton said.

"No," Hap replied, "No, I'm not leaving the kid."

"We're ready. Let's go. Let's get him to the hospital," one of the paramedics yelled. They wheeled him out on a gurney, lifted it into the ambulance, and slammed the doors. One of the medics banged twice on the doors.

"Move out!" he yelled.

"Wait! Wait!" Libby yelled back at them. "Please, let me go with him."

"Climb in, Miss Libby, but do it in a hurry."

"I'm going, too," Hap said.

"No, son. Just hold it." Burton said. "Let him be, for right now. He's in good hands." The strange look on Burton's face, one of dead-right insistence, convinced Hap that he'd better do as he said. When Eagle saw the ambulance pull out, he looked to Hap for instructions. Just then, Wheelan came running down the planked walkway carrying the handler. "How's Joey?" he asked.

No one answered until Burton suggested, "You boys get a move on. I'll stay here and help catch that rattler. We're going to find out who's responsible. I swear it, son."

Hap nodded, waved to Wheelan, and climbed into the van.

"Get yourself moving," he said to Eagle.

"You okay?" Eagle asked.

"Yeah, I'm just dandy," he said. "Just dandy. The next time I get a bright idea to come to a God-forsaken place like this one, you tell me to just shoot myself in the head and get it over with. It would cause a lot less misery."

They burned rubber as the tires squealed out of the parking lot and headed for the hospital.

Wheelan and Burton stood outside the bathroom door listening for the slightest sound. They heard nothing.

"I'm going to ease the door open. You better stand aside," Wheelan said.

He eased the door open ever so slightly. Still nothing. He pushed it a little further and stopped. In the corner by the commode was a small, writhing lump. Carefully, Wheelan scooted the handler along the floor as quietly as he could. Then, in one swift movement, he aimed and plunged the handler toward the snake. It squirmed from around the tip of the handler and, as quick as lightning, crawled into the opposite corner, the one Wheelan couldn't see without stepping into the bathroom.

"I'll have to step inside, Chief."

"Watch yourself, boy," Burton said. Wheelan stepped into the bathroom, peeked over the commode, and saw the viper curled in the corner. "It's scared," Wheelan said.

"Good," Burton said.

Once again, Wheelan positioned the handler. This time, he aimed more carefully, plunged the handler toward the back corner, and held it fast against the wall. "Hand me the bag," he said. "I've got it."

"Kill it before it kills somebody else."

"Shh," he said. "Just hand me the bag."

As soon as he felt the bag in his hand, he heard the rattling, a faint sound from a tiny assassin. He twisted the crook of the handle just right, trapped the viper, and lowered the bag to the floor. In an instant, he had swept the snake into the bag and pulled the drawstring.

"Got it," he said.

"Whew, you had me goin' there for a minute or two," Burton said.

Sweat dripped from Wheelan's hair and beaded across his upper lip. His hands trembled and his knees felt like rubber. The vodka settled in his throat like a lump of stone. "Let's get this thing outside," he said, his voice quivering so that Burton could barely understand him. "I need to get a good look at it. If it's like the other one, then we've got big trouble, Chief, real big trouble."

41

Libby looked down at the young man on the gurney. As the paramedics kept working, she reached over and slid her hand into his. The chill in his hands frightened her. *Maybe he's too far gone,* she thought. When she closed her eyes and summoned the energy in her body, Joey's hand began to warm slightly. For a moment, her hopes soared. But within seconds, the chill returned and as she held his hand in hers, it seemed to turn to mush, as if her own hand slid right through it. When she squeezed his hand just slightly, it reminded her of those childhood times when she used to squeeze oatmeal through her hands, just because she liked the feel of it. She tried again, this time wrapping both of her hands around his. She closed her eyes and imagined the lovely White Maiden soaring above. Silently, she called to her for help. When she felt her eyes burning, she knew that she must keep them closed. The glowing seemed to frighten people, narrow-minded sorts who refused to believe that what happened to her was not Satan's work. It was simply nature's way of helping her to help others. Libby imagined the Maiden standing close beside her, whispering in her ear. "Take heart, child," the White Maiden whispered. "Let him sleep."

Immediately, Libby removed her hands and opened her eyes. The gentle, dissolving glow faded quickly. She placed Joey's hand on his chest, gave it a soft pat, and stroked his cold forehead.

"Sleep, child," she said.

"Beg your pardon?" one of the paramedics said.

"He needs his rest," Libby said, tears streaming down her face.

"Maybe your prayers helped him," the man said. "Praying helps when nothing else will, you know."

"Yes," she said. "Maybe they helped."

The pain she felt increased as they neared the hospital. Sobbing almost uncontrollably, she found it difficult to stay seated. She needed to do something, anything to relieve the heartache. "We're almost there," the paramedic said. "Hang on, lady."

A thunder clap boomed in the distance. "Sweet Jesus!" one of the medics yelled. "Another one's coming."

When they pulled into the Emergency entrance, all of them except Libby piled out of the ambulance. They hurried Joey into the hospital, yelling about pulse, respiration, IV fluids, and blood pressure. Libby felt light-headed. She scooted back on the bench and leaned her head back against the wall of the interior. Her heart felt heavy in her chest, her breathing labored. Fatigued from expending such energy—and failing—she closed her eyes. Memories flooded her brain; a great tidal wave of images and emotions washed over her, and even though she squeezed her eyes tightly shut, the images spilled forth. She remembered a night some twenty years earlier, when she and her husband Alton stood outside listening to a low rumbling of thunder in the distance. The sky, clear and beautiful, puffed with clouds of billowy white cotton. For three years, she and Alton enjoyed a life of hard work, hefty profit, and cordial companionship. When she had consented to marry him, after his weekly visits from Georgia lasted first a day, then a weekend, then a full week, Libby felt that Alton truly loved her. She did her best to return his love. On that night, when they heard the low rumbling, neither would admit the fear they felt. Some things they found better left unsaid. But when the rumbling grew louder and the sky darkened, Libby told Alton that they should go inside. "It's the devil's growl, you know," she said.

"The thunder won't hurt you, honey. We have plenty of time," Alton said.

Libby had left him, then, and gone inside to find Lucy. As soon as she walked inside, she heard Wheelan screaming. She remembered the horrible sound...a thirteen-year-old terrified of his mother. She had not heard a sound like it since. She prayed to God that she wouldn't. Poor Wheelan, backed into the corner of a flaming bed, begged her to help him. She remembered the look of terror in his eyes. She remembered the utter lack of emotion from Lucy's. Wild-eyed, she looked, at that moment, like the monster everyone thought she was. Outside, the thunder bellowed. Inside, the boy screamed. Alton ran to him, and with pitchers of water, they doused the flames, and as quickly as she could, Libby led Lucy and Wheelan down to the kitchen. When she heard the booming outside once again and felt the floor beneath them tremble, her heart literally skipped a beat. "Stay right here, Lucy, with Alton Don't you move."

A luminescent green sky hovered over Preacher's Cove. Occasional bursts of brilliant pink light snaked through the green radiance, casting a kaleidoscope of silent, stunning color. Alton stood there looking amazed, as if he'd never seen anything as beautiful. Libby screamed at him, "Alton, come in, please come in. Alton, come in NOW!"

Wheelan yelled at his beloved uncle to get inside. When Alton heard them, he turned to run back to the porch. Then he stopped to take one last look at the brilliance above him, as if to savor it... as if he might never see it again.

He was right.

Libby remembered the sounds of her own screams shattering the silence of luminescence. In a matter of seconds, the awesome electrical force of greenflash snatched Alton off the ground, jerked him up to its bosom, and kissed him with the kiss of death. A deadly bolt of lightning seared his lifeless body to sickening, smoldering crispness. Alton hit the ground with a deafening thud. As Libby watched, the rain hammered down and reduced Alton's body to a smoldering mound of flesh, as it had done to Frankie all those years earlier. With his own burned hands, Wheelan led Libby through the rain. When they reached the body, their muscles trembled. The rain ended as quickly as it had started.

Alton lay at their feet.

Libby remembered thinking that maybe this time was different. Maybe greenflash had spared him, and he would turn over any second, reach out to her and whisper her name. Maybe he would wake up and say, "Libby, I love you so much."

And she would have one last chance to say, "Alton, you are the best man I've ever known. You loved me even when I treated you mean and hateful. You came into my life and rescued me and my family. You smiled when you watched me. You gave me flowers every day and kisses every night. You've saved my life, Alton, and given me happiness. I love you so much."

Tears remembered and present rolled down Libby's cheeks. She realized on that night long ago that she had never said any of those things to Alton. She had never told him what a wondrous presence he had been in her life. She had never told him how grateful she was that he had stayed in love with her even when she treated him like a fixture in the house. She had never run up to him and hugged him madly or called out to the world, "I love you, Alton."

At that moment long ago, she had wanted nothing more than to hold him, to kiss his face and tell him everything would be all right. She needed to tell him that she would never turn away from his caresses again, that she would thank him for the flowers, and that she would, from now on, speak softly and gently instead of nagging him to do even more than he had already done. And she would never say to him again, "Can't you work any faster? Do I have to do everything myself? Can't you for once do anything without me having to nag you about it?"

She heard her own harsh words from that day echoing inside her brain. She remembered earlier that morning when Alton had playfully sneaked up behind her and hugged her tight. "Stop that. Don't get all over me right here in the kitchen," she'd said.

It had been a hug, a simple hug. He had looked so hurt, but had said only, "Yes, dear."

As the images continued to flood her mind, she remembered that, standing there after the storm, she had yelled at him, "I want you to get up now, Alton. Do you hear me? I want you to wake up. Don't you dare leave me here all alone. Don't you dare. You wake up, now, Alton. Wake up!"

By then, her eyes glowed a soft, luminescent green.

Alton didn't listen that time. His body had shifted slightly, and in one final motion, he sloshed face down in the mud.

42

A sudden trembling in the ambulance jolted Libby swiftly into present tense again. The thunderclaps, closer and louder, sent a chill down her spine. She climbed out of the ambulance, stretched, straightened her hair, smoothed her skirt, and walked toward the entrance. All she could think of now was that poor young man that her niece, Caillin, found so appealing. Caillin would be devastated at the news. "Hello, Ms. Libby," someone called to her.

When she turned back to look, she saw Billy Ray, Ike Madison's handyman and harmonica maestro.

She managed a weak smile. "How are you, Billy Ray?" she asked.

"Good, real good," he said, a toothpick dangling between his teeth. "Excuse me. I need to go inside."

"Right," he said. "I'm headin' to the restaurant later to grab some breakfast."

Libby had almost reached the door when Billy Ray called to her again. "Ms. Libby, I was sorry to hear about the accident. You gotta be real careful. Snakes can kill ya if ya ain't careful."

Libby nodded at him and went inside. She stopped at the entrance and looked back at Billy Ray. She wondered who had told him about the accident, but in the Cove, word travels fast. She walked toward the desk and asked about Joey. With a formality that Libby found almost insulting, the nurse announced that the doctor would be out shortly and directed her toward the waiting area where Hap and the others were already seated. Then it occurred to her that the strangers, the visiting non-residents accounted for the nurse's guarded manner. Strangers made everyone uneasy, and in Preacher's Cove, anyone who hadn't lived there for at least ten years was a stranger. Tourists didn't stand a chance of getting anywhere with anyone. Formality veiling secrecy was the order of the day, every day, for them.

Libby walked to the waiting area and sat next to Hap.

"Have you heard anything?" she asked him.

"Does it matter?" he answered.

The look on his face said it all. He looked at her as if she were... a stranger. No warm smile, no pat on the hand, nothing. He simply turned away. She touched his arm, and he turned to look at her.

"Of course, it matters," she said. "Why would you ask such a thing?"

"Oh yes, it matters," he said. "When the owner of a place climbs into an ambulance to accompany an injured guest, I guess it does matter. After all, you *should* put on a concerned face to show that you're not responsible for the accident and that your only concern is the safety and well-being of the guest."

She stared at him in disbelief, searching his face with her eyes for any sign of affection. She found none. "It's not what you think, Hap. Not at all what you think."

"I'll tell you, Libby. I'm just a little sick of all this secrecy. My friend is dying. He was dying when you got into that ambulance, when Burton kept me back. If I had gone, at least I could have been with Joey. I could have talked to him. But no, you rushed in there like he was your best friend. And why? You barely know him."

Libby sat back in her chair, folded her hands in her lap, and stared down at them. Hap was right. He should have gone with the boy. She had no right to turn him away from the last chance he might have with his friend. "I'm sorry," she whispered.

Hap ran his hands through his hair, propped his elbows on the arms of the chair, and rested his chin on his folded hands. When the doctor came out, Hap recognized him immediately... the idiot who had accused him of being a drug addict. He sighed so loudly that Eagle and the others heard him. They stood up and waited.

"Jesus Christ," he said. "Nice to see you again, Mr. Murray," the doctor said. "I'm sorry it had to be under such unfortunate circumstances."

"How is he?" they all asked at once.

The doctor shook his head.

"There was not much we could do," he said. "The venom worked so fast. There was nothing anyone could have done. We weren't able to revive him. I'm so sorry."

"He's dead?" Hap asked and jumped up out of his chair. "Joey's dead?"

"Oh, my God," Libby whimpered. "No, not that young boy."

Eagle covered his face with his hands and let out a low moan. "No, not the kid, not the kid."

Hap's knees buckled and he slipped back into the chair. Unable to think coherently, he stared at the floor and wondered when he would wake up from this nightmare. The doctor sat down next to him and apologized again. Then, he said something so bizarre that he shook the cobwebs out of Hap's brain immediately.

"Mr. Murray," he said, "your young friend died in a matter of minutes. I'm not sure what has happened here, but to my knowledge albeit limited, no snake indigenous to Alabama is venomous enough to kill that quickly."

"What are you saying?'

"All I'm saying is that after what happened to you and what has happened to your friend, you can do one of two things."

"Two things?"

"Yes. You can leave town immediately or you and your buddy there can use those reporter's instincts of yours to find out what is really going on."

The doctor got up, then, and walked over to talk to Libby. Within minutes, Burton and Wheelan came in carrying a drawstring bag that Hap recognized. It was the same one that Wheelan had used before.

"Is that it?" Hap asked and came up out of his seat. "Did you get it?"

"How is Joey?" Wheelan asked.

Hap wiped a tear from his eye, looked down at the floor and shook his head.

"He didn't make it," he said.

Wheelan put a hand on Hap's shoulder. "I'm so sorry," Wheelan said. "Is there anything I can do?"

"Yes, you can find out what kind of snake that is and what it's doing in Alabama territory. The doctor said that no snake indigenous to Alabama has venom strong enough to kill as quickly as it killed Joey."

"We already know what kind it is, son," Burton said. "It's a massasauga, a kind of pygmy rattler. They've been around here for a while, but we've never had anyone die from a bite before, not to my knowledge anyway."

"And how many times before now has a guest at Cove's End been bitten?" Hap asked.

"Never," Libby said. "This has never happened before."

"Then you see my point, don't you?" he asked. "Either someone's trying to kill me or...."

"That doesn't make sense, Hap. Why would someone want to kill you?"

"I don't know, but I'm sure going to find out."

"I've got a team out there now, son. Maybe they'll find something useful."

"I need to get back there. Someone has to contact Joey's dad and Mr. James. Someone has to try to explain."

"Come back to my place," Libby said. "Both of you can stay and you can do your calling from there, and I don't want you staying in your room again. The police will clear it so that you can get your things. In the meantime, you and Eagle can rest up with me and Wheelan."

Her eyes pleaded with him to accept her offer. "Please," they seemed to say. "Please."

Hap nodded, whispered something to Eagle, and looked to see if the doctor was still around. He was standing at the desk filling out papers. Hap walked over to him and asked if he could see Joey. The doctor nodded and led him to the room.

Joey lay stiff and still on the table, surrounded by tubes, bags, and machines. Purple-lipped and wide-eyed, he bore little resemblance to the young man who'd been Hap's buddy for four years. When they first met, Joey was only eighteen, straight out of high school, a rookie kid with a yearning for fame and fortune and a keen eye for detail. It was Joey who spotted the first irregularities in "the Senator's" accounts, reported them, and landed the job at Channel 12 as a part-time driver and hound. The hound's job was to sniff out stories by following one or two noted senators or judges. Having a prominent lawyer as a father both helped and hindered him. The Senator he accused of irregularities was a family friend, but not for long. Still though, he did his job, kept snooping, and found more "dirt," and in his spare time, drove the others from location to location without complaint.

"I'm sorry, kid," Hap said as tears rolled down his cheeks. "I'm so very sorry." An image of his mother's headstone came into his mind. He figured that the inscription was suitable for his friend.

"May God hold you in His arms and sing you a song of peace," he quoted.

As he walked out the door, he thought of how his mother always knew the right thing to say. "Good job, Mom," he whispered. "Take care of the kid for me."

When he joined the others in the waiting room, Eagle told him that he had called Joey's father.

"He's flying in immediately," Eagle said. Hap was relieved that he didn't have to call Mr. Donovan. Joey was his only child. The loss, especially under these circumstances, would be unbearable, Hap imagined.

"I should have called him myself," Hap said.

"He asked if you'd meet him at the airport in Monteagle. He said he'd call the hotel before he landed. Should be three hours or so from New York."

"Is there anything we need to do in the meantime?" Hap asked.

"No." Eagle said. "He wants Joey left alone. Nothing before he gets here."

"You need to get back to the hotel. I'll be there in a little while. Something I want to check out here first."

"Okay," Eagle said. "I'll call Herb when we get back."

He patted Hap on the shoulder.

"It wasn't your fault, partner."

Hap nodded and returned the gesture.

"It feels like my fault," he said. "I'm going to get to the bottom of this if it's the last thing I do."

As they were about to walk out, a man strode through the door as if he owned the place, head held high, shoulders back, voice booming like thunder. "Nurse!" he called to the person sitting at the desk. "Make sure these people have everything they need. You attend to their physical needs, and I'll attend to the spiritual."

When Libby saw him walk in, the expression on her face changed immediately. She looked at Hap and sighed. The preacher came right over to them, shook their hands one by one, and said loudly enough for even poor Joey to hear, "I came as quickly as I heard," he said.

Once again, Ike Madison was dressed fit to kill. Hap still liked his taste in clothes, and wondered where he would get a fine Italian suit around Preacher's Cove. The man looked as if he'd just stepped out of a GQ photo shoot: he had style.

"Libby, are you holding up all right? What a shock this must have been for you. Imagine such a terrible thing happening at your place of business," he said. "Oh, I hope it doesn't ruin you. And Chief Riggs, I see you're ahead of me, as usual. Good to see you, but not under such unfortunate circumstances. Dr. Addams, this must be quite a terrible time for you, as well. Tragedy seems to follow you around."

He turned to Hap. "I'm so sorry for your loss, as well. I know you were responsible for the boy. Such a young man with such promise." Ike shook his head. "But it isn't your fault. I've come to offer my services and, of course, my prayers."

Burton rolled his eyes and sighed. "Reverend," he said, "nice of you to come. How did you hear about the accident?"

"You know how word spreads in a small town! And this is *my* small town, Chief. I keep watch over my sheep. Is there anything you need? If there is anything I can do, please don't hesitate to ask."

"Thank you, Reverend." Hap said. "We appreciate it, but there's really nothing we can think of."

"Prayer is sufficient, my friends. It will sustain you in these times of trouble. I'll be praying for all of you. Please excuse me. I am utterly famished this morning, for some reason. I think I'll go by the restaurant, Libby, and have one of those Early Bird Country Specials. Mmm, you just can't beat it," he said and moved toward the door. He stopped after a few strides and turned toward them again.

"Oh, Libby, where in the world are my manners this morning? I didn't ask about your sister. How is she?"

"She's doing well, Ike. Thank you for asking."

"I must watch over my sheep," he said. "Even those who cannot follow must be led."

He nodded, adjusted his tie, smiled at them and left as confidently as he had entered. "A little too enthusiastic, isn't he?" Hap asked.

"Oh, I don't know, son," Burton said. "We think the good reverend is quite a piece of work."

"Burton, Ike asked about Lucy again. Did you notice?" Libby asked.

"Indeed he did," Burton said. "He never ceases to surprise me."

Hap glared at Ike Madison as the man strode so confidently out the door. *This is the man, he thought, who married Taylor and raised our child.* Remorse and regret washed over him like a flood. He longed to see Taylor and explain, and he longed to get to know his daughter. *Maybe, he thought, maybe I will....*

43

Two hours later, Hap, Burton, and Wheelan, dressed out in white lab coats politely provided by the young doctor, stood in the hospital's largest lab staring down at a coiled pit viper encased in a large Rubbermaid container with holes punched in the lid. It lay coiled on a bed of grass and hay. Beside it lay another, this one stretched to its full length of approximately eleven inches. Hap shuddered. "I hate snakes," he said. "I've always hated them, even when I was a kid. They make my stomach feel like it's tied up in knots. I just want to run as far away from them as possible. Nah, I won't even go in the reptile house at the zoo. The things just scare me to death."

"A true ophidiophobe," Wheelan said. "Now you know why."

"Huh?"

"Well, maybe your brain knew something it just wasn't telling. Maybe your innate fear of snakes was a warning that something of a dangerous nature would happen if you were around them. A precognitive sort of thing."

"Oh, so now I'm psychic?" Hap joked.

"Not really. It's just one of my theories about why people develop unexplained phobias."

"This boy's got theories out the ying-yang," Burton said. "Smart people are like that, you know. Theories about why we think what we think, why we do what we do. He's got all sorts of theories."

Hap chuckled. Wheelan just shook his head.

"He sure does loosen up around you," Hap said. "Yeah, always has."

"*He* is in the room, gentlemen. No need to refer to him in third person when he's standing right beside you."

"Okay, okay, now give me what you've got on those snakes, Professor."

The three of them gathered closely around the lab table. Wheelan pointed to two large glass jars. "This coiled one is the one that bit you, Hap."

"God, you kept it? But you chopped it in half."

"I kept the remains, of course I did. I wanted to examine what was left of it. The one next to it is the one that killed Joey. Both are massasaugas, not indigenous to this area, but seen occasionally. The interesting thing is that both of these snakes are pygmies. They shouldn't have enough venom to kill a human being quickly, as in Joey's case and almost in yours."

"So...we're waiting for your brilliant deductions," Burton said. "Share with us, please."

"That's why I needed the lab. I'm going to dissect this one and find out what makes its venom so lethal. The other one that bit Joey has some kind of mark, like a tiny incision, in its underbelly. I want to find out if this one has it, too."

He reached in carefully to retrieve the dead viper. "Geez! Be careful," Hap said.

Wheelan jerked his hand back. "It would help if you would be a little quieter," he said, his heart racing. "Why don't you both step back."

Wheelan took a deep breath, exhaled slowly, and closed his eyes for a few seconds. Another deep breath slowed his heart rate and calmed him down. He reached into the container and slid his fingers around the tail of the dead viper. Slowly, he slid it up the side of the plastic and out of reach of the other viper. Once he cleared the container, he dangled the snake by its tail and held it up in front of his face. He looked at every inch of the dangling viper, searching for the mark. "Bingo," he said. "Gentlemen, we have a match!"

"What kind of match?" Burton asked.

"Give me a second," Wheelan said. He positioned the snake under the largest of the microscopes, adjusted the lens to bring it into focus, and found exactly what he was looking for. An incision about three-quarters of an inch ran alongside the underbelly of the snake. "Chief, take a look at this."

Burton walked over to the microscope and looked into the

eyepiece. "Never seen a snake with a scar before," he said.

"What is it, Wheelan?" Hap asked.

"This snake has the same mark."

"What kind of mark?"

"An incision. Both of these snakes have undergone some type of surgery."

"Why would anyone operate on a snake?" Hap asked.

"I don't have any idea, but if you'll slide that tray of instruments over this way, I'll try to find out." Re-opening the incision, Wheelan performed his own reptilian surgery. He removed something from the opening and held it up to the light. "What in the world is that?" Burton asked. "A computer chip," Wheelan said. "A *what*?" Burton asked.

"This little piece of engineering is a computer chip, some sort of device for monitoring, I believe. Someone has been monitoring our little killers."

"Why would anyone monitor these snakes?" Hap asked.

"Scientists all across the world implant chips into animals of all types, expressly for the purpose of following movement, determining behavior patterns." Wheelan said.

"Let me rephrase that," Hap said. "Why would anyone in Preacher's Cove need to monitor the behavior patterns of these snakes? Isn't it illegal for people to own venomous animals?"

"Nope, not in Alabama. It's illegal to sell them, but if they're indigenous to the state, people can have them," Burton said. "Wheelan, are you aware of any scientific studies going on anywhere around here that involve pit vipers?"

"No, Chief. This is not exactly the place where grant money would fund projects of that sort."

"Do you remember the night of my accident outside the workshop?" Hap asked. "When you were in my room, you told me that Preacher's Cove had lots of things, like little bitty snakes that would kill you. Are these the snakes you were talking about?"

Burton Riggs looked over at Wheelan, hoping he was still busy with the examination. Then, he looked at Hap and lowered his eyes. "I was stupid," he said. "I didn't make the connection. I guess sometimes I act like that backwoods jerk of a cop."

"What's going on?" Wheelan asked. "You two must have some secrets. I'm obviously missing something.

"Burton grabbed Hap's arm. "Have you told Libby yet?" he asked Hap.

Hap shook his head, "No, not yet."

"Then, maybe you should just let this ride until you tell her," Burton said.

"What's going on here, guys?" Wheelan asked. "Come on. Somebody level with me."

The three of them huddled closer together in the laboratory, occasionally glancing around to make sure that no one else was in there. Hap stood straight and tall as he told his story about his relationship with Belinda to Wheelan, but as he continued, he felt himself begin to slump. When he had finished, he stood very quietly and waited for some reaction from Wheelan. Once again, beads of perspiration dotted his upper lip. His stomach churned, and his heart felt as if it would split wide open. Wheelan said nothing for a few seconds. He looked down at the floor, then at Hap, then down again. His silence was as difficult for Hap to bear as any display of anger would have been. He almost wished that Wheelan would cold-cock him and get it over with. The first indignation was the comments about his mother, followed closely by the relationship with Libby, and now...the final blow.

Not only was he "seeing" Wheelan's aunt, but he had fathered a child by another of his aunts, a younger version of Libby, but one who had met with a tragic death. He couldn't blame Wheelan for anything he might want to do to him at this point. But worst of all, the daughter of the woman he had once loved but turned away, had been living all these years with a man who was suspected of having killed her mother. He could barely stand the thought of his beautiful Taylor—and his daughter—being trapped with Ike Madison.

Finally, Wheelan spoke to him. "Ike Madison will kill you, Hap, if he knows who you are," he said. "I suspect that's exactly what he was trying to do with the snake. Poor Joey. Ike got the wrong person. It's more important than ever for you to tell Aunt Libby and soon. You don't want her to find out from someone other than you. If she did, she'd never get over it."

"Yes, I know," Hap said. "I will, just as soon as we get back."

Then Hap reached into his pocket and grabbed his notepad and pen. He turned to Burton.

"Tell me more about the deaths."

"Juliianna was building a rock garden near a pond in our back yard. She turned over a large rock. She was bitten about 9:00 in the morning. I didn't get home until after eight that night and found her outside...eleven hours after the bite."

"And what about Belinda?" Hap asked.

"Belinda liked to hike these mountains. She took long walks in the mountains, on back trails that only she knew about. On the last hike, she was gone for a full day. Ike was visiting a friend in Huntsville, gone for two days. Caillin was with Libby."

"In other words," Hap said as he scribbled in his pad, "no one was home for two days to know whether or not Belinda returned safely from her hike."

Burton shook his head. "Ike reported her missing. We called a search party and found her about a mile or so from the house. Strange, isn't it? She made it all the way down the mountain and died only a mile from her home."

"So, what about the snake?"

"We never found it. I guessed the size from the tiny punctures."

Hap put his hand on Burton's shoulder. "I'm sorry about Julianna."

"Three years... you'd think a fellow could get over it. But she helped you out. That was her way."

"I beg your pardon?"

"I had been visiting her grave and was on my way back to the Cove. And then, there you boys were. Stuck on the side of the road to nowhere! I took it as a sign from my sweet Juls that I was supposed to be there to lend a hand."

Hap smiled at him. "Next time you visit, tell her I said thank you."

Burton nodded, wiped a hand across his forehead, and cleared his throat.

"I'd say we've got a real problem on our hands, wouldn't you?" he said to them.

"Yes, I'd say so," Wheelan answered. "These monitoring devices could become controlling devices."

"That's a little far-fetched," Hap said. "Remote controls for snakes?"

The three of them looked at one another, then at the snake in the container, then back at each other. The same thought crossed their minds simultaneously. "Put the lid on that thing," Hap said, "and make sure it's on tight!"

44

At 6:15, when the three of them left the hospital, the early morning sky embraced them in a soft orange delight. Hap said that he'd never seen an orange sky before. Burton and Wheelan said nothing. They had both seen it plenty of times...Mother Nature's caution signal, her proverbial calm before the storm. They climbed into Burton's car and headed toward Cove's End. Too exhausted to talk, they traveled along in separate worlds admiring the wondrous sights of the mountains. Ancient, towering oak trees rose as proud kings along the landscape. As the men drove further up the mountain, each one noticed, deep in the crevices of the mountainside, the pristine waters of natural springs etched by years of nature's sculpting. Alongside the road, bright purple blooms amid a flourish of dense emerald leaves appeared at steady intervals...tiny royal sentinels guarding the majestic oaks. Enthroned above it all, from Mother Nature's palette issued a billowing angel whose feathery white wings enfolded her artistry with a brilliant orange caress. The hypnotic purr of the engine as it braced itself for the steep climb entranced them all in silent whirls of fragmentary illusions...reflections of promise, pain, and absolute terror.

As Burton neared the restaurant, he could barely remember the drive up the mountain. It was as if he had stepped out of the hospital and presto...he was at Cove's Inn. He glanced around to make sure his passengers were all right, then lowered his eyes lest the men discover his mental lapse. "I'm going back to work," he said. "Lots to do. You boys hold down the fort for me and call if you need me before I get back. Wheelan, be sure to check on your mother and Libby. And Hap, give my sympathies to Joey's father. I'm real sorry about the kid."

Hap nodded and was about to wave and leave when he felt a slight tremor beneath his feet. "Don't worry," Wheelan said. "It's just another one of Mother Nature's warnings."

"Another? Did I miss one?"

"Yes, this illusion above you: the orange sky. Reminds me of Dreamsicles. I used to love those things."

"Yeah, me, too. So, this is a warning?"

"This illusion, my friend, hides the only *real* monster in Preacher's Cove."

They both looked up, awestruck by the sheer beauty of this wonder of nature. Hap turned to walk back to the room and felt the hair on the back of his neck prickle. "What else could possibly happen?" he asked, rubbing his neck to soothe it.

But then, he was in Preacher's Cove. God's little corner of the world...where just about anything could happen. He was almost at the door of Eagle's room when he stopped and stood dead still. A sharp pain pierced his right eye. "Oh, God," he whispered, "not again."

Flashes of his dreams darted across his mind, the images almost blinding. Strobe light pictures of the coffin, the woman inside it, the woman in the river, the snake, the tall man—one right after the other—bombarded him. The baby, dead, blue, its face covered with thick clear slime. The images zoomed closer, every detail of them crystal clear. He saw the tall man looking down at the coffin as clumps of dirt slapped across it. He felt the tremble of the earth, saw the coffin lid set askew, revealing the corpse's hand. Porcelain-white skin showed through streaks of blood. In the palm of the hand was a small round mark. This time, though, the images disappeared as quickly as they had flashed into his mind. Hap shook his head to clear it and steadied himself on one of the columns of the walkway.

"Hey, are you okay?" For a split second, Hap thought it was Joey talking to him. He smiled and looked up to see Eagle standing in the doorway. Disappointment washed over him and revealed itself in the look on his face. "Hap, are you all right?" Eagle asked.

Hap answered, "For a minute there, I thought you were the kid. I have these weird pictures in my brain, and...never mind."

"You hoped I was Joey. Come on in and sit down and then I want you to tell me about those pictures."

Hap sat down on the edge of one of the beds. "Is he here yet?" he asked. "Has he called?"

"No, not yet. Tell me about the pictures."

"Weird pictures. Probably just stress." Hap said.

"Can you be a little more specific than just 'weird'?"

Eagle got up, went over to the counter and opened a cooler. He grabbed two cans of soda and handed one to Hap.

"Thanks," Hap said. "The pictures are nothing to worry about. I've been having these attacks since...well, for a long time. They've been a little different since we've been in Preacher's Cove, though. Same images from the dreams. I told you, it's probably just stress."

Hap congratulated himself, once again, on his expert lying. It wasn't stress. He believed that the woman in the coffin had something to do with Libby and Lucy. And the tall man was a dead ringer for Wheelan. He couldn't explain any rational connection, but the similarities of the mark, the snake, the same color hair and skin. Too many similarities to be merely coincidence.

"Something's wrong," Hap said. "I have to go see Libby for a minute. I'll be back as soon as I can. If Joey's dad calls, please meet him at the airport. I'll see him as soon as I can."

"Hap, listen. I barely know Joey's dad. He wants you to meet him, not me. And what do you mean that something's wrong? With whom, with what? Every time I turn around, you're running off somewhere. What is it with you and this place? I mean, geez, I know you're a reporter. I've seen you chase stories before, but I've never seen you this way."

Eagle stood up and glared down at Hap. "You're obsessed with this place and these people. And we've got the story. Joey sacrificed his life, but by God, he gave us a story. Face it, man, there's no other story here except the one you're gonna write about that kid. So, just let it be. Let's meet Mr. Donovan and then get out of here."

"We don't have anything on Ike Madison, yet. And we're not leaving until we do. I know how this looks, Eagle. Believe me. I know exactly how it looks, but I need your help here. Please, bear with me just a little while longer. When it's over, I'll explain everything, but right now, I don't have time. Something is wrong, and I'm the only one who can fix it. I can't give you a better explanation than that. Okay?"

Eagle finished the soda in one big gulp, and looked at his friend. He shook his head, shrugged his shoulders and motioned toward the door. "Do what you've gotta do, man," he said. "But you're not doing this by yourself again. I'm not going back to face James without any pictures. So as soon as Donovan gets here and gets settled, I'm finding you and we're gonna take care of this together. Do what you've gotta do right now, but in an hour or so, I'll be right there beside you, taking pictures...recording these precious moments for posterity!"

Hap smiled and patted his friend on the shoulder. "I knew I could count on you," he said. "If I'm not back here in a while, I'll be in one of two places. Libby's house—it's as far as you can go down at the end of the property—or a place Wheelan showed me called the Hallows. Take a left when you leave the parking lot and go about two or three miles. The sign's old and beat up, but if you watch, you'll see it. Think you can find it?"

"Yeah, I think so," Eagle said.

"I'm supposed to stay with Libby—and Wheelan—tonight...."

"You dog!"

Hap smiled and shook his head. Eagle just looked at him and nodded.

"I'll be as glad to leave this place, and everything in it, as you are."

"Well, that sounds real convincing, man. Keep talking and maybe you'll believe it yourself," Eagle claimed.

Hap waved to him and opened the door to leave, but instead of walking out, he stopped dead still.

A familiar stranger stood at the door.

45

A girl wearing sunglasses, her red hair pulled back into a pony-tail, stared up at him. Her hand was raised as if she had been caught in mid-knock. She put her hand down quickly, lowered her head, and mumbled something Hap couldn't quite hear.

"Caillin?"

"Yes, sir?"

"What are you doing here?"

The girl turned to look behind her and then on both sides down the long, planked walkways. Hap stepped closer to her and looked around. He saw nothing suspicious.

"Is something wrong?" Hap asked. "Would you like to come in?"

He stepped back away from the doorway. The girl looked around once more, then slipped into the room. With her arms folded in front of her, she stood very still and said nothing. Hap looked at Eagle as if to ask what to do next. Eagle shrugged and lifted his hands to signal that he didn't have a clue. The girl took off her sunglasses and Hap knew why she had worn them. Her eyes were swollen and red-rimmed, her cheeks tear-stained and hollow. Her pale skin seemed even paler against the dark rings under her eyes. In that face was little trace of the beautiful young girl that attracted Joey. Hap looked at Eagle once again.

"Miss, would you like a soda?" Eagle asked. "It's a little warm outside. Something cool to drink might...." His voice trailed off when the girl spoke.

"I'm so sorry about Joey," she said. "I just wanted to tell you."

"He was a good kid," Hap said and sat down on the foot of the bed right across from the chair where the girl sat. Eye level usually worked best for him. "Thank you for coming here to tell us."

"My father," she whispered.

The words cut through Hap like a knife in his heart. For a split second, he thought that she had somehow found out about him. He looked at her, his mouth forming words to speak, but his brain sending no message. He couldn't tell her, not right now. He had to tell Libby first. Then he had to get information about Ike Madison so that he could send him away. So much to do. "My father," she said once again.

She looked at Hap and began to whimper like a frightened child. Neither Hap nor Eagle knew what to do, so they did nothing except exchange nervous looks. Two grown men were no match for the tears of a trembling teenage female. "It was very nice of your father to come to the hospital," he said and immediately felt his face flush. Lies seemed to be the order of the day.

"He's..." she whispered again.

"He's what, Caillin? Please, if you need help, just tell us." Hap said, the charmer in him emerging at last. "Is there something about your father that I should know?"

He got up, then, and sat closer to the girl. He reached over and patted her small, cold hands.

"Be careful," she said. "Just be careful."

"Why?" he asked.

The girl wiped her eyes, put on her sunglasses and walked to the door. Hap jumped up and opened it for her. She looked up at him one last time before she left.

"I'm next in line," she said and walked out the door. "He'll never let it happen."

Hap hurried after her. "Caillin," he said. "Please don't go. We'll do everything we can to help you, but we need to know more."

The girl stopped and looked back at him. She slid her sunglasses down to the tip of her nose and stared at Hap. He looked back, directly into her eyes. He stepped toward her, held out his hand, and waited. She pushed her sunglasses back into place, glanced around, and gently touched his fingers. "He's watching," she said. "I must get back home."

Hap looked out onto the parking lot, scanning each car for the limo that he'd seen Madison climb into at the hospital. Then he looked out across the street. Parked parallel to the sentinel of trees sat a large black car, its engine purring. The windows, almost black themselves, protected the passenger from the prying eyes of reporters. Slowly, the window by the passenger side lowered about two inches. All Hap could see was a pale forehead topped with black hair. He glanced down at Caillin, but she had disappeared, scampered away like a frightened little animal. He looked back inside and saw Eagle standing a few feet behind him. The two men stared at each other for a few seconds, both of them mystified at the girl and the visit.

"Okay," Eagle said. "She got my attention. This place gets creepier by the second, but I'm going to hang around just to find out what she meant by that."

"She's scared," Hap said to Eagle. "I have to get something big on Ike Madison. Caillin's scared out of her mind. I don't know why she came here, but it's obvious that she needs our help."

"Another stellar example of the kid's idea."

"Huh?"

"You just happened to be in the right place at the right time. So, your job now is to find us a story so big that we'll be buckin' for a Pulitzer."

"And more importantly, that will help us save my daughter's life. I have something to tell you, Eagle. Let's sit down for a minute."

46

On his walk down to the office, Hap could hear the elusive "Billy Whoever" playing the harmonica, sending eerie strains of "Edelweiss" across Preacher's Cove. As he went in the front doors, the bell over the door rang to announce his entrance. He nodded at the clerk and walked over to the mantle above the fireplace. The pictures seemed more familiar than before, each one a step back into the past. Behind the framed family photos was a smaller one, a sepia-toned portrait of a young woman who looked very much like Libby. The clothes and hairstyle seemed early 1900s, but except for those, there was such a remarkable resemblance that Hap picked up the photo to see if there might be a name on it, or a date...anything that would identify the woman.

"Late 1800s," a familiar voice whispered.

Hap turned around to see Wheelan standing beside him. He wondered how he had come through the doors without the bell announcing his arrival.

"The photo," he said. "Late 1800s when sepia was popular... and cheap."

"She looks so much like Libby."

"Yes, she does. It's a family trait. All the women look alike. Small-framed with red hair and green eyes. My mother and Aunt Libby, and Belinda if you noticed, used to look exactly alike. Lots of twins in this family."

"Who is she?" Hap asked.

"Her name is Maribeth. She's Aunt Libby's great-great-grand-mother. She died shortly after the photo was made, so I'm told. Only twenty years old when she died."

"Something about her is so familiar," Hap said.

Wheelan shrugged and reminded his friend of the family

resemblance. As they talked about the photo, Libby walked out of her office.

"Have you heard from Joey's father yet?" she asked.

"No, but he'll be calling soon. Listen, Libby, there's something I need to tell you."

She stared up at him without smiling.

"Please, may I come into your office for a moment? It's urgent."

"Sure," she said.

She smiled at him, then, and led him into her office.

"Once I'm finished, Libby, you can decide whether or not you ever want to see me again. You probably won't feel the same when you've heard my story."

They sat down on the sofa, but Hap felt uncomfortable sitting next to Libby. He wanted, instead, to face her, so he got up, moved one of the high-back chairs close to the sofa, arranged it precisely, and sat down to face her. He studied her pretty face for a moment. Her green eyes, her porcelain-colored complexion, the soft tendrils of red hair curled daintily around her face...exactly like Taylor's. Libby filled a void for him, a void left by her younger sister sixteen years ago. He realized as he studied her that he would destroy their relationship with what he was about to tell her. His heart ached. He did not want to lose Libby, not now, especially now. But, for once in his life, he had to be completely honest. No more reporter's tricks, no more evading the truth, no more inventing. He had to be straight-forward, no matter what the cost...even if it meant losing Libby for good.

When Libby shifted her position and cleared her throat, Hap realized that his steady gaze made her uncomfortable.

"Forgive me for staring," he started and inched closer to her. When he had scooted to the very edge of his chair and was as close as he could get without actually sitting in Libby's lap, he touched her hands, neatly folded in her lap, and spoke again.

"You are such a beautiful woman, Libby," he said then immediately regretted it. She was beautiful, yes, but mentioning it now was the same as taking advantage of her feelings for him.

"Thank you. Now, please tell me what is wrong," she said, a soft smile forming on her face.

He hesitated for a few seconds, trying to find exactly the right words. Then he blurted out, "Caillin is my daughter."

The smile on Libby's face seemed to freeze. She didn't move, didn't blink her eyes, didn't speak. She stared at him with that soft smile frozen in place.

He continued, "Years ago, sixteen to be exact, I met a girl named Taylor Winters. Remember, Libby? I mentioned this when we were in the gazebo, but I didn't know it was...I didn't know that Taylor Winters was Belinda Madison. I noticed the resemblance, but it had been so long since I'd seen her that I didn't put the two together. I'm sorry, Libby. I didn't know that she was your sister."

"How did you find out?" she asked, that smile still frozen on her face.

"Burton showed me a letter that she'd written to Julianna."

Libby's expression changed, then, the frozen smile replaced by a wrinkled brow and a slight frown. Her warm hands turned icy underneath his.

"Burton knows?"

"Yes, he does, and so does Wheelan."

"So, I'm the last one you've told," she said and shook her head as if she were remembering the old adage about always the woman always being the last to know.

"No, Libby, you're not the last. I haven't told Caillin," he said, his head lowered, his voice crackling. Suddenly, Libby stood up. Hap was sure she'd had enough and would leave and never want to see him again. He braced himself to remain calm while he watched this wonderful woman walk out of his life for good.

"So, why are you just sitting there, Hap? Get your butt up and let's get started."

She walked over to him and held out her hand, a genuine smile forming on her perfect rose-colored lips. Hap sat in the chair, so surprised that he was unable to move.

"Come along," she said. "We have work to do. If Burton knows, then Ike Madison knows. Joey's death was no accident, Hap. Ike was trying to kill you."

"Caillin," he said. "She came to my room to see me, well, to tell me how sorry she was about Joey."

Libby stopped and waited for him to stand up. Then, she smiled broadly and said, "She was trying to warn you, Hap."

"She mentioned her father, but that's all she said," Hap said, "other than a warning about my being careful."

"Then, she was asking for your help, as well. And you damn well better be careful if you intend to tangle with Madison. She's right about that part."

"But, would he hurt her? How could he hurt her? It's insane," he shouted.

"Consider what he's done so far, Hap. Julianna and Belinda are dead. Snakes in your room and the workshop...*that* is insane, but it's his work. You can't take anything for granted where he is concerned."

"Caillin said she was next in line but that he'd never let it happen. I don't have a clue what she meant, but it seemed like a big deal to her. Do you know?"

Libby's heart felt like a hammer in her chest. "We have to help her," she said. Libby went to her office and picked up the phone. She pressed 2 and waited for an answer.

"Madison Manor," the voice said.

"Hello, Louisa, this is Ms. Libby. Is Caillin there?"

"Yes, Ms. Libby, I'll get her."

In a few moments, Libby heard the strained voice of her niece.

"Hello," she said.

"Caillin, I need you to come in and work this morning, if you're up to it, sweetie."

"I'm not feeling very well this morning, Aunt Libby."

"Caillin, listen. It would be better for you if you were here with me. The reporter is on his way to your house. Please get Jeffrey to bring you over here as quickly as possible. I'll explain to your father. Is he there?"

"Yes, he's here. I'll get him."

"Caillin, let Louisa get him. You find Jeffrey and tell him I said to bring you here, right this minute."

"All right, Aunt Libby."

The girl handed the phone to the housekeeper.

"Lulu, will you get Daddy to the phone?" she asked. "Aunt Libby needs to talk to him. She wants me to come to Cove's End. Can Jeffrey take me?"

"Yes, Missy. I'll call for him. But the two of you had better behave." Louisa reached up and pressed a button on a keypad. "Jeffrey," she said. "Miss Caillin needs to go to Cove's End immediately."

"Okee dokee," he said. "I'll meet her out back."

Louisa nodded at Caillin. She wondered how the child would have managed without them, especially without her Jeffrey. He loved the girl like his own. He had taken over all the fatherly duties. He talked to her, taught her how to drive, listened to her problems, and comforted her when her real father became unbearable. He had become her surrogate grandfather, and he took the job seriously. "Run along, Miss. I'll get your father to the phone. Jeffrey's waiting for you out back."

Louisa put the phone down and walked toward the study, her heels clicking on the marble flooring in the foyer. She looked back to make sure the girl had left the house; then she knocked softly on the door.

"Come in," the voice called.

When she opened the door, she saw Reverend Madison pacing back and forth, his Bible in his hands. She had seen him practice his sermon this way many times before.

"I am sorry to interrupt your work, Reverend, but Ms. Libby would like to speak to you on the phone."

"Thank you, Louisa. Close the door as you leave," he said. "And Louisa, the next time you hear me practicing my sermon, please be kind enough not to disturb me. Haven't we talked about this before? I do not want to be disturbed when I'm trying to perfect a message to my sheep. Don't you know how important my job here is?"

"Yes, sir. I'm sorry, sir."

She left the study and closed the door, but not before she heard Ike mumble, "Moron."

Louisa sighed and walked back to hang up the phone in the living room. "I'm not a moron," she whispered to herself. Sometimes, she wondered why she stayed with him, why she had endured his insults for almost twenty years, but then she remembered his father, Isaiah, the kindest man she'd ever known. He had given her a job when no one else would hire her and her husband. He not only gave them jobs, but he paid them very well and trusted them with everything in the house. She made allowances for his snotty son because she loved and respected his father. When he died, she and Jeffrey were sure that the young reverend would fire them, but he didn't. He assured them that their places were secure, as long as they did exactly as he wanted. By then, they had grown so attached to little Caillin that they didn't want to leave, especially when her mother died. The girl was different. She needed them. So, they stayed and put up with the young reverend because they loved the girl and because he didn't change their salaries. There was nowhere in the Cove that they could work and make the money Reverend Isaiah paid them. "Louisa!" Ike yelled. "Be still my heart," she whispered. "He calls."

She went immediately to the study.

"Where is Caillin?" he demanded.

Louisa didn't know exactly what to say. She didn't know what Ms. Libby had told him and she didn't want to get the girl in trouble.

"Are you deaf *and* mute?" Ike said.

He continued the pacing with his Bible in hand.

"Tell her she should get dressed for work. My sister-in-law needs her."

47

With a cue from Libby, Hap followed her out of the office. Her pace was quick, her footsteps light as she scurried out the door, into the lobby, and out onto the planked flooring outside. He ran as quickly as he could to keep up. When they finally reached the house, she bolted up the steps and slung open the door. "Wheelan!" she yelled. Her nephew came into the room, his eyes red-rimmed and bloodshot.

"Hap's explained things to me," Libby said. "I've called for Caillin to come in to work. I want you to take Hap out to Madison Manor. Get Louisa to let you in. Maybe the two of you can rattle him a little. Should I call Burton to go with you?"

"No, Burton's working on something. He's got a lead on something Ike's done. I think he wants to follow up. He'll do more good if he can get some tangible evidence," Wheelan said, rubbing his eyes.

"Fine," Hap said. "Let's go."

"I'll go get the car," Wheelan said. "I'll meet you here in a couple of minutes."

"No, meet me at the room. I need to see if Joey's dad has called."

"I'm going to call Louisa again and tell her you're coming. She'll see that you get in," Libby said. "Ike doesn't like unannounced visits, but Louisa will be thrilled when I explain things."

Wheelan nodded and they both went in opposite directions. As he walked to the room, Hap looked once again across the street. The mighty oaks stood tall and majestic. He nodded in their direction. "We could use some help," he whispered to them.

His footsteps heralded by the creaks on the planked floor, he strode to the room, stopped once again and looked at the trees, and opened the door. Eagle sat in one of the chairs, drinking another soda.

"Hi," he said to Eagle. "Did Donovan call?"

"Yep," he said, "he called a few minutes ago. I'm going to meet him at the airport. Then he's coming here to make the arrangements. He was pretty angry that you weren't coming with me."

"Sorry, man. I'll make it up to you...and to him. Did Mr. James call?"

"Yep, he called, too. Says he faxing something to Chief Burton Riggs that you'll want to see. I swear I thought I could hear the old coot laughing."

"Yeah," Hap said. "I need to tell him how things are going."

"I wish you'd tell me!" Eagle said.

"I'm going to go see Ike Madison. Wheelan's going to take me."

"What for?" Eagle asked. "I mean, do you have anything we can use against him?"

"Not yet," Hap said. "But it's rolling along nicely."

"Whatever you say, buddy, but don't forget that once I get back here with Donovan and get him squared away, I'm finding you, and I'm bringing the video camera."

The horn outside signaled that Wheelan was waiting.

"Gotta run. See you in a little while."

Eagle waved but didn't look at him.

"If I'm not back within an hour or so, I'm counting on you to find me. I might need a rescue."

Eagle smiled then and nodded.

Hap walked out to the Jeep and climbed in. "Ready?" Wheelan asked.

"As I'll ever be," Hap said.

They drove the three miles to The Estates, turned in, and saw The Manor immediately. The gold cross reflected the sunlight like a beacon. "It's his calling card, of sorts," Wheelan said, pointing toward the cross.

"Yes," Hap said. "Burton brought me out here. The cross isn't nearly as spectacular as that stained-glass window. It's amazing."

"Oh, yeah," Wheelan said and rolled his eyes. "Not many people can take a beautiful work of art and turn it into a beacon of destruction."

"What do you mean?" Hap asked.

"That stained-glass window is what Madison uses as his whip... you know, to keep the parishioners in line. He calls it his Eye of God, and he uses it as a powerful weapon."

"But all the homes have them, right? So, how can Madison use his against them?"

"Well, the homes have them because of Belinda. She and Julianna found a local artist who needed work desperately when these homes were being built, and as it turned out, Ike liked the guy so much that he hired him."

"Who?" Hap asked.

"Billy Ray, the harmonica player, is also the artist who designed these windows. He didn't create them, but he helped Ike design them. And Ike's twisted it so much that the parishioners—especially the ones who don't live in the Estates—and that's about seventy percent of them—believe that Ike was inspired by God to have Billy Ray create these just for him. Ike's a sneaky, conniving sort. You can't imagine the influence he has over this town."

"These places are like palaces," Hap said. "They are absolutely astounding."

"Well, we're a small town, but there's a lot of money here. Lots of wealth."

"The one down the street there is really beautiful. It's unique," Hap said.

"You can tell the Chief next time you see him. He'll be pleased."

"Ratty old Riggs lives in that house?"

Wheelan laughed at the look of shock on Hap's face.

"Don't let him fool you, Hap. I thought you'd be a better judge of character than that."

"So tell me," Hap said.

"Well, Ratty old Riggs graduated magna cum laude from Sewanee University, then went to Yale and finished a Ph.D. in Criminal Justice. You know what they say. A book and its cover. He came back to Preacher's Cove because he was in love with Julianna. Burton built that house for her. Actually, she built it for herself and for him. Burton's parents and grandparents were some of the wealthiest around. Don't tell him I said it, though. He doesn't like to talk about it."

"So all of his joking about your being so educated?" Hap said as they pulled into a long winding drive that circled the Madison place.

"Just another load of crap," Wheelan said. "He tries to maintain an image of a country bumpkin police chief. I think it gives him an edge because people underestimate him."

"He got me!" Hap said. They stepped out of the Jeep and stood at the bottom of a set of bright white steps that led up to the porch of the main house. Six enormous white columns graced the front of the porch, staunch sentinels guarding the entrance to hallowed ground.

"Let's go," Wheelan said.

They walked up the steps and stood at the front double doors, massive wooden structures embellished with ornate carvings. Above the doors, perfectly centered, was a stained-glass rendering of Jesus surrounded by a flock of sheep.

"My father carved the doors," Wheelan said. "You're kidding," Hap said. "They are works of art."

"My father was a carpenter, but more of an artist," Wheelan said. "He could do practically anything with his hands. If he could picture something in his mind, he could craft it in wood. He made a good living because people loved his work. But, the important thing to him was creating something of lasting beauty."

"You have a very talented family. I can see that none of that talent rubbed off on you, though!" Hap said and laughed.

The double doors swung wide and a short, pudgy dark-haired woman wearing a maid's uniform stood before them.

"May I help you?" she asked with a definite Spanish accent.

"Hello, Louisa. How are you?" Wheelan asked.

"Oh, Mr. Wheelan, nice to see you again. I just spoke with Ms. Libby. She sounded good. And your mother? How is she these days?"

"She's doing well, Louisa. She's working more than ever, I think."

"The dolls, oh, they are so beautiful. Every time I go in Miss

Caillin's room, I have to remind myself that it isn't a real child sitting in that little rocker."

She laughed a nervous little titter of laughter, wrung her hands, and looked at Hap.

"How is Jeffrey?"

"Oh, he is fine, just fine, busy as always. Lots to do 'round here."

"Is Reverend Madison at home?" Hap asked. Wheelan looked at him as if he'd made a grand faux-pas.

"Louisa, this is Mr. Murray. He is a reporter from Channel 12. If the Reverend is home, we'd like to visit with him for just a few minutes."

"I'm sorry," she said, "about the young man who died. He was Miss Caillin's friend."

"Yes, he was, and thank you," Hap said in his most gracious Southern tone.

"I will see if Reverend Madison is accepting visitors. Please, come in and wait."

When they walked into the enormous foyer, Hap was stunned. His eyes widened, his jaw dropped open, and he inhaled sharply. Marble flooring, lavish antique furnishings, beautiful art work, and an enormous crystal chandelier...it was something out of a movie.

At the end of the foyer rose a sweeping staircase that widened as it reached the next floor. The banisters were brightly polished and beautifully carved. Thick white carpet covered the stairs, and against the background of marble and bright gold, gave the look of a magical palace. "Please, follow me. Reverend Madison will be with you shortly," Louisa said.

They moved into another spacious, elegant room decorated with thick green carpet, long white draperies, and white wicker furniture with a floral pattern covering it. Ferns hung in the huge bay windows, four of them surrounding the room, each with a cushioned window seat that matched the pattern on the furniture. In the center of the room, rays of sunlight shone through two vast skylights.

"Feels as if you're in a garden, doesn't it?" Louisa asked.

"Glorious," Hap said. "I've never seen anything like it."

"It was Mrs. Madison's favorite room," she said.

Hap could imagine her working in this room, reading a book and sipping tea. He could almost see her talking to the flowers, insisting they would grow if only they had her voice as a guide.

"Please, sit down. The Reverend will be right in," Louisa said.

When they had been sitting only a moment or two, Louisa emerged again carrying a tray filled with two large glasses of iced tea, an elegant china bowl brimming with all manner of raw vegetables with crackers and dip on the side, and a small matching plate of cookies.

"Help yourselves," she said.

"Thank you, Louisa," Wheelan said. "It looks delicious. Everything is stunning, as usual."

She smiled and nodded then left the room. Twenty minutes later, when they had almost finished their tea and devoured the goodies, Ike Madison walked in.

"Gentlemen," he called. "How good of you to visit."

Hap and Wheelan stood up immediately. Once again, the Reverend displayed immaculate style, his suit and shoes perfect, right down to the gold and diamond cufflinks and tasseled wing-tips. A striking figure of a man, Ike Madison commanded attention. Wheelan held out his hand. "Nice to see you, Ike."

They shook hands briefly. Ike grabbed a napkin from the tray and wiped his hands. Hap extended his before he realized what Ike had done. He shook. Ike wiped.

"Hap Murray," he said to Hap. "Welcome to my home. I trust you find it pleasing."

"Beyond measure," Hap said. "It is truly magnificent."

Ike smiled and sat down on one of the wicker chairs.

"Please, sit down, gentlemen. How may I be of service to you today?"

Hap spoke quickly, afraid that he would decide against speaking at all. "Reverend, I wanted to ask about your daughter."

The expression on Ike Madison's face froze, as if some mechanism in his brain had ground suddenly to a halt. "My daughter," he said, the expression on his face unwavering, with no hint of emotion in his fixed eyes.

"Yes, Reverend," Hap continued, "she seemed upset by Joey's death. I just wanted to make sure that she was all right."

"You've seen my Caillin, have you?"

"Only briefly when she came by to tell us how sorry she was about Joey."

Ike stared at Hap with such intensity that Hap could almost feel the piercing gaze. He knew, then and there, that he had angered Madison to the point of action. Although his heart fairly hammered in his chest, he did not shift in his seat. He stared back at Ike Madison with equal intensity.

Eventually, Madison spoke. "So you drove out here to inquire about the health and well-being of my daughter," Ike said. With his words, the expression on his face finally changed. He shifted his gaze to Wheelan. "Wheelan, you should have told Mr. Murray that my daughter's concerns are certainly none of his. I'm sure that his time could have been spent in a much more productive manner, given the unfortunate circumstances of losing a young friend to tragedy. How disappointing it must be for the family, in these most critical moments, to realize that you are occupying yourself with other matters." Ike Madison stood up. Immediately, Hap and Wheelan followed his lead. Ike walked over to the wall which held the keypad. He pushed one large white button. Louisa answered immediately.

"Yes, Reverend," she said.

"Louisa, the gentlemen are ready to leave. Will you kindly show them to the door?"

"Right away, sir."

In seconds, Louisa appeared in the parlor's doorway.

"Gentlemen," he called from across the room, "feel free to visit anytime, whenever I may be of service. And Mr. Murray, don't hesitate to call if the grieving parents need my services. When family and friends are unavailable, assistance must come from the kindness and wisdom of a stranger."

Then he turned and walked across the marble foyer, his shoes clacking against the glossy surface. He opened the door to his study, went in and slammed it shut without looking back at either of them. Louisa winced when she heard the door slam. "You'd better be going now," she whispered to Wheelan. "The Reverend is very busy today."

As they left the house and walked towards the Jeep, Wheelan called to Louisa, "Louisa, would it be all right if I showed my friend the gardens before we leave?"

She hesitated, then nodded in agreement.

"The gardens?" Hap whispered. "You want me to see the gardens after I've just been insulted and thrown out of the house?"

"Smile," Wheelan said. "Ike takes great pride in the gardens. Maybe it will make up for your asking him so bluntly about Caillin. That was kind of stupid, don't you think? I mean, you're a reporter, for God's sake. Couldn't you think of a more appropriate question?"

"I wanted to make him angry enough to make a move. Maybe I screwed up. I'm sorry. I know the rules: never go into an interview—and unless you're talking to yourself, you're in an interview—never go in unprepared. But with that man sitting across from me, all I could think of was the look on Caillin's face and the sound of fear in her voice. Besides, he knew I had seen her, Wheelan. He was parked across the street watching the girl. Madison is some piece of work."

"And of all the things to ask about, you asked him about Caillin, in a very personal way, I might add."

"Well, she came to my room, for Christ's sake. Something is wrong in this house, and I have to find out what it is."

"You'll never get in again. You know that, don't you? You've committed the ultimate sin, and I'm sure that Ike knows the whole story."

"Exactly! He set me up to die by snakebite, did the same thing to your mother, and killed my friend. There's no telling what else he'll do. I'm not leaving until I have some proof that I can use against him."

"I understand, but did you happen to think that maybe Caillin came by simply out of respect for Joey? Caillin's unusual, very timid. Don't read into that brief meeting—and your newly-found feelings—something that isn't there."

As they moved across the expansive grounds of the manor, someone came from the side of the house and almost ran into the two of them. Startled by the encounter, a bearded man in overalls gasped and grabbed his chest.

"What the...."

"Billy Ray?" Wheelan asked. "Whew, that was a close one. I wasn't expecting anyone else to be out here," he said and wiped his brow with an old handkerchief that he'd grabbed from his back pocket. "I was just about to show Mr. Murray the gardens. He's leaving soon, and I didn't want him to miss out on seeing such a beautiful display as that of the Reverend's gardens."

"Yep, that'd be a shame," Billy Ray said. "I'm the gardener, handy-man, too. I do just about everything for the Reverend."

Hap held out his hand. "I'm Hap Murray. I'm a reporter for Channel 12, and I'm doing a story about Preacher's Cove. I'd love to see your gardens, Billy Ray."

The three of them walked around to the far end of the grounds. As they approached, Hap looked up and was amazed at the size of the house. It seemed to go on forever, with rooms and side rooms everywhere. A winding covered walkway on the back led to even more rooms attached fifty yards or so away from the main house. Hap could see what seemed to be two additional small cottages at the end of the additional rooms.

"Good grief," he said. "How many people live in this house?"

"Four, I think," Wheelan said. "Ike, Caillin, Louisa and Jeffrey. They live on the east wing, I believe."

"Yep, that's right," Billy Ray said, "and me, you forgot about me. I live way out there in that first cottage. Me and the missus. We got our own driveway. The Reverend's good to us."

They walked further along the grounds until they came to two large Doric columns, the entrance to the gardens. Enormous oak trees grew at the sides of the columns, and just beyond them, centered perfectly, a large fountain with water gushing out, then cascading down three separate levels welcomed visitors to the Reverend's pride and joy. Colors in every shade burst from the ground in a brilliant display. The gardens obviously meant a great deal to Ike Madison. The only place Hap had ever seen that compared was the Botanical Gardens in Birmingham. "Roses are in full bloom. Pretty, ain't they?" Billy Ray asked.

"It's like the house," Hap said. "Truly magnificent. I don't know much about flowers, but these have to be some of the prettiest I've ever seen. If my photographer were here, I'd ask if I could get a picture."

When Billy Ray heard that, he launched into a discourse on each species of plant in the garden, how it grew best, and what his particular gardening secrets happened to be.

As he talked, Wheelan surveyed, as inconspicuously as possible, the rooms attached to the house. He had visited the Manor several times but hadn't noticed the room at the farthest end. He wondered how long it had been there, and then figured it had been there all along. He'd just failed to notice it.

"Billy Ray," he interrupted, "these rooms on the back are fairly new, aren't they? I've never noticed them before...not that I've been here that much, but...."

"Yep," he said. "Them two on the back there was just built a few years ago. Three maybe. 'Course, the first one's been here since the house was built. But the others are fairly new. I helped build 'em."

"Look at the time," Hap said. "I really need to get back to the hotel."

"Thank you, Billy Ray," Wheelan said, "for showing the gardens. We appreciate it."

"You bet. Y'all come back anytime. Hey, and bring that photographer fella with you next time. The Reverend would love that."

"See you later, Billy Ray. We can find our way out."

"Hey, Mister," he called to Hap. "I was sorry to hear about your friend. You be careful, now. Some of these snakes 'round here, well, they can be a might ornery unless you know how to handle them."

48

The two of them walked across the grounds until they came to the winding driveway in the front of the house. Just as they climbed into the Jeep, they saw a white limousine drive around the side of the house and disappear. "Jeffrey," Wheelan said. "He's the chauffeur."

"I've never known a small-town preacher who made the kind of money it takes to have all this. What's his sideline?"

"No one knows, for sure, although his family owns a good deal of property. He owns the whole stretch of land on which The Estates are built."

"Madison owns all this?"

"Yes, his great-great grandfather bought this land and most of Preacher's Cove, so naturally, he named it after himself!"

"That's what Madison meant when he said this was *his* town. Of course, it's his if he owns most of it."

"No, not the whole town, just part of it. The rest of it is owned by several different people, Aunt Libby among them. She owns the land on which Cove's End is built. It's some prime acreage now, especially since Best Western has been making offers."

"Best Western? The hotel chain? They want Cove's End?"

"Oh yeah. They've been after it for a couple of years now. Aunt Libby would be set for life if she sold, but then, she is pretty much set as it is. She doesn't really need the money, and she'd never sell that place. She built it from nothing and has spent all of her adult life making it the place it is now. She loves it. She and Mother are at home there."

"How did she buy the land? I know she didn't have a lot of money before Cove's End became famous. What happened to bring in the money for all that land?"

"Isaiah Madison, Ike's father. He sold it to her for $1,000."

"What? Prime property like that?"

"Isaiah loved my Aunt Libby, and before that, he loved my mother. He was good to both of them, especially after Mother was hurt. He was so impressed with Aunt Libby's skills and with Mother's artistry—he owned four of the Firelight Angels—that he sold her the land so that she would never have to worry about a place to live."

"Good Lord! I'll bet Ike didn't like that."

"Actually, Ike didn't know anything about it until his father died a couple of years ago. He found out when the will was read. When Isaiah drew up the deed to all the properties he owned he divided it two-fold. One half went to Aunt Libby, the other to Mother."

"And who inherits from them?"

"A little nosy, aren't we?"

"I'm a reporter, remember? I'm naturally nosy."

"We'd better get out of here."

Wheelan started the Jeep and drove down the winding driveway. As they left, the two of them could see Ike Madison staring at them from behind a partially drawn set of drapes in the study.

"Creepy, isn't he?" Wheelan said.

"Yeah, so who inherits after Libby and your mother?"

"Caillin and I get the majority of it. Ike gets the remainder, but it isn't very much. He'll have the land his house is on, a few acres more, and the land the church is on."

"I'll bet Ike doesn't like that very much."

Wheelan chuckled. "Not one little bit, but he'll just have to deal with it. Anyway, it's done. Family business."

"You're right," Hap said. "It's none of my business."

"If you have time, I need to go by the Hallows. Is that all right with you?"

"Sure," Hap said. They drove out of The Estates and took the on-ramp to Highway 24. The distant rumbling of thunder persisted, and as they drove, they heard Billy Ray's harmonica. Strains of "Edelweiss" again drifted across the mountainous terrain. The wind grew stronger, bending the limbs of some of the smaller trees along the highway. The sky seemed a little darker than when they had left Madison Manor, the air heavy with moisture. When they reached the dilapidated sign that marked the Hallows, Wheelan turned in and drove as far up into the wooded area as the Jeep would go. "We have to hurry," he said. "I know the look and the smell of this sky."

They climbed out of the Jeep and hiked the trail up to the Hallows, pushing aside tree limbs that hung so far down that they brushed the ground. A clap of thunder roared in the sky. After fifteen minutes of fighting overgrowth, they plowed through the last of it and into the open area of the digging site. Another thunderclap bellowed across the mountains. Wheelan picked up shovel and pushed it into the ground at the center of the site. He used his foot, positioned carefully at the top of the scoop, to drive it through the rocks and dirt, only to find more rocks and dirt. He drove it a second time while Hap watched. Finally, on the third try, the shovel struck something different, something unyielding.

"What is it?" Hap asked.

"I don't know," Wheelan said, struggling to talk and breathe at the same time. "Help me with this. I'll use the axe. You take the shovel. We need to remove the dirt around it carefully."

Meticulously, Wheelan maneuvered the axe so that it barely grazed the dirt, yet moved it, bit by bit, away from the object. Hap, not as skillful as his friend, shoveled the dirt in clumps that fell back into the ground when he tried to remove them. With both of them working, they managed to clear away two feet of earth. Out of breath but eager to continue, to see his treasure, Wheelan asked Hap to stop while he used his hands to dig a little deeper. The treasure beckoned to him, irresistible in its song. A third blast of thunder exploded around them.

"Geez!" Hap yelled. "Let's get out of here."

"Bear with me for just a few more minutes," Wheelan said as he scooped more handfuls of dirt from around the buried treasure. "We're still quite safe. I know these storms, remember? I'll know when we need to leave."

Suddenly, Hap looked beyond Wheelan and into the sky. His

jaw dropped open as he watched a lightning bolt strike the ground only yards from where they stood. "We have to get out of here, Doc. I can't take it." Hap said. "I don't think I can...."

"Just a few more minutes, please," Wheelan said.

"I, uh, I think I'm going to throw up," Hap said.

Wheelan looked up from his work and stopped when he saw Hap's pale complexion and sunken eyes. "I'm sorry, Hap. I didn't realize that you were serious. If you can give me five more minutes, I promise that I'll finish up. Okay?"

Hap nodded.

"Approximately one hundred fifty million volts of electricity per strike," Wheelan said, "each one heating the atmosphere to almost 60,000 degrees Fahrenheit. But remember, only about a hundred people die each year from lightning strikes. You're more likely to get eaten by a shark or hit by a diesel truck."

"Well, of those one hundred people who die each year, how many of them live here? I mean, Jesus, Doc, ten people died right here not two weeks ago."

Wheelan stopped his scooping again and looked at his friend. He wiped his hands on his pants, wiped his forehead, and stood up. He fished inside one of the large crates in an unusually large, make-shift tent, the bottom of which was precisely formed atop a pebbled floor. On top of the rocks was a large piece of canvas spread evenly across the stones. And on top of the canvas was a rolled-out sleeping bag. He grabbed a large piece of canvas from inside. As he spread it over the spot that held his treasure, he looked up again at Hap.

"Will you get a couple of those stakes out of the crate for me? I'll tie this down and take you back to the hotel."

Hap took a deep breath, forced his feet and hands to move and obliged him. He reached into the crate and felt several large metal stakes inside. He grabbed two of them and turned around to hand them to Wheelan. A thunderous blast came again from the sky, and Hap dropped the two stakes. The ground beneath them trembled slightly, and as the tremors shook the ground, the stakes rolled down into the hole where Wheelan had been digging. "Buggers, I'm sorry," Hap said. "I'll get them, just hold on for a minute."

He stretched himself across the open space and braced himself with his legs. Then he bent over to pick up the stakes. As he did, he looked above Wheelan's head, far beyond into the large oaks and saw one perfect silent lightning bolt strike and snake into the ground. Wheelan's treasure, still partially buried, buzzed and glowed. The two men stared at something that reminded them of a bug-zapper. It made the same sound—zapzap—and glowed with the same greenish-white fluorescent light.

49

Thirty minutes before his shift would end, his first full day at his new job, a lab technician named Roscoe made a final stop in the lab to check the results of some "stat" requests for Dr. Anderson. To his surprise, he found no other techs in the lab. The place was fairly deserted. He walked over to the workstation, checked on a few cultures, and held another up to get a closer look. Just as he raised the dish, a muffled thumping sound stopped him cold. He turned and looked behind him, but saw nothing. Roscoe held up the culture a second time. When the thumping sounded again, he jumped and almost dropped the dish. He put the culture back on the workstation, took a deep breath, and stepped towards the station on the opposite side of the room. Rumors about practical jokes in the labs—one tech in particular bragged about making fake dishes filled with red Jell-O with oatmeal bits on top, a classic botulism-looking mold—made him feel a little foolish about being nervous. "Come on, Roscoe, lighten up," he said loudly enough to convince himself.

But when the muffled thumping sounded again, it scared him so much that his hands trembled. He took another step closer to the station, leaned forward to see if he could find anything that would cause the sound, and finding nothing, took another step. The thumping grew louder and more frequent, as if someone were banging on the lid of a coffin—from the inside. One final thump, then a snap...the noise stopped. "You watch too many horror movies," he mumbled. "Your mama tried to warn you, but NO, you wouldn't listen."

Roscoe took another step toward the workstation and found an empty plastic container, the lid askew. He peered down at it. Reddish droplets lined the inside of the container. Other drops, smeared across the table top, formed a pattern, a winding pattern as if someone smeared the drops with a finger. Roscoe dipped his forefinger into the smeared liquid, rubbed it between his thumb and middle finger, smelled it, and looked at it. "Looks like blood," he said.

"Ouch!"

When he looked at the fleshy area between the thumb and forefinger on his hand, he saw two tiny puncture marks, minute droplets of blood welling from underneath each one. Instinctively, he flexed the wounded hand and cradled it against his chest. By the time he noticed the red streaks moving up his arm and toward his heart, his legs would no longer support him. As he fell, he thought he saw a small snake slither across the table. Roscoe fought to fill his lungs with air even as he hit the floor with a sickening thud—the sound of dead weight coming to a sudden stop. When his head smacked against the linoleum, he drifted mercifully into painless darkness.

50

Libby stood in front of the mantle in the office at Cove's End. The photos, some so old that they barely maintained an image, gave her a long-overdue connection to the reality of her life. She was one of them, one of the women of the Taylor Curse, one of the shareholders of the power of the Eye of God. At times, she forgot. It was so easy to allow Lucy to be the holder, so easy. There were things to do, after all, everyday things that required her attention. She couldn't let Cove's End run itself. She balanced the books, managed the restaurant, kept the assets flowing and growing. She was a busy woman, a self-made successful woman of the 21st century. When was there time to be a priestess?

But now...the photos beckoned to her. The more she looked at them, the more intense her feelings grew. She remembered stories her great-grandmother had told her, stories of women blessed with life-giving power, but cursed with merciless tragedy. She remembered, in particular, the story of Maribeth Taylor, her great great-grandmother. Maribeth, the holder of the Eye of God, died in Big Springs, bitten so savagely by giant rattlesnakes that very little of her face remained intact. Why she was in the Springs, no one knew. Only a month before her death, she gave birth to a baby boy who died, in some bizarre twist of fate, the same day that his mother did. At their funerals, deep in the forest by the circle of stones now known as The Hallows, Sidney Taylor, Maribeth's husband, walked off into the woods and was never seen again. The stories say he died of grief in those woods.

"Aunt Libby?" a voice called.

Libby jumped and looked around to see Caillin standing behind her.

"I didn't mean to startle you," Caillin said. "I need your help, yours and Aunt Lucy's."

"What's wrong, honey?" Libby asked and put her arm around the girl.

"I need to find out what happened to Joey. I've tried to see it in my mind, but I can't. Something is keeping me from being able to see. Will you help? Will you talk to Aunt Lucy?"

"Yes, sweetie. I'll do the best I can. But you must promise me that you won't give up. The power is there. Right now, your emotions are getting in the way. You will have to learn to put them aside if you are to be of help to people. Don't be afraid." The girl smiled at her and kissed her on the cheek.

"Thank you, Aunt Libby. I'd better get back to work now," she said.

"Caillin," Libby said.

"Yes, Aunt Libby?"

Libby watched the girl, the sweet innocence of her youth evident in every movement. She wondered what Caillin would do now that she knew bout her father's terrible plans. And she wondered about Hap. She wondered how Caillin would react if she ever found out that Hap Murray was her real father. "Is something wrong, Aunt Libby?"

"No, sweetie. One of these days, though, you and I need to sit down and have a long talk. There are some very important things I need to tell you." Caillin smiled at her and nodded. Then she walked away. Libby left the office and walked down the back of the complex to her house, dreading the confrontation with her sister. There was no choice now, no alternative. Caillin's pleas made her feel almost ashamed that the child had to ask for help. She stopped at the bottom of the stairs that led to her front door and stood for a few seconds listening to the voices in the air around her. One voice, that of her precious niece, compelled her to climb the stairs.

Libby walked back toward Lucy's room, listened at the door for a few seconds, and heard the steady rhythm of her breathing. She eased the door open. Immediately the scent of lavender wafted across her face. Libby chuckled to herself. Lucy couldn't tie her own shoes, but she had to have those lavender air-fresheners. She walked quietly over to the bed centered in the massive room where her sister lay sleeping. The room, darkened by the heavy pulled shades and draperies, felt as familiar as her own airy bedroom and provided relief from the sunlight that burned Lucy's tender skin and eyes. Libby pulled an ottoman beside the bed and sat down. She took one of Lucy's hands in hers.

"Lucy," she whispered. "Lucy, we have work to do. They need our help again."

Lucy groaned and turned over in her bed. "Please, Lucy," Libby said. "I can't do this without you. You're the strength. You are the holder."

After a few seconds, Lucy turned over again to face Libby. With the mangled side of her face pressed against the pillow, she seemed as beautiful as ever to her sister. Libby reached over and ran her fingers along Lucy's face. "You will always be beautiful to me, Lucy," she said. "Always."

Lucy rested her arm on the bed and opened her hand to reveal the mark in her palm. Her eyes met Libby's, the gazes between them rock-solidly intense. Libby held her hand, and when she felt the heat begin in Lucy's, she knew that it had begun in hers, too. "Think of the baby, Lucy, the blonde baby who was bitten by the snake, the one you saved. Remember him? You saved his life. You put him in the glow. He is in danger now, Lucy. Someone in the Cove is trying to hurt him. Someone is trying to hurt all of us."

Lucy sat up and dangled her legs over the side of the bed.

"Bah...bee," she mouthed. "Yes, Lucy, someone is trying to hurt the baby. Think of him. Tell me who it is."

Libby closed her eyes and waited for the gunshot. With their hands held tightly together, the women exchanged thoughts. In her mind, Lucy saw Hap in the workshop, watched as he fell, and watched as her sister—is that her or me—straddled him and breathed into him the breath of life. She watched as the glow began. It started at his feet, worked its way to his chest, pulsating, searching for the source of the poison. The green glow searched until it found the lethal spot, the spot most weakened, and then the glow engulfed the man from the top of his head to the bottom of his feet. Pulsing, humming, it saturated his body, until at last, the man gasped. Libby braced herself for the sound that filled her head with almost unbearable pain. It came as she expected, a powerful blast of energy that echoed through the chambers of her brain and left her head throbbing. She felt the surge of power and gasped as well. Immediately, she let go of Lucy's hand. "Lucy," she said, "show me who put the snake in the workshop."

Lucy whined like a little child. "Please help me," Libby said.

Lucy looked at her sister. She remembered, in a flash of images, when they used to stand in front of the cheval-glass mirror in their bedroom, holding hands and watching each other. Lucy would think of something. Libby would tell her what it was. They played like that for hours at a time. Lucy's job was to think of something and send it to Libby. It never worked the other way around. The image disappeared, the laughter replaced by wails of grief.

Lucy whined again and lowered her head.

"Um...um...um..." she said as she rocked back and forth on the bed, whimpering and drawing in her shoulders. She pressed a smooth hand to her mouth and shook her head slowly.

"Lucy, look at me," Libby said. "Look at me. You're safe now. Nothing bad can happen in here. You are safe."

Lucy looked up again and stared into Libby's eyes. She took a deep wheezing breath and squeezed her sister's hand. They both closed their eyes, waiting for Lucy's images to reappear, but their concentration was broken when Libby thought she heard a noise in the living room. "Wait," she said. She listened for other intrusive sounds, but by the time she had decided that everything was quiet—stone quiet—Lucy had already begun the journey into the deep recesses of her mind. Libby felt the images coming, braced herself again for the gunshot, and squeezed her sister's hand again. The blast came, and Libby squeezed her eyes tightly shut to abate the pain. But nothing worked against that kind of pain, nothing short of death, she imagined. She saw a wondrous sky filled with brilliant green lights. Intermittent pink streaks danced through the green light. She could hear thunder in the background and could feel the earth tremble, but the kaleidoscopic sky held her in rapt attention.

From the sky came several blinding white streaks of lightning, each one poised over a victim, the first being a large white oak. When the lightning struck, Libby felt the energy surge through her body, burning her eyes and heating her skin. A second bolt of lightning found another victim, a man who screamed in agony, but only for a split second. When the scream stopped, the man lay in a crumpled heap on the ground, his eyes bulging from their sockets, the rest of him smoldering in the dirt. Lightning showered across the yard, alighting everything it touched. When the flames began, they consumed the grand old house as if it were made of kindling. At the large front window of the house stood two blonde-haired children, their horrified faces and small hands pressed against the window. They were trapped inside the house by a fallen beam and ceiling-high flames. Lucy ran inside, tripped but fell face-first onto the body of her husband, and heard her babies screaming, "Mama, help us, Mama."

"Mama's here, boys. Mama's here," she reassured them. She barely felt her face melting away. She squirmed around until, at last, she grabbed hold of young Will's hand. "Mama!" they screamed together.

When the screams stopped, young Will's hand fell to the floor. The images in Lucy's mind propelled her outside the house where she saw, for the first time, a thirteen-year-old boy standing on the lawn. His face expressionless, he stood frozen in place, his feet like lead. The last thing he saw before merciful unconsciousness overtook him was the contorted faces of his baby brothers pressed hard against the window, screaming for their mama.

Sobbing and gasping for breath, Libby fought to free herself from Lucy's grasp.

"Lu...cy...please..." she moaned. Her sister loosened her grasp and sobbed. Downstairs in the restaurant, Caillin Madison gasped and dropped a tray filled with food and drinks, the images in her mind too horrible to comprehend.

And miles away, standing on trembling ground at The Hallows, Hap Murray gasped, a blinding pain searing through his brain.

51

Libby got up, paced around the room for a moment, and poured a glass of water from the pitcher beside the bed. She took a sip and held the glass for Lucy. "We have to try again," Libby said. "You have to help me see what's going on in the Cove, Lucy. Burton, Wheelan, and Caillin are depending on us. We must help them."

Libby grabbed a tissue from the box and wiped her eyes. She blotted the tissue gently across Lucy's mangled socket, then across her perfect, beautiful green eye. "Once more," she said. "Just once more. Then, I will let you rest."

She sat down on the ottoman again, grabbed Lucy's hand, and waited. In the distance, she heard thunder rumbling and the tune of Edelweiss playing. "He loves that harmonica, doesn't he?" she asked. She didn't hear the door ease slightly open. She didn't see the intruder that slithered across the floor and into a cozy slipper. Once again, the power surged into her body with a painful, deafening blast as they began the exchange. Lucy thought about the blond-haired baby in the workshop. She saw him fall, felt the poison consume the healthy tissues in his body, and saw herself atop his long body. In her mind, she scanned the room. "Go back, Lucy, go back," Libby whispered.

Within seconds, Lucy's mental vision shifted. Some force pulled her—swoosh, swoosh—to a place outside the workshop, a strange place where a truck driver unloaded cumbersome crates. Standing beside the crates was a man in overalls. He lifted each crate with care. A voice startled them both. "Be careful, you idiot," the voice demanded.

Swoosh....

The lights in the room flickered on and off. The television set popped on, then off again, and one candle beside the bed melted onto the nightstand. The rocking chair in the corner rocked gently back and forth, while streams of green and yellow light danced across the room, swirled around the two women, and hovered there. Lucy traveled into another strange place, a place filled with glass tanks. She saw frogs inside some of them, snakes inside others. But in one corner of the room, she saw a large crate with the letters RCT. Immediately, Lucy's eyes burned, her skin heated, and she moaned. Thunder blasted outside and shook the windows. Lucy's eyes opened wide, and she saw her sister staring back at her. From their eyes issued a brilliant green glow. Their hands squeezed tighter together and the twin sisters breathed in unison. After a few seconds, the glow subsided, their skin cooled, and they inhaled slowly, held the breath inside, and loosened their grasps. With one long exhaled breath, their eyes and skin returned to normal and the brilliant streams of light dissipated. Weakened and trembling, Libby reached up and stroked Lucy's face. "Thank you," she said. "I have the answer. Go to sleep, sweet sister."

She helped Lucy lie down, covered her with the down comforter on her bed, and kissed her on the cheek.

"I love you, Lucy," she said. She turned to walk out of the room, stopped dead still, and screamed. Standing in the doorway was a man with a video camera perched on his shoulder and the word Eagle embroidered on his shirt. When he saw that Libby had turned around, he tried to run but tripped and fell over a large mirrored stand that held a vase filled with large silk flowers. Immediately, Lucy sat up, saw the man lying in the doorway, and stared at him. She thought of a bolt of lightning, pictured it in her mind so clearly that she felt its power. The mark in her palm throbbed with energy. Libby looked back at her, saw her eyes glowing, and yelled, "NO!" But it was too late. A bolt of energy shot from her eyes and into the intruder. He screamed and squirmed, his body convulsing. Then he stilled and released his grip on the camera.

"Stop it, Lucy! Stop it now," Libby said. Lucy blinked her eyes and fell back onto the pillows. "Bah...bee," she mouthed. "Hur da bah bee." Libby checked the man for a pulse. Slight, irregular, but a pulse nonetheless. She stepped over him, went to the phone in the kitchen, and called the paramedics.

Then she beeped Burton. He returned her call within seconds. "Come up here," she said. "We've got trouble."

52

"Don't touch the stakes," Wheelan whispered. "Move out of the dig and get under the tent. You're big, but it will hold you. It's raised off the ground. You'll have to crawl up onto those rocks inside, but you will fit. I've slept in there, so I know there's room. Keep yourself on top of the rocks until I'm finished. Okay? Go!"

Hap did exactly as Wheelan instructed. He lifted himself away from the dig site, stood up, and walked toward the tent. He had taken only a few steps when another clap of thunder sounded. The pain that had seared through his brain diminished.

"Hurry!" Wheelan said. "Get in there."

Maneuvering his full 6' 3" into the tent space wasn't as easy as he'd first thought, but he managed to climb onto the rocked bottom and slide atop the sleeping bag. Just as he pulled his feet into the tent, another bolt of lightning struck only a few yards from where Wheelan crouched. Again, the charge hit the ground, seared through the upper mantle of earth, and snaked down deeper, searching for something, some hidden magnetic force of such attraction that it was irresistible. Wheelan felt the tremors underneath his feet, this time more violent than before. Several of the dig stakes toppled and landed on top of his treasured hole in the ground.

"Get out of there, Doc!" Hap yelled.

Wheelan slid away from the site and motioned for Hap to follow. "Come on," he said. "Let's go."

Hap squirmed out of the tent, and together, the two of them dashed down the trail that led to the safety of the Jeep. Out of breath, their hearts pounding in their chests, they opened the doors and climbed in. Beads of sweat dotted their upper lips and pooled under their arms. "I don't want to end up another statistic,"

Hap said, his breathing heavy. Wheelan backed down along the wooded trail and stopped when he came to the entrance of the Hallows. The sky had turned from bright blue to dusty gray, the air heavy with moisture. "It's coming," Wheelan said, "but we have time. Don't worry."

Hap nodded, wiped his forehead and rolled down the window. Fifteen minutes later, they pulled into the back lot of Cove's End. They clamored out of the Jeep, took the steps two at a time, and slammed the door behind them.

Wheelan and Hap burst into the living room and stood absolutely still. Pale and trembling, Libby looked first at them, then down at the man lying on the floor. Bending over the man was Chief Riggs.

"The paramedics are on their way," Riggs said. "He'll be all right."

Hap took a few steps closer, saw the video camera, and cried out.

"Eagle?"

He hurried over to his friend and bent down beside him. "What happened?" he yelled. "What have you done to my friend?"

Thunder roared in the background with a blast so strong that it shook the floor. In only a few seconds, a spray of lightning lit up the Cove. Eagle's hand jerked as if he had touched something hot. Then he moaned, coughed and opened his eyes. "Eagle, are you okay, buddy?" Hap asked. "Don't worry. The paramedics are coming. You'll be fine."

Hap glared at Libby as if she were the original carrier of the bubonic plague. "What happened to him?" he asked her. "What did you do to him?"

When the paramedics pounded at the door, Wheelan opened it and ushered them in. "Clear away, please," one of them said.

Hap got up, grabbed Libby's elbow, and pulled her to the other side of the room.

"What happened to him?" he demanded.

"You're hurting my arm," she said. "Let go of me."

He squeezed her arm tighter. "I asked you a question," he said.

"I want an answer."

As Libby stared up at him, she felt the change come over her body, the heat rising, the hands throbbing, the eyes burning. She felt it, but was powerless to stop it.

"Please let me go," she whispered, "before we both regret it."

But it was too late. Her eyes took on a soft green glow. Just as Hap was about to speak, Wheelan stepped in between him and his aunt. "Don't say anything you'll regret," he said. "The paramedics are ready to take your friend to the hospital. He's all right, and he doesn't want to go to the hospital, so why don't you go over and convince him that he needs to be examined by a doctor." Hap stepped aside, looked over at Eagle, and did as Wheelan asked. Tears streamed down Libby's cheeks. She wiped them away with her fingers, closed her burning eyes for a few seconds, then looked up at her nephew. "I'm sorry," she said, "for everything."

Libby felt as if she could no longer stand up. Her energy drained, she grabbed Wheelan's arm to steady herself. Wheelan hugged her and told her to go lie down. "You look terrible," he said. "You need rest."

"Yes," she said. "I need some rest. Will you check on Hap's friend in a little while? Just to make sure he's all right? I've told Burton something Hap might be interested in, but I'm sure he's in no mood to talk to me. Will you tell him that I know who owns the snakes. I don't know why, but I know."

"Why didn't you tell me?" he asked, the look of disappointment on his face apparent. "I didn't know until a little while ago. Your mother...."

"What?"

"No, honey, your mother is the one who helped me see. She's so much more gifted than we realize, so strong."

"Come and lie down. Then you can tell me everything," Wheelan said. Wheelan glanced over at Burton, nodded toward Hap, and hoped he'd made his point. He hoped that the Chief would tell his friend what he wanted to know.

At 2:00 in the afternoon, after only an hour of examination

and treatment, the photographer for Channel 12 walked out of the hospital with his friend. They took a cab back to the hotel and found Joey's father, Mr. Donovan, sitting in their room, just where Eagle had left him. Hap shook his hand, embraced him, and told him how sorry he was about Joey.

"I wanted to see you," Donovan said, "to tell you how much that boy of mine respected you and to thank you for the help you've given him these past few years. I don't think he would have been able to keep that job if you hadn't been pulling for him. His mother and I are grateful."

"He was a good kid, bright and funny. He was always making us laugh," Hap said. "I'll miss him."

"Well," Donovan said, fighting back tears, "I'd better get going. I'm taking him back with me. The police chief, Mr. Riggs, has been very helpful. I'll see that I thank him properly after the...."

His voice trailed off as his eyes welled up with tears. His throat felt as if it were engorged with some huge mass that would not allow it to function. He cleared his throat several times, then addressed them both. "I'd better be going," he said. "My pilot is waiting. As I said, the Chief has made all the arrangements for transporting the, uh...the body. I'll call you when I have the specific details. I'll provide your transportation, if you want. For the funeral, I mean."

"Thank you, Mr. Donovan. We appreciate it. Give Mrs. Donovan our sympathies."

"Yes, certainly."

As Donovan left, he glanced back at them. "You'll find out for me, won't you, the truth about this accident? I can count on you, can't I?"

"You can count on me, sir."

Mr. Donovan smiled, nodded his approval of Hap's words, and left. "Whew!" Hap said. "That was awkward."

"Poor guy. It must be terrible to lose a son, especially one like Joey. If it had been my boy, I think I'd have been a whole lot less composed."

"You up to a little adventure?" Hap asked.

"What kind of adventure?" Eagle responded.

"I thought we'd pay a visit to Wheelan and Libby, just to let them know you're all right."

"I'm a little shaky, but I'm up to it. I'd like to talk to them." Eagle said. "But first let me check out the camera. I want it fully functional for this little visit."

Hap picked up the phone and dialed Libby's home number, and when Wheelan answered, he felt relieved.

"Wheelan, is it all right if I come by for a little while?"

"Sure, I'm glad you called. Did the Chief tell you who owns the snakes?"

"Riggs? No, I didn't see him after we left for the hospital. You *know* who owns the snakes?"

"Yes, and that's not all. Look, I've got to go out to the Hallows for a little while. The storm seems to have subsided a bit. Do you want to go with me? We can talk about this mess while we're there."

"Sure, but I'm bringing Eagle along. Is that okay with you?"

"Yes, it's fine. Is he doing all right?"

"Well, for an old guy, he seems to be okay."

Eagle rolled his eyes then held up his middle finger. "He's a real charmer," Hap said. "We'll see you in a few minutes."

Eagle finished checking the camera, packed it into the case, and grabbed the small bag that held extra batteries, flashes, and blank tapes. Hap patted his shirt pocket to make sure he had the notebook and pen. "You might need a bigger notebook," Eagle said. "This might be one heck of a story."

Hap stopped before they walked to the door.

"Is something wrong?"

"This is a big story, Eagle, but there are people who must be protected. We have to be careful.

The two of them left, prepared they thought, for their visit. But then, they forgot that they were in Preacher's Cove, where just about anything, especially the unexpected, can happen.

53

A few miles away, at Madison Manor, Chief Riggs was paying a call to Ike Madison. The Chief, too, thought he'd left prepared for anything. But he was wrong.

Fifteen minutes into their meeting, Ike Madison asked Burton to leave his house, and although the Chief had anticipated that move, he did not anticipate what happened next. "Louisa!" Ike yelled. "Kindly show the Chief out the door. He's ready to leave."

Louisa appeared almost immediately, and when Ike went into his study to continue practicing his sermon, she whispered something to Riggs that sent a chill down his spine. "He will kill her if she doesn't obey."

With her eyes, Louisa beseeched Riggs not to say anything else. Riggs left, got in his car, and drove away. He pulled into his own driveway, positioned the car so that he could see any movement in the back of the Manor, and waited. He lit a cigarette and watched. By the time he had finished the cigarette, he saw Ike walk out the back door of the house. He glanced around to see if anyone suspicious might be watching, and headed down the walkway that led to the rooms attached to the Manor. He reached into his pocket, drew out what looked like a large key ring, and fumbled around until he found the one he needed. He disappeared into one of the rooms. Almost immediately thereafter, Billy Ray appeared out of nowhere and disappeared into the same room. Burton got out of the car, walked across the driveway and hesitated at the side entrance yard of Madison Manor. Muffled sounds of a harmonica playing filtered into his ears. He crossed the side yard and listened as his shoes clicked on the walkway. "Real cool," he muttered, "trying to sneak up on someone wearing these things."

He kept on walking until he reached the room that Ike and

Billy Ray had entered. He knocked on the door and waited. Nothing.

He knocked again. When no one answered, he pounded on the door and called to Ike.

"Reverend Madison!" he yelled. "Open the door. There's something I forgot to tell you."

"It's no use," someone behind him said.

Riggs gasped and turned around. "It's no use. He can't hear you in there. If you want to talk to him, you have to press this button right here."

"Jeffrey, you startled me."

"Sorry, Chief. It's spooky around here even in broad daylight. Clouds seem to be drifting, though. Did you notice? Maybe the storm's fizzled out."

"Jeffrey, why don't you call the Reverend and ask him to come out?"

"It's not allowed, Chief. Not unless something's wrong."

"But Jeffrey, there is something wrong. I forgot to tell the Reverend about a new deal I've found. It might make him a healthy profit."

Jeffrey smiled at the Chief, and nodded a big, "Yes!"

He pressed the button to the intercom. "What is it?" Ike screamed. "This better be important, Jeffrey."

Burton stepped up to the small speaker.

"Ike? It's Riggs here. I need to speak with you, if you can tear yourself away from your duties. May I come in?"

"Riggs, I thought you'd left," Ike said in a sugary voice. "If you can come back later this evening, I'll be glad to talk to you in the privacy of my home."

"It's pretty important, Ike. It would be to your, uh, financial advantage to speak with me."

In a few seconds, Ike eased the door open slightly and slipped out. He glared at Riggs, drew close to him, and spoke.

"Ike? You called me Ike in the presence of my employees? Have you no respect for my position?" His voice sounded almost like hissing. Burton noticed beads of sweat that dotted the man's upper lip.

"I have the utmost respect for you, Reverend, which is exactly why I'm here."

Ike straightened his tie, cleared his throat, and dismissed Jeffrey. Then he asked Riggs what on earth was so important that it would keep him from his business.

"You'll probably think this is silly, but I'd like to ask you about Billy Ray and that harmonica of his."

"I thought you said this was about financial matters! I'm not going to discuss something as trivial as Billy Ray's harmonica. If you want to talk to him about that, be my guest. I won't waste my time with it. Excuse me, Chief. I have work to do."

Riggs watched as Ike huffed away, mumbling to himself.

"Have a nice day, Reverend."

Ike didn't respond to him but kept walking toward the house. Riggs turned around and walked back to his car thinking about Ike's reaction. *A little too over-the-top for a question about a harmonica,* he thought. His mind reeling with possibilities, probabilities, and speculations, he got into the car and headed straight to Cove's End. On his way, he called his friend, Judge Paden, and told him he needed a search warrant ASAP for Ike Madison's house and grounds. Paden laughed and said, "Sure, you do. I guess you're tired of your job here."

When he kept talking and convinced the Judge that he was serious, there was silence on the other end of the phone for a few seconds. "I'll have it ready in an hour," he said to Burton. "I hope you know what you're doing."

"Me, too," Burton said. "See you soon."

54

Inside his study, Ike Madison made one phone call; then he sat down on his plush leather sofa and poured himself a glass of water. On the coffee table in front of him was a photograph, a small family portrait of him, his late wife Belinda, and Caillin. The photograph, taken when Caillin was only five, brought back memories that flooded his mind and washed him in melancholia. He traced the picture with his fingers, half hoping that the gesture might bring back his wife and put an end to his loneliness and constant depression about Caillin. Belinda had been so much better with her. She always knew exactly what to say, how to react, and when to step in and administer discipline. Ike remembered Belinda's laugh, her slim body, her beautiful face. His body ached for her, for her love and laughter, for her constant support. He picked up the photo, framed in gold and sterling silver, and held it to his chest. A single tear rolled down his cheek. "I miss you, baby," he said. "I need you here with me. I need your help with our daughter. She's on that path we both feared. She wants to be like Libby, a pagan madwoman. I can't let that happen. She will condemn herself to Hell if I don't keep her away from them. I've tried to be a good father, but I feel helpless without you."

Then he thought about Murray, and his mood shifted.

"He's come to get her, Belinda. See what you did? Your sins are about to be visited on our daughter. God forgive your poor soul, Belinda."

Ike smiled as he remembered the look on Belinda's face as the life drained out of her body. He wondered briefly if she had known in those last few minutes that he was the one who had followed her to the woods. And he wondered if, when she heard that last twig snapping, she knew that Caillin—and the Eye of God—

would forever be his.

He would control the power. He would wait for the emotional upheaval that created the glowing eyes in all of these foul women, and he would seize control, especially of his Caillin. He had seen that faint glowing in Caillin's eyes, even when she was a child. "The work of the devil," he whispered. Under his control, his daughter would forsake her ties with the devil. She would become, instead, a righteous warrior for God. He smiled at the thought of it.

The phone rang and interrupted his melancholy. He looked over at his desk and saw the red light flashing. His private line needed his attention immediately. "Forgive me, darling," he whispered. "Business beckons as always." While Ike Madison took his call, Burton Riggs leaned against the door on his car, his arms folded across his chest, and talked face to face with Wheelan, Hap and Eagle.

"So, you have proof," Hap said, "that Madison owns these snakes."

"Will have shortly. A search warrant should do the trick," Burton said. "He won't like it, but he can't ignore it."

"There's no motive, Riggs. Ike Madison can have anything he wants in this town. Why would he use snakes to kill people if he already has everything he wants? It doesn't make a whole lot of sense to me, but then, there's very little in this place that does make sense."

"Look, Son, you've had a hard time of it here. You and your buddies have gotten a raw deal, but this isn't a bad place to live. We've got our problems, but so does every other town in the world. Idiosyncrasies...that's all they are. Every place has them."

"Let's think about this," Wheelan said. "What is the one thing in this town that Madison cannot control?"

No one said anything for a few seconds.

Then Hap spoke up.

"The weather?"

The four of them laughed together.

"Think again," Wheelan said.

"Cove's End?" Hap asked. "The complex here, he can't control that. Can he?"

"No, he can't," Wheelan said. "But does he want to?"

"Yes, he wants to," Burton said. "He's a control freak or haven't you noticed? He wants to control everything in the town."

"Well, he can't control his daughter!" Eagle said. "She came here looking for Hap and even went into his room. I'd bet Madison didn't know anything about it."

"I'd be careful what I put up for a wager in this town," Wheelan said. "If you lose, someone will call you on it for sure!

"You're wrong, Eagle," Hap said. "Madison was watching us from his limo across the street. He knew every move Caillin made, except when she was inside with us."

They talked for a few more minutes about Ike Madison. Then Hap asked, "Why would he use snakes?" Hap asked.

"Professional courtesy...one snake to another!" Eagle said.

"An even better question is how would he import snakes that have RCT chips implanted in them?"

"I beg your pardon," said Eagle. "What kind of chips?"

"RCT chips. Radio Control Transmission. Scientists use them to track the movement of endangered species of animals, all kinds of animals all over the world. But how would Ike Madison know that, and how would he get his hands on snakes that have been implanted?"

"With enough money, you can buy just about anything, Wheelan. Research would be right at his fingertips. Anybody could find out about the RCT's if they wanted to. Rattlesnakes with implants. I know Ike is cunning, but I'd never have thought even HE could think of something like this."

"What purpose could it serve?" Eagle asked. "I mean, what good is it to know where they are and they send signals back to him? Nah, man, that makes absolutely no sense.

"These are snakes we're talking about, not people." Hap said. "This gets crazier and crazier. A man like Ike Madison, from what little I know of him, doesn't need snakes to do his dirty work. There are plenty of people who would do it for him."

"Maybe the snakes are more dependable and predictable," Wheelan said. "And they won't talk or ask for payment," Hap added.

"I think you two are carrying this a little too far," Eagle said. "I'll admit that I've seen some pretty odd things in my time, but this is, by far, the wackiest idea I've ever heard. There has to be another explanation. I mean, even if he owns those snakes, maybe they just got loose and he's afraid to tell anyone for fear that people will blame him. Then his pristine reputation would be tarnished."

When they had exhausted all manner of speculation about the how and why, the only thing left was Ike's obsession with control. But it seemed so ludicrous that not one of them believed it.

And then they saw Libby walking down the stairs. Barefoot and disheveled, she walked over to where they stood, surveyed the four of them, and stated quite factually,

"Obsession has no rationale, except to the obsessed."

The four of them stared at her, expecting more information.

"And?" Hap asked.

Libby lowered her eyes and spoke so softly that they could barely hear her. "He won't stop until he rids himself of all liabilities according to God's laws."

Hap stepped forward and bent down closer to Libby's face.

"Are you all right?" he asked with genuine sincerity.

He thought that she had been drinking, maybe just an afternoon nip or two. Libby backed away from him and walked back toward the house.

"How kind of you to ask," she called to him.

Hap blushed and looked down at the ground. He shook his head as if he would never again know the right thing to say or do when it came to that woman. He had screwed up big time. As she walked away, pangs of desire stirred in him. Her bare feet and tousled hair reminded him of the passion they shared for each other. Now, he felt certain that he would never see that look of passionate longing in her eyes, and for a few seconds, he wanted to run after her and explain. He wanted to grab her by the arm, spin her around, and kiss her so hard that he would feel her knees weaken. Then he remembered the faint green glow in her eyes, and his desire for her turned to abject fear.

"I've gotta run, boys," Burton said. "Y'all keep those brilliant minds working for me now. I'm counting on you." He pointed to

Wheelan. "And you go see after your Aunt Libby. She looks pale."

They waved as Burton pulled out of the lot and agreed to meet in back in the parking lot in an hour. The three of them left in separate directions: Wheelan back home, Eagle to his room, and Hap to the restaurant.

55

Hap brushed past the crowd waiting to be seated and went directly to the gift shop where the four children stared down at him from a shelf above the cash register. For the first time, he didn't shudder when he saw them. Images of their creator, the woman the townspeople called Crazy Lucy, flashed in his mind. He saw that hideous mangled mess of a face. Then, the light shifted in his brain, and he saw the beautiful smooth features of the portion that the flames did not claim. When he thought of the tragedy that she endured—the tragedy for the whole family—he was ashamed that he had judged her only by the ugliness that she could neither control nor change. Crazy Lucy's face had given him a new perspective. He asked the woman behind the counter if he could hold one of the dolls.

"Certainly," she said. "We're very proud of them. The Firelight Angels, we call them. Which one would you like to see?"

He asked for the one on the end.

"Oh, she's our newest one. Such a lovely angel, isn't she?"

Hap held the doll in his arms, amazed at the artistry that could turn red clay into a work of such staggering resemblance to a human child. The doll was posed with one hand in her lap, the other at her lips. He found himself waiting for the doll to say, "Shh."

She looked as if she held some forbidden secret, the expression on her face both mysterious and playful. As he handed the doll back to the clerk, he hesitated. Then he turned the hand held to her mouth very carefully. On the palm of her hand was a small blue dot. The clerk took the doll and, using a step stool, replaced her carefully on the shelf beside the others. "There's no card for her," Hap said. The clerk looked puzzled, glanced around the area, and said, "Ah, here it is. It must have fallen."

She steadied the card and positioned it.

"There we go," she said.

The card read, "Sweet Caillin Murray: A Firelight Angel, Hand-made by Lucy Addams."

"Would you like to see another one?" the clerk asked.

"No, thank you," he said, his voice trembling, his knees weak as rubber.

Hap smiled at the clerk, ran his hand through his hair, and walked toward the seating area. His height gave him the advantage of being able to scan the crowd for the person he sought. He found her balancing a tray filled with drinks. As he made his way through the customers, he called to her. "Excuse me, Caillin. May I speak with you for a few moments?"

The girl looked at him, shook her head, and went about her duties. Hap pushed his way closer to her until he was standing right beside her. "Just for a few minutes?" he asked.

Caillin distributed the glasses to the guests, took their order, and told them she would return in a few minutes to check on them. Then she led Hap into the main kitchen and out a side door that took them into a large storage room. She stared up at him but said nothing.

"Are you all right?" he asked.

"Yes, thank you," she said and smiled at him. "I am fine."

"Caillin, I was a little confused about your visit. You warned me to be careful, but you didn't give me many details. Is your father threatening you?"

The expression on her face did not change. "I was upset," she said. "I apologize for disturbing you."

Hap nodded his head to indicate that he knew she was hiding something.

"Okay, sure," he said, "I'll let you get back to work. But Caillin...."

"Yes, sir?" she asked.

"You call me if you need me."

"Likewise," she said and brushed past him. Hap sighed and wondered how he could convince her to trust him. Then he chucked to himself. *Oh, yeah,* he thought, *she's gonna trust a reporter about as much as she trusts one of those little snakes.*

He left the storage room, walked through the kitchen, and made his way past the lingering crowd and out the door. When he was outside, he stood for a moment and looked up into the sky, now a grayish blue streaked with thin stratus clouds. His untrained eye detected no sign of an impending storm, another of the killers that stalked the Cove.

Hap decided to go to Libby's. He wondered if he should call first, but decided that Wheelan was planning to meet him in a few minutes, anyway, so he might be expecting him. He walked down the wooden walkway, turned and went toward the back, found the steps leading to the house and walked up. He stopped at the door and knocked, expecting Wheelan to answer. When Libby answered instead, he felt awkward. A long silence between the two of them followed. Finally, Libby stepped aside and invited him in. "Please, make yourself comfortable. Would you like something to drink?"

"I'd love some iced tea, but why don't you let me get it myself?" he asked. "I'm a big boy now, and I can manage a glass of tea. Besides," he said, "you look a little tired."

"Wheelan will be here in a minute," she said. She walked down the hallway and knocked on Wheelan's door. "Hap is here," she said, her voice a mixture of fatigue and uneasiness.

"Libby?" Hap called after her. "May I talk to you for a few minutes?"

He patted the sofa.

"Please, come and sit beside me," he said.

"Your tea," she said as she walked back into the living room.

"It can wait," he said.

Libby sat down on the sofa beside him and stared down at the cushions, shielding his direct vision of her eyes. She knew that her eyes were still red-rimmed and watery because she could feel the slight burning that persisted.

"Libby," he said, "I want to apologize. I made some callous assumptions about you and about Lucy. I was wrong. I shouldn't have doubted you, but...."

"Yes, you should have," she said. "You don't really know us, after all. Lucy and I are, well, we are...different from most people. We have a long family history, a legacy of sorts that we must continue. It is our job, Hap, to protect the Cove, to make sure her treasures are safe. Our heritage dates backs to the ancient Druids to the call of an ancient princess. We are her descendants and we must carry on her work. Forgive me, I'm rambling. If most people bothered to trace their own ancestry, they might find that theirs dates back even farther than the Druids."

She rubbed her eyes, ran her hands through her long hair, and sat up a little straighter. "You really don't have to apologize," she said. "I understand how...."

"No," he interrupted, "you're wrong. I do need to apologize. I tried to trick you."

"I know, Hap," she said. "You wanted a story, and I wanted you. It's as simple as that. Maybe we used each other."

He slid closer to her and cupped her chin. "Libby, forgive me," he said. "I wanted a story, but I also wanted you. I still do. I don't care about your heritage or the work you have to do. All I care about is the two of us right here right now."

Wheelan walked into the room, cleared his throat, and headed toward the kitchen. Libby stood up immediately and smoothed her skirt. "Tea, anyone?" Wheelan called and chuckled.

"No, no thank you, Doc," Hap said. "It's about time for us to meet Riggs, isn't it?"

Wheelan walked into the living room carrying two big glasses of iced tea. He put them down on the coasters and looked at Hap.

"Let's talk and have some tea. Burton's already been out there. He got the search warrant, took two cops with him, and searched Madison's storage houses. They were virtually empty, with the exception of one aquarium tank that housed several tree frogs. That's all. Tree frogs. No snakes. He searched the study, the den, and the bedrooms for invoices, some kind of paperwork, but found nothing. When he called me, he was headed for Ike's office downtown in the church."

"So, there's no proof," Hap said.

"None."

"What about Billy Ray? Wouldn't he be able to give us something?"

"You're kidding, right? Billy Ray Henderson and practically everyone else in his family have worked for the Madisons for thirty years, since he was just a kid. His father worked for Madison, Sr. and his grandfather for the elder Madison. No, this goes back for generations. He'd never say anything against them."

"What now?" Hap asked. "Well, we have two options, I guess. We could try to catch one of them in the act of committing the crime, an impossibility from my viewpoint since the snakes are the killers. Or, we could hope that something happens to make Billy Ray talk, and even that is highly unlikely."

"No, there has to be a way," Hap said. "Sooner or later, every criminal makes a mistake. Everyone slips up. I've gotten half my stories from just those mistakes. So, even Ike Madison will eventually make a mistake. It's inevitable."

"Well, if you'd be so kind as to enlighten me, I'd be glad to listen to your suggestions," Wheelan said. The silence that filled the room was almost deafening. The three of them looked at one another, but no words came. Finally, Wheelan made a suggestion.

"Let's ride out to the Hallows," he said. "I still have work to do out there. Maybe some bright idea will strike us while we're digging."

"Interesting choice of words, Doc. Let's hope that's all that strikes us."

"The storm's coming back, but I think we'll be safe for a little while."

"Didn't you say that the last time we were out there?"

"Yes, I did, and here we sit safely in the living room."

Hap shrugged an okay, and the two of them walked out the door. Libby stood in the living room wondering what she could do to catch Ike Madison. Suddenly, the door flew open. Hap rushed in, grabbed her by the shoulders, and kissed her hard on the lips.

"I'll be back," he said in his very worst Arnold impersonation.

Libby laughed out loud and walked back into her bedroom. *What a guy*, she thought. She stretched out on the bed and closed her eyes. A smile crossed her lips, and she imagined Hap lying beside her. She turned onto her side and reached out for the pillow. But when she opened her eyes, she saw Alton Anderson's charred body smoldering next to her.

She whimpered.

56

Wheelan drove by Eagle's room on the way out of the parking lot. Hap jumped out of the Jeep and banged on the door of the room. When Eagle stumbled to the door, half-asleep in his T-shirt and boxers, Hap laughed at him. "Buggers! Put on some clothes and grab the camera. We're going out to the Hallows. You don't want to miss this."

Eagle just stared at him as if he had lost his mind.

"You know, you live in Alabama. Nobody in Alabama says, 'buggers.'"

Hap laughed again and bent close to him.

"You gonna stand there in your buggery shorts all day or are ya gonna get the buggers ready and come with us?"

"Get outta here, Yank. I'm comin. Blond and Yank...whew!" he said as he walked over to get his clothes. "It's a bloody miracle you can breathe on your own."

Hap went back to the Jeep and climbed inside. "He's on his way," he said. "That Eagle, he's a corker, a real corker."

"Sometimes," Wheelan said, "you actually have a bit of an English accent. Are you aware of it?"

"So I've been told on more than one occasion. Actually, I believe my accent—Southern and British—is one of the things that got me the job at Channel 12. That, of course, combined with my stunning good looks and natural charm."

"Do you ever stop talking?" Eagle said as he clamored over Hap and into the back of the Jeep.

"Well, I have a list of women you can ask about that. I'm sure they'll tell you that, on the most wonderful occasions, I do stop talking and get down to business."

Suddenly, Hap thought of Libby. His stomach felt tied in knots when he realized what he'd said. He squeezed his eyes shut and muttered,

"Oh, man, I'm sorry. I didn't mean anything...."

Wheelan nodded at him and put the Jeep in gear. He was overwhelmed with an urge to punch him right in the mouth, but instead, he pulled out of the lot and onto the road. He took a deep breath.

"It's none of my business," he said to Hap. "Forget about it."

Once again, the silence filled the car with such disquietude that Wheelan reached down and turned on the radio for relief. News from the Weather Channel blared into the Jeep, and Wheelan fumbled to turn down the volume.

"Sorry about that," he said. The three of them laughed and listened to the latest broadcast. The beep-beep-beep sounded to indicate severe weather. They listened as the announcer told of severe thunderstorm warnings for north Alabama. "I suppose that means us," Hap said.

"Yes, it does," Wheelan said. "But we have time."

Wheelan pulled into the Hallows and issued a warning.

"Hold on, fellas," he said. "I'm pulling this baby as far up onto that trail as she will go."

Twigs and small bushes snapped as the Jeep ran over them, but Wheelan was determined to get closer to the dig site this time. He pressed hard on the accelerator and plowed over large rocks and even a sapling. The Jeep crept upwards toward the site and stopped only when a good-sized boulder blocked the way. "Well, how did you like that? Is she a trooper or what?" Wheelan asked. "Let's get going."

They climbed out of the Jeep, gathered the gear, and walked to the spot where Wheelan's treasure lay still buried under the earth. He approached the site with some trepidation. He hoped that no one had disturbed it. He peered into the hole and saw the grayed metal breaking through the ground. "Is it there?" Hap asked.

"Yes, it's here."

"Okay, big guy, let's get some tape going."

"What? Of this hole? You want me to film this hole?"

"No, not the hole. It's what's inside the hole that's important."

"Right," Eagle said and shook his head.

He positioned the camera onto his shoulder and stepped gingerly beside the site. He leaned in close, adjusted the focus and the flash, and ran the tape. He stopped after a few seconds and said, "I'm not getting anything except dirt."

Wheelan knelt beside the site and scooped away as much dirt as he could. Hap knelt beside him, helping with a plastic scoop he'd found in the Jeep. Between the two of them, they unearthed more of the treasure. Wheelan grabbed a large, fine paintbrush and flicked the bristles over the outer portion of the object.

"Any ideas, yet?" Hap asked.

"No, not yet."

"And we're taping this because...."

"Point of origination," Hap said.

"What?" Eagle asked.

"The point of origination. Doc believes that the severity of the storms here is caused by a conductor buried deep inside the mantle of the earth. Whatever is buried here may be what he considers the point of origination, meaning that the conductor picks up the lightning, or maybe even draws it like a magnet, then intensifies it. Hence, the killer electrical charge that sweeps through this area originates first in the sky then at this spot. The two feed off each other and strengthen each other."

"Very good, Mr. Murray," Wheelan said.

"So, this little treasure of yours is the conductor you're trying to find?"

"Exactly!" he said. "If I can remove it from this spot, the storms will lessen in severity. Maybe our townspeople won't have to live in fear every time they hear thunder."

A gentle trembling in the earth startled them all. In the distance, thunder rumbled. "Speak of the devil," Eagle said.

The trembling loosened the dirt around the object. "Help me!" Wheelan yelled. "Let's get this thing out of here."

Eagle filmed every move, right down to the time when Wheelan withdrew the metal object from its grave and held it up to the sky.

"What in the world is that?" Hap asked.

"Gentlemen, behold the mark of a nobleman, the status symbol of the wealthy, and the handiwork of a creative genius."

Eagle and Hap looked at each other and shrugged. Neither of them had a clue as to what it was.

"Please, kind sirs, tell me that you are familiar with this precious object, especially you, Mr. Murray...he of semi-Celtic ancestry."

They stood without saying a word, struck dumb by ignorance. "Oh ye of little knowledge!" Wheelan said. "This, my friends, is a torq, the necklace of noblemen, the more ornate the carving, the wealthier the man who wore the piece."

"I'd say the guy was loaded, then," Hap said.

Wheelan knelt down to brush away the remaining pieces of earth from the torq. He admired the artistry, the ornate carvings on filigreed metal of a crown and a serpent, both clearly visible. Wide along the front, narrowing in the back with each end formed into perfectly symmetrical balls, the torq was still pliable. He moved it gently and smiled from ear to ear. Then, he set it down on the ground and walked over to the crates. From inside one of them he pulled a large zip bag lined with two large pieces of felt. He walked back and slipped the torq into the bag. He barely noticed that the sky had taken on a darker hue, that the air had become thick with moisture, and the wind had begun a fierce stirring within the enormous white oak trees. He knelt down again and began scooping earth away.

"What are you doing?" Hap asked. "Come on! We have to leave before the storm gets any worse. Please, we have to get out of here."

"Maybe there's another piece," Wheelan said. "I can't leave right now. We'll be all right. I promise."

Hap took a deep breath, wiped the sweat from his upper lip, and helped him dig around in the site until they did, indeed, feel another piece of metal. Wheelan got so excited that he dug like a madman. "Come on," he said, almost breathless, "help me out here."

The three of them dug out the dirt until they uncovered the

tip of another crafted piece. "Gently," Wheelan said. They were still digging when the wind toppled one of the stake poles. The earth beneath them seemed to sigh, then to groan, and finally to scream. It shook so hard that not one of them kept their balance. Sprawled on the ground, they felt the trembling of the earth beneath them. A thunderclap blasted through the Hallows, followed in seconds by a bolt of fiery hot lightning. Eagle squirmed around and grabbed the camera. He filmed as one mighty bolt struck high in the trees, down along the bark, and onto the ground. It snaked down into the earth as if it were searching for something. Instantly, Wheelan shouted at them to get up off the ground.

"Jump up!" he screamed, "as high as you can. Now!"

Just as their feet lifted from the ground for a fraction of a second, a deafening popping sound burst from the ground and set the partially-covered metal aglow with a soft green light. "Roll!" Wheelan screamed, and they did. When their feet touched the ground, they rolled away from the site and tumbled down into the brush, each one emitting a loud "umph." Only seconds later, the ground cooled and steadied. Covered by leaves, twigs, and dirt, the three men sat up slowly.

"Bugger!" Hap said, his stomach in knots. "I can't take this, Wheelan. The storms are too much. Please, let's get out of here." Bruised, cut, and aching, they moaned like children.

"I think Hap's right," Eagle said as he brushed off the camera. He held it up to the graying sky and peered through the lens. "Ah, that's my baby," he said and patted the side of the camera.

Wheelan scurried back to the site and began scooping away more handfuls of dirt. He dug so hard that he blistered his fingers, but he kept digging until he unearthed part of the treasure. "I have it!" he cried.

Eagle and Hap, in spite of their common-sense internal warnings, knelt down to help him. This one was much bigger than the first, broader and heavier. With all the effort the three of them could muster, they dug. Eagle, down inside the hole, dug from beneath. Hap dug from around one side, while Wheelan dug from the other. When the object loosened from their work, they worked even harder. Within minutes, the three accomplished what

Wheelan would have spent days trying to do by himself. At last, the men lifted it from its tomb. Gently, ever so gently, Eagle gripped the bottom portion and held fast to it. Hap did the same with the side portion. Gingerly, they raised it and laid it on the ground beside Wheelan. Paintbrush in hand, he whisked the last particles of loose dirt from around it.

"What is it?" Hap asked.

"A breastplate," Wheelan responded, "the breastplate of an ancient warrior."

The wind whipped through the trees, whispering of ancient times, ancient rituals held deep in the Hallows. It called to the sky, beckoned to the powers that empowered the wind to breathe life into the stagnant recesses of mortal limitations. The sky responded with thunderous resounding. Then, in a reaffirmation of glorious light and power, it sent a messenger, a silent, silver slash that sparked across the land. To this magnificent dance of wind and light, the Earth applauded in a moment of quivering admiration. Beyond the sight of the three mortals, five ancient stones glowed in unison. The call of an ancient land allowed the mortals to return unharmed.

57

Safely back at home, Wheelan, Hap, and Eagle stared down at the treasure unearthed in the Hallows. Still in their plastic bags, each object carefully laid along the kitchen table, Wheelan's treasures had the three men transfixed. "Maybe now, the Cove can rest," Wheelan said. "These artifacts may have been attracting the lightning all these years. I believe that I've found the answer to the question of why we have such killer storms."

"But maybe it's just the opposite," Eagle said. "They've been in the ground for years. Suppose the storms get worse. Or suppose your point of origination shifts to follow them. It's wild, but it fits this place."

"No, I believe that I'm right this time," Wheelan said. "All my research, my first-hand experience living here, my theories, they all lead to this conclusion. These objects, buried so many years ago that we probably couldn't date them, are the sources of conduction. But you see, all of it combined made them so strong."

"Explain, please," Libby said as she walked into the room. The knock at the door interrupted the beginning of another of Wheelan's explanations, so he merely stopped. Burton opened the door and asked, "Wheelan, honey, are you decent?"

Wheelan's face turned beet red when the rest of the bunch laughed so hard that they could barely stay in their seats. "Burton, you're such a scalawag," Libby said, "such a scoundrel."

He walked in grinning. "Well, I have to keep the boy on his toes," he said.

They laughed even harder. Even Libby blushed at that one. "Burton, go home if you're not going to play nice," she said.

He stood at the table looking at the treasures. "At least somebody in the group has had some luck. I'm still trying to figure out a way to nail Madison to the wall, and I'll do it...eventually. Wheelan, I assume these are the treasures you've been digging for since you came back here. A breastplate, is it? And a torq. Amazing! These little goodies will make you richer than you are now!"

"I'm impressed, Riggs. Imagine a country jerk-off cop like you knowing about these things," Hap said and winked at him. He thought of Joey, and a feeling of sadness crept into his heart and mind. He looked away from the group when his eyes began to tear.

"Wheelan, please continue with your explanation," Eagle said. "I need it to go along with the tape. You mind if I put you on camera?"

"No, he doesn't mind," Burton said. "Go ahead, kiddo, do your stuff."

Wheelan smiled and began. "These objects represent what I call the points of origination for the killer storms here in Preacher's Cove. Their metals, combined with the electromagnetic field produced by an inactive volcano—over which we are situated—create a magnetic field so powerful that it not only attracts and guides the lightning, but it strengthens it as well. When lightning strikes here, the main leader seeks out these objects, located at this particular spot, and draws energy from them. Since the point of origination is atop the tallest hill in the Cove, that, too, lends to the attraction of the lightning. So, there are many forces combined that perpetuate the deadly strikes and the greenflash, as well."

"Good, very good," Hap said.

"Was that clear?" Wheelan asked.

"Yeah," Eagle said, "and it makes sense, too!"

"So," Libby said, "with these objects no longer buried deep in the earth, the lightning should become less lethal in Preacher's Cove. Is that right?"

"I'm hoping," Wheelan said. "Without their being buried atop the charge from the volcano, maybe, just maybe, things will be better for us."

"Looks like you might be a hero," Burton said.

"Well, let's not give out any accolades until after the next storm...the one that's steadily approaching as we speak," Wheelan said. "So, Wheelan, how exactly do you think these objects came to be in Alabama, of all places?" Eagle asked.

"Migration. The ancient ones, forced out of their communities, fled to other areas. Centuries of family legacies, treasures passed down from generation to generation, moved along with the families. The Druids left Gaul, fled from Rome, and traveled to the territories we know today as Wales, Scotland, and Ireland. But some colonies of Druids traveled constantly, never establishing roots in one place for very long. Persecution followed them wherever they went, so they kept moving. Wheelan rubbed the back of his neck and stretched. "These treasures are, I believe, remnants of several families' legacies which made their way to the Southeastern coastline, then inward to lands that resembled Wales, Scotland, and Ireland...places like Tennessee and northern Alabama. It's not as far-fetched as you might think considering the times and the circumstances. Now, these treasures will become a part of my family's legacy. Centuries of life are represented in these works of art, and I will guard them with my own life."

"Wow," Eagle said, "that was even better than the first shot."

"But aren't you afraid that people will try to steal them? I mean, you're going on TV talking about these treasures, and people are bound to try to see them, even if all they want to do is look."

"No," Wheelan said, "showing the tape will be all right. The Chief and I have already made plans for the treasures. He can keep them hidden and safe from harm. And after tonight, he will see to it that they are placed in the proper hands, so the objects will disappear from Preacher's Cove and make their way to the museums for study. In essence, they will simply disappear."

58

"Did you find it?" Ike Madison asked.

"Yes, sir. It was just about a goner, but I got it. Poor little critter almost killed itself trying to get out of that plastic container."

"I don't understand people sometimes, Billy Ray. Imagine trapping a helpless animal in a box. Some people are just no good, no sense of compassion for God's creatures."

"He's back with us now, Reverend. No worries."

"We have one last duty, Billy Ray. Are you prepared?"

"Yes, Reverend. I'm prepared and so is our little friend. Everything's already in place."

Ike Madison opened his wallet and drew out ten crisp one-hundred-dollar bills. He counted them out and handed them to Billy Ray.

"You're a good man. I'm fortunate to have your loyalty and support."

"Always, Reverend, always."

At 5:00, exhausted from the emotional and physical toll of Joey's death and the events at the Hallows, Hap excused himself from the bunch and snuggled down onto the sofa in the living room of Libby's house. He leaned back on the thick cushions, squirmed around until he had made himself a cushy little nest, and drifted off to sleep. Only a few minutes later, he was propelled once again into a land of strangers. He dreamt of a man, a tall man standing alone by an open grave surrounded by a circle of trees. The tall man looked down into the grave, his eyes as hollow as the pit itself. Dirt splashed onto the open wooden coffin deep

inside and with each splay of rocks and dirt, the tall man clasped his hands tighter. The hollow eyes gave no hint of awareness. The dull, lifeless pallor of his face, and the steady crease of his sunken cheeks made him appear no more alive than the woman whose name was crudely carved onto a small, flat piece of board propped against the nearest tree. As he clasped his large, rough hands ever tighter, he showed the only sign of visible life: glaring white knuckles.

From deep inside the pit issued a whimper, barely audible. The tall man twitched. The sky darkened, thunder rumbled in the distance, and the earth trembled beneath him. The lid of the coffin slid open. Inside were two bodies, one of a young woman dressed in blue, the other of the baby cradled in her arms. The trembling earth disturbed the woman's body. One arm slid from around the baby and fell against the side of the coffin. Another tremor skewed the lid with such force that it smashed sideways into the loose earth around the grave. The young woman's eye popped open. Beneath her right eye were two gorged marks...fang marks. And in her hand, matched perfectly to an exact replica in the baby's hand, was the Eye of God. When one fierce bolt of lightning struck beside the circle of trees, a light shone inside the pit. The tall man's hollow eyes widened in horror. Another cry from the grave startled him so that he took a single step back, and when the earth trembled a second time beneath his feet, he opened his mouth to scream. But it was Hap Murray, once again, whose scream pierced the stillness of evening calm in Preacher's Cove. "Lucy!" he said. "It's Lucy in the coffin."

"Are you all right?" Libby asked, sitting down beside him on the sofa. "Tell me what's wrong, Hap. Please."

"The woman in the coffin is Lucy. There are fang marks on her face. The tall man standing in front of the grave is Wheelan."

"No, Hap, you're just dreaming. Wheelan is here. Lucy's asleep."

The group gathered around him. Burton sat across from him, leaned over and patted his knee playfully. "Hey, it's all right, son. Nightmares are common here. Everyone has them."

"Listen to me," Hap insisted. "The woman in the coffin is Lucy.

There are fang marks on her face. Lucy is in danger."

"Hap," Libby said, "do you remember the photograph on the mantle? There is a photograph, a portrait of Maribeth Taylor. She was killed by rattlesnakes at a place called Big Springs. Her baby died on the same day, and they were buried together. The tall man you're seeing, I believe, is Sidney, her husband...Wheelan's great great-grandfather. Everyone in our family looks alike."

"But Lucy also has the mark," he said. "She has the mark and she's in danger. I think my dream is a warning about Lucy, not about the ancestors."

Libby stood up, took him by the hand and motioned for him to follow her. They walked the length of the long hallway and stopped outside the last door on the right. Libby eased the door open, just enough so that Hap could see inside. "It's dark in the room, but wait a few seconds while your eyes adjust. She's sleeping, and she's perfectly fine."

Hap waited until he could see inside the room. He scanned the interior, amazed at the size of her bedroom. After several seconds had passed, he looked at the bed. Lucy was there, curled up, nestled amidst several pillows. He stepped inside the doorway and looked around the massive room. When he was convinced that Lucy was all right, he looked down at Libby and stepped out, closing the door gently behind him. As Libby walked in front of him, he put his hands on her shoulders. When she took another step, he stopped, pulled her close to him, and wrapped his arms around her. Then, he bent down and kissed the top of her head.

"Okay, now you can go," he said. "Just wanted you to know what I was thinking."

"Thanks for sharing," she said and giggled like a school girl.

"Hey, you two, it doesn't take *that* long to walk down the hallway!" Burton called. "I trust there's no illegal activity going on. I'd hate to have to arrest you both."

"Mind your own business, such as it is," Libby said and winked at him.

"But yours is so much more interesting right now," he said.

Eagle chimed in and said that he was enjoying all the activity, but that he was starving. He suggested that they all go down to the restaurant. Everyone agreed, and while Wheelan gathered his treasure and tucked it away in a locking trunk in his room, the others stood at the doorway and waited patiently. Wheelan locked his bedroom door, lumbered down the hallway and then ushered them out the door. He secured the locks and headed down the stairs. The air, heavy with moisture, wrapped them in damp heat. Filled with gray clouds, the sky enveloped them, holding them hostage in the Cove. Wheelan stood outside and sniffed toward the sky.

"Lightning," he said. "There's a monster in those clouds."

"Should we go back?" Hap asked, his stomach in knots.

"No, we have time," Wheelan said.

"You say that every single time it's going to storm," Hap teased.

"Yes, and I'm always right, Mr. Murray. I'm an amateur meteorologist, remember? We're always right."

A thunderclap sounded, a huge one that rumbled and rocked the ground. "Bugger!" Hap said, his stomach churning, his heart fairly racing in his chest. "Please, let's just get inside."

Hap followed Libby and the others into the restaurant. He stood beside Libby as she stopped at the counter and whispered something to the clerk. After a few moments, a young hostess appeared and whispered to Libby. Hap smiled as Libby grabbed his hand and led him into the private dining area. She invited him and the others to be seated as the young hostess placed a menu in front of them. Hap decided on the buffet with iced tea and suggested it to the others.

They ate as if they would never have food again, and after their meal, they sat around the table and talked, smoked cigarettes, and laughed. At 7:00, content and happy, they decided to leave. But before they got up, Libby gestured to one of the servers. The server nodded and walked away.

"I never got a chance to thank Lucy for the doll she made," Hap said. "May I go and thank her? I won't bother you again about it. I just want to tell her how grateful I am."

"What do you think, Wheelan? Should Hap venture in to thank your mother for the doll?"

"I left her only a few minutes ago," Wheelan said. "She seemed fine."

"Just one last time," Hap said. "That nightmare has me spooked. I'd like to see for myself if she's okay."

"Nightmare?"

Wheelan looked at Libby then back to Hap.

"Let's go check again," he said and patted his shirt pocket. "This time, I've come prepared for those snakes of Ike's."

When they reached Lucy's door, Libby knocked. "Lucy, honey, it's me. I'd like to talk to you."

Libby eased the door open. "Lucy? Are you all right?"

Libby flipped on the light switch and saw Lucy lying on the floor. She dropped to her knees beside her.

"Oh, God." The sickly pallor of Lucy's skin made her queasy. "She's been bitten," Libby sobbed. "She's dying."

"Where's the snake?" Hap asked and knelt next to her.

"Dead," Wheelan said, his tone flat, lifeless, "under my foot." He held up the hypodermic. "Antivenom. It might work. Might not. It's all I know to do for my mother."

Wheelan plunged the needle into Lucy's vein, squeezed the serum into her, and watched. Then he scooted back. The small rocker behind him toppled. The doll tumbled to the floor. Hap leaned over and picked it up.

"It's Caillin, but look. She has the mark in her palm." He held it for Libby to see. "Caillin...she's the next...is she still working?"

"No," Wheelan said. "I saw her earlier and she said she had urgent business to take care of."

"No," Libby said. "She's gone to confront Ike. I just know it. But right now, we have to get Lucy out of here, Wheelan. We have to get her to The Hallows. She'll recover there. I'll explain later."

"But what about Caillin?" Hap said.

"You and I will go check on her," Burton said.

"Oh," Wheelan said. "Libby, we need to take Lucy to The Hallows."

"Okay," Libby said.

"One of the servers handed me this note from Caillin," Wheelan said. I didn't read it."

"Let me see it," Hap said and he unfolded the paper.

He looked at the words and felt the blood drain from his face.

"What is it, Hap?"

Burton took the note.

"Not good news, I'm afraid." Burton handed it to Hap. Scrawled in a jerky script was a simple message, "*I'll have proof.*"

Hap closed his eyes.

"Keep her safe, please. Just keep her safe until I can find her."

"Why don't you go with Libby and Wheelan. I'll take care of Caillin," Burton said to Hap.

"But she's my daughter," Hap said. "I'm the one who needs to protect her."

"Right now, Hap, Lucy needs your help. She'll die if they're not able to get her to The Hallows. Please, stay with them and help her. I'll be with Caillin. She'll be all right. Besides, Ike will go to The Hallows. He'll probably take her there with him. He's all twisted inside. Trust me on this."

Hap sighed.

"I'll do as you ask, but I don't like it one bit."

"Have a little faith," Burton said. "It isn't just Caillin that Ike wants, Hap. The stone's there, as well."

Libby gasped.

"He might as well know," Burton said. "Ike knows where it is and he will use it."

"Wait, what are you talking about?" Hap asked.

"The stone, the Eye of God. With it, he can rule as he chooses. He will have unlimited power. We must get it back. We're its rightful owners."

"But why haven't you mentioned it, Libby?" Hap asked. "Why didn't I know about it?"

Burton broke in.

"You didn't need to know about it, Hap. It's really no concern of yours. So, just drop it, okay? That stone belongs to Libby and Lucy. It's part of their heritage."

"Let's get moving," Libby said.

59

"Look, the gate is closed," Wheelan said.

Libby listened as Wheelan revved the engine. "Just hold on."

Libby grabbed the back of the bucket seat just as he drove through the gates at The Hallows. The car bounced along in the clearing until it hit the foot of the embankment and stopped.

"We're fine. Head for the stones."

Libby hurried out of the car then opened the door for Hap.

"It's her only hope."

With Lucy in his arms, Hap climbed up the embankment, Wheelan and Libby right behind. They moved as quickly as they could through the hedges, the low-hanging branches slapping across their faces, the tangle of rose bushes attaching themselves to their legs. Wheelan walked in front. He cleared the trail as he moved forward.

"Hurry!" Libby said, the voice drenched with fear. "Please, please hurry!"

"She moved, Libby," Hap said, his voice in short, raspy bursts. "Lucy moved. Maybe the antivenom is working."

Wheelan jumped over the stream then turned and held out his arms.

"Give her to me, Hap. Lean over. Come on. We're tall, our arms can reach across this."

Hap leaned out over the stream. Wheelan grabbed Lucy, hugged her to him, and ran toward the stones.

"Jump, Libby," Hap said. "You can make it."

Libby hesitated. The stream that she'd crossed a hundred times seemed too wide now, her legs too weak to hold her if she jumped. "Hurry, Libby," Hap said. "I'm right here. I'll help you."

Libby took a step forward but stopped at the slope that ran into the stream.

"Hurry!"

Libby took a deep breath, jumped, and felt Hap's arm around her back. He pulled her onto the damp ground.

"Good girl," he said then took her hand.

Together, they dashed to catch up with Wheelan.

"They're not far, just over that little rise," she said, brushing away branches, stepping over dried twigs and rustling leaves. A sheet of lightning spread across the sky, the buzzing of it almost deafening. They stopped, looked at the splay of green light in the sky, and huddled together.

"We have to keep going," Libby said. "Just keep going."

As they neared the circle, they heard voices, human voices. They slowed, listened, and strained to hear. Libby indicated they should move ahead and when they'd taken several more steps, they heard:

"No, Daddy, no! Please don't. Please. I'm begging you, Daddy. Don't do it."

Libby looked up at Hap.

"Caillin! She's in trouble. Hurry."

60

They entered the clearing. The great circle of standing stones glimmered in the hazy morning light. A thunderclap bellowed around them. Ike covered his ears. He stood at the foot of the largest stone, holding something above his head.

"I'm in control, now," he said, his voice barely above a whisper, his eyes glazed.

"Call the goddess, Libby, if you know what's good for you."

"You idiot!" Libby yelled and raced toward him.

He held out a stone in front of him.

"Not so fast, girlie."

Libby stopped a few inches from him and took a deep breath.

"I can't call her without Lucy, and Lucy's dying, Ike. She's dying from snakebite, from the snake you put in her matchbox. She's dying like Belinda and Julianna died, all because of you! You slimy bastard!"

Ike smiled, his eyes still glazed.

"Now, now. Watch your language in front of the child. I just wanted to leave her a gift, Libby. It's what she deserves. She's insane, you know, a madwoman, and she bears the mark."

Lucy moaned. Blood seeped out of her mouth and nose.

"We need help, Ike. For God's sake, we need help," Hap yelled. "She won't last much longer."

"Oh, I know you need help. All of you need help, especially my precious girl. I'll not have her in your cult, Libby. She's mine, and she'll follow my orders and my path for her. I'll not have her accepting your special brand of evil."

"Daddy, please, can we just go back home now? I promise to be good and to do whatever you want."

Ike smiled.

"Caillin, my love, my daughter, look at your hand. Just look at it. You have the mark, my darling girl. You have the mark. It must be destroyed. The living God will not stand for His name to be so blasphemed."

A frantic Caillin screamed,

"Please, Daddy. Please, let me go."

She broke down into sobs and fell limp against the tree to which she was tied. Libby stepped closer to Ike.

"What is that you're holding, Ike? Have you found it?"

Ike looked at her, his eyes glassy.

"Dear sister, Libby. It's true. I hold in my hand the Eye of God, from which all power on earth is derived. Because you are my blood kin, Libby, I will allow you to live, as long as you serve me as God intends."

Libby smiled and curtsied.

"My brother, I will gladly do whatever you ask."

"Will you, Libby?" Ike asked. "Will you work with me, serve me, be the family we should have been all those years ago?"

Libby moved even closer.

"Yes, dear brother. I will do whatever you command."

While Libby talked, she glanced to her right and saw Hap move closer to the trees.

"Shall I demonstrate, dear sister?" Ike asked.

"Please do."

Ike held the Eye at arm's length.

"I command the powers of the earth and sky to show themselves. Show yourselves," he shouted, "to the true holder of the Eye of God."

Wind whipped through the trees and bent the large branches almost to the ground. Blinding sheets of lightning crackled and buzzed, setting aflame a spindly young oak that grew in front of Ike. A deafening roar of thunder bellowed in the Cove. Ike flinched.

Libby watched Hap pull at the rope around Caillin's hands. Then he reached into his pocket and slipped out a small Swiss Army knife that his dad had given him twenty years earlier.

"Be quiet, Caillin. I think I can cut the rope. Lucy needs you, Caillin. Hurry." He sliced through the rope and it slipped to the ground.

Caillin rubbed her hands. She looked up at Hap then back at Ike.

"Caillin," Hap whispered.

She looked up at him.

"Don't let him kill me," she said. "He's my father, but I hate him. I hate him!"

"Caillin, listen to me," Hap said.

Libby watched him bend down and kiss the top of Caillin's head.

"I loved your mother with all my heart. *I'm* your father, Caillin. Me, Hap Murray. I'm your father."

Her hands covered her mouth.

"It's true," Hap said. "I'm your real father. Now, please, help Lucy. Do it for your mother."

"I heard that," Ike roared. "Caillin, he's lying to you. Can't you see that?"

Gnarled fingers of lightning spread across the sky, buzzing and humming, the smell salt water mixing with the sweet scent of lavender and roses.

Ike gagged and coughed.

"Brother," Libby said. "Call them again. Take control. Demand they appear."

"I command you!" Ike shouted. "Show yourselves."

The ground, then, shifted beneath them and gave off a shrill scraping sound. The hairs on Libby's arm prickled and rose. She watched the silhouettes of great tree branches illuminated by the flashbulb glare of lightning. Gray-black clouds tumbled over the forest and emptied themselves over the stones.

Caillin squeezed Hap's hand.

"For my mother," she said and glanced at Ike as she ran to Lucy. Her voice sounded frantic. "What do I do, Libby? Show me what to do."

Libby watched as Hap moved closer.

"Ike, dear," she said, "I must give Caillin some direction. Would you agree to that?" Ike said nothing. Libby put her hand gently on his face.

"The goddess will respond, I believe."

"Very well," he said. "Try your useless tricks."

"Caillin, stretch out beside Lucy," Libby called, her hands cupped over her mouth. "When the mark in your palm begins to throb, you'll know the power is in you. All you have to do is concentrate and let it work."

Libby gave Ike a sweet smile. "What can it hurt?"

Libby watched as Caillin uncurled the misshapen fingers on Lucy's hand then put her face close to her.

"Help me, Lucy," Caillin cried. "Please, help me. Help me save you!"

Torrents of rain poured from the sky in cold pellets that stung their skin.

"NO!" Ike cried. "I will NOT have rain now. Cease this minute."

The stone in his hand shone, the colors of it almost blinding. The rains subsided, but from the earth below issued a wailing sound. Ike smiled and wrapped his hand around the stone, the Eye of God. A laser of green light shone from it.

"Behold its power," Ike shouted. "Sister, do you see it? Can you feel it?"

"It's magnificent," Libby said. "You have what you've always wanted, Brother. The power of the Eye of God is yours!"

Ike turned and smiled at her.

"Yes, yes it is," he said. "But sadly, it is not yours, Sister, and it never will be. Once you and Caillin are gone, there's no one to threaten me, no other Holder. Caillin is the last, and poor girl, she won't live to claim her power. God will command the Stone to destroy all who interfere with His plan for its power."

Libby's heart hammered in her chest.

"Now, my sweet daughter, my precious Caillin, because you are evil, branded with the mark of Satan, you must be next."

Again, Ike wrapped his hand around the Eye and pointed it at Caillin.

"Goodbye, daughter."

When the green light shone from it, Hap lunged forward. He smashed into Ike with such force that it knocked them both to the ground. The Eye slipped from Ike's grasp and rolled away. The two giants tussled, each trying to stop the other from reaching the stone.

Ike pulled himself free and was on his feet in an instant. He brought up his foot and kicked Hap on the side of the head. Hap groaned and curled his legs toward his chest. When Libby screamed, Ike laughed, stepped beside Hap and bent down.

The Eye shone amidst the wet leaves. He scooped it into his hands, kissed it, then slipped it into his pants pocket. He laughed again, then struggled, using both hands, to pick up a large round rock on the ground. He hefted it above his head and held it. Still laughing, he said to Hap,

"I'm going to enjoy killing you almost as much as I enjoyed killing that whore of yours and her bleeding-heart sister."

Libby watched him steady himself and take a deep breath.

"My brother," she said in a calm, soft voice, though her heart was racing.

"Why not let our goddess kill him?" Libby stepped closer to Ike, her hands at her sides. She wanted desperately to hold his attention.

"Our *angel* knows what a threat he is to you. The job of the high priest is to command. Killing the traitor with a rock is beneath you." Libby smiled and inched closer to Ike. "Don't you agree?" Ike stared down at her then tossed the rock onto the ground.

"I agree," he said and rubbed his hands together. "Shall I do it now?"

Libby could hear rustling sounds behind her. "Perhaps," she whispered to Ike, "we could save the best for last." She hoped she'd given Hap enough time to move out of the way. Ike smiled at her.

"You truly are my sister."

Fear and anger welled inside her, but she swallowed hard and willed them back down inside. She smiled at Ike and pretended to hang on his every word. *Think of something,* she thought. *Think of something to save us.*

The sky turned dark as more clouds amassed above the forest, bringing with them a thunderous explosion. Libby covered her ears and glanced around for Hap. She felt relieved when she saw that he'd gotten up and moved away. Ike picked up the stone again and held it in front of him and grinned.

"Caillin, honey," he called. "It's your turn. Everything I've ever tried to do, I've done for you. I've spent my life trying to keep you from turning into one of those evil creatures. But now you bear the mark. Evil cannot live in my Cove."

"Angel of the woods, please help us," Libby whispered. "Through God's power in Heaven, please help us."

"Shut up, Libby. Shut your mouth right now!" Ike yelled.

Wheelan called to Libby,

"She's not responding. She won't wake up!"

Another clap of thunder sounded, and this time, the earth trembled with such force that no one remained standing. Below the standing stones, great chunks of earth splayed open, a hissing steam rising from deep inside.

The Eye rolled around in Ike's hand and then dropped to the ground. It stopped at the very edge of the open pit. He clambered toward it. The earth heaved again, spewing out steam and debris. Branches of the majestic oaks swayed in the mighty winds.

Then, slowly, one by one, shapes began crawling out of the earth. They moved to the top of the fissure, pulled themselves up, and formed a straight line. Each one held a large staff. One of them slammed his staff onto the ground with a heavy thud.

"Libby!" Caillin screamed.

Libby watched as the wind whipped Caillin's hair around her head, saw the long ends of it slap her face.

"Libby help me. She's not breathing! I can't do this by myself."

Thunder bellowed around them as if gigantic boulders had broken free and tumbled down the mountains. The force of it collided with the ground and vibrated beneath their feet. The wind whipped through the trees, whispering of ancient times, ancient rituals held deep in The Hallows. It called to the sky, beckoned to the forces that empowered the wind to breathe life into the stagnant recesses of mortal limitations.

The sky responded with thunderous resounding. A silent, silver slash sparked across The Hallows. Five ancient stones glowed in unison as if they'd received the call of an ancient land.

"Caillin," Ike roared, "Caillin, don't do it. Don't let yourself be overcome by this evil. Please, child, I beg you."

The forest stilled. A quiet hovered around them.

Swirls of brightness swooped from the sky and bathed the forest in green light. Pink sparks blazed through it. The sparks crackled along the ground, seeking the heat of bodies. A touch of its charge stiffened each of them, one by one, until they all stood stunned, held in place by a powerful electric charge.

The winds wailed for a return of deep peace in the grove. The clouds spilled a cooling mist scented with lavender. The Angel of The Hallows rose in an explosion of golden light, rose from the ground in search of one person. Her diaphanous gown billowed around her then floated out and hovered across the forest floor. Her porcelain skin shone, the round emerald eyes glowed, and the sea of hair tumbled around her in waves of luminescent white. From the glorious radiance of her presence fell a single beam of incandescent light, twirling in spirals toward her beloved Lucy.

The ray of light pulsed at Lucy's feet, shimmered up her legs, hovered at her chest, then floated across her face. Years of mutilation and madness melted away. Lucy inhaled, her chest rising, her body arching, her arms, both perfectly formed, stretching out beside her. Her fingers clutched handfuls of earth and leaves.

"A gift," the angel called, and in the distance, a resounding "Yes" filled the forest, the sound of far-away applause carried through the great branches of the huge oak trees. Lucy sat up and gazed at the beautiful White Maiden floating before her. As she watched the brilliant display of golden light, two small figures appeared. Extending each arm, the Maiden took their hands and led them forward.

The two young boys beside her, little boys, both blonde haired and bright, smiled. "Mama," they called. "Mama, we've missed you."

Lucy stood on two perfectly formed legs and walked toward the light.

Hap opened his eyes. The Maiden hovered closer, the children only a few feet from Lucy.

"My babies," she said. "My sweet babies."

Tears cascaded along her cheeks. She held out her arms.

"How I've missed you."

The angel called again, "Remember!"

Lucy closed her eyes. A tap on her forehead from the angel brought the images clearly into her mind. On that night years ago, lightning lit up the yard. When the flames began, they consumed Lucy's grand old house as if it were made of kindling. At the large front window of the house stood two blonde-haired children, their horrified faces and small hands pressed against the window. They were trapped inside the house by a fallen beam and ceiling-high flames. Lucy watched herself as she ran inside, tripped, and fell face-first onto the body of her husband.

Her babies screamed, "Mama! Help us, Mama!"

"Mama's here, little ones. Mama's here," she reassured them.

"Mama!" they screamed together, their little faces pressed hard against the window.

She barely felt her face melting away. She squirmed around until she felt young Will's hand. She grabbed hold and wrapped her fingers tightly around it. When the screams stopped, Lucy held to all that was left of little Will: the hand she held so tightly to. She loosened her grip and watched it fall to the floor. Just outside the house in one long row stood men with torches. Lucy wiped her tears and recalled the moment. The man who held his torch the highest was Ike Madison.

Now, Lucy buried her face in her hands. "Mama," the little ones called. "Come with us, Mama. It's beautiful here."

She took her hands away and smiled up at the two precious children.

"Yes, sweethearts, Mama's coming. Mama's coming."

The Maiden drifted closer, close enough so that Lucy could reach out and touch their fingers. Sobbing, Lucy took their hands and stepped up into the light. They wrapped their thin arms around her waist.

"Mama," they cried. "You've come home."

"Yes, babies, I'm here. Mama's here."

Ike Madison stood and held the Eye in front of him.

"You're mine now," he said and turned toward the spot where Caillin lay.

"Do it!" he screamed. "Kill the evil heretic!"

The Maiden delivered at his command, sending one quick bolt of green lightning speeding across the ground. It sought the girl. Caillin screamed as it neared. When it reached her feet, it slowed and tapped the toes of her shoes. Caillin scooted backwards, but it followed, engulfing her feet in its brilliant green light. It snaked up her leg, hissing and popping against her jeans, then traveled to the mark in her palm. It glowed and throbbed.

Suddenly, the lightning traveled under her, lifting her into the air. The Maiden's gown swept beneath her and cushioned her on a cloud of light. Caillin held out her hand, palm to the Maiden. The angel greeted her with another bolt of brilliant green that touched her palm and ricocheted straight into Ike Madison's chest.

He screamed once.

The lightning lifted him off the ground, smashed him against a tree, and dropped him to the earth in a sizzling heap of charred flesh. The Maiden withdrew, then, her gown rushing out from under Caillin. She fell from the sky but landed safely on her feet.

Hap was up on his feet, the lightning bursting around him, the force of it so strong that he had to put his hand on a large boulder to balance himself. But he did not move. "Lucy," he called, lightning sparking around him. "Thank you. Thank you for saving my life." Hap held out his hand to her, tears spilling onto his cheeks.

"Lucy!" Libby screamed.

She jumped to reach the hem of the Maiden's gown.

"Please, Lucy, don't go." Then she looked at Hap. "Help me, please."

Hap lifted her up onto a large boulder. Libby scrambled to touch the hem. The jagged surface of the rock dug into her knees, but she inched forward.

"Lucy!"

Suddenly, Libby felt a hand on hers, a smooth, fine hand. Lucy pulled her onto the billows of the gown and the two of them stood together. Libby wrapped her arms around her sister. "Please, Luce, please, can't you stay with me?"

Little William tugged at his mother's arm.

"Come on, Mama."

Lucy looked down at him. When Libby saw the precious face staring up at her, she hugged her sister one last time. She gently cupped Lucy's face in her hands.

"I love you," she whispered. The sisters kissed each other, then embraced. Libby saw her nephews, so happy, so perfect. Her heart felt as if it would break.

"Journey sweet, dear sister. Journey sweet."

Lucy knelt and wrapped her arms around her boys.

"Let's go home, my babies."

The Maiden hovered just above the forest floor, the golden light streaming across the standing stones.

When she vanished, the Maiden left behind one woman, cradled in the arms of a good man. Libby sobbed and nestled her head against Hap's chest. In her heart, she held the precious memories of her beloved sister. In her hand, she held the precious stone. A gentle rain washed her tears away.

61

Nestled in the northern-most corner of Alabama, at the toes of the Smoky Mountains, is a town called Preacher's Cove. Enormous white oak trees brimming with mistletoe encircle the place and feed from the once rattlesnake-infested waters of crystal springs. Dotted with magnificent mansions and a hallowed circle of stones, the Cove houses three thousand residents. Reigning over the gentle community is a compassionate young minister, a replacement for the one who defied all laws, both of church and state, and who paid with his life; his harmonica-playing assistant, the sole heir to the vanquished reverend's beliefs, spends his time converting strangers in the Cove to his own bizarre form of Christianity, whispering tales of evil that lives in small towns.

People come to Preacher's Cove because they've heard the stories of the killer storms and the crazy, mangled woman who made dolls called the Firelight Angels. The visitors, unaware of the truth, come back time and time again to the familiar sound of a voice that says, "Hello, I am Libby Murray. Welcome to Preacher's Cove...God's little corner of the world." Sometimes, she mentions her husband's Associated Press Award hanging above the mantle in the lobby. And occasionally, when the mood is just right, she tells the story of her late twin sister, a beautiful woman and a brilliant artist. People come to the Cove even though they do not know that at the center of this place is a wooded area called The Hallows, a place where Druids once worshipped. Buried deep within the earth's mantle is an ancient golden scepter on which is carved the head of a serpent, and along whose sides is the name, "Julian."

The scepter, at times, glistens with the power of lightning strikes. It calls to a forgotten goddess to lift it from its burial site and free it into the air. Crafted long ago by a young girl with startling talent, the scepter shares her power and the power of the young one who fulfills the legacy.

The scepter rests forever in Preacher's Cove, the perfect place for such a magnificent piece.

The perfect place for the holder of the Eye of God.

The End

CPSIA information can be obtained
at www.ICGtesting.com
Printed in the USA
FSHW012142150420
69217FS